About the Authors

Kate Hardy has been a bookworm since she was a toddler. When she isn't writing Kate enjoys reading, theatre, live music, ballet and the gym. She lives with her husband, student children and their spaniel in Norwich, England. You can contact her via her website: www.katehardy.com

Caroline Anderson's been a nurse, a secretary, a teacher, and has run her own business. Now she's settled on writing. 'I was looking for that elusive something and finally realised it was variety – now I have it in abundance. Every book brings new horizons, new friends, and in between books I juggle! My husband John and I have two beautiful daughters, Sarah and Hannah, umpteen pets, and several acres of Suffolk that nature tries to reclaim every time we turn our backs!'

Cathy Williams is a great believer in the power of perseverance as she had never written anything before her writing career, and from the starting point of zero has now fulfilled her ambition to pursue this most enjoyable of careers. She would encourage any would-be writer to have faith and go for it! She derives inspiration from the tropical island of Trinidad and from the peaceful countryside of middle England. Cathy lives in Warwickshire her family

D1331469

000003103806

Italian Playboys

Italian Playboys: Proposals

KATE HARDY

CAROLINE ANDERSON

CATHY WILLIAMS

MILLS & BOON

All rights reserved including the right of reproduction in whole or in part in any form. This edition is published by arrangement with Harlequin Books S.A.

This is a work of fiction. Names, characters, places, locations and incidents are purely fictional and bear no relationship to any real life individuals, living or dead, or to any actual places, business establishments, locations, events or incidents. Any resemblance is entirely coincidental.

This book is sold subject to the condition that it shall not, by way of trade or otherwise, be lent, resold, hired out or otherwise circulated without the prior consent of the publisher in any form of binding or cover other than that in which it is published and without a similar condition including this condition being imposed on the subsequent purchaser.

® and TM are trademarks owned and used by the trademark owner and/or its licensee. Trademarks marked with ® are registered with the United Kingdom Patent Office and/or the Office for Harmonisation in the Internal Market and in other countries.

First Published in Great Britain 2021
by Mills & Boon, an imprint of HarperCollins*Publishers* Ltd,
1 London Bridge Street, London, SE1 9GF

www.harpercollins.co.uk

HarperCollins*Publishers*
1st Floor, Watermarque Building,
Ringsend Road, Dublin 4, Ireland

ITALIAN PLAYBOYS: PROPOSALS
© 2021 Harlequin Books S.A.

It Started at a Wedding... © 2015 Pamela Brooks
Valtieri's Bride © 2012 Caroline Anderson
Wearing the De Angelis Ring © 2016 Cathy Williams

ISBN 978-0-263-30262-2

MIX
Paper from
responsible sources
FSC™ C007454

This book is produced from independently certified FSC™ paper to ensure responsible forest management.

For more information visit: www.harpercollins.co.uk/green

Printed and bound in Spain
by CPI, Barcelona

IT STARTED AT A WEDDING...

KATE HARDY

DUDLEY LIBRARIES	
000003103806	
Askews & Holts	07-Oct-2021
AF ROM	£7.99
2GL	

To the Mills & Boon Romance authors, with much love and thanks for being such brilliant colleagues and friends—and for letting me bounce mad ideas off them!

CHAPTER ONE

No.

This couldn't be happening.

The box had to be there.

It *had* to be.

But the luggage carousel was empty. It had even stopped going round, now the last case had been taken off it. And Claire was the only one standing there, waiting with a small suitcase and a dress box—and a heart full of panic.

Where was her best friend's wedding dress?

'Get a grip, Claire Stewart. Standing gawping at the carousel isn't going to make the dress magically appear. Go and talk to someone,' she told herself sharply. She gathered up her case and the box containing the bridesmaid's dress, and went in search of someone who might be able to find out where the wedding dress was. Maybe the box had accidentally been put in the wrong flight's luggage and it was sitting somewhere else, waiting to be claimed.

Half an hour of muddling through in a mixture of English and holidaymakers' Italian got her the bad news. Somewhere between London and Naples, the dress had vanished.

The dress Claire had spent hours working on, hand-stitching the tiny pearls on the bodice and the edge of the veil.

The dress Claire's best friend was supposed to be wearing at her wedding in Capri in two days' time.

Maybe this was a nightmare and she'd wake up from it in a second. Surreptitiously, Claire pinched herself. It hurt. Not good, because that meant this was really happening. She was in Naples with her luggage, her own bridesmaid's dress...and no wedding dress.

There was nothing else for it. She grabbed her mobile phone, found a quiet corner in the airport and called Ashleigh.

Whose phone was switched through to voicemail.

This definitely wasn't the kind of news Claire could leave on voicemail; that would be totally unfair. She tried calling Luke, Ashleigh's fiancé, but his phone was also switched through to voicemail. She glanced at her watch. It was still so early that they were probably in the middle of breakfast and they'd probably left their phones in their room. OK. Who else could she call? She didn't have a number for Tom, Luke's best man. Sammy, her other best friend, who was photographing the wedding, wasn't flying to Italy until tomorrow, after she'd finished a photo-shoot in New York. The rest of the wedding guests were due to arrive on the morning of the wedding.

Which left Ashleigh's brother. The man who was going to give Ashleigh away. The man who played everything strictly by the rules—and Claire had just broken them. Big time. He was the last person she could call.

But he wasn't in Capri yet, either. Which meant she had time to fix this.

What she needed was a plan.

Scratch that. What she *really* needed was coffee. She'd spent the last two weeks working all hours on Ashleigh's dress as well as the work she was doing for a big wedding show, and she'd skimped on sleep to get everything done in time. That, plus the ridiculously early flight she'd taken out here this morning, meant that she was fuzzy and unfocused.

Coffee.

Even thought she normally drank lattes, this called for desperate measures. She needed something strong and something fast. One espresso with three sugars later, Claire's head was clear enough to work out her options. It meant more travelling—a lot more travelling—but that didn't matter. Claire would've walked over hot coals for Ashleigh. She was more than Claire's best friend; she was the sister Claire would've chosen.

She tried calling Ashleigh again. This time, to Claire's relief, her best friend answered her mobile phone.

'Claire, hi! Are you in Naples already?'

'Um, yes. But, Ash, there's a bit of a problem.'

'What's wrong?'

'Honey, I don't know how to soften this.' There wasn't a way to soften news like this. 'Is Luke with you?'

'Ye-es.' Ashleigh sounded as if she was frowning with concern. 'Why?'

'I think you're going to need him,' Claire said.

'Now you're really worrying me. Claire? What's happened? Are you all right?'

'I'm fine.' Claire had no option but to tell her best friend the news straight. 'But I'm so sorry, Ash. I've really let you down. Your dress. It's gone missing somewhere between here and London.'

'What?'

'I've been talking to the airline staff. They phoned London for me. They said it's not in London, and it's definitely not in Naples. They're going to try and track it down, but they wanted us to be prepared for the fact that they might not be able to find it before the wedding.'

'Oh, my God.' Ashleigh gave a sharp intake of breath.

'I know. Look—we have options. I don't have time to make you another dress like that one, even if I could get the material and borrow a sewing machine. But we can go looking in Naples and find something off the peg, something I can maybe tweak for you. Or I can leave the bridesmaid's dress and my case here in the left luggage, and get the next flight back to London. I'm pretty much the same size as you, so I'll Skype you while I try on every single dress in my shop and you can pick the ones you like best. Then I'll get the next flight back here, and you can try the dresses on and I'll do any alterations so your final choice is perfect.'

Except it wouldn't be perfect, would it?

It wouldn't be the dress of Ashleigh's dreams. The dress Claire had designed especially for her. The dress that had gone missing.

'And you'll still be the most beautiful bride in the world, I swear,' Claire finished, desperately hoping that her best friend would see that.

'They lost my dress.' Ashleigh sounded numb. Which wasn't surprising. Planning the wedding had opened up old scars, so Ashleigh had decided to get married abroad—and the dress had been one of the few traditions she'd kept.

And Claire had let her down. 'I'm so, so sorry.'

'Claire, honey, it's not your fault that the airline lost my dress.'

That wasn't how Sean would see it. Claire had clashed with Ashleigh's brother on a number of occasions, and she knew that he didn't like her very much. They saw the world in very different ways, and Sean would see this as yet another example of Claire failing to meet his standards. She'd failed to meet her own, too.

'Look, I was the one bringing the dress to Italy. It was my responsibility, so the fact it's gone wrong is my fault,' Claire pointed out. 'What do you want to do? Meet me here in Naples and we'll go shopping?'

'I'm still trying to get my head round this. My *dress*,' Ashleigh said, sounding totally flustered—which, considering that Ashleigh was the calmest and most together person Claire knew, was both surprising and worrying.

'OK. Forget Naples. Neither of us knows the place well enough to find the right wedding shops anyway, so we'll stick with London. Have a look on my website, email me with a note of your top ten, and we'll talk again when I'm back in the shop. Then I'll bring your final choices on the next flight back.' She bit her lip. 'Though I wouldn't blame you for not trusting me to get it right this time.'

'Claire-bear, it's not your fault. Luke's here now—he's worked out what's going on and he's just said he'd marry me if I was wearing a hessian sack. The dress isn't important. Maybe we can find something in Capri or Sorrento.'

Ashleigh was clearly aiming for light and breezy, but Claire could hear the wobble in her best friend's voice. She knew what the dress meant to Ashleigh: the one big tradition she was sticking to for her wedding day. 'No,

Ash. It'll take us for ever to find a wedding shop. And what if you don't like what they have in stock? That's not fair to you. I know I'll have something you like, so I'm going to get the next flight back to London. I'll call you as soon as I get there,' she said.

'Claire, that's so much travelling—I can't make you do that.'

'You're not making me. I'm offering. You're my best friend and I'd go to the end of the earth for you,' Claire said, her voice heartfelt.

'Me, too,' Ashleigh said. 'OK. I'll call the spa and move our bookings.'

So much for the pampering day they'd planned. A day to de-stress the bride-to-be. Claire had messed that up, too, by losing the dress. 'I'm so sorry I let you down,' Claire said. 'I'd better go. I need to get my luggage stored and find a flight.' And she really hoped that there would be a seat available. If there wasn't... Well, she'd get to London somehow. Train, plane, ferry. Whatever it took. She wasn't going to let Ashleigh down again. 'I'll call you when I get back to London.'

'Please don't tell me something's come up and you're not going to make it in time for the wedding.'

'Of course not,' Sean said, hearing the panic in his little sister's voice and wondering what was wrong. Was this just an attack of last-minute nerves? Or was she having serious second thoughts? He liked his future brother-in-law enormously, but if Ashleigh had changed her mind about marrying him, then of course Sean would back her in calling off the wedding. All he wanted was to see Ashleigh settled and happy. 'I was just calling to see if you needed me to bring any last-minute things over with me.'

'Oh. Yes. Of course.'

But she sounded flustered—very unlike the calm, sensible woman he knew her to be. 'Ashleigh? What's happened?'

'Nothing.'

But her response was a little too hasty for Sean's liking. He deliberately made his voice gentle. 'Sweetie, if there's a problem, you know you can always talk to me. I'll help you fix it.' OK, so Ashleigh was only three years younger than he was, and he knew that she was perfectly capable of sorting out her own problems—but he'd always looked out for his little sister, even before their parents had been killed in the crash that had turned their lives upside down six years ago. 'Tell me.'

'The airline lost my dress,' Ashleigh said. 'But it's OK. Claire's gone back to London to get me another one.'

Sean paused while it sank in.

There was a problem with his sister's wedding.

And Claire Stewart was smack in the middle of the problem.

Why didn't that surprise him?

'Wasn't Claire meant to be bringing the dress with her?' he asked.

'It wasn't her fault, Sean.'

No. Of course not. It would never be Miss Follow-Your-Heart's fault that something went wrong and everyone else had to pick up the pieces.

But he wasn't going to spoil his sister's wedding by picking a fight with her best friend. At least, not in front of Ashleigh. He fully intended to discuss the matter with Claire herself—sooner, rather than later. 'OK. Is there anything else you need?'

'No, it's fine.'

But his little sister didn't sound fine. She sounded shaky. 'Is Luke there with you?' he asked.

'Yes. He said the dress didn't matter and he'd marry me if I was wearing a hessian sack. He says it's our marriage that matters, not the trappings.'

Sean mentally high-fived his brother-in-law-to-be. And thank God Luke was so sensible and reliable. Ashleigh's last boyfriend had been selfish, thoughtless and flaky—and he'd just so happened to be the best friend of Claire's boyfriend at the time. Which figured. Claire always seemed to leave chaos in her wake.

'I could've told you that, sweetheart. Luke's a good bloke and he loves you to bits. Look, I'll be there later tonight, OK? If there's anything you need, anything at all, just call me. And I'm with Luke. Even if you're wearing a hessian sack, you're going to be the most beautiful bride ever.' The bride his father should've been giving away. His throat tightened. If only. But the crash had happened and they'd had to make the best of it ever since. And Sean was determined that his little sister was going to have the wedding she really wanted. He'd *make* it happen.

'Thanks, Sean.' She blew out a breath. 'I'm fine. Really. This is just a little hiccup and Claire's fixing it.'

Yes, Sean thought grimly, because he'd make quite sure that Claire did exactly that.

'See you tonight,' she said.

'See you tonight.'

Sean checked his diary when he'd put down the phone. All his meetings that afternoon could be moved. Anything else, he could deal with in Capri. A quick word with his PA meant that everything would be sorted. And then he called Claire.

Her phone went straight through to voicemail.

So that meant either she was on the phone already, her phone was switched off completely, or she'd seen his name on the screen and wasn't answering because she was trying to avoid him. OK, then; he'd wait for her at the shop. And he'd make absolutely sure that Ashleigh's dress didn't get lost, this time round.

It didn't take Sean long to get to the terraced house in Camden which held Dream of a Dress on the ground floor and Claire's flat on the top storey. Although the sign on the door said 'closed', he could see light inside—meaning that Claire was there, or whoever she'd employed to man the shop in her absence. Either would do.

He rang the doorbell.

No reply.

OK. Play dirty it was, then. This time, he leaned on the doorbell until a figure hurried through to the door.

A figure wearing a wedding dress.

Claire narrowed her eyes at him when she opened the door. Though he noticed that she didn't ask him why he was here. Clearly she had a pretty good idea that he already knew she'd lost his sister's wedding dress and he wasn't happy about the situation.

'I'm Skypeing Ash right now,' she said quietly. 'And I don't want her upset any more today, so can we leave the fight until she's chosen another dress and I've said goodbye to her?'

Claire clearly realised that they were about to have a fight. A huge one. But Sean agreed with her about not rowing in front of his sister. Right now, Ashleigh's feelings had to come first. 'OK.'

'Good. Come in. If you want a drink, feel free to make yourself something. There's tea, coffee and mugs in the cupboard above the kettle, though I'm afraid there's only long-life milk.' She gestured to a doorway which obviously led to the business's kitchen.

'Thank you,' he said. Though he wasn't about to accept any hospitality from Claire Stewart, even if it was do-it-yourself hospitality.

'If you'll excuse me, I have a wedding dress to sort out.' She gave him a level look. 'And I'm modelling the dresses for Ash, which means I'll need to change several times—so I'd appreciate it if you didn't come through to the back until I'm done.'

'Noted,' he said.

She locked the shop door again, still keeping the 'closed' sign in place, and vanished into the back room. Feeling a bit like a spare part—but wanting to know just how Claire had managed to lose a wedding dress—Sean waited in the main area of the shop until she walked back out, this time dressed in faded jeans and a strappy top rather than a wedding dress.

'No coffee?' she asked.

'No.'

She folded her arms. 'OK. Spit it out.'

'Firstly, does Ashleigh actually have a dress?' he asked.

'There are three she likes,' Claire said. 'I'm taking them all over to Capri as soon as I can get a flight. Then she can try them on, and I'll make any necessary alterations in time for the wedding.'

'What I don't understand is how you managed to lose her dress in the first place.' He shook his head in exasperation. 'Why wasn't it with you in the plane?'

'Believe it or not,' she said dryly, 'that was my original plan. I cleared it with the airline that I could put the boxes with her dress and mine in the overhead storage compartments, and if there was room they'd hang Ash's dress on a rail in the stewardesses' cabin. I packed both the dresses in boxes that specifically met the airline's size guidelines. Your waistcoat and cravat, plus Luke's and Tom's, are packed in with my dress.'

So far, so sensible. But this was Claire—the woman who was chaos in high heels with a snippy attitude. 'But?'

'It turned out there were three other brides on the flight. One of whom was a total Bridezilla and demanded that her dress should be the one in with the stewardesses. There was a massive row. In the end, the captain intervened and ordered that all the bridal dresses should go in the hold with the rest of the luggage—even those belonging to people who weren't involved in the argument with Bridezilla. He wouldn't even let us put the dresses in the overhead lockers. The atmosphere on the plane was pretty bad.' She shrugged. 'The airline staff have looked in London and in Naples, and there's no sign of the box with Ash's dress. They're still checking. It might turn up in time. But it probably won't, so these dresses are my contingency plan—because I don't intend to let Ash down. Ever.'

It hadn't been *entirely* Claire's fault, Sean acknowledged. But, at the same time, she *had* been the one responsible for the dress, and right now the dress was missing. 'Why didn't you buy a seat for the dress?'

'They said I couldn't—that if I wanted the dress to come with me, it would have to be treated as additional cabin luggage. Which,' she pointed out, 'is what I organised and what I paid for.' Her blue eyes were icy as she added, 'And, just in case you think I'm perfectly OK about the situation, understand that I've spent weeks working on that dress and I'm gutted that my best friend doesn't get to wear the dress of her dreams—the dress

I designed especially for her. But moaning on about the situation isn't going to get the dress back. I'd rather do something practical to make sure Ash's wedding goes as smoothly as possible. So, if you'll excuse me, I have three wedding dresses to pack and a flight to book.' She shrugged again. 'But, if it makes you feel better, do feel free to storm and shout at me.'

Funny how she was the one in the wrong, but she'd managed to make him feel as if *he* were the one in the wrong, Sean thought.

Though she had a point. Complaining about the situation or losing his temper with her wouldn't make the dress magically reappear. And Claire had spent most of today travelling—two and a half hours each way on a plane, plus an hour each way on a train and waiting round in between. Now she was just about to fly back to Italy: yet more travelling. All for his sister's sake.

Claire Stewart was trying—in both senses of the phrase. But maybe he needed to try a bit harder, too.

'Do you want me to find you a flight while you pack the dresses?' he asked.

She looked at him as if he'd just grown two heads.

'What?' he asked.

'Are you actually being *helpful*?' she asked. 'To *me*?'

He narrowed his eyes at her. 'Don't make it sound as if I'm always the one in the wrong.'

'No. That would be me,' she said. 'In your regimented world view.'

'I'm not regimented,' he said, stung. 'I'm organised and efficient. There's a difference.'

Her expression suggested otherwise.

'I was,' he pointed out, 'trying to call a truce and work with you. For Ashleigh's sake.'

She looked at him for a long, long time. And then

she nodded. 'Truce. I can do that. Then thank you—it would save me a bit of time if you could find me a flight. I don't care which London airport it's from or how much it costs—just let me know as soon as they need paying and I'll come to the phone and give them my credit card details. But please put whichever airline in the picture about what happened to the dress this morning, and I want cast-iron guarantees that *these* dresses are going to make it out to Italy with me. Otherwise I'll be carving their entire check-in staff into little pieces with a rusty spoon.'

He couldn't help smiling. 'Spoons are blunt.'

'That,' she said, 'is entirely the point. Ditto the rusty.'

'You really care about Ashleigh, don't you?' he said.

'Sean, how can you not already know that?' Claire frowned. 'She's been my best friend for more than half my lifetime, since I moved to the same school as her when I was thirteen. I think of Ash practically as my sister.'

Which would technically make her his sister, too. Except Sean didn't have any sibling-like feelings towards Claire. What he felt for Claire was…

Well, it was a lot easier to think of it as dislike. When they weren't being scrupulously polite to each other, they clashed. They had totally opposite world views. They were totally incompatible. He wasn't going to let himself think about the fact that her hair was the colour of a cornfield bathed in sunshine, and her eyes were the deep blue of a late summer evening. And he certainly wasn't going to let himself think about the last time he'd kissed her.

'Of course. I'll get you a flight sorted.'

Though he noticed her movements while he was on the phone. Deft and very sure as she packed each dress in tissue paper to avoid creases, put it inside a plastic cover to protect it from any damage and then in a box. As if she'd done this many times before. Which, he realised, she probably had.

He'd never seen Claire at work before. Apart from when she'd measured the three men in the wedding party for their waistcoats, and that had been at Ashleigh and Luke's house. He'd been too busy concentrating on being polite and anodyne to her for his sister's sake to take much notice of what she was actually doing.

And, OK, it was easy to think of dress designers as a bit kooky and not living in the same world as the rest of the population. The outlandish outfits on the catwalks in Milan and the big fashion shows left him cold and wondering what on earth was going on in the heads of the designers—real people just didn't wear stuff like that. But the woman in front of him seemed business-like. Organised. Efficient.

Like someone who belonged in his world.

He shook himself. That was just an illusion. Temporary. Claire didn't belong in his world and he didn't belong in hers. They'd be civil to each other over the next few days, purely for Ashleigh's sake, and then they'd go back to avoiding each other.

Safely.

CHAPTER TWO

As Claire worked on packing up the dresses, she found herself growing more and more aware of Sean. He looked every inch the meticulous businessman in a made-to-measure suit, handmade shirt, and perfectly polished shoes; as part of her job, Claire noticed details like that. Sean wouldn't have looked out of place on a catwalk or in a glossy magazine ad.

And he was actually helping her—working with her as a team. Which was rarer than a blue moon. They didn't get on.

Apart from a few occasions, and some of those were memories that still had the ability to make Claire squirm. Such as Ashleigh's eighteenth birthday party. Claire's life had imploded only a couple of weeks before and, although she'd tried so hard to smile and be happy for her best friend's sake, she'd ended up helping herself to too much champagne that evening to blot out the misery that had threatened to overwhelm her.

Sean had come to her rescue—and Claire had been young enough and drunk enough to throw herself at him. Sean had been a perfect gentleman and turned her down, and her adult self was glad that he'd been so decent, but as a teenager she'd been hideously embar-

rassed by the whole episode and she'd avoided him like
the plague for months and months afterwards.

Then there was his parents' funeral, three years
later. Claire had been there to support Ashleigh—just
as Ashleigh had supported Claire at her own mother's
funeral—and she'd glanced across at Sean at a moment
when he'd looked utterly lost. Wanting to help, Claire
had pushed past the old embarrassment and gone to
offer him her condolences. Sean hadn't been quite approachable enough for her to give him a hug, so she'd
simply squeezed his hand and said she was sorry for
his loss. At the time, her skin had tingled at the contact
with his—but the timing was so inappropriate that she
hadn't acted on it.

They'd fought again when Ashleigh had decided not
to join the family business. Sean had blamed Claire for
talking Ashleigh out of what he clearly saw as her duty.
OK, so Claire had been a sounding board and helped
Ashleigh work out what she really wanted to do, encouraging her to follow her dreams; but surely Sean
had wanted his sister to be happy instead of feeling
trapped and miserable in a job she really didn't want
to do? And surely, given that his parents had died so
young, he understood how short life was and how you
needed to make the most of every moment? It wasn't
as if being a maths teacher was some insecure, fly-
by-night job. And Ash was a really gifted teacher. She
loved what she did and her pupils adored her. It had
been the right decision.

The problem was, Sean had always been so overprotective. Claire could understand why; he was Ashleigh's
elder brother and had been the head of the family since
he was twenty-four. But at the same time he really
needed to understand that his sister was perfectly ca-

pable of standing on her own two feet and making her own way in the world.

She forced herself to concentrate on packing the dresses properly, but she couldn't help noticing the deep tone of Sean's voice, his confidence and sureness as he talked to the airline.

Most of the time Claire didn't admit it, even to herself, but she'd had a secret crush on Sean when she'd been fourteen. Which was half the reason why she'd thrown herself at him at Ashleigh's birthday party, three years later.

Another memory seeped back in. Ashleigh's engagement party to Luke. Sean had asked her to dance; Claire had been well aware that he was only being polite for his sister's sake. Which was the same reason why she'd agreed to dance with him. Though, somewhere between the start and the middle of the song, something had changed. Claire couldn't even blame it on the champagne, because she hadn't been drinking. But something had made her pull back slightly and look up at Sean. Something had made her lips part slightly. And then he'd dipped his head and kissed her.

The kiss had shaken her right to the core. Nobody had ever made her feel like that with a single kiss—as if her knees had turned to mush and she needed to cling to him to keep herself upright. It had panicked her into backing away and cracking some inane joke, and the moment was lost.

Since then, she'd been scrupulously polite and distant with Sean. But in unguarded moments she wondered. Had he felt that same pull of attraction? And what if…?

She shook herself. Of course not. Apart from the fact that her judgement when it came to men was totally rubbish, she knew that Sean just saw her as his baby sister's super-annoying best friend, the woman he ended up bickering with every time they spoke to each other for more than five minutes. It rankled slightly that he still didn't take her seriously—surely the fact that she'd had her own business for the last three years and kept it going through the recession counted for *something*?

Then again, she didn't need to prove anything to him. She was perfectly comfortable with who she was and what she'd achieved.

She finished packing the last box.

'Any luck with my flight?' she asked when Sean ended his call.

'There's good news and bad,' he said.

'OK. Hit me with the bad first.'

He frowned. 'Why?'

'Because then I've faced the worst, and there's still something good to look forward to.'

He looked surprised, as if he'd never thought of it in that way before. 'OK. The bad news is, I can't get you a flight where they'll take the dresses on board.'

The worst-case scenario. Well, she'd just have to deal with it. 'Then if planes are out, I'll just have to go by train.' She thought on her feet. 'If I get the Eurostar to Paris, there'll be a connecting train to Milan or Rome, and from there to Naples. Though it means I probably won't get to Capri until tomorrow, now.'

'Hold on. I did say there was good news as well,' he reminded her. 'We can fly to Naples from London.'

She frowned, not understanding. 'But you just said you couldn't get me a seat where they'll take the dresses.'

'Not on a commercial flight, no. But I have a friend with a private plane.'

'You have *what*?'

'A friend with a private plane,' he repeated, 'who's willing to take us this afternoon.'

'Us.' The word hit her like a sledgehammer and she narrowed her eyes at him. 'Are you saying that you don't trust me to take the dresses on my own?'

'You need to go to Naples. I need to go to Naples. So it makes sense,' he said, 'for us to travel together.'

She noticed that he hadn't answered her question. Clearly he didn't trust her. To be fair to him, she had already lost his sister's wedding dress—but it hadn't been entirely her fault. 'But don't you already have a flight booked?'

'I cancelled it,' he said. 'I promised Ashleigh I'd be there tonight or I would've offered you my original booking and flown in later. This seemed like the best solution to the problem.'

'You have a friend with a private plane.' She still couldn't get over that one. 'Sean, normal people don't have friends with private planes.'

'You barely accept that I'm human, let alone normal,' he pointed out.

And they were heading towards yet another fight. She grimaced. 'Sorry. Let's just rewind and try this again. Thank you, Sean, for coming to the rescue and calling in whatever favour you had to call in to get me a flight to Naples. Please tell your friend that if he ever needs a wedding dress or a prom dress made, I'll do it for nothing.'

'I'll tell her,' Sean said dryly.

Her. Girlfriend? Probably not, Claire thought. Ashleigh was always saying that Sean would never settle down and never dated anyone for more than three weeks in a row. So maybe it was someone who'd gone to university with him, or a long-standing business acquaintance. Not that she had any right to ask.

'Thanks,' she said. 'So what time does the flight leave?'

'When we want it to, give or take half an hour,' he said. 'My car's outside. I just need to drop it back home and collect my luggage.' He looked at her. 'You might as well come with me.'

Gee, what an invitation, Claire thought. But she wasn't going to pick a fight with him now. He'd already gone above and beyond. It was for Ashleigh's sake rather than hers, she knew, but she still appreciated it. 'Ready when you are.'

He drove them back to his house and parked outside. His luggage was in the hallway, so it only took a few seconds for him to collect it; Claire noticed that he didn't invite her in. Fair enough. It was his space. Though she was curious to know whether his living space was as organised and regimented as the rest of him.

They took the tube through to London City airport. Claire used the noise of the train as an excuse not to make conversation, and she knew that he was doing exactly the same. Being with Sean wasn't easy. He was so prickly. He had to have a charming side, or he wouldn't have made such a success of running the family business—clients wouldn't want to deal with him. But the sweetness of the toffee that Farrell's produced definitely didn't rub off on him where Claire was concerned.

The check-in process was much faster than Claire was used to; then again, she didn't know anyone with a private plane. It was more the sort of thing that a rock star would have, not a wedding dress designer. The plane was smaller than she'd expected, but there was plenty of room to stretch out and the seats were way, way more comfortable than she was used to. She always travelled economy. This was another world.

'Welcome aboard,' the pilot said, shaking their hands. 'Our flight today will be about two and a half hours. If you need anything, ask Elise.'

Elise turned out to be their stewardess.

And, most importantly, Elise stored the dress boxes where Claire could see them. This time, she could be totally sure that none of the dresses would be lost.

'Do you mind if I...?' Sean gestured to his briefcase.

Claire would much rather work than make small talk with him, too. 'Sure. Me, too,' she said, and took a sketchpad from her bag. She'd had a new client yesterday who wanted a dress at short notice, plus there was the big wedding show in two months' time—a show where Claire was exhibiting her very first collection, and she was working flat out to get enough dresses ready in time. Six wedding dresses plus the bridesmaids' outfits to go with each, as well as colour co-ordinating the groom's outfit with each set. She could really do with an extra twenty-four hours in a day for the next few weeks—twenty-four hours when she didn't need to sleep. But, as that wasn't physically possible, she'd have to settle for drinking too much coffee and eating too much sugary stuff to get her through the next few weeks.

As he worked, Sean was aware of the quick, light strokes of Claire's pencil against her sketchpad. Clearly she was working on some preliminary designs for someone else's dress. When the sound stopped, he looked over at her.

She'd fallen asleep mid-sketch, her pencil still held

loosely in one hand, and there were deep shadows beneath her eyes.

Right at that moment, she looked vulnerable. And Sean was shocked by the sudden surge of protectiveness.

Since when did he feel protective about Claire Stewart?

That wasn't something he wanted to think about too closely. So he concentrated on his work and let her sleep until the plane landed. Then he leaned over and touched her shoulder. 'Claire, wake up.'

She murmured something and actually nestled closer, so her cheek was resting against his hand.

It was his second shock of the afternoon, how her skin felt against his. It made him feel almost as if he'd been galvanised. Very similar to that weird sensation when she'd measured him for the waistcoat—even though her touch had been as professional and emotionless as any tailor's, it had made him feel strange to feel the warmth of her fingers through his shirt.

Oh, help.

Sexual attraction and Claire Stewart were two things that definitely didn't go together, in his book.

OK, so there had been that night, all those years ago—but Claire had been seventeen and his mother had dispatched him to rescue the girl and get her safely to bed back at their house. Of course he'd been tempted when she'd tried to kiss him—he was a man, not an automaton—but he also knew that he was responsible for her, and no way would he ever have taken advantage of her.

And the times since when their eyes had met at one of Ashleigh's parties...

Well, she'd normally had some dreadful boyfriend

or other in tow. In Sean's experience, Claire's men were always the type who'd claim that artistic integrity was much more important than actually earning a living. Sean didn't have much time for people who wouldn't shoulder their fair share of responsibility and expected other people to bail them out all the time, but he still wouldn't encourage their girlfriend to cheat on them. He'd never made a move.

Except, he remembered with a twinge of guilt, for the night Ashleigh had got engaged to Luke. He'd asked Claire to dance—solely for his sister's sake. But then Claire had looked up at him, her blue eyes huge and her mouth parted, and he'd reacted purely on instinct.

He'd kissed her.

A kiss that had shaken him to the core. It had shaken him even more when he analysed it. No way could he feel like *that* about Claire Stewart. She was his total opposite. It would never, ever work between them. They'd drive each other crazy.

He'd been too shocked to say a word, at first, but then she'd made some terrible joke or other and he'd somehow managed to get his common sense back. And he'd blanked out the memory.

Except now it was back.

And he had to acknowledge that the possibility of something happening between himself and Claire had always been there. Right now, the possibility hummed just a little harder. Probably because he hadn't dated anyone in the last three months—this was a physical itch, he told himself, and Claire definitely wasn't the right woman to scratch said itch. Their approach to life was way too different for it ever to work between them.

'Claire.' This time, he shook her a little harder, the

way he would've liked to shake himself and get his common sense back in place.

She woke with a jolt. She blinked, as if not quite sure where she was, and he saw her expression change the second that she realised what had happened. 'Sorry,' she said. 'I didn't intend to fall asleep. I hope I didn't snore too loudly.'

He could tell that this was her way of trying to make a joke and ease the tension between them. Good idea. He'd follow her lead on that one. 'Not quite pneumatic drill mode,' he said with a smile.

'Good.'

Like him, she thanked the pilot and the stewardess for getting them there safely. And then they were in the bright Italian sunshine, so bright that they both needed to use dark glasses. And Sean was secretly glad of the extra barrier. He didn't want Claire guessing that she'd shaken his composure, even briefly.

And no way was he going to let her struggle with three dress boxes. 'I'll take these for you.'

She rolled her eyes. 'They're not that heavy, Sean. They're just a bit bulky.'

'Even so.'

'I can manage.'

Did she think that he was being sexist? 'I'm taller than you and my arms are longer,' he pointed out. 'So it makes sense for me to carry the boxes.'

'Then I'll carry your suitcase and briefcase.'

He'd almost forgotten just how stubborn she could be. But, at the same time, he had a sneaking admiration for her independence. And he always travelled light in any case, so his luggage wouldn't be too heavy for her.

On the way from the plane to the airport terminal, Claire said to Sean, 'Perhaps you can let me have your friend's name and address, so I can send her some flowers.'

'Already done,' he said.

'From you, yes. I want to send her something from *me*.'

'Sure,' he said easily. 'I'll give you the details when we get to the hotel.'

'Thank you.' She paused. 'And I need to pick up my case and the bridesmaid's dress. I checked them in to the left luggage, this morning.'

'Wait a second.' He checked his phone. 'Good. Jen—my PA—has booked us a taxi from here to Sorrento and arranged the hydrofoil tickets.'

They went through passport control, then collected Claire's luggage. He waited while she checked with the airline whether Ashleigh's original dress had turned up yet. He knew from her expression that there was still no luck.

The taxi driver loaded their luggage into the car. Claire and Sean were sitting together in the back seat. She was very aware of his nearness, and it made her twitchy. She didn't want to be this aware of Sean. And how did you make small talk with someone who had nothing in common with you?

She looked out of the window. 'Oh, there's Vesuvius.' Looming over the skyline, a brooding hulk of a mountain with a hidden, dangerous core.

'You went there with Ashleigh, didn't you?' he asked.

'And Sammy. Three years ago. It was amazing—like nothing any of us had ever seen before. It was what I imagine a lunar landscape would look like, and we squeaked like schoolkids when we saw steam coming out of the vents.' She smiled at the memory. 'I think that's why Ash chose to get married in Capri, because she fell in love with the island when we came here and had a day trip there.'

They both knew the other reason why Ashleigh hadn't planned to get married in the church where she and Sean had been christened and their parents had got married—because their parents were buried in the churchyard and it had been too much for Ashleigh to bear, the idea of getting married inside the church while her parents were outside.

'It's a nice part of the world,' Sean said.

'Very,' Claire replied. She ran out of small talk at that point and spent the rest of the journey looking out of the window at the coastline, marvelling at the houses perched so precariously on the cliffsides and the incredible blueness of the sea. At the same time, all her senses seemed to be concentrating on Sean. Which was insane.

Finally the taxi dropped them at the marina in Sorrento. Claire waited with their luggage while Sean collected their tickets—and then at last they boarded the hydrofoil and were on their way to Capri.

There were large yachts moored at the marina. As they drew closer she could see the buildings lining the marina, painted in brilliant white or ice cream shades. There were more houses on the terraces banking up behind them, then the white stone peak of the island.

Once they'd docked, they took the funicular railway up to the Piazzetta, then caught a taxi from the square; she noticed that the cars were all open-topped with a stripy awning above them to shade the passengers. So much more exotic than the average convertible.

The taxi took them past more of the brilliant white buildings, in such sharp contrast to the sea and the sky.

There were bougainvillea and rhododendrons everywhere, and terracotta pots full of red geraniums. Claire had always loved the richness and depth of the colours on the south European coast.

At last, they reached the hotel.

'Thank you for arranging this,' she said as they collected their keys. 'And you said you'd give me your friend's details?' She grabbed a pen and paper, ready to take them down as Sean gave them to her. 'Thanks. Last thing—milk, white or dark chocolate?'

'I have no idea. You're sending her chocolate?'

'You've already sent flowers.' She smiled. 'I guess you can't really send anyone confectionery, with your business being in that line.' Admittedly Farrell's specialised in toffee rather than chocolates, but it would still be a bit of a *faux pas*. 'I'll play it safe and send a mixture.'

'Good plan,' he said. 'See you later.'

He'd made it clear that he didn't plan to spend much time with her. Which suited Claire just fine—the less time they were in each other's company, the less likelihood there was of another fight.

She let the bellboy help her carry her luggage to her room. She'd barely set the dress boxes on the bed in her room when there was a knock on the door.

'Come in,' she called with a smile, having a very good idea who it would be.

Ashleigh walked in—physically so like Sean, with the same dark eyes and dark hair, but a million times easier to be with and one of Claire's favourite people in the whole world. Claire hugged her fiercely. 'Hey, you beautiful bride-to-be. How are you?'

Ashleigh hugged her back. 'I'm so glad to see you! I can't believe you've been flying back and forth between England and Italy all day. That's insane, Claire, even for you.'

Claire shrugged. 'You're worth it. Anyway, I'm here now.' She held her friend at arm's length. 'You look gorgeous. Radiant. Just as you should be.'

'And you look shattered,' Ashleigh said, eyeing her closely. 'You were up before dawn to get your first flight here.'

'I'm fine. I, um, had a bit of a nap on the plane,' Claire admitted.

'Good—and you must be in dire need of something to eat and a cold drink.'

'A cold drink would be nice—but, before we do anything else, I need you to try on these dresses so I can get the alterations started.' Claire hugged her again. 'I'm so sorry that it's all gone so wrong.'

'It wasn't your fault,' Ashleigh said loyally.

That wasn't how Sean saw it, but Claire kept that thought to herself.

Ashley tried on the dresses and looked critically at herself in the mirror. Finally, she made her decision. 'I think this one.'

'Good choice,' Claire said.

Thankfully, the dress didn't need much altering. Claire took the dressmaking kit from her luggage and pinned the dress so it was the perfect fit.

'You're not doing any more work on that tonight,' Ashleigh said firmly. 'It's another day and a half until the wedding, and you've been travelling all day, so right now I want you to chill out and relax.'

'I promise you, I plan to have an early night,' Claire said. 'But I still need to check the waistcoats on the men. And I would kill for a shower.' All the travelling had made her feel tired, as well as sticky; running some cool water over her head might just help to keep her awake a bit longer.

'Sort the men's fitting tomorrow after breakfast,' Ashleigh said. 'Just have your shower, then come and meet us on the terrace when you're done. I'll have a long, cold drink waiting for you. With lots and lots of ice.'

'That sounds like heaven,' Claire said gratefully.

When Ashleigh had gone, Claire hung up all the dresses and waistcoats, and had a shower. Then she joined her best friend, her husband-to-be and their best man on the terrace. To her relief, Sean wasn't there.

'He had some phone calls to make,' Ashleigh explained. 'You know Sean. He always works crazy hours.'

Probably, Claire thought, because he'd been thrown in at the deep end when he'd had to take over the family business at the age of twenty-four after their parents had been killed in a car crash. Working crazy hours had got him through the first year, and it was a habit that had clearly stuck. 'Well—cheers,' she said, and raised her glass as the others echoed her toast.

Somehow Claire managed to avoid Sean for most of the next day; their only contact was just after breakfast, when she did the final fitting of the waistcoats and checked that they went perfectly with the suits and shirts. She was busy for most of the day making the last-minute alterations to Ashleigh's dress, and when she was finished Sean was still busy making phone calls and analysing reports.

Then again, the sheer romance of the island of Capri would be wasted on a man like Sean, Claire thought. He was too focused on his work to notice the gorgeous flowers or the blueness of the sea. So much so that she'd half expected him not to join them for the surprise that she and Luke had organised for Ashleigh that evening; when he joined them in the taxi, she had to hide her amazement.

'So where are we going?' Ashleigh asked.

'You'll see. Patience, Miss Farrell,' Claire said with a grin. Actually, it was something that she was looking forward to and dreading in equal measure, but she knew that it was something her best friend would love, so she'd force herself to get over her fears. It was just a shame that Sammy wasn't there to join them as her flight from New York had been delayed. Which meant that, instead of being able to let Sammy defuse the awkwardness between herself and Sean, Claire was going to have to make small talk with him—because she could hardly talk only to the best man and the groom-to-be and ignore Sean completely.

Finally they arrived at the chairlift.

'Oh, fabulous!' Ashleigh hugged Claire and then her husband-to-be. 'I love this place. I didn't think we'd get time to do this.'

'It was Claire's idea,' Luke said with a smile. 'She said sunset at the top of Monte Solaro would be incredibly romantic.'

'Especially because it's outside the usual tourist hours and we'll have the place all to ourselves. I can't believe you arranged all this.' Ashleigh looked thrilled. 'Thank you so much, both of you.'

Twelve minutes, Claire reminded herself as she was helped onto the chair. It would only take twelve minutes to get from the bottom of the chairlift to the very top of the island. She wasn't going to fall off. It was perfectly safe. She'd done this before. Thousands and thousands of tourists had done this before. The chairs were on a continuous loop, so all she had to do was let them help her jump off at the top. It would be *fine*.

Even so, her palms felt slightly damp and she clung on to the green central pole of her chair for dear life. Thankfully, her bag had a cross-body strap, so she didn't have to worry about holding on to that, too. Her hands ached by the time she reached the top, but she managed to get off the chair without falling flat on her face.

Just as she and Luke had arranged, there was a table at the panoramic viewpoint overlooking the *faraglioni*, the three famous vertical columns of rock rising out of the sea. There was a beautiful arrangement of white flowers in the centre of the table, and white ribbons on the wicker chairs. When they sat down, the waiter brought over a bottle of chilled Prosecco and canapés.

'Cheers. To Ashleigh and Luke—just to say how much we love you,' Claire said, lifting her glass, and the others echoed the toast.

'I really can't believe you did this.' Ashleigh was beaming, and Claire's heart swelled. The night before the wedding, when Ashleigh should've been happily fussed over by her mum...Claire had wanted to take her best friend's mind off what she was missing, and she and Luke had talked over the options. The scary one had definitely been the best decision.

'It wasn't just me. It was Luke as well,' Claire said, wanting to be fair. 'It's just a shame Sammy couldn't make it.'

'She'll be here tomorrow,' Tom said confidently.

'You know, some brides actually get married up here,' Ashleigh said. 'Obviously they're not going to walk for an hour uphill in a wedding dress and high heels, so they ride on the chairlift. I've seen photographs where the bride carried her shoes in one hand and her bouquet in the other.'

'And I suppose Claire showed them to you,' Sean said.

Claire didn't rise to the bait, but she wished she hadn't already done the final fitting of his waistcoat, because otherwise she would've had great pleasure in being totally unprofessional and sticking pins into him.

'No,' Ashleigh said. 'Actually, she talked me out of it.'

'Because the design of your dress means you wouldn't fit in the seat properly and I didn't want your dress all creased in the photographs,' Claire said with a smile.

Ashleigh laughed. 'More like because you wouldn't be able to hang on to your shoes and your flowers and cling on to the central bar for dear life all at the same time.'

Claire laughed back. 'OK, so I'm a wuss about heights—but I would've done it if that's what you'd really wanted, Ash. Because it's your day, and what *you* want is what's important.' Her words were directed at her best friend, but she looked straight into Sean's eyes, making it very clear that she meant every word.

He had the grace to flush.

It looked as if he'd got the message, then. Ashleigh came first and they'd put their differences aside for her sake.

Luke and Tom chatted easily, covering up the fact that Claire and Sean were barely speaking to each other. And gradually Claire relaxed, letting herself enjoy the incredibly romantic setting. They watched as the sun began to set over the sea; mist rose around the distant islands as the sky became striped with yellow and pink and purple, making them seem mysterious and otherworldly.

Claire took a few shots with her camera; she knew they wouldn't be anything near as good as Sammy's photographs, but it would at least be a nice memory. She glanced at Sean; he looked as if he was lost in thought, staring out at the sunset. Before she quite realised what she was doing, she took the snap.

Later that evening, back in her hotel room, she reviewed her photographs. There were some gorgeous shots of the sunset and the sea, of Ashleigh and Luke and Tom. But the picture she couldn't get out of her head was the impulsive one she'd taken of Sean. If they'd never met before, if there were no history of sniping and backbiting between them, she would've said he was the most attractive man she'd ever met and she would've been seriously tempted to get together with him.

But.

She'd known Sean for years, he was far from an easy man, and she really didn't need any complications in her life right now.

'Too much Prosecco addling your brain, Claire Stewart,' she told herself with a wry smile. 'Tomorrow, you're on sparkling water.'

Tomorrow.

Ashleigh's wedding day.

And please, please, let it be perfect.

CHAPTER THREE

'MISS STEWART?' THE woman from the airline introduced herself swiftly on the phone. 'I'm very pleased to say we've found the dress box that went missing.'

It took a moment for it to sink in. They'd actually found Ashleigh's original dress?

'That's fantastic,' Claire said. She glanced at her watch. Ashleigh's wedding wasn't until four o'clock. Which meant she had enough time to get the hydrofoil across to Sorrento and then a taxi to the airport to collect the dress, and she'd be back in time to get the dress ready while Ashleigh was having her hair and make-up done. Thankfully, she'd brought her portable steam presser with her in her luggage, so although the dress would be quite badly creased by now, she'd be able to fix it. 'Thank you very much. I'll be with you as soon as possible.'

'And if you could bring some identification with you, it would be helpful,' the airline assistant added.

'I'll bring my passport,' Claire said. Even before she'd said goodbye and ended the call, she was unlocking the safe in her wardrobe and taking her passport out.

When she went to tell Ashleigh the good news, Sean was there.

'It'd be quicker to get the dress couriered here,' he said.

'I've already lost the dress once. If you think I'm taking the risk of that happening again...' Claire shook her head. 'No chance.'

It also meant she had a bulletproof excuse to avoid Sean for the next few hours. Though that was slightly beside the point. She kissed Ashleigh's cheek. 'I'll text you when I've picked it up and I'm on my way back. But I'll be back well before it's time to have our hair and make-up done, I promise.'

Ashleigh hugged her back. 'I know. And thanks, Claire.'

'Hey. That's what best friends are for,' she said with a smile.

When Claire collected the dress, the box was in perfect condition, so she didn't have to worry that the contents had been damaged in any way. It didn't matter any more where the dress had been; the important thing was that she had it now, and Ashleigh would wear the dress of her dreams on her wedding day.

'Miss Stewart? Before you go,' the airline assistant said, 'I have a message for you. You have transport back to Capri. Would you mind coming this way?'

'Why?' Claire asked, mystified. She'd planned to get another taxi back to Sorrento, and then the hydrofoil across to Capri.

Before the airline assistant could answer, Claire's phone pinged with a message. 'Sorry, would you mind if I check this?' she asked, just in case it was Ashleigh.

To her surprise, the message was from Sean.

Transport arranged. Don't argue. Ashleigh worrying. Need to save time.

Sean had arranged transport for her? She swallowed hard. She knew Sean had done this for his sister's sake, not for hers, but it was still such a nice thing to do.

And the transport wasn't a taxi back to Sorrento. It was a helicopter. And the pilot told her that the flight from Naples to Capri took less time than the hydrofoil from Sorrento to Capri, so Sean had saved her the time of the taxi journey on top of that.

She texted back swiftly. Thank you. Tell her the dress is absolutely fine. Let me know how much I owe you for the transport. She knew Sean's opinion of her was already low and she was absolutely not going to let him think she was a freeloader, on top of whatever else he thought about her. She'd always paid her own way.

A text came back from him.

Will tell her. Transport on me.

Oh, no, it wasn't. Dress my responsibility, so *I* will pay. Not negotiable, she typed back pointedly. No way was she going to be in debt to Sean.

She'd half expected a taxi to meet her at the helipad, but Sean was in the reception area, waiting for her. He was wearing formal dark trousers and a white shirt—Claire didn't think he actually owned a pair of jeans—but for once he wasn't wearing a tie. His concession to casual dress, perhaps.

He looked gorgeous.

And he was totally off limits. She really needed to get a grip. Like *now*.

'What are you doing here?' she asked.

'Transport,' he said, gesturing to an open-topped sports car in the car park.

She didn't have much choice other than to accept. 'Thank you.' She looked at him. 'Is Ash OK?'

'She's fine,' he reassured her.

'Good.'

'And I owe you an apology.'

Claire frowned, surprised. Sean was apologising to her? 'For what?'

'Sniping at you last night—assuming that you'd given Ashleigh that crazy idea of getting married at the top of the mountain and going up by chairlift.'

'Given that I'm scared of heights,' she said dryly, 'I was quite happy to talk her out of that one on the grounds of dress practicalities.'

'But you went up on the chairlift last night.'

She shrugged. 'Luke and I wanted to distract her and we thought that would be a good way.'

'Yeah.'

She looked at him. He masked his feelings quickly, but she'd seen the flash of pain in his eyes. On impulse, she laid her hand on his arm. 'It must be hard for you, too.'

He nodded. 'It should be Dad walking down the aisle with her, not me.' His voice was husky with suppressed emotion. 'But things are as they are.'

'Your parents would be really proud of you,' she said.

'Excuse me?' His voice had turned icy.

She took her hand off his arm. 'OK. It's not my place to say anything and I wasn't trying to patronise you. But I thought a lot of your parents. Your mum in particular was brilliant when my mum died. And they would've been proud of the way you've always been there for Ash, always supported her—well, *almost* always,' she amended. To be fair, he'd been pretty annoyed about Ashleigh's change of planned career. He hadn't supported it at first.

'She's my little sister. What else would I do?'

It was a revelation to Claire. Sean clearly equated duty with love, or mixed them to the point where they couldn't be distinguished. And discussing this was way beyond her pay grade. She changed the subject again. 'So how much do I owe you for the flight?'

'You don't.'

'I've already told you, the dress is my responsibility, so I'll pay the costs. But thank you for organising it, especially as it means Ash isn't worrying any more.'

'We'll discuss it later,' he said. 'Ashleigh comes first.'

'Agreed—but that doesn't mean I'm happy to be in your debt,' she pointed out.

'I did this for Ashleigh, not for you.'

'Well, *duh*.' She caught herself before she said something really inflammatory. 'Sean, I know we don't usually get on too well.' That was the understatement of the year. 'But I think we're going to have to make the effort and play nice while we're on Capri.'

He slanted her a look that said very clearly that he didn't believe she could keep it up.

If she was honest, she wasn't sure she could keep it up, either. Or that Sean could, for that matter. But they were at least going to make the effort. Though they had a cast-iron excuse not to talk to each other for the next few minutes, because he needed to concentrate on driving.

She put the dress box safely in the back of the car, took her sunhat from her bag and jammed it on her head so it wouldn't be blown away, then sat in the front seat next to Sean. She still had her dark glasses on from the helicopter flight, so the glare of the sun didn't bother her.

Sean was a very capable driver, she noticed, even though he was driving on the right-hand side of the road instead of the left as he was used to doing in England. The road was incredibly narrow and winding, with no verges and high stone walls at the edges; it was busy with vans and scooters and minibuses, and every so often he had to pull over into the tiniest of passing places. If Claire had been driving, she would've been panicking that the car would end up being scraped on one of those stone walls; but she knew that she was very safe with Sean. It was an odd feeling, having to rely on someone she normally tried to avoid. And even odder that for once she didn't mind.

'Is there anything you need for the dress?' he asked as they pulled up outside the hotel.

'Only my portable steam presser, which I brought with me on my first trip.'

He looked confused. 'Why do you need a steam presser?'

'This dress has been in a box for three days. Even though I was careful when I packed it, there are still going to be creases in the material, and I don't have time to hang the dress in a steamy bathroom and wait for the creases to fall out naturally. And an ordinary iron isn't good enough to give a professional finish.'

'OK. Let me know if you need anything organised.'

He probably needed some reassurance that it wasn't going to go wrong, she thought. 'You can come and have a sneak peek at the dress, if you want,' she said.

'Isn't that meant to be bad luck?'

'Only if you're the bridegroom. Remember that the

dress needs pressing, so you won't be seeing it at its best,' she warned, 'but it will be perfect by the time Ash puts it on.'

Sean looked at Claire. Her sunhat was absolutely horrible, a khaki-coloured cap with a peak to shade her eyes; but he supposed it was more sensible than going out bareheaded in the strong mid-morning sun and risking sunstroke.

He wondered if she'd guessed that he wanted reassurance that nothing else was going to go wrong with the dress—just as she'd clearly noticed that moment when the might-have-beens had shaken his composure. She'd been a bit clumsy about it, but she hadn't pushed him to talk and share his feelings. She'd been kind, he realised now, and that wasn't something he associated with Claire Stewart. It made him feel weird.

But, if she could make the effort, then so could he. 'Thanks. I would appreciate that.'

'Let's go, then,' she said.

He followed her up to her room. Everywhere was neat and tidy. Funny, he'd expected the room to be as messy and chaotic as Claire's life seemed to be—even though her shop had been tidy. But then he supposed the shop would have to be tidy or it would put off potential clients.

She put the dress box on the bed. 'Right—how much do I owe you for that flight?'

'We've already discussed that,' he said, feeling awkward.

'No, we haven't, and I don't want to be beholden to you.'

'Ashleigh is my sister,' he reminded her.

'I know, and she's my best friend—but I still don't want to be beholden to you.'

He frowned. 'Now you're being stubborn.'

'Pots and kettles,' she said softly. 'Tell me how much I owe you.'

Actually, he liked the fact that she was so insistent on paying her fair share. It showed she had integrity. Maybe he'd been wrong to tar her with the same brush as her awful boyfriends. Just because she had a dreadful taste in men, it didn't necessarily mean that she was as selfish as they were—did it? 'OK.' He told her a sum that was roughly half, guessing that she'd have no idea how much helicopter transfers would cost.

'Fine. Obviously I don't have the cash on me right at this very second,' she said, 'but I can either do a bank transfer if you give me your account details, or give you the cash in person when we're back in England.'

'No rush. I'll give you my bank details, but making the transfer when you get back to England will be fine,' he said.

'Good. Thank you.' She opened the box, unpacked the dress, and put it on a hanger.

The organza skirt was creased but Sean could already see how stunning the ivory dress was. It had a strapless sweetheart neckline, the bodice was made of what he suspected might be handmade lace, and it looked as if hundreds of tiny pearls had been sewn into it. It was worthy of something produced by any of the big-name designers.

And Claire had designed this for his little sister. She'd made it all by hand.

Now he understood why she'd called her business that ridiculous name, because she was delivering exactly what her client wanted—a dream of a dress.

Clearly his lack of response rattled her, because she folded her arms. 'If you hate it, fine—but remember that this is what Ash wanted. And I'm giving you fair warning, if you tell Ash you hate it before she puts it on, so she feels like the ugliest bride in the world instead of like a princess, then you're so getting the rusty spoon treatment.'

'I don't hate it, actually. I'm just a bit stunned, because I wasn't expecting it to be that good,' he admitted.

She dropped into a sarcastic curtsey. 'Why, thank you, kind sir, for the backhanded compliment.'

'I didn't mean it quite like that,' he said. 'I don't know much about dresses, but that looks as if it involved a lot of work.'

'It did. But she's worth every second.'

'Yeah.' For a moment, he almost turned to her and hugged her.

But this was Claire 'Follow Your Heart' Stewart, the mistress of chaos. Their worlds didn't mix. A hug would be a bad, bad idea. 'Thanks for letting me see the dress,' he said. 'I'd better let you get on.'

'Tell Ash her dress is here safely, and I'll come and find her the second it's ready.'

He nodded. 'Will do.'

Once Claire was satisfied with the dress, she took it through to Ashleigh's room. Sammy opened the door. 'Claire-bear! About time, too,' she said with a grin. 'Losing the dress. Tsk. What kind of dressmaker does that?'

'Don't be mean, Sammy,' Ashleigh called. 'I'd cuff her for you, Claire, but I have to sit still and let Aliona take these rollers out of my hair.'

Claire hung up the dress, then enveloped Sammy with a hug. 'Hello to you, too. How was your flight?'

'Disgusting,' Sammy said cheerfully, 'but when I've finished taking photographs tonight then I'm going to drink Prosecco until I don't care any more.'

'Hangover on top of jet lag. Nice,' Claire teased. 'It's so good to see you, Sammy.'

'You, too. And oh, my God. How amazing is that dress? You've really surpassed yourself this time, Claire.'

Claire smiled in acknowledgement. 'I'm just glad we got it back.'

The hotel's hairdresser and make-up artist cooed over the dress, too, and then Claire submitted to being prettied up before putting on her own dress and then helping Ashleigh with hers.

Sammy posed them both for photographs on the balcony. 'Righty. I need to do the boys, now,' she said when she'd finished. 'See you at the town hall.'

'OK?' Claire asked when Sammy had gone.

Ashleigh gulped. 'Yes. Just thinking.'

'I know.' It would be similar for Claire, if she ever got married: she'd be missing her mum, though her dad would be there—*if* he approved of Claire's choice of man—and her mum's family would be there, with Ashleigh and Sammy to support her.

Not that Claire thought she'd ever get married. All the men she'd ever been involved with had turned out to be Mr Wrong. Men she'd thought would share her dreams, but who just couldn't commit. Men who'd been so casual with her emotions that she'd lost trust in her judgement.

'But I think they're here in spirit,' Claire said softly.

'They loved you so much, Ash. And Luke can't wait to make you his bride. You've got a good guy, there.'

'I know. I'm lucky.' Ashleigh swallowed hard.

'Hey. If you cry and your make-up runs, Sean will have my guts for garters,' Claire said. She went into a dramatic pose. 'Help! Help! Save me from your scary big brother!'

To her relief, it worked, and Ashleigh laughed; she was still smiling when Sean knocked on her door to say they needed to go.

CHAPTER FOUR

SEAN HAD ALREADY seen the dress—albeit not at its best—but seeing his little sister wearing it just blew him away. The ivory dress emphasised Ashleigh's perfect hour-glass shape by skimming in at the waist, then falling to the floor in soft folds. Her dark hair was drawn back from her face and pinned at the back as a base for her veil, and then flowed down in soft curls. She wore a discreet and very pretty tiara with sparkling stones and pearls to reflect the pearls in the bodice. And finally she was carrying a simple posy of dusky lavender roses, the same colour as Claire's dress; the stems were tightly bound with ivory ribbon.

'You look amazing, Ashleigh,' he said. 'Really amazing.'

Then he glanced at Claire. Again, he was shocked. He hadn't seen the bridesmaid's dress before, though he'd had a fair idea that it would be dusky lavender, the same colour as his waistcoat and the rose in his buttonhole. Although it, too, was strapless and had a sweetheart neckline, it was much plainer than Ashleigh's dress and ended at the knee. Claire's hair was dressed in a similar style to his sister's, though without a veil and with a discreet jewelled headband rather than a tiara. Her roses were ivory rather than lavender, as a counterpoint to the bride's bouquet, and her satin high heels were dyed to match her dress.

If he'd seen her across a crowded room as a complete stranger, he would've been drawn to her immediately. Approached her. Asked her out.

He pushed the thought away. This was Claire. He *did* know her. And, if they hadn't made a truce for Ashleigh's sake, they would've been sniping at each other within the next five minutes. She was absolutely not date material.

'Ready?' he asked.

'Ready,' they chorused.

The official civil ceremony was held at the town hall in Anacapri. Only the main people from the wedding party were there: Ashleigh and Luke, with Luke's best friend, Tom, as the best man, Claire as the bridesmaid and one of the witnesses, and himself as the other witness. Sammy was there, too, to take photographs.

After everything had been signed, the two open-topped cars took them to the private villa where the symbolic ceremony was being held and the rest of their family and friends were waiting to celebrate with them.

Luke and Tom went ahead to wait at the bridal arch, which was covered with gorgeous white flowers.

Then Ashleigh stood at the edge of the red carpet, her arm linked through Sean's. He could feel her trembling slightly. Nervous, excited and a little sad all at the same time, he guessed. 'Ashleigh, you're such a beautiful bride,' he said softly. 'Our parents would be so proud of you right now.'

Ashleigh nodded, clearly too overcome to speak, and squeezed his arm as if to say, 'You, too.'

'Come on. Let's get the party started,' he said, and

gave the signal to the traditional Neapolitan guitar and mandolin duo.

Their version of Pachelbel's 'Canon' was perfect. And Sean was smiling as he walked his little sister down the aisle to marry the man she loved.

Claire had seen the photographs and knew that the garden where Ashleigh and Luke were getting married was spectacular, but the photographs really hadn't done the place justice. The garden was breathtaking, overlooking the sea; lemon trees grew around the edge of the garden, their boughs heavy with fruit, and the deep borders were filled with rhododendrons and bougainvillea. There seemed to be butterflies everywhere. A symbol of good luck and eternal love, she thought.

She took the bouquet from Ashleigh and held it safely during the ceremony, and she had to blink back the tears as Ashleigh and Luke exchanged their vows, this time in front of everyone. She glanced at Sean, who was standing beside her, and was pleased to see that for once he was misty-eyed, too. And so he should be, on Ashleigh's wedding day, she thought, and she looked away before he caught her staring at him.

Everyone cheered when the celebrant said, 'You may now kiss the bride,' and Luke bent Ashleigh back over his arm to give her a show-stopping kiss.

'Let them have it, guys,' Sammy called as Ashleigh and Luke started to walk back down the aisle, and the confetti made from white dried flower petals flew everywhere.

Once the formal photographs had been taken, waiters came round carrying trays filled with glasses of Prosecco. Ashleigh and Luke headed the line-up to welcome their guests; and then, finally, it was time for the meal. Ashleigh had chosen a semi-traditional top table layout, so Claire as the chief bridesmaid was at one end, next to Luke's father. As Sean was standing in for the bride's father, he was at the other end, between Ashleigh and Luke's mother. And there were enough people between them, Claire thought, for them to be able to smile and hide their relief at not having to make small talk.

It was an amazing table, under a pergola draped with white wisteria. Woven in between the flowers were glass baubles, which caught the light from the tea-light candles set in similar glass globes on the table, and reflected again in the mirrored finish of the table. The sun was already beginning to set, and Claire had never seen anything so romantic in her life. And the whole thing was topped off by the traditional Neapolitan guitar and mandolin duo who played and sang softly during the meal.

If she ever got married, Claire thought, this was just the kind of wedding she'd want, full of love and happiness and so much warmth.

Finally, after the excellent coffee and tiny rich Italian desserts, it was time for the speeches. Luke's was sweet and heartfelt, Tom's made everyone laugh, but Sean's made her blink back the tears.

He really did love Ashleigh. And, for that, Claire could forgive the rest.

The cake—a spectacular four-tier confection, which Claire knew held four different flavours of sponge—was cut, and then it was time for the dancing.

Ashleigh and Luke had chosen a song for their bridal dance that always put a lump in her throat—'Make You Feel My Love'—and she watched them glide across the temporary dance floor. The evening band played it in waltz time, and Claire knew that Luke had been tak-

ing private lessons; he was step-perfect as he whirled
Ashleigh round in the turns. The perfect couple.

Tradition said that the best man and the chief bridesmaid danced together next, and Claire liked Tom very
much indeed; she was pleased to discover that he was
an excellent dancer and her toes were perfectly safe
with him.

'I love the dresses,' Tom said. 'If I wasn't gay, I'd *so*
date you—a woman who can create such utter beauty.
You're amazing, Claire.'

She laughed and kissed his cheek. 'Aww, you're such
a sweetie, Tom. Thank you. But I wouldn't date you because I have terrible taste in men—and you're far too
nice to be one of *my* men.'

He laughed. 'Thank *you*, sweetie. You'll find the
right guy some day.'

'If I could find someone who'd make me as happy
as Luke makes Ash,' she said softly, 'I'd consider myself blessed.'

'Me, too,' Tom said. 'And the other way round.
They're perfect for each other.'

'They certainly are,' she said with a smile, though
at the same time there was a nagging ache in her heart.
Would she ever find someone who'd make her happy,
or was she always destined to date Mr Wrong?

Sean knew it was his duty—as the man who'd given
the bride away—to dance with the chief bridesmaid at
some point. For a second, he stood watching Claire as
she danced with Luke's father. She was chatting away,
looking totally at ease. And then Sean registered what
the band was playing: 'Can't Take My Eyes Off You'.
He was shocked to realise that it was true: he couldn't
take his eyes off Claire.

Which was absolutely not a good thing.

Claire Stewart was the last woman he wanted to get involved with.

And yet he had to acknowledge that he was drawn to her. There was something about her. He couldn't pin it down, which annoyed him even more—he couldn't put his feelings in a pigeonhole, the way he usually did. And that made her dangerous. He needed to stay well away from her.

Though, for tonight, he had to do the expected thing and make the best of it.

As the song came to an end, he walked over. 'I guess we need to play nice for Ashleigh.'

'I guess,' she said.

Even as the words came out of his mouth, he knew he was saying the wrong thing, but he couldn't stop himself asking, 'So is one of your awful boyfriends joining you later?'

'If that's your idea of nice,' Claire said, widening her eyes in what looked like annoyance, 'I'd hate to see how caustic your idea of snippy would be.'

He grimaced, knowing that he was in the wrong this time. 'Sorry. I shouldn't have put it quite like that.'

'Not if you were being nice. Though,' she said, 'I do admit that I have a terrible taste in men. I always seem to pick Mr Wrong.' She shrugged. 'And the answer's no, nobody's joining me. I'm happily single right now. And I'm way too busy at work right now to get involved with someone.'

Was that her way of telling him she wasn't interested? Or was she just giving him the facts?

Her perfume wasn't one he recognised; it was something mysterious and deep. Maybe that was what was scrambling his brain, rather than her nearness. Scrambling his brain enough to make him think that she was the perfect fit. The way she felt, in his arms...

'So isn't one of your sweet-but-temporary girlfriends joining you later?' Claire asked.

Ouch. Though Sean knew he deserved the question. He'd started it. 'No. Becca and I broke up three months ago. And I'm busy at work.' Which was his usual excuse for ending a relationship before things started to get too close.

'Two peas in a pod, then, us,' she said with a grin.

'I always thought we were chalk and cheese.'

She laughed. 'I was going to say oil and vinegar. Except they actually go together.'

'And we don't,' Sean said. 'So would you be the vinegar or the oil?'

'Difficult to say. A bit of both, really,' she said. 'I make things go smoothly for my clients. But I'm sharp with people who have an attitude problem. You?'

'Ditto,' he said.

This was *weird*.

They were actually laughing at themselves. Together. Not sniping at each other.

And this felt sparky. Fun. He was actually enjoying Claire's company—something that he'd never thought would happen in a million years.

This was the second song in a row they were dancing to. The music was slower. Softer. And, although he knew it was a seriously bad idea, he found himself drawing Claire closer. Swaying with her.

Oh, help, Claire thought. She'd been here before. Today, she'd paced herself and only drunk a couple of small glasses of Prosecco, well spaced out with sparkling water. But she could still remember the first night she'd kissed Sean Farrell. The way his mouth had felt against hers before he'd pulled away and given her a total dressing-down about being seventeen years old and in a state where an unscrupulous man could've taken advantage of her.

And again, at Ashleigh and Luke's engagement party, where they'd ended up dancing way too close and then Sean had kissed her, his mouth warm and sweet and so tempting that it terrified her.

Right now, it would be all too easy to let her hands drift up over his shoulders, curl round the nape of his neck, and draw his mouth down to hers. Particularly as they were no longer on the dance floor, in full view of the rest of the guests; at some point, while they'd been dancing together, they'd moved away from the temporary dance floor. Now they were in a secluded area of the garden. Just the two of them in the twilight.

'Claire.' His voice was a whisper.

And she knew he was going to kiss her again.

He dipped his head and brushed his mouth against hers, very lightly. It felt as if every nerve-end had been galvanised. He did it again. And again. This time, Claire gave in and slid her hands into his hair. His arms tightened round her and he continued teasing her mouth with those light, barely there kisses that made her want more. Maybe she made some needy little sound, because then he was really kissing her, and it felt as if fireworks were exploding all around them.

When he broke the kiss, she was shaking.

'Claire.' He sounded dazed.

That made two of them.

Part of her wanted to do this. To go with him—her room or his, it wouldn't matter. She knew they both needed a release from the tension of the last few days.

But the sensible part of her knew that doing that would make everything so much worse. How would they face each other in the morning? They certainly didn't have a future. Yes, Sean was reliable, unlike most of her past boyfriends—but he was also too regimented for her liking. Everything had to go within his twenty-year plan. Which was fine for a business, but it wasn't the way she wanted to live her personal life. She wanted to take time to smell the roses. Spontaneity. A chance to seize the day and enjoy whatever came her way. Live life to the full.

'We need to stop,' she said. While she could still be sensible. If he kissed her once more, she knew she'd say yes. So she'd say the word while she could still actually pronounce it. 'No.'

'No.' He looked at her, his eyes haunted. For a second, he looked so vulnerable. She was about to crack and place her palm against his cheek to comfort him, to tell him that she'd changed her mind, when she saw his expression change. His common sense had snapped back into place. 'You're absolutely right,' he said, and took a step back from her.

'I have bridesmaid stuff to do,' she said. It wasn't strictly true—the rest of the evening was all organised—but it was an excuse that she thought would save face for both of them.

'Of course,' he said, and let her go.

Even as she walked away, Claire regretted it. Her old attraction to Sean had never quite gone away, no matter how deeply she thought she'd buried it or how much she denied it to herself.

But she knew it had been the right thing to do. Because no way could things work out between her and Sean, and she'd had enough of broken relationships and being let down. Keeping things platonic was sensible, and the best way to avoid heartbreak.

Claire spent the rest of the evening socialising with the other guests, encouraging the younger ones to dance. All the time, she was very aware of exactly where Sean was in the garden, but she didn't trust herself not to make another stupid mistake. She'd got it wrong with him in the past. She couldn't afford to get it wrong in the future.

Finally, she went back to the hotel with the last few guests, kicked off her high heels, and curled up in one of the wrought iron chairs on the balcony of her room, looking out at the moon's sparkling path on the sea. She'd been sitting there for a while when there was a knock at her door.

She wasn't expecting anyone, especially this late at night—unless maybe someone had been taken ill and needed help?

She padded over to the door, still in bare feet, and blinked in surprise when she saw Sean in the doorway. 'Is something wrong?'

'Yes,' he said.

She went cold. 'Ash?'

'No.'

Then she saw that he'd removed his jacket and cravat. He looked very slightly dishevelled, and it made him much more approachable. And much, much harder to resist.

He was also carrying a bottle of Prosecco and two glasses.

'Sean?' she asked, completely confused.

'I think we need to talk,' he said.

Again, for a split second, she glimpsed that vulnerability in his eyes. How could she turn him away when she had a good idea of how he was feeling—the same way she was feeling herself? 'Come in,' she said, and closed the door behind him.

'I saw you sitting on your balcony,' he said.

She nodded. 'I was a bit too wired to sleep, so I thought I'd look out over the sea and just chill for a bit.'

'Good plan.' He gestured to her balcony. 'Shall we?'

Sean, the sea and moonlight. A dangerous combination. It would be much more sensible to say no.

'Yes,' she said.

He uncorked the bottle with a minimum of fuss and without spilling a drop of the sparkling wine, then poured them both a glass.

Claire held hers up in a toast. 'To Ashleigh and Luke,' she said, 'and may they have every happiness in their life together.'

'Absolutely,' he said, clinking his glass against hers. 'To Ashleigh and Luke.'

'So you're too wired to sleep, too?' she asked.

He nodded. 'I was walking in the hotel gardens. That's when I saw you sitting on the balcony.'

'So why do we need to talk, Sean?'

He blew out a breath. 'You and me.'

The idea sent a shiver of pure desire through her.

'I think it's been a long time coming,' he said softly.

'But we don't even like each other. You think I'm a flake, and I think you're…well…a bit *too* organised,' she said, choosing her words carefully.

'Maybe,' he said, 'because it's easier for us to think that of each other.'

She took a sip of Prosecco, knowing that he was right but not quite wanting to admit it. 'You turned me down.'

'Nearly ten years ago? You know why,' he said. 'I think we've both grown up and got past that.'

'I guess.' She turned her glass round. 'Though I'm not in a hurry to put myself back in that situation.'

'You won't be,' he said softly. 'Because you're not seventeen any more, you're not drunk, and I'm not responsible for you.'

The three barriers that had been in the way, back then. It had hurt and embarrassed her at the time, but later Claire had appreciated how decent he'd been. Not that they'd ever discussed it. It was way too awkward for both of them.

But, now he'd said it, she needed to know. 'Back then, if I hadn't been drunk, if I'd been eighteen, and if you hadn't been responsible for me—would you have...?'

'Let you seduce me?' he asked.

She nodded.

His breath shuddered through him. 'Yes.'

Heat curled in her belly. That night, she'd wanted him so desperately. And, if the circumstances had been different, he would have made love with her. Been her first lover.

All the words were knocked out of her head. Because all she could think about was the way he'd kissed her tonight in the garden, and the way he looked right now. Sexy as hell.

'Ashleigh's engagement,' he said softly. '*You* turned *me* down, that time.'

'Because I was being sensible.' She paused. 'This isn't sensible, either.'

'I know. But your perfume's haunted me all evening,' he said, his voice low and husky and drenched in desire. 'Your mouth. And you've been driving me crazy in that dress.'

She made a last-ditch attempt at keeping the status quo. 'This is a perfectly demure bridesmaid's dress,' she said. 'It's down to my knees.'

'And I can't stop thinking about what you might be wearing under it.'

Her breath hitched. 'Can't you, now?'

The same heat that curled in her belly was reflected in his eyes. 'Going to show me?' he invited.

'We're on my balcony. Anyone could see us. *You* saw me,' she pointed out.

'Then maybe,' he said, 'we should go inside. Draw the curtains.'

She knew without a shadow of a doubt what was going to happen if they did.

There would be repercussions. Huge ones.

But the old desire had lanced sharply through her, to the point where she didn't care about the repercussions any more. 'Yes.'

Without a word, he stood up and scooped her out of her chair. Carried her into the room and set her down on her feet. He turned away just long enough to close the curtains, then pulled her into his arms and kissed her

That first kiss in the garden had been tentative, sweet. This was like lighting touchpaper, setting her on fire. By the time he broke the kiss, they were both shaking.

'Show me,' he said softly.

She reached behind her back to the zip and slid it down; then she held the dress to her.

He raised an eyebrow. 'Shy?'

She shook her head. 'I'm waiting for you to get rid of your waistcoat and undo your shirt.'

He looked puzzled, and she explained, 'Because, if we're going to do this, it's going to be equal. Both of us. All the way.'

'All the way,' Sean repeated huskily. He removed his waistcoat, then undid his shirt and pulled it out of the waistband of his trousers. 'Better?'

'Much better. It makes you look touchable,' she said.

'Good—because I want you to touch me, Claire. And I want to touch you.' He gestured to her dress. 'Show me.'

She felt ridiculously shy and almost chickened out; but then took a deep breath and stepped out of the dress before hanging it on the back of a chair.

'Now that I wasn't expecting—underwear to match your dress.' He closed the gap between them and traced the outline of her strapless lacy bra with the tip of his finger.

'I had it dyed at the same time as my shoes,' she said.

'Attention to detail—I like that,' he said approvingly.

She slid her palms against his pectoral muscles. 'Very nice,' she said, and let her hands slide down to his abdomen. 'A perfect six pack. I wasn't expecting that.'

'I don't spend the whole day in a chair. The gym gives me time to think about things,' he said.

'Good plan.' She slipped the soft cotton from his shoulders.

'So now I'm naked to the waist, and you're not. You said we were in this together, Claire.'

'Then do something about it,' she invited.

Sean smiled, unclipped her bra and let the lacy garment fall to the floor. Then scooped her up, carried her to the bed, and Claire stopped thinking.

CHAPTER FIVE

CLAIRE'S MOBILE SHRILLED. Still with her eyes closed, she groped for the phone on the bedside table. 'Hello?'

'C'mon, sleepyhead! You went to bed before I did—you can't *still* be snoozing,' Sammy said cheerfully. 'There's a pile of warm pastries and a bowl of freshly picked, juicy Italian peaches down here with our name on them. And the best coffee ever.'

Breakfast.

Claire had arranged to meet Sammy for breakfast.

And right now she was still in bed. *With Sean.* Whose arms were still wrapped round her, keeping her close.

'Uh—I'll be down as soon as I can,' Claire said hastily. 'If you're hungry, start without me.'

'Don't blame me if the pastries are all gone by the time you get here. See you soon,' Sammy said, her voice full of laughter.

'Who was that?' Sean asked when Claire put the phone down.

'Sammy. We arranged to have breakfast together this morning.' Claire dragged in a breath. 'Except…Sean, I…' She frowned. 'And now I'm being incoherent and stupid, and that isn't me.'

'Lack of sleep,' he said, nuzzling her shoulder. 'Which is as much my fault as yours.'

Oh, help. When he was being sweet and warm like this, it made her want what she knew she couldn't have. And she really had to be sensible about this. 'Sean—we really can't do this,' she blurted out.

'Do what?'

'Be together. Or let anyone know about what happened last night.' She twisted round to face him. 'You and me—you know it would never work out between us in a month of Sundays. We're too different. You have a twenty-year plan for everything, and I hate being boxed in like that. We'd drive each other bananas.'

'So, what? We're going to pretend last night didn't happen?' he asked.

'That'd probably be the best thing,' she said. 'Because then it won't be awkward when Ash asks us both over to see the wedding photos and what have you.'

'Uh-huh.' His face was expressionless.

And now she felt horrible. Last night had been a revelation about just how much attention Sean paid to things and how good he'd made her feel. And it had been better between them than she'd ever dreamed it would be as a starry-eyed teenager. If only they weren't so different, she'd be tempted to start a proper relationship with him. Seriously tempted. But she knew it wasn't going to work out between them, and she didn't want her oldest friendship to become collateral damage of a fling that didn't last. She swallowed hard. 'Last night... You made it good for me. Really good.'

'Dear John—it's not you, it's me,' he intoned, raising an eyebrow.

'It's both of us, and you know it,' she said. 'You hate the fact that I follow my heart. I know what you call me, Sean.' Just as she was pretty sure that he knew what she called him.

He shrugged. 'I guess you're right.'

So why did it make her feel so bad—so *guilty*? 'I'm not dumping you, and you're not dumping me, because we were never really together in the first place,' she said. 'We'd be a disaster as a couple.'

'Probably,' he agreed.

'Sammy's waiting for me downstairs. I don't get to see her that much, with her job taking her away so much. I promised her I'd be there. I really have to go,' Claire said, feeling even more awkward. She wanted to stay. She wanted to pretend that she and Sean were two completely different people and that it would have a chance of working out between them.

But she had to face the facts. Tomorrow they'd both be back in London. And no way could things work between them there. Their lives were too opposite, and they just wouldn't fit.

'I know I'm being rude and bratty and everything else, but would you mind, um, please closing your eyes while I grab some clothes and have the quickest shower in the world?' she asked.

'It's a little late for shyness,' he said dryly, 'given that we saw every millimetre of each other last night.'

Not just saw, either. The memory made her face hot. They'd touched. Stroked. Kissed.

'Even so,' she said.

'As you wish.' He rolled over and closed his eyes. 'Let me know when it's safe to look.'

'I'm sorry. I really wish things could be different,' she said, meaning it. 'But this is the best way. A clean break.'

'Apart from the fact that my little sister is your best friend, and we'll still have to see each other in the future.'

'And we'll do exactly the same as we've done for years and years,' she said. 'We'll be polite to each other for her sake, and avoid each other as much as we can.'

'Uh-huh.'

'Like you said, last night—well, it's been a long time coming. And now we've done it and it's out of our systems.' Which was a big, fat lie, so it was just as well that he couldn't see her face. She had a nasty feeling that Sean Farrell would never be completely out of her system. Especially now she knew what it was like to kiss him properly. To touch him. To make love with him.

She shook herself and grabbed some clothes. 'It's OK to look,' she said as she closed the bathroom door.

She showered and dressed in record time. When she walked back into the bedroom, Sean was already dressed and sitting on the bed, waiting for her. Well, he would. He had impeccable manners. 'Thank you,' she said. 'Um—I guess I'll see you in London when Ash gets back. And I'll sort out the money I owe you for that helicopter flight.'

Downstairs, Sammy was pouring a cup of coffee from a cafetière when Claire walked over to her table. 'So who was he?' she asked.

'Who was what?' Claire asked.

'The guy who kept you awake last night and gave you that hickey on the left-hand side of your neck.'

Claire clapped a hand to her neck and stared at her friend in utter dismay. She hadn't noticed a hickey while she was in the bathroom—well, not that she'd paid much attention to the mirror, because she'd been too busy panicking about the fact that Sean Farrell was naked and in her bed, and she'd just messed things up again.

And he'd given her a hickey?

Oh, no. She hadn't had a hickey since she was thirteen, and her dad had been so mad at her that she'd never repeated that particular mistake. Until now.

When Claire continued to be silent, Sammy laughed. 'Gotcha. There's no hickey. But clearly I wasn't far wrong and there *was* a guy last night.'

'You don't want to know,' Claire said.

'I wouldn't be fishing if I didn't,' Sammy pointed out.

'It was a one off. And I feel suitably ashamed, OK? I said I wouldn't date any more Mr Wrongs.'

'Forgive me for saying, but you didn't have a date for Ash's wedding,' Sammy said. 'So I think he doesn't count as one of your Mr Wrongs.'

'Oh, he does. You couldn't get more wrong for me than him,' Claire said feelingly. More was the pity.

'Was the sex good?'

'Sammy!' Claire felt the colour hit her face like a tidal wave.

Her friend was totally unrepentant. 'Out of ten?'

Claire groaned. 'I need coffee.'

'Answer the question, Claire-bear.'

'Eleven,' Claire muttered, and helped herself to coffee, sugaring it liberally.

'Then maybe,' Sammy said, 'he might be worth working on. Sort out whatever makes him Mr Wrong.'

'That'd be several lifetimes' work,' Claire said wryly.

'Your call. Pastries or peaches?'

Claire couldn't help smiling. Only Sammy would ask something so outrageous followed by something so practical and mundane. 'I thought you'd already scoffed all the pastries? But if there are any left I'll have both,' she said.

'Attagirl.' Sammy winked at her. 'And I hope you

don't have a hangover. Because we're taking that boat out to the Blue Grotto this afternoon before we catch our flights—I've got a commission.'

'Do you ever stop working?' Claire asked.

'About as much as you do,' Sammy said with a grin. 'Anyway, mixing work and play means you get to fit twice as much into your day—and you enjoy it more.'

'True.'

'Pity about Mr Wrong.'

Yeah.

And Claire really wasn't looking forward to facing Sean, the next time they met. Somehow, before then she needed to get her emotions completely under control.

Claire enjoyed her trip to the Blue Grotto, and the colours and textures gave her several ideas for future dress designs; but on the plane home she found herself thinking about Sean. He'd been a very focused lover, very considerate. She still felt guilty about the way she'd called a halt to it, but she knew she'd done the right thing. Sean planned things out to the extreme, and she preferred to follow her heart, so they'd never be able to agree on anything.

Back at her flat, she unpacked and put the laundry on, checked her mail and her messages, and made notes for what she needed to do in the morning. Though she still couldn't get Sean out of her head. When she finally fell asleep, she had the most graphic dream about him—one that left her hot and very bothered when her alarm went off on the Monday morning.

'Don't be so ridiculous. Sean Farrell is completely off limits,' she told herself firmly, and went for her usual pre-breakfast run. Maybe that would get her common sense back in working order. But even then she couldn't stop thinking about Sean. How he'd made her feel. How she wanted to do what they'd done all over again.

After her shower, she opened her laptop and logged in to her bank account so she could transfer the money she owed Sean for the flight into his account. And, once that was done, she knew she wouldn't need any contact with him until Ashleigh and Luke were back from honeymoon. By which time, her common sense would be back.

She hoped.

She went down to open the shop, then headed for her workroom at the back to start work on the next dress she needed to make for the wedding show. She'd just finished cutting it out when the old-fashioned bell on her door jangled to signal that someone was coming through the front door.

She came out from the workroom to see a delivery man carrying an enormous bunch of flowers. 'Miss Stewart?' he asked.

'Um, yes.'

'For you.' He smiled and handed her the flowers. 'Enjoy.'

'Thank you.'

It wasn't her birthday and she wasn't expecting any flowers. Or maybe they were from Ashleigh and Luke to say thanks for her help with the wedding. She absolutely loved dusky pink roses; the bouquet was stuffed with them, teamed with sweet-smelling cream freesias and clouds of fluffy gypsophila. She'd never seen such a gorgeous bouquet.

She opened the envelope that came with it and felt her eyes widen with shock; she recognised the strong, precise handwriting immediately, because she'd seen it on cards and notes at Ashleigh's flat over the years.

Saw these and thought of you. Sean.

He'd sent her flowers.

Not just any old flowers—glorious flowers.

And he hadn't just asked his PA to do it, either. The handwriting was his, so he'd clearly gone to the florist in person, and maybe even chosen the flowers himself.

Sean Farrell had sent her flowers.

Claire couldn't quite get her head round that.

Why would he send her flowers?

She didn't quite dare ring him to ask him. So, once she'd put them in water, she took the coward's way out and texted him.

Thank you for the flowers. They're gorgeous.

He took his time replying, but eventually the text came through. Glad you like them.

Where was he going with this?

Before she could work out a way to ask without sounding offensive, her phone beeped again to signal the arrival of another text.

Thank you for the flight money. Bank just notified me. Do you have an appointment over lunch?

Why? No, that sounded grudging and suspicious. She deleted the message and started again. No worries, and no, she typed back.

You do now. See you at your shop at one.

What? Was he suggesting a lunch date? Dating her? But—but—they'd agreed that the thing between them would be a disaster if they let it go any further.

Sean, we can't.

But he didn't reply. And she was left in a flat spin.

By the time the bell on the front door jangled and she went through to the shop to see Sean standing there—and he'd turned her sign on the door to 'closed', she noticed—she was wound up to fever pitch.

'What's this about, Sean?' she asked.

'I thought we could have lunch together.'

'But…' Her voice faded. They'd already agreed that this was a bad idea—hadn't they?

'I know,' he said softly, and walked over towards her.

He was dressed in another of his formal well-cut suits, with his shoes perfectly shined and his silk tie perfectly knotted; he was a million miles away from the sensual, dishevelled man who'd spent the night in her bed in Capri. And yet he was every bit as delectable. Even though he wasn't even touching her, being this close to him made all her senses go on red alert.

'I can't get you out of my head,' he said.

Well, if he could be brave enough to admit it, so could she. She swallowed hard. 'Me, neither,' she said.

'So what do we do about this, Claire?' he asked. 'Because I have a feeling this isn't going away any time soon.'

'That night in Capri was supposed to—well—get it out of our systems,' she reminded him.

'And it didn't work,' he said. 'Not for me.'

His admission warmed her and terrified her at the same time.

'Claire?' he asked softly.

He deserved honesty. 'Me, neither.'

He leaned forward and brushed his lips against hers, ever so gently. And every nerve end on her mouth sizzled.

He tempted her. Oh, so much. But it all came back to collateral damage.

'We have to be sensible,' she said. 'And why am I the one saying this, not you? You're the one with—'

'—the twenty-year plan,' he finished. 'For the record, it's five years. Not twenty.'

'Even so. You have your whole life planned out.'

'There's nothing wrong with being responsible and organised,' he said.

'There's nothing wrong with being spontaneous, either,' she retorted.

He smiled. 'Not if it's like Saturday night, no.'

Oh, why had he had to bring that up again? Now her temperature was spiking. Seriously spiking. 'We're too different,' she said. 'You're my best friend's brother.'

'And?'

'There's a huge risk of collateral damage. I can't take that risk.' The risk of losing Ashleigh. Claire had already lost too much in her life. She wasn't prepared to risk losing her best friend as well. 'If it goes wrong between us. *When* it goes wrong between us,' she amended.

'Why are you so sure it will go wrong?'

That was an easy one. 'Because my relationships always go wrong.'

'Because you pick the kind of man who doesn't commit.'

She didn't have an answer to that. Mainly because she knew he was right.

'You pick men who say they're free spirits. And you

think that'll work because you're a free spirit, too. Except,' he said softly, 'they always let you down.'

Claire thought of her last ex. The one who'd let her down so much that she'd temporarily sworn off relationships. He definitely hadn't been able to commit. She'd found him in bed with someone else—and then she'd discovered that he was cheating on both of them with yet *another* woman. Messy and a half.

And the worst thing was that he'd assumed she'd be OK with it, because she was a free spirit, too... It had been a wake-up call. Claire had promised herself that never again would she date someone who could be so casual with her feelings. But it had shaken her faith in her judgement of men. In a room full of eligible men, she was pretty sure she'd pick all the rotten ones.

'I guess,' she said. 'And anyway, what about you? You never date anyone for longer than three weeks.'

'It's not quite that bad.'

'Even so, that's not what I want, Sean. Three weeks and you're out. That's just...' She grimaced. 'No.'

'I'm always very clear with my girlfriends. That it's for fun, that I'm committed to the factory and won't have time to...' His voice faded.

'Actually, that makes you the kind of man who won't commit,' she said softly. 'Like every other man I date.'

Sean had never thought of himself in that way before. He'd thought of the way he conducted his relationships as protecting his heart. Not letting himself get too involved meant not risking losing someone. He'd already lost too much in his life, and he didn't want to lose any more. So he'd concentrated on his career rather than on his relationships. Because the business was *safe*. Staying in control of his emotions kept his heart safe.

'What do you want, Sean?' she asked.

Such an easy answer—and such a difficult one. Though he owed her honesty. 'You. I can't think beyond that at the moment,' he admitted. And that was scary. Claire had accused him of having a twenty-year plan; although it wasn't anywhere near that long-range, he had to admit that he always planned things out, ever since his parents had died and he'd taken over the family business.

Planning had helped him cope with being thrown in at the deep end and being responsible for everything, without having the safety net of his father's experience to help him. And planning meant that everything was always under control. Just the way he liked it.

She bit her lip. 'I've got a wedding show in two months. My first collection. This could make all the difference to my career—this could be what really launches me into the big time. I'm hoping that one of the big wedding fashion houses might give me a chance to work with them on a collection. So I really don't have time for a relationship right now.'

'And I've just finished fighting off a takeover bid from an international conglomerate who wanted to add Farrell's to their portfolio,' he said. 'The vultures are still circling. I need to concentrate on the business and make absolutely sure they don't get another opening. If anything, I need to expand and maybe float the company on the stock market to finance the expansion. It's going to take all my time and then some.'

'So we're agreed: this is the wrong time for either of us to start any kind of relationship. By the time it *is* the right time, we'll both be back to our senses and we'll know it'd be the wrong thing to do anyway.'

That was something else she'd thrown at him—he

was the sensible one, the one who planned things out and was never spontaneous. So why wasn't he the one making this argument instead of her? Why had he sent her flowers and moved an appointment so he could see her for lunch?

It was totally crazy. Illogical.

And he couldn't do a thing to stop it.

Which exhilarated him and terrified him at the same time. With Claire, there was a real risk of losing control. And if he wasn't in control…what then? The possibilities made his head spin.

The only thing he could do now was to state the facts. 'I want you,' he said softly. 'And I think you want me.'

'So, what? We have a stupid, crazy, insane affair?'

He grimaced. 'Put like that, it sounds pretty sleazy.'

'But that's what you're offering.'

Was it? 'No.'

She frowned. 'So what *are* you suggesting, Sean?'

'I don't know,' he said. And it was a position he'd never actually been in before. He'd always been the one to call the shots. The one who initiated a relationship and the one who ended it. He shook his head, trying to clear it. But nothing changed. It was still that same spinning, out-of-control feeling. Like being on the highest, fastest, scariest fairground ride. 'All I know is that I want you,' he said.

'There's too much at stake. No.'

'Unless,' he said, 'we have an agreement.'

Her eyes narrowed. 'What kind of agreement?'

'We see each other. Explore where this thing goes. And then, whatever happens between us, we're polite to each other in front of Ashleigh. Nobody gets hurt. Especially her.'

'Can you guarantee that?' she asked softly.

'I can guarantee that I'll always be polite to you in front of Ashleigh.' He paused. 'The rest of it—I don't think anyone could guarantee that. But maybe it's worth the risk of finding out.' Risk. Something he didn't usually do unless it was precisely calculated. This wasn't calculated. At all. He needed his head examined.

'Maybe,' she said.

He curled his fingers round hers. His skin tingled where it touched her. 'Come and have lunch with me.'

She smiled then. Funny how it made the whole room light up. That wasn't something he was used to, either.

'OK,' she said. 'I just need to get my bag.'

'Sure.' He waited for her; then, when she'd locked the shop door behind them, he took her hand and walked down the street with her.

CHAPTER SIX

CLAIRE WAS WALKING hand in hand with Sean Farrell. Down the high street in Camden. On an ordinary Monday lunchtime.

This was surreal, she thought.

And she couldn't quite get her head round it.

But his fingers were wrapped round hers, his skin was warm against hers, and it was definitely happening rather than being some kind of super-realistic dream—because when she surreptitiously pinched herself it hurt.

'So what do you normally do for lunch?' Claire asked.

'I grab a sandwich at my desk,' he said. 'In the office, we put an order in to a local sandwich shop first thing in the morning, and they deliver to us. You?'

'Pretty much the same, except obviously I eat it well away from my work area so I don't risk getting crumbs or grease on the material and ruining it,' she said.

'So we both work through lunch. Well, that's another thing we have in common.'

There was a gleam in his eye that reminded her of the first thing they had in common. That night in Capri. She went hot at the memory.

'So how long do you have to spare?' he asked.

'An hour, maybe,' she said.

'So that's enough time to walk down to Camden Lock, grab a sandwich, and sit by the canal while we eat,' he said.

'Sounds good to me.' The lock was one of her favourite places; even though the area got incredibly busy in the summer months, she loved watching the way the narrow boats floated calmly down the canal underneath the willow trees. 'But this is a bit strange,' she said.

'How?'

'I've been thinking—we've known each other for years, and I know hardly anything about you. Well, other than that you run Farrell's.' His family's confectionery business, which specialised in toffee.

'What do you want to know?' he asked.

'Everything. Except I don't know where to start,' she admitted. 'Maybe we should pretend we're speed-dating.'

He blinked. 'You've been speed-dating?'

'No. Sammy has, though. I helped her do a list of questions.'

'What, all the stuff about what you do, where you come from, that sort of thing?' At her nod, he said, 'But you already know all that.'

'There's other stuff as well. I think the list might still be on my phone,' she said.

'Let's grab some lunch, sit down and go through your list, then,' he said. 'And if we both answer the questions, that might be a good idea—now I think about it, I don't really know that much about you, either.'

She smiled wryly. 'I can't believe we're doing this. We don't even like each other.'

He glanced down at their joined hands. 'Though we're attracted to each other. And maybe we haven't given each other a proper chance.'

From Claire's point of view, Sean was the one who hadn't given her a chance; but she wasn't going to pick a fight with him over it. He was making an effort, and she'd agreed to see where this thing took them. It was exhilarating and scary, all at the same time. Exhilarating, because this was a step into the unknown; and scary, because it meant trusting her judgement again. Her track record where men were concerned was so terrible that...

No. She wasn't going to analyse this. Not now. She was going to see where this took them. Seize the day.

They walked down to Camden Lock, bought bagels and freshly squeezed orange juice from one of the stalls, and sat down on the edge of the canal, looking out at the narrow boats and the crowd.

Claire found the list on her phone. 'Ready?' she asked.

'Yup. And remember you're doing this, too,' he said.

'OK. Your favourite kind of book, movie and music?' she asked.

He thought about it. 'In order—crime, classic film noir and anything I can run to. You?'

'Jane Austen, rom-coms and anything I can sing to,' she said promptly.

'So we're not really compatible there,' he said.

She wrinkled her nose. 'We're not that far apart. I like reading crime novels, too, but I like historical ones rather than the super-gory contemporary stuff. And classic noir—well, if Jimmy Stewart's in it, I'll watch it. I love *Rear Window*.'

'I really can't stand Jane Austen. I had to do *Mansfield Park* for A level, and that was more than enough for me,' he said with a grimace. 'But if the rom-com's witty and shot well, I can sit through it.'

She grinned. 'So you're a bit of a film snob, are you, Mr Farrell?'

He thought about it for a moment and grinned back. 'I guess I am.'

'OK. What do you do for fun?'

'You mean you actually think I might have fun?' he asked.

She smiled. 'You can be a little bit too organised, but I think there's more to you than meets the eye—so answer the question, Sean.'

'Abseiling,' he said, his face totally deadpan.

She stared at him, trying to imagine it—if he'd said squash or maybe even rugby, she might've believed him, but abseiling? 'In London?' she queried.

'There are lots of tall buildings in London.'

She thought about it a bit more, and shook her head. 'No, that's not you. I think you're teasing me.' Especially because he knew she was scared of heights.

'Good call,' he said. And his eyes actually *twinkled*.

Sean Farrell, teasing her. She would never have believed that he had a sense of humour. 'So what's the real answer?' she asked.

'Something very regimented,' he said. 'Sudoku.'

'There's nothing wrong with doing puzzles,' she said. Though trust Sean to pick something logical.

'What about you? What do you do for fun?' he asked.

Given how he'd teased her, he really deserved this. She schooled her face into a serious expression. 'Shopping. Preferably for shoes.' Given what she did for a living, that would be totally plausible. 'Actually, I have three special shoe wardrobes. Walk-in ones.'

'Seriously?' He looked totally horrified.

'About as much as you go abseiling.' She laughed. 'I like shoes, but I'm not that extreme. No, for me it's cooking for friends and watching a good film and talking about it afterwards.'

'OK. We're even now,' he said with a smile. 'So what do you cook? Anything in particular?'

'Whatever catches my eye. I love magazines that have recipes in them, and it's probably one of my worst vices because I can never resist a news stand,' she said. 'What about you?'

'I can cook if I have to,' he said. 'Though I admit I'm more likely to take someone out to dinner than to cook for them.'

She shrugged. 'That's not a big deal. It means you'll be doing the washing up, though.'

'Was that an offer?' he asked.

'Do you want it to be?' she fenced.

He held her gaze. 'Yes. Tell me when, and I'll bring the wine.'

There was a little flare of excitement in her stomach. They were actually doing this. Arranging a date. Seeing each other. She could maybe play a little hard to get and make him wait until Friday; but her mouth clearly had other ideas, because she found herself suggesting, 'Tonight?'

'I'd like that. I've got meetings until half past five, and some paperwork that needs doing after that—but I can be with you for seven, if that's OK?' he asked.

'It's a date,' she said softly.

He took her hand and brought it up to his mouth. Keeping eye contact all the way, he kissed the back of her hand, just briefly, before releasing it again; it made Claire feel warm and squidgy inside. Who would've thought that Sean Farrell was Prince Charming in disguise? Not that she was a weak little princess who needed rescuing—she could look after herself perfectly well, thank you very much—but she liked the charm. A lot.

'Next question,' he said.

'OK. What are you most proud of?' she asked.

'That's an easy one—my sister and Farrell's,' he said.

His family, and his family business, she thought. So it looked as if Sean Farrell had a seriously soft centre, just like the caramel chocolates his factory made along with the toffee.

'How about you?' he asked.

'The letters I get from brides telling me how much they loved their dress and how it really helped make their special day feel extra-special,' she said.

'So you're actually as much of a workaholic as you think I am?'

'Don't sound so surprised,' she said dryly. 'I know you see extreme things on a fashion catwalk and the pages of magazines, but it doesn't mean that designers are all totally flaky. I want my brides to feel really special and that they look like a million dollars, in a dress I've made just for them. And that means listening to what their dream is, and coming up with something that makes them feel their dream's come true.'

'Having seen the dress you made for Ashleigh, I can understand exactly why they commission you,' he said. 'Next question?'

'What are you scared of?'

'Easy one. Anything happening to Ashleigh or the business.'

But he didn't meet her eye. There was clearly something else. Something he didn't want to discuss.

'You?' he asked.

'Heights. I'm OK in a plane, but chairlifts like that

one in Capri make my palms go sweaty. Put it this way, I'm never, ever going skiing. Or abseiling.'

'Fair enough. Next?'

She glanced down at her phone to check. 'Your most treasured possession.'

'I can show you that.' He took his wallet out of his pocket, removed two photographs and handed them to her. One was of himself with Ashleigh, and the other was himself on graduation day with his parents on either side of him. Claire had a lump in her throat and couldn't say a word when she handed them back.

'You?' he asked.

'The same,' she whispered, and took her own wallet from her bag. She showed him a photograph of herself and her parents on her seventeenth birthday, and one of her with Ashleigh and Sammy and the Coliseum in the background.

He took her hand in silence and squeezed it briefly. Not that he needed any words; she knew he shared her feelings.

She put the photographs away. 'Next question—is the glass half full or half empty?'

'Half full. You?'

'Same,' she said, and glanced at her watch. 'We might have to cut this a bit short. Last one for now. Your perfect holiday?'

'Not a beach holiday,' he said feelingly. 'That just bores me silly.'

'You mean, you get a fit of the guilts at lying on a beach doing nothing, and you end up working.'

'Actually, I'm just not very good at just sitting still and doing nothing,' he admitted.

'So you'd rather have an active holiday?'

'Exploring somewhere, you mean?' He nodded. 'That'd work for me.'

'Culture or geography?'

'Either,' he said. 'I guess my perfect holiday would be Iceland. I'd love to walk up a volcano, and to see the hot springs and learn about the place. You?'

'I like city breaks. I have a bit of an art gallery habit, thanks to Sammy,' she explained. 'Plus I love museums where they have a big costume section. I should warn you that I really, really love Regency dresses. And I can spend hours in the costume section, looking at all the fine details.'

'So you see yourself as Lizzie Bennett?'

'No,' she said, 'and I'm not looking for a Darcy—anyway, seeing as you hate Austen, how come you know more than just the book you did for A level?'

'Ex-girlfriends who insisted on seeing certain films more than once, and became ex very shortly afterwards,' he said dryly.

'Hint duly noted,' she said. 'I won't ever ask you to watch *Pride and Prejudice* with me. Even though it's one of my favourite films.'

'Nicely skated past,' he said, 'but let's backtrack—you said you like holidays where you go and look at vintage clothes. And you said you look at details, so I bet you take notes and as many photos as you can get away with. Isn't that partly work?'

'Busted.' She clicked her fingers and grinned. 'I have to admit, I don't really like beach holidays, either. It's nice to have a day or two to unwind and read, but I'd rather see a bit of culture with friends. I really loved my trips in Italy with Ash and Sammy.'

'So what's your perfect holiday?' he asked.

'Anywhere with museums, galleries and lots of nice

little places to eat. Philadelphia and Boston are next on my wish list.'

'This is scary,' he said. 'A week ago I would've said we were total opposites.'

She thought about it. 'We still are. We have a few things in common—probably more than either of us realised—but you like things really pinned down and I like to go with the flow.' She smiled. 'And I bet you have an itinerary on holiday. Down to the minute.'

'If you don't know the opening times and days for a museum or what have you, then you might go to see it when it's closed and not get a chance to go back,' he pointed out. 'So yes, I do have an itinerary.'

'But if you go with the flow, you discover things you wouldn't have known about otherwise,' she pointed out.

'Let's agree to disagree on that one.' He glanced at his watch. 'We'd better head back.'

'You don't have to walk me back, Sean. Go, if you have a meeting.'

'I was brought up properly. I'll walk you back,' he said.

'I'm planning a slight detour,' she warned.

He looked a little wary, but nodded. 'We'll do this your way, then.'

Her detour was to an ice cream shop where the ice cream was cooled with liquid nitrogen rather than by being put in a freezer. 'I love this place. The way they make the ice cream is so cool,' she said, and laughed. 'Literally.'

'It's a little gimmicky,' he said.

'Just wait until you taste it.'

To her surprise, he chose the rich, dark chocolate. 'I would've pegged you as a vanilla man,' she said.

'Plain and boring?'

'Not necessarily. Seriously good vanilla ice cream is one of the best pleasures in the world—which is why I just ordered it.'

'True. But remember what I do for a living. And my favourite bit of my job is when I work with the R and D team. Am I really going to pass up chocolate?'

This was a side of Sean she'd never really seen. Teasing, bantering—*fun*. And she really, really liked that.

She watched him as he took a spoonful of ice cream. He rolled his eyes at her to signal that he thought she was overselling it. And then she saw his pupils widen.

'Well?' she asked.

'This is something else,' he admitted. 'I can forgive the gimmicky stuff. Good choice.'

'And if you hadn't gone with the flow, you wouldn't have known the place was there.' She grinned. 'Admit it. I was right.'

'You were right about the ice cream being great. That's as far as I go.' He held her gaze. 'For now.'

It should've been cheesy and made her laugh at him. But his voice was low and sexy as hell, and there was the hint of a promise in his words that made her feel hot all over, despite the ice cream. It was enough to silence her, and she concentrated on eating her ice cream on the walk back to her shop.

'Well, Ms Stewart,' he said on her doorstep. 'I'll see you later. Though there is something you need to attend to.'

She frowned. 'What's that?'

'You have ice cream on the corner of your mouth.' Just as she was about to reach up and scrub it away, he stopped her. 'Let me deal with this.'

And then he kissed the smear of sweet confection away. Slowly. Sensually. By the time he'd finished, Claire was close to hyperventilating and her knees felt weak. Sean was kissing her *in the street*. This was totally un-Sean-like behaviour and it put her in a flat spin.

'Later,' he whispered, and left.

Although Claire spent the rest of the day alternately talking to customers and working on the dress, in the back of her head she was panicking about what to cook for him. She had no idea what he liked. She could play safe and cook chicken—she was fairly sure that he wasn't a vegetarian. Wryly, she realised that this was when Sean's 'plan everything down to the last microsecond' approach would come in useful.

She could text him to check what he did and didn't like. But that meant doing it his way and planning instead of being spontaneous—and she didn't want to give him the opportunity to say 'I told you so'. Then again, she didn't want to cook a meal he'd hate, or something he was allergic to, so it would be better to swallow her pride.

She texted him swiftly.

Any food allergies I need to know about? Ditto total food hates.

The reply came back.

No and no. What's for dinner?

She felt safe enough to tease him.

Whatever I feel like cooking. Carpe diem.

When he didn't reply she wondered if she'd gone too far. Then again, he'd said that he was going to be in meetings all afternoon. She shrugged it off and concentrated on making the dress she'd cut out that morning.

Though by the end of the afternoon she still hadn't decided what to cook. She ended up having a mad dash round the supermarket and picked up chicken, parma ham, asparagus and soft cheese so she could make chicken stuffed with asparagus, served with tiny new potatoes, baby carrots and tenderstem broccoli.

Given that Sean was a self-confessed chocolate fiend, she bought the pudding rather than making it from scratch—tiny pots of chocolate ganache, which she planned to serve with raspberries, as their tartness would be a good foil to the richness of the chocolate.

Once she'd prepared dinner, she fussed around the flat, making sure everywhere was tidy and all the important surfaces were gleaming. Then she changed her outfit three times, and was cross with herself for doing so. Why was she making such a big deal out of this? She'd known Sean for years. He'd seen her when she had teenage spotty skin and chubby cheeks. And this was her flat. It shouldn't matter what she wore. Jeans and a strappy vest top would be fine.

Except they didn't feel fine. Sean was always so pristine that she'd feel scruffy.

In the end, she compromised with a little black dress but minimal make-up and with her hair tied back. So he'd know that she'd made a little more effort than just dragging on a pair of jeans and doing nothing with her hair, but not so much effort that she was making a big deal out of it.

The doorbell rang at seven precisely—exactly

what she'd expected from Sean, because of course he wouldn't be a minute late or a minute early—and anticipation sparkled through her.

Dinner.

And who knew what else the evening would bring?

CHAPTER SEVEN

HE WAS ACTUALLY *NERVOUS*, Sean realised.

Which was crazy.

This was Claire. He'd known her for years. There was nothing to be nervous about. Except for the fact that this was a date, and in the past they'd never really got on. And the fact that, now he was getting to know her, he was beginning to realise that maybe she wasn't the person he'd thought she was.

Would it be the same for her? He had no idea.

He took a deep breath and rang the doorbell.

When she opened the door, she was barefoot and wearing a little black dress, and her hair was tied back at the nape with a hot pink chiffon scarf. He wanted to kiss her hello, but was afraid he wouldn't be able to stop himself—it had been tough enough to walk away at lunchtime. So instead he smiled awkwardly at her. 'Hi. I wasn't sure what to bring, so I brought red and white.'

'You really didn't need to, but thank you very much.' She accepted the bottles with a smile. 'Come up.'

She looked so cool, unflustered and sophisticated. Sean was pretty sure that she wasn't in the slightest bit nervous, and in turn that made him relax. This was just dinner, the getting-to-know-you stuff. And he really should stop thinking about how easy it would be to untie that scarf and let her glorious hair fall over her shoulders, then kiss her until they were both dizzy.

He followed her up the stairs and she ushered him in to the kitchen.

'We're eating in here, if that's OK,' she said. 'Can I get you a drink? Dinner will be ten minutes.'

'A glass of cold water would be fabulous, thanks.' At her raised eyebrows, he explained, 'It's been a boiling hot day and I could really do with something cold and non-alcoholic.'

'Sure.' She busied herself getting a glass and filled it from the filter jug in the fridge, adding ice and a frozen slice of lime. When she handed the glass to him, her fingers brushed against his; it sent a delicious shiver all the way down his spine.

Her kitchen was a place of extremes. The work surfaces had all been used, and it looked as if most of her kitchen equipment had been piled up next to the sink. The fridge was covered with magnets and photos, and a cork board on one wall had various cards and notes pinned to it, along with what looked like a note of a library fine. Chaos. And yet the bistro table was neatly set for two, and there was a compact electric steamer on the worktop next to the cooker, containing the vegetables. So there was a little order among the chaos.

Much like Claire herself.

'Something smells nice,' he said.

'Dinner, I hope,' she said, putting the white wine into the fridge.

He handed her a box. 'I thought these might be nice with coffee after dinner.'

'Thank you.' She smiled. 'Toffee, I assume?'

'Samples,' he said, smiling back. 'There have to be some perks when you're dating a confectioner.'

'Perks. Hmm. I like the sound of that, though if we're talking about a lot of calories here then I might have to start doubling the length of my morning run.' She did a cute wrinkly thing with her nose that made his knees go weak, then looked in the box. 'Oh, you brought those lovely soft caramel hearts! Fabulous. Thank you.'

Clearly she liked those; he made a mental note, and hoped she wouldn't be disappointed with what these actually were. 'Not *quite*,' he said.

'What are they, then?'

'Wait until coffee. Is there anything I can do to help?'

'No, you're fine—have a seat.' She gestured to the bistro table, and he sat down on one of the ladder-back chairs.

Small talk wasn't something Sean was used to doing with Claire, and he really wasn't sure what to say. It didn't help that he was itching to kiss her; but she was bustling round the kitchen, and he didn't want to distract her and ruin the effort she'd put into making dinner. 'It's a nice flat,' he said.

She nodded. 'I like it here. The neighbours are lovely, the road's quiet, and yet I'm five minutes away from all the shops and market stalls.'

Work. An excellent subject, he thought. They could talk about that. 'So how did the dressmaking go today? Are you on schedule for your big show?'

'Fine, thanks, and I think I am. How about your meetings?'

'Fine, thanks.' Then it finally clicked that she wasn't as cool and calm as she seemed. She was being super-polite. So did that mean that she felt as nervous about this as he did? 'Claire, relax,' he said softly.

'Uh-huh.' But she still looked fidgety, and he noticed that she didn't sit down with him. Was she just feeling a little shy and awkward because of the newness of their situation, or was she having second thoughts?

'Have you changed your mind about this?' he asked, as gently as he could.

'No-o,' she hedged. 'It's not that.'

'What is it, then?'

'I'm usually a reasonable cook.' She bit her lip. 'What if it all goes wrong tonight?'

Nervous, then, rather than second thoughts. And suddenly his own nerves vanished. He stood up, walked over to her and put his arms round her. 'I'm pretty sure it'll be just fine. If it's not, then it doesn't matter. I'll carry you to your bed and take your mind off it—and then I'll order us a pizza instead.' He kissed the corner of her mouth, knowing he was dangerously close to distracting her, but wanting to make her feel better. 'Claire, why are you worrying that the food's going to be bad tonight?'

'Because it's *you*,' she said.

Because she thought he'd judge her? He had to acknowledge that he'd judged her in the past—and not always fairly. 'You already know I'd rather wash up or take someone out to dinner than cook for them, so I'm in no position to complain if someone cooks me something that isn't Michelin-star standard.'

'I guess.' She blew out a breath. 'It's just… Well, this is you and me, and it feels…'

He waited. What was she going to say? That it felt like a mistake?

'Scary,' she finished.

He could understand that. Claire fascinated him; yet, at the same time, this whole thing scared him witless. Her outlook was so different from his. She didn't have a totally ordered world. She followed her heart. If he let her close—what then? Would he end up with his heart broken? 'Me, too,' he said.

The only thing he could do then was to kiss her, to stop the fear spreading through him, too. So he covered her mouth with his, relaxing as she wrapped her arms round him, too, and kissed him back. Holding her close, feeling the warmth of her body against his and the sweetness of her mouth against his, made his world feel as if the axis was in the right place again.

A sharp ding made them both break apart. 'That was the steamer. It means the vegetables are done,' Claire said, looking flustered and adorably pink.

'Is there anything I can do to help?' he asked again.

This time, to his relief, she stopped treating him like a guest who had to be waited on. 'Could you open the wine? The corkscrew's in the middle drawer.'

'Sure. Would you prefer red or white?'

'We're having chicken, so it's entirely up to you.'

He looked at her. 'You'd serve red wine with chicken?'

'Well, hey—if you can cook chicken in red wine, then you can serve it with red wine.'

He wrinkled his nose at her. 'Am I being regimented again?'

'No. Just a teensy bit of a wine snob,' she said with a grin. 'You need to learn to go with the flow, Sean. *Carpe diem*. Seize the day. It's a good motto to live by.'

'Maybe.' By the time he'd taken the wine from her fridge, found the corkscrew in the jumble of her kitchen drawer, uncorked the bottle and poured them both a glass, she'd served up.

He sat down opposite her and raised his glass. 'To us, and whatever the future might bring.'

'To us,' she echoed softly, looking worried and uncertain—vulnerable, even—and again he felt that weird surge of protectiveness towards her. It unsettled him, because he didn't generally feel like that about his girl-friends.

'This is really lovely,' he said after his first mouthful. Chicken, stuffed with soft cheese and asparagus, then wrapped in parma ham. Claire Stewart was definitely capable in the kitchen, and he could tell that this had been cooked from scratch. He'd assumed that she'd be the sort to buy ready-made meals from the supermarket; clearly that wasn't the case.

'Thank you.' She acknowledged his compliment with a smile.

'But you're not reasonable.'

She frowned. 'Excuse me?'

'You called yourself a reasonable cook,' he said. 'You're not. You're more than that.'

'Thank you. Though I wasn't fishing for compliments.' She shrugged. 'I used to like cooking with my mum. Not that she ever followed a recipe. She'd pick something at random, and then she'd tweak it.'

'So I'm guessing that you didn't follow a recipe for this, did you?' he asked.

'I cooked us dinner. It's not exactly rocket science,' she drawled.

Why had he never noticed how deliciously sarcastic she could be?

'What?' she asked

He blinked. 'Sorry. I'm not following you.'

'You were smiling. What did I say that was so funny?'

'It was the way you said it.' He paused. 'Do you have any idea how delectable you are when you're being sarcastic?'

It was her turn to blink. 'Sarcasm is sexy?'

'It is on you.'

She grinned. 'Well, now. I think tonight has just got a whole lot more interesting. Are you on a sugar rush, Sean?'

'Excuse me?'

'Working where you do, you have toffee practically on tap. Eat enough of the stuff and you'll be on a permanent sugar rush. Which, I think, must be the main reason why you're complimenting me like this tonight.'

No. It was because it was as if he'd just met her for the first time. She wasn't the girl who'd irritated him for years; she was a woman who intrigued him. But he didn't want to sound soppy. 'Honey,' he drawled, 'the only sugar I want right now is you.'

She laughed at him. 'Now you've switched to cheese.'

'No. You're the one who's served cheese.' He indicated the stuffing for the chicken. 'And very nice it is, too.'

Her mouth quirked. 'Keep complimenting me like this, and...'

'Yeah?' he asked, his voice suddenly lower. What was she going to do? Kiss him? That idea definitely worked for him.

'Oh, shut up and eat your dinner,' she said, looking flustered.

'Chicken,' he said, knowing that she'd pick up on the double use of the word—and he was seriously enjoying fencing with her. Why had he never noticed before that she was bright and funny, and sexy as hell?

Probably because he'd had this fixed idea of her as a difficult girl who attracted trouble. That was definitely true in the past, but now...Now, she wasn't who he'd always thought she was. She'd grown up. Changed.

And he really liked the woman he was beginning to get to know.

She served pudding next—a seriously rich chocolate ganache teamed with tart raspberries. 'Come and work for my R and D department,' he said, 'because I think you'd have seriously good ideas about flavouring.'

She smiled. 'I know practically nothing about making toffee, and if I make banoffee pie I always buy a jar of *dulce de leche* rather than making my own.'

'That's a perfectly sensible use of your time,' he said.

She grinned. 'It's not so much that you have to boil a can of condensed milk for a couple of hours and keep an eye on it.'

'What, then?'

'I had a friend who tried doing it,' she explained. 'The can exploded and totally wrecked her kitchen.'

'Ouch.' He grimaced in sympathy, and took another spoonful of pudding. 'This is a really gorgeous meal, Claire.'

'I didn't make the ganache myself—it's a shop-bought pudding.'

'I don't care. It's still gorgeous. And I appreciate the effort. Though, for future reference, you could've ordered in pizza and I would've been perfectly happy,' he said. 'I just wanted to spend time with you.'

'Me, too,' she said softly. 'But I wanted to—well...'

Prove to him that she wasn't the flake he'd always thought she was? 'I know. And you did.'

And how weird it was that he could follow the way she thought. Scary, even. She was the last woman in the world he'd expected to be so in tune with.

Once he'd helped her clear away, she said, 'I thought we could have coffee in the living room.'

'Sounds good to me.'

'OK. You can go through and put on some music, if you like,' she suggested.

Claire's living room had clearly been hastily tidied, judging by the edges of the magazines peeking from the side of her sofa—he remembered her telling him that she was addicted to magazines; but the flowers he'd sent her that morning were in a vase on the coffee table, perfectly arranged. Clearly she liked them and hadn't just been polite when she'd thanked him for them earlier. And, given the pink tones in the room, he'd managed to pick her favourite colours.

Her MP3 player was in a speaker dock. He took it out and skimmed through the tracks. Given what she'd said at lunchtime, he'd expected most of the music to be pop, but he was surprised to see how much of it was from the nineteen-sixties. In the end, he picked a general compilation and switched on the music.

She smiled when she came in. 'Good choice. I love the Ronettes.' She sang a snatch of the next line.

'Aren't you a bit young to like this stuff?' he asked.

'Nope. It's the sort of stuff my gran listens to, so I grew up with it—singing into hairbrushes, the lot,' she said with a smile. 'Best Friday nights ever. Totally girly. Me, Mum, Gran, Aunt Lou and my cousins. Popcorn, waffles, milkshake and music.'

It was the first time she'd talked about her family. 'So you're close to your family?' he asked.

'Yes. I still clash quite a bit with my dad,' she said, 'but that's hardly tactful to talk about that to you.'

'Because I'm male?'

'Because,' she said softly, 'I'd guess that, like Ash, you'd give anything to be able to talk to your dad. And here am I grumbling about my remaining parent.

Though, to be fair, my dad 's nothing like yours was. Yours actually *listened.*'

Fair point. He did miss his parents. And, when the whole takeover bid had kicked off, Sean would've given anything to be able to talk about it to his dad. But at the same time he knew that relationships were complicated. And it was none of his business. Unless Claire wanted to talk about it, he had to leave the subject alone.

She'd brought in a tray with a cafetière, two mugs, a small jug of milk and the box he'd given her earlier. 'Milk and sugar?' she asked.

'Neither, thanks. I like my caffeine unadulterated,' he said with a smile.

Claire, he noticed, took hers with two sugars and a lot of milk. Revolting. And it also made him worry that she wouldn't like the samples he'd brought; she probably preferred white chocolate to dark. Then again, he'd been wrong about a lot of things where Claire was concerned.

'Right. This box of utter yumminess. Whatever else I might have said about you in the past,' she said, 'I've always said that you make seriously good toffee.'

Honesty compelled him to say, 'No, my staff do. I'm not really hands-on in the manufacturing department.'

'Now that surprises me,' she said. 'I would've pegged you as the kind of manager who did every single job in the factory so you knew exactly what all the issues are.'

'I have done, over the years,' he said. 'Everything from the manufacturing to packing the goods, to carrying the boxes out for delivery. And every single admin role. And, yes, I worked with the cleaning team as well. Nowadays, I have regular meetings with each department and my staff know that I want to know about any problems they have and can't smooth out on their own.'

'Attention to detail.'

Her voice sounded almost like a purr. And there was a suspicious glow of colour across her cheeks.

'Claire?'

'Um,' she said. 'Just thinking. About Capri. About...'

And now he was feeling the same rush of blood to the head. 'Close your eyes,' he said.

Her breathing went shallow. 'Why?'

'Humour me?'

'OK.' She closed her eyes.

He took one of the dark salted caramel chocolates from the box and brushed it against her lips. Her mouth parted—and so did the lashes on her left eye.

'No peeking,' he said.

In return, she gave him an insolent smile and opened both eyes properly. 'So we're playing, are we, Mr Farrell?'

'We are indeed, Ms Stewart. Now close your eyes.' He teased her mouth with the chocolate and made her reach for it before finally letting her take a bite.

'You,' she said when she'd eaten it, 'have just upped your game considerably. I love the caramel-filled hearts, but these are spectacular.'

'You liked them?' Funny how that made him feel so good.

'Actually, I think I need another one, to check.'

He laughed. 'Oh, really?'

'Yes, really.' She struck a pose.

No way was he teasing her with chocolate when she looked like that, all pouting and dimpled and sexy as hell. Instead, he leaned over and kissed her.

The next thing he knew, they were both lying full length on the sofa and she was on top of him, his arms were wrapped tightly round her, and one of his hands was resting on the curve of her bottom.

'You're telling me that was chocolate?' she dead-panned.

'Maybe. Maybe not.' He moved his hand, liking the softness of her curves. 'Claire. You're…'

'What?'

'Unexpectedly luscious,' he said. 'None of this was supposed to happen.'

'Says the man who made me close my eyes and lean forward to take a bite of chocolate. Giving him a view straight down the front of my dress, if I'm not mistaken.'

'It was a very nice view,' he said, and shifted slightly so she was left in no doubt of his arousal.

'This is what chocolate does to you?' she asked.

'No. This is what *you* do to me.'

She leaned forward and caught his lower lip between hers, teasing him. 'Indeed, Mr Farrell.'

'Yeah.' He was aware that his voice sounded husky. She'd know from that exactly how much she affected him.

'So did you come prepared?' she asked.

He couldn't speak for a moment. And then he looked into her eyes. 'Are you suggesting…?'

'Capri, redux?' She held his gaze and nodded.

He blew out a breath. 'I didn't come prepared.'

'Tsk. Not what I expected from Mr Plan-Everything-Twenty-Years-in-Advance,' she teased.

'How do you manage to do that?' he asked plaintively.

'Do what?'

'Make me feel incredibly frustrated and make me want to laugh, all at the same time?'

'Go with the flow, sweetie,' she drawled.

He kissed her again. 'OK. Tonight wasn't about expectations. It wasn't about sending you flowers this morning so you'd sleep with me tonight. It was about getting to know you better.'

'Platonic, you mean?'

'I'd like to be friends.'

'Uh-huh.' She sounded unaffected, but he'd seen that little vulnerable flicker in her expression and he didn't let her move. He pulled her closer.

'I didn't say *just* friends. I want to be your lover as well.'

Her pupils went gratifyingly large.

'But I didn't come prepared because I'm not taking you for granted.'

To his surprise, he saw a sheen of tears in her eyes. 'Claire? What's wrong?'

She shook her head. 'I'm being wet.'

'Tell me anyway.'

'That's not how it usually is, for me,' she admitted.

Not being taken for granted? He brushed his mouth very gently against hers. 'That's because you've been dating the wrong men, thinking they're Mr Right.'

'I always thought you'd be Mr Wrong,' she admitted.

'And I always thought you'd be Ms Wrong,' he said. 'But maybe we should give each other a little more of a chance.'

'Maybe,' she said softly. 'But next time—I think I'm going to be prepared.'

'You and me, both.' He nuzzled the curve of her neck. 'Careful, Claire. You might turn into a bit of an *über*-planner if you keep this up.'

As he'd hoped, she laughed. 'And you might start going with the flow without having to be reminded.'

He laughed back. 'I think we need to move. While we still both have some self-control.'

'Good plan.' But when she climbed off him, he didn't

let her move away and sit in a different chair. He kept hold of her hand and drew her down beside him.

'This works for me,' he said. 'Just simply holding hands with you.'

For a moment, she went all dreamy-eyed. 'Like teenagers.'

'What?'

She shook her head. 'Ah, no. I'm not confessing that right now.'

Confessing what? He was intrigued. 'I could,' he suggested sweetly, '*make* you confess. Remember, I'm armed with seriously good chocolate.'

She drew his hand up to her mouth and kissed each knuckle in turn. 'But I also happen to know you're a gentleman. So you won't push me right now.'

So even when she hadn't liked him, she'd recognised that he had integrity and standards and knew that she was safe with him? That warmed him from the inside out. 'I won't push you right now,' he agreed. He handed her the box. 'Help yourself.'

'Salted caramel in dark chocolate. Fabulous. Are they all like that?'

'No. There's a Seville orange version and an espresso.'

'Nice choices. And you said earlier they were samples.' She looked thoughtful. 'So are you experimenting with new lines?'

'Possibly.'

She rolled her eyes. 'Sean, I'm hardly going to rush straight off to one of your competitors and sell them the information.'

'Of course you're not.' He frowned. 'Do you think I'm that suspicious?'

'You sounded it,' she pointed out.

'It's an experiment, moving into a slightly different form of toffee,' he said, 'but I need to put them through some focus groups first and see what my market thinks.'

'Ah, research. Looking at growing your market share.' She smiled. 'So either you sell the same product to more people, or you sell more products to the same people.'

At his raised eyebrow, she sighed. 'I'm not a total dimwit, you know. I've had my own business for three years.'

'I know, and it's not just that. Ashleigh told me you turned down an unconditional offer from Cambridge for medicine, and I know you wouldn't get that sort of offer if you weren't really bright.' He looked at her. 'I always wondered why you became a wedding dress designer instead of a doctor.'

She looked sad. 'It's a long story, and I don't really want to tell it tonight.'

Because she didn't trust him not to judge her? 'Fair enough,' he said coolly.

'I wasn't pushing you away, Sean,' she said. 'I just don't want to talk about it right now.'

'So what do you want, Claire?' He couldn't resist the question.

'Right now? I want you to kiss me again. But we've both agreed that's, um, possibly not a good idea.'

'Because I'm not prepared, and neither are you. So we'll take a rain check,' he said.

'How long?' She slapped a hand to her forehead. 'No. I didn't ask that and you didn't hear me.'

'Right. And I wasn't thinking it, either,' he retorted. 'When?'

'Wednesday?'

Giving them two days to come to their common sense. 'Wednesday,' he agreed. 'I would offer to cook for you, except you'd get a sandwich at best.'

She laughed. 'I can live with sandwiches.'

'No, I mean a proper date.'

'Planned to the nth degree, Sean-style?' she asked.

Why did planning things rattle her so much? In answer, he kissed her. Hard. And she was breathless by the time she'd finished.

'That was cheating,' she protested.

'Yeah, yeah.' He rubbed the pad of his thumb along her lower lip. 'And?'

'Go home, Sean, before we do something stupid.'

'Rain check,' he said. 'Wednesday night. I'll pick you up at seven.' He leaned forward and whispered in her ear, 'And, by the time I've finished with you, you won't remember what your name is or where you are.'

Her voice was gratifyingly husky when she said, 'That had better be a promise.'

'It is.' He stole one last kiss. 'And I always keep my promises. Which reminds me—I have washing-up duties.'

'I'll let you off,' she said.

'The deal was, you'd cook and I'd wash up.'

'Do you really think it's a good idea for us to be that close to each other, in the presence of water, and while neither of us is, um, prepared?'

He didn't quite get the reference to water, but he agreed with the rest of it. 'Good point. Rain check on the washing up, then, too?'

She laughed. 'No need. I have a dishwasher. It's horribly indulgent, given that I live on my own, but it's nice when I have friends over for dinner.' She paused, and added in a softer, sexier, deeper tone, 'Or my lover.'

Which sounded as if she was going to invite him back.

And that set his pulse thrumming.

'Right.' He couldn't resist one last kiss, one that sent his head spinning and left her looking equally dazed. 'Enjoy the chocolate,' he said. And then he left, while he was still capable of being sensible.

CHAPTER EIGHT

SEAN SENT CLAIRE a text later that evening.

Sweet dreams.

Yes, she thought, because they'd be of him. She typed back, You, too x.

He'd turned out to be unexpectedly sweet, so different from how he'd always been in the past. He was still a little regimented, but there was huge potential for him to be…

She stopped herself. No. This time she wasn't going to make the same old mistake. She wasn't going into this relationship thinking that Sean might be The One, that there would definitely be a happy-ever-after. OK, so he wasn't like the men she usually dated; but that didn't guarantee a different outcome for this relationship, either.

And this was early days. Sean had a reputation for not dating women for very long; the chances were, this would all be over in another month. Claire knew that she needed to minimise the potential damage to her heart and make sure that her best friend didn't get caught in any crossfire. Which meant keeping just a little bit of distance between them.

Even though Claire tried to tell herself to be sensible, she still found herself anticipating Wednesday. Wondering if he'd kiss her again. Wondering if they'd end up at his place or hers. Wondering if this whole thing blew his mind as much as it did hers.

Wednesday turned out to be madly busy, and Claire spent a long time on the phone with one of her suppliers, sorting out a mistake they'd made in delivering the wrong fabric—and it was going to cost her time she didn't have. A last-minute panic from one of her brides took up another hour; and, before she realised it, the time was half past six.

Oh, no. She still needed to shower, wash her hair, change and do her make-up before Sean arrived. She called him, hoping to beg an extra half an hour, but his line was busy. Swiftly, she tapped in a text as she went up the stairs to her flat.

Sorry, running a bit late. See you at half-seven?

She pressed 'send' and dropped the phone on her bed before rummaging through her wardrobe to find her navy linen dress.

She'd just stepped out of the shower and wrapped a towel round her hair when her doorbell rang.

No. It couldn't be Sean. It couldn't be seven-thirty already.

Well, whoever it was would just have to call back another time.

The bell rang again.

Arrgh. Clearly whoever it was had no intention of being put off. If it was a cold-caller, she'd explain firmly and politely that she didn't buy on the doorstep.

She blinked in surprise when she opened the door

to Sean. 'You're early!' And Sean was never early and never late; he was always precisely on time.

'No. We said seven.'

She frowned. 'But I texted you to say I was running late and asked if we could make it half past.'

'I didn't get any text from you,' he said.

'Oh, no. I'm so sorry.' She blew out a breath. 'Um, come up. I'll be twenty minutes, tops—make yourself a coffee or something.'

'Do you want me to make you a drink?'

She shook her head. 'I'm so sorry.'

He stole a kiss. 'Stop apologising.'

'I'll be as quick as I can,' she said, feeling horribly guilty. Why hadn't she kept a better eye on the time? Or called him rather than relying on a text getting through?

She had to dry her hair roughly and tie it back rather than spending time on a sophisticated updo, but she was ready by twenty-five past seven.

'You look lovely,' he said.

'Thank you.' Though she noticed that he'd glanced at his watch again. If only he'd lighten up a bit. It would drive her crazy if he ran this evening to schedule, as if it were a business meeting. 'Where are we going?' she asked brightly.

'South Bank.'

'Great. We can play in the fountains,' she said with a smile. 'It's been so hot today that it'd be nice to have a chance to cool down.'

He simply glanced at his suit.

And she supposed he had a point. Getting soaked wouldn't do the fabric any favours. Or her dress, for that matter. But the art installations on the South Bank were *fun*.

'I called the restaurant to say we'd be late,' he said.

Sean and his schedules. Though if they didn't turn up when they were expected, the restaurant would be perfectly justified in giving their table to someone else, so she guessed it was reasonable of him. 'Sorry,' she said again.

This was the side of Sean she found harder to handle. Mr Organised. It was fine for business; but, in his personal life, surely he could be more relaxed?

They caught the tube to the South Bank—to her relief, the line was running without any delays—and the restaurant turned out to be fabulous. Their table had a great view of the river, and the food was as excellent as the view. Claire loved the fresh tuna with mango chilli salsa. 'And the pudding menu's to die for,' she said gleefully. 'It's going to take me ages to choose.'

'Actually, we don't have time,' Sean said, looking at his watch,

'No time for pudding? But that's the best bit of dinner out,' she protested.

'We have to be somewhere. Maybe we can fit pudding in afterwards,' he said.

Just as she'd feared, Sean had scheduled this evening down to the last second. If she hadn't been running late in the first place, it might not have been so much of a problem. But right now she was having huge second thoughts about dating Sean. OK, so he managed to fit a lot in to his life; but all this regimentation drove her crazy. They were too different for this to work.

'So why exactly do we have to rush off?' she asked.

'For the next bit of this evening,' he said.

'Which is?'

'A surprise.'

Half past eight was too late for a theatre performance to start, and if they'd been going to the cinema she thought he would probably have picked a restaurant nearer to Leicester Square. She didn't work out what he'd planned until they started walking towards the London Eye. 'Oh. An evening flight.'

'It's the last one they run on a weeknight,' he confirmed. 'And we have to pick up the tickets fifteen minutes beforehand. Sorry I rushed you through dinner.'

At least he'd acknowledged that he'd rushed her. And she needed to acknowledge her part in the fiasco. 'If I hadn't been running late, you wouldn't have had to rush me.' She bit her lip. 'I'm beginning to think you might be right about me being chaotic. I should've checked that the text had gone or left you a voicemail as well.'

'It's OK. Obviously you had a busy day.'

She nodded. 'There were a couple of glitches that took time to sort out,' she said. 'And I'm up to my eyes in the wedding show stuff.'

'It'll be worth it in the end,' he said.

'I hope so. And I had a new bride in to see me this morning. That's my favourite bit of my job,' Claire said. 'Turning a bride-to-be's dreams into a dress that will suit her and make her feel special.'

'That's why you called your business "Dream of a Dress", then?' he asked.

'Half of the reason, yes.'

'And the other half?' he asked softly.

'Because it's my dream job,' she said.

He looked surprised, as if he'd never thought of it that way before. 'OK. But what if a bride wants a dress that you know wouldn't suit her?'

'You mean, like a fishtail dress when she's short and curvy?' At his nod, she said, 'You find out what it is she loves about that particular dress, and see how you can adapt it to something that will work. And then you need tact by the bucketload.'

'Tactful.' He tipped his head on one side and looked at her. 'But you always say what you think.'

'I do. But you can do that in a nice way, without stomping on people.'

The corners of his mouth twitched. 'I'll remember that, the next time you don't mince your words with me.'

She laughed back. 'You're getting a bit more bearable, so I might be nicer to you.'

He bowed his head slightly. 'For the compliment.' Then he took her hand and lifted it to his mouth, pressed a kiss into her palm, and folded her fingers round it.

It made her knees go weak. To cover the fact that he flustered her, she asked, 'How was your day?'

'Full of meetings.'

No wonder he found it hard to relax and go with the flow. He was used to a ridiculously tight schedule.

But at least he seemed to relax more once they were in the capsule and rising to see a late summer evening view of London. Claire was happy just to enjoy the view, with Sean's arm wrapped round her.

'I was thinking,' he said softly. 'I owe you pudding and coffee. I have good coffee back at my place.'

'Would there be caramel hearts to go with it?' she asked hopefully.

'There might be,' he said, the teasing light back in his eyes.

This sounded like a spontaneous offer rather than being planned, she thought. So maybe it could make up for the earlier part of the evening. 'That sounds good,' she said. 'Coffee and good chocolate. Count me in.'

And, to her pleasure, he held her hand all the way

back to his place. Now they weren't on a schedule any more, he was less driven—and she liked this side of him a lot more.

The last time Claire had been to Sean's house, she'd waited on the path outside while he picked up his luggage. This time, he invited her in. She discovered that his kitchen was very neat and tidy—as she'd expected—but it clearly wasn't a cook's kitchen. There were no herbs growing in pots, no ancient and well-used implements. She'd guess that the room wasn't used much beyond making drinks.

His living room was decorated in neutral tones. Claire was pleased to see that there were lots of family photographs on the mantelpiece, but she noticed that the art on the walls was all quite moody.

'It's Whistler,' he said, clearly realising what she was looking at. 'His nocturnes—I like them.'

'I would've pegged you as more of a Gainsborough man than a fan of tonalism,' she said.

He looked surprised. 'You know art movements?'

'I did History of Art for GCSE,' she said. 'Then again, I guess those paintings are a lot like you. They're understated and you really have to look to see what's there.'

'I'm not sure,' he said, 'if that was meant to be a compliment.'

'It certainly wasn't meant to be an insult,' she said. 'More a statement of fact.'

He poured them both a coffee, added sugar and a lot of milk to hers, and gestured to the little dish he'd brought on the tray. 'Caramel hearts, as you said you liked them.'

'I do.' She smiled at him, appreciating the fact that he'd remembered and made the effort.

'You can put on some music, if you like,' he suggested, indicating his MP3 player.

She skimmed through it quickly and frowned. 'Sean, I don't mean to be horrible, but all your playlists are a bit—well...'

'What?' he asked, sounding puzzled.

'They're named for different types of workouts, so I'm guessing all the tracks in each list have the same number of beats per minute.'

'Yes, but that's sensible. It means everything's arranged the way I want it for whatever exercise I'm doing.'

'I get that,' she said, 'but don't you enjoy music?'

He frowned. 'Of course I do.'

'I can't see what you listen to for pleasure. To me this looks as if you only play set music at set times.' Regimented again. And this time she couldn't just let it go. 'That works for business but, Sean, you can't live your personal life as if it's a business.'

'Right,' he said tightly.

So much for reaching an understanding. She sighed. 'I'm not having a go at you. I'm just saying you're missing out on so much and maybe there's another way of doing things.'

'Let's agree to disagree, shall we?'

Sean had closed off on her again, Claire thought with an inward sigh—and now she could guess exactly why his girlfriends didn't last for much longer than three weeks. He'd drive them crazy by stonewalling them as soon as they tried to get close to him, and then either he'd gently suggest that they should be just friends, or they'd give up trying to be close to him.

She also knew that telling him that would be the quickest way of ending things between them; and from the few glimpses she'd had she was pretty sure that, behind his walls, the real Sean Farrell was someone really worth getting to know.

'OK, I'll back off,' she said. 'But you have absolutely nothing slushy and relaxing on here.'

He coughed. 'In case you hadn't noticed, I'm male.'

She'd noticed, all right.

'I don't do slushy,' he continued. 'But…' He took the MP3 player gently from her and flicked rapidly through the tracks.

When the music began playing, she recognised 'Can't Take My Eyes Off You', but it was a rock version of the song.

'The band played this at Ashleigh's wedding,' he said, 'and I found myself looking straight at you—that's why I asked you to dance.'

'And there was I thinking it was because it was traditional,' she deadpanned.

'No. I just wanted to dance with you.'

His honesty disarmed her. Just when he'd driven her crazy and she was thinking of calling the whole thing off, he did something like this that made her melt inside.

He drew her into his arms, and Claire was surprised to discover that, even though the song was fast, they could actually dance slowly to it.

'And then, when I was dancing with you,' he continued, 'I wanted to kiss you.'

She found herself moistening her lower lip with her tongue. 'Do you want to kiss me now, Sean?'

'Yes.' He held her gaze. 'And I want to do an awful lot more than just kiss you.'

Excitement thrummed through her, but she tried to play it cool. 'Could you be more specific?'

'I want to take that dress off,' he said, 'lovely as it is. And I want to kiss every inch of skin I uncover.'

'That sounds like a good plan,' she said. 'So what do I do?'

He smiled. 'I'm surprised you don't already know that one. Isn't it what you're always saying? Be spontaneous. Follow your heart. Go with the flow.'

'So that means,' she said, 'I get to take that prissy suit off you?'

'Prissy?' he queried. 'My suit's *prissy*?'

'It's beautifully cut, but it's so neat and tidy. I'd like to see you dishevelled,' she said, 'like you were that morning in Capri.'

'Would that be the morning you threw me out of your bed?'

'Yes, and don't make me feel guilty about it. That was mainly circumstances,' she said.

'Hmm.'

'Besides, I can't throw you out of your own bed,' she pointed out.

'Now that's impeccable logic.' He frowned. 'Though, actually, if you said no at any point I hope you realised I'd stop.'

She stroked his face. 'Sean, of course I know that. You're...'

'Dull?'

She shook her head. 'I was going to say honourable.'

He brushed the pad of his thumb across her lower lip, making her skin tingle. 'You normally call me regimented.'

'You can be. You were tonight, and I nearly left you to it and went home.' She smiled. 'But there's a huge difference between regimented and dull.'

'Is there?'

'Let me show you,' she said. 'Take me to bed.'

'I thought you'd never ask.'

To her surprise, he scooped her up and actually carried her up the stairs. She half wanted to make a snippy comment about him being muscle-bound, to tease him and push him, but at the same time she didn't want to spoil the moment. She was shocked to discover that she actually quite liked the way he was taking charge and being all troglodyte.

Once they were in his room, he set her down on her feet.

His bedroom was painted in shades of smoky blue—very masculine, with a polished wooden floor, a rug in a darker shade that toned with the walls and matched the curtains, and limed oak furniture. But what really caught Claire's eye was his bed. A sleigh bed, also in limed oak, and she loved it. She'd always wanted a bed like that, but there really wasn't the room for that kind of furniture in her flat. Sean's Victorian terraced house was much more spacious and the bed was absolutely perfect.

'The last time you took your dress off for me,' he said, 'your underwear matched. Does it match today?'

'That's for me to know,' she said, 'and for you to find out.'

'Is that a challenge?'

'In part. It's also an offer.' She paused. 'Um, before this goes any further, do we have Monday's problem?'

'We absolutely do not,' he confirmed.

'Good.' Because she was going to implode if she had to wait much longer.

He drew the curtains and turned on the bedside light; it was a touch lamp, so he was able to dim the glow. Then he sat on the edge of the bed. 'Show me,' he invited.

She unzipped her dress and stepped out of it, then hung it over the back of a chair.

'What?' she asked, seeing the amusement in his face.

'You're a closet neat freak,' he said.

'No. Just practical. This is linen. It creases very, very badly. And I'm not walking out of here looking as if I've just been tumbled in a haystack.'

He gave her a slow, sexy smile. 'I like that image. Very much. You, tumbled in a haystack.'

She shook her head. 'It's not at all romantic, you know. Straw's prickly and itchy and totally unsexy.'

'And I assume you know that because you've, um, gone with the flow?'

'Listen, I haven't slept with everyone I've dated, and I certainly haven't slept with anyone else as fast as I fell into bed with *you*,' she said, folding her arms and giving him a level stare.

He stood up, walked over to her and brushed his mouth against hers. 'I'm not calling you a tart, Claire. We both have pasts. It's the twenty-first century, not the nineteen-fifties. I'm thirty and you're twenty-seven. I'd be more surprised if we were both still virgins.' He traced the lacy edge of her bra with one fingertip. 'Mmm. Cream lace. I like this. You have excellent taste in clothing, Ms Stewart.'

'It's oyster, not cream,' she corrected.

He grinned. 'And you have the cheek to call me prissy.'

'Details,' she said. 'You need to get them right.'

'We're in agreement there.'

She coughed.

'What?' he asked.

'I'm in my underwear. You can see that it matches,

so I've done my half of the bargain. And right now, Mr Farrell, I have to say that you're very much overdressed.'

'So strip me, Claire,' he said, opening his arms to give her full access to his clothes.

It was an offer she wasn't going to refuse.

Afterwards, curled in Sean's arms, Claire turned her face so she could kiss his shoulder. 'I'd better go.'

'Not yet. This is comfortable.' He held her closer. 'Stay for a bit longer. I'll drive you home.'

So Sean the super-efficient businessman was a cuddler? Ah, bless, Claire thought. And, actually, she rather liked it. It made him that much more human. 'OK,' she said, and settled back against him.

Funny how they didn't really need to talk. Just being together was enough. It was *peaceful*. Something else she would never have believed about herself and Sean; but she liked just being with him. When he wasn't being super-organised down to the last microsecond. And it seemed that he felt the same.

So maybe, just maybe, this wasn't all going to end in tears.

When she finally got dressed and he drove her home, he parked outside her flat. 'So. When are you free next?' he asked.

'Sunday?' she suggested. 'I have the shop on Saturday.'

'Sunday works for me.'

'You organised tonight, so I'll organise Sunday,' she said. 'And that means doing things my way.'

'Going with the flow.' He looked slightly pained.

'It means being spontaneous and having fun,' she said. 'I'll pick you up at nine. And I won't be late.'

'No?' he asked wryly.

'No.' She kissed him. 'The first bit of tonight was, um, a bit much for me. But I loved dinner. I loved the London Eye and just being with you. Those kind of things works for me. It's just…' She shook her head. 'Schedules are for work. And I keep my work and my personal life separate.'

'Hmm,' he said, and she knew he wasn't convinced. But then he made the effort and said, 'I enjoyed being with you.'

But the fact she'd been late had really grated on him. He didn't have to tell her that.

He kissed her lightly. 'I'll walk you to your door.'

'Sean, it's half a dozen paces. I think I'm old enough to manage.'

He spread his hands. 'As you wish.'

'I'm not pushing you away,' she said softly. 'But I don't need protecting—the same as you don't.' She already had one overprotective male in her life, and that was more than enough for her. And it was half the reason why she'd always chosen free-spirited boyfriends who wouldn't make a fuss over everything or smother her.

Though maybe she'd gone too far the other way, because they'd all been disastrous.

But could Sean compromise? Could they find some kind of middle ground between them? If not, then this was going to be just as much a disaster as her previous relationships.

'Thank you for caring,' she said, knowing that his heart was in the right place—he just went a bit too far, that was all. 'I'll see you Sunday.'

'Spontaneous. Go with the flow.'

'You're learning. *Carpe diem*,' she said with a smile, and kissed him. 'Goodnight.'

CHAPTER NINE

WHEN CLAIRE WENT to pick Sean up on Sunday morning he was wearing formal trousers, a formal shirt and a tie. At least this time it wasn't a complete suit, but it still didn't work for what she wanted to do. And they looked totally mismatched, given that Claire was wearing denim shorts, a strappy vest and matching canvas shoes. Sean looked way too formal.

'Do you actually own a pair of jeans?' she asked.

'No.'

It was just as well she'd second-guessed. 'Right, then.' She delved into her tote bag and brought out a plastic carrier bag bearing the name of a department store.

'What's this?' he asked.

'Pressie. For you.' When he still looked blank, she added, 'The idea is that you wear it. As in right now.'

He looked in the bag. 'You bought me a pair of jeans?'

'Give the monkey a peanut,' she drawled.

'How do you know my size?'

She rolled her eyes. 'I measured you for a wedding suit, remember?'

He sighed. 'Claire, you didn't need to buy me a pair of jeans.'

'You don't own any. So actually, yes, I did.'

He looked at her, and she sighed. 'Sean, don't be difficult about this. I bought you a present, that's all. It's what people do when they date.'

He still didn't look convinced.

'Look, you bought me those gorgeous flowers, and I don't think you'd enjoy it if I bought you flowers— well, not that I think you *can't* buy a man flowers,' she clarified, 'but I don't think you're the kind of man who'd really appreciate them.'

'Probably not,' he admitted.

'Most people would buy their man some chocolate, but I can hardly give chocolate to someone who owns a confectionery company, can I? Which leaves me pretty stuck for buying you a gift. It's just an ordinary pair of jeans, Sean. Nothing ridiculously overpriced. So come on. Do something you haven't done since you were a teenager,' she coaxed, 'and wear the jeans. And swap those shoes for your running shoes.'

'My running shoes?' he queried.

She nodded. 'Because I bet you don't have a pair of scruffy, "go for a walk and it doesn't matter if they're not perfectly polished" shoes.'

'There's nothing wrong with looking smart at work,' he protested.

'I know, but you're not at work today, Sean. You're playing. You can keep the shirt, but lose the tie.'

'Bossy,' he grumbled, but he did as she asked. By the time he'd changed into the jeans and his running shoes, he looked fantastic—much more approachable. *Touchable.* Claire was glad she'd picked a light-coloured denim that looked slightly worn. It really, really suited him.

She folded her arms and looked at him.

'What now?' he asked. 'I'm not wearing the tie.'

'But your top button is still done up. Fix it, and roll your sleeves up.'

'Claire…'

'We did your date your way,' she said. 'And you agreed that we'd do this one my way.'

'This is the giddy limit,' he said, and for a moment she thought he was going to refuse; but finally he indulged her.

'That's almost perfect,' she said, then sashayed over to him, reached up to kiss him, and then messed up his hair.

'Why did you do that?' he asked, pulling back.

'It's the "just got out of bed" look. Which makes you look seriously hot,' she added. 'Like you did in Capri.'

He gave her a predatory smile. 'So if you think I look hot…'

'Rain check,' she said. 'Because we're going out and having fun, first.'

There was a bossy side to Claire, Sean thought, that he'd never seen before. The whole idea of giving up control—that just wasn't how he did things.

Claire Stewart was dangerous with a capital D where his peace of mind was concerned.

'This is your car?' He looked at the bright pink convertible Mini stencilled with daisies that was parked on the road outside his house. 'Oh, you are kidding me.'

'What's wrong with my car?' She put her finger into the keyring and spun her keys round.

What was wrong with the car? Where did he start?

He closed his eyes. 'OK. I know, I know, go with the flow.' He groaned and opened his eyes again. 'But, Claire. *Pink.* With daisies. Really?'

Finally she took pity on him. 'I borrowed it from a friend. I don't have a car of my own at the moment.'

'Then we could go wherever it is in mine,' he suggested hopefully.

'Nope—we're doing this my way.' She gave him another of those insolent grins. 'Actually, my friend wants to sell this. I was thinking about buying it from her.'

He pulled a face, but said nothing.

'Very wise, Sean, very wise,' she teased.

She tied her hair back with a scarf, added some dark glasses that made her look incredibly sexy, and then added the disgusting khaki cap he remembered from Capri and which cancelled out the effect of the glasses. Once they were sitting in the car, she put the roof down, connected her MP3 player, and started blasting out sugary nineteen-sixties pop songs. Worse still, she made him sing along; and Sean was surprised to discover that he actually knew most of the songs.

By the time they got to Brighton, he'd stopped being embarrassed by the sheer loudness of the car and was word-perfect on the choruses of all her favourite songs.

'Brighton,' he said.

'Absolutely. Today is "Sean and Claire do the seaside",' she said brightly.

'And this isn't planned out?'

She rolled her eyes. 'Don't be daft—you don't plan things like going to the seaside. You go with the flow and you have *fun*.' She parked the car, then took his hand and they strolled across to the seafront.

This was so far removed from what he'd normally do on a Sunday. He might sit in his garden—perfectly manicured by the man he paid to mow the lawn, weed the flower beds, and generally make the area look tidy— but nine times out of ten he'd be in his study, working.

He couldn't even remember the last time he went to the seaside. With one of his girlfriends, probably, but he hadn't paid much attention.

But with Claire, he was definitely paying attention.

He hung back slightly. 'Those are very *short* shorts.' And it made him want to touch her.

She just laughed. 'I have great legs—I might as well show them off before they go all wrinkly and saggy when I'm old.'

'You're...' He stopped and shook his head.

'I'm what, Sean?'

'A lot of things,' he said, 'half of which I wouldn't dare utter right now.'

'Chicken,' she teased.

'Discretion's the better part of valour,' he protested.

She laughed and took him onto the pier. They queued up to go on the fairground rides.

'You couldn't get fast-track tickets?' he asked.

She rolled her eyes. 'Queuing is part of the fun.'

'How?' he asked. In his view, queuing was a waste of time. If something was worth visiting, you bought fast-track tickets; otherwise, you didn't bother and you used your time more wisely.

'Anticipation,' she said. 'It'll be worth the wait.'

He wasn't so sure, but he'd agreed to do this her way. 'OK.'

But then they queued for the roller coaster.

'I thought you hated heights?'

'I do, but it'll be worth it if it loosens you up a little,' she said. 'It's OK to stop and smell the roses, Sean. If anything it'll enrich the time you spend on your business, because you'll look at things with a wider perspective.'

'Playing the business guru now, are you?'

'I don't play when it comes to business,' she said, 'but I do remember to play in my free time.'

'Hmm.'

He wasn't that fussed about the thrill rides, but for her sake he pretended to enjoy himself.

They grabbed something quick to eat, then went over to the stony, steeply sloping beach next. The sea was such an intense shade of turquoise, they could have been standing on the shore of the Mediterranean rather than the English Channel. He'd never seen the sea in England look so blue. And this, he thought, was much more his style than waiting in a queue for a short thrill ride that did nothing to raise his pulse.

Claire, on the other hand, could seriously raise his pulse...

'Shoes off,' she said, removing her own canvas shoes, 'and roll up your jeans.'

'You're so bossy,' he grumbled.

She grinned. 'The reward will be worth it.'

'What reward?'

She fluttered her eyelashes at him. 'Wait and see.'

He had to admit that it was nice walking on the edge of the sea with her, his shoes in one hand and her hand in his other. The sound of the waves rushing onto the pebbles and the seagulls squawking, the scent of the sea air and the warmth of the sunlight on his skin. Right at that moment, he'd never felt more alive.

It must have shown in his face, because she said softly, 'Told you it was rewarding.'

'Uh-huh.' He smiled at her. 'Talking of rewards...' He leaned forward and kissed her. But what started out as a sweet, soft brush of her lips against his soon turned hot.

He pulled back, remembering that they were in a

public place and with families around them. 'Claire. We need to…'

'I know.' Her fingers tightened round his. 'And this was what I wanted today. For you to let go, just a little bit, and have some fun with me.'

'I *am* having fun,' he said, half surprised by the admission.

'Good.' Her face had gone all soft and dreamy and it made him want to kiss her again—later, he promised himself.

When they'd finished paddling, they had to walk on the pebbles to dry off—Claire clearly hadn't thought to bring a towel with her—and then she said, 'Time for afternoon tea. And I have somewhere really special in mind.'

'OK.' He didn't mind going with the flow for a while, especially as it meant holding her hand. There was something to be said about just wandering along together.

As they walked into the town, he could see the exotic domes and spires of Brighton Pavilion.

Another queue, he thought with a sigh. It was one of the biggest tourist attractions in the area. Again, if she'd planned it they could've bought tickets online rather than having to queue up. He hated wasting time like this.

But, when they got closer, he realised there was something odd. No queues.

A notice outside the Pavilion informed them that the building was closed for urgent maintenance. Just for this weekend.

Sean just about stopped himself pointing out that if Claire had planned their trip in advance, then she would've known about this and she wouldn't have been disappointed.

'Oh, well,' she said brightly. 'I'm sure we can find a nice tea shop somewhere and have a traditional cream tea.'

Except all the tea shops nearby were full of tourists who'd had exactly the same idea. There were queues.

'Sorry. This is, um, a bit of a disaster,' she said.

Yes. But he wasn't going to make her feel any worse about it by agreeing with her. *'Carpe diem,'* he said. 'Maybe there's an ice cream shop we can go to instead.'

'Maybe,' she said, though he could tell that she was really disappointed. He guessed that she'd wanted to share the gorgeous furnishings of the Pavilion with him—and there had probably been some kind of costume display, too.

They wandered through the historic part of the town, peeking in the windows of the antiques shops and little craft shops, and eventually found a tea shop that had room at one of the tables. Though as it was late afternoon, the tea shop had run out of scones and cream.

'Just the tea is fine, thanks,' Sean said with a smile.

They had a last walk along the beach, then Claire drove them home. 'Shall I drop you back at your house, or would you like to come back to my place and we can maybe order in some Chinese food?' she asked.

Given what she'd said to him by the sea, Sean knew what she wanted to hear. 'I think,' he said, 'we'll go with the flow.'

Her smile was a real reward—full of warmth and pleasure rather than smugness. 'We won't go home on the motorway, then,' she said. 'We'll find a nice little country pub where we can have dinner.'

Except it turned out that every pub they stopped at didn't do food on Sunday evenings.

'I can't believe this,' she said. 'I mean—it's the summer. Prime tourist season. Why on earth wouldn't any of them serve food on Sunday evenings?'

Sean didn't have the heart to ask why she hadn't planned it better. 'Go back on to the motorway,' he said. 'We'll get a takeaway back in London.'

'I'm so sorry. Still, at least we can keep the roof down and enjoy the sun on the way home,' Claire said.

Which was clearly all she needed to say to jinx it, because they were caught in a sudden downpour. By the time she'd found somewhere safe to stop and put the car's soft top back up, they were both drenched. 'I'm so sorry. That wasn't supposed to happen,' Claire said, biting her lip.

'So we were literally going with the flow. Of water,' Sean said, and kissed her.

'What was that for?' she asked.

'For admitting that you're not always right.' He stole another kiss. 'And also because that T-shirt looks amazing on you right now.'

'Because it's wet, you mean?' She rolled her eyes at him. 'Men.'

He smiled. 'Actually, I wanted to cheer you up a bit.'

'Because today's been a total disaster.'

'No, it hasn't. I enjoyed the sea.'

'But we didn't get to the Pavilion, we missed out on a cream tea, I couldn't find anywhere for dinner and we just got drenched.' She sighed. 'If I'd done things your way, it would've been different.'

'But when I planned our date, we ended up rushing and that was a disaster, too,' he said softly. 'I think we might both have learned something from this.'

'That sometimes you need to plan your personal life?' she asked.

'And sometimes you need to go with the flow,' he said. 'It's a matter of compromise.'

'That works for me, too. Compromise.' And her smile warmed him all the way through.

On the way back to London, he asked, 'So are you seriously going to buy this car?'

'What's wrong with it?'

'Apart from the colour? I was thinking, it's not very practical for transporting wedding dresses.'

'I don't need a car for that. I'm hiring a van for the wedding show,' she said.

'So why don't you have a car?' he asked.

'I live and work in London, so I don't really need one—public transport's fine.'

'You needed a car today to take us to the seaside,' he pointed out.

'Not necessarily. We could have gone by train,' she said.

'But then you wouldn't have been able to sing your head off all the way to Brighton.'

'And we wouldn't have got wet on the way home,' she agreed ruefully.

'We really need to get you out of those wet clothes,' he said, 'and my place is nearer than yours.'

'Good point,' she said, and drove back to his.

Sean had the great pleasure of peeling off her wet clothes outside the shower, then soaping her down under the hot water. When they'd finished, he put her clothes in the washer-dryer while she dried off. And then he had the even greater pleasure of sweeping her off her feet again, carrying her to his bed, and making love with her until they were both dizzy.

Afterwards, she was all warm and sweet in his arms. He stroked her hair back from her face. 'You were going to tell me how come you're not a doctor.'

'It just wasn't what I wanted to do,' she said.

'But you applied to study medicine at university.'

She shifted onto her side and propped herself on one elbow so she could look into his face. 'It was Dad's dream, not mine. It's a bit hard to resist pressure from your parents when you're sixteen. Especially when your father's a bit on the overprotective side.' She wrinkled her nose. 'Luckily I realised in time that you can't live someone else's dream for them. So I turned down the places I was offered and reapplied to design school.'

He frowned. 'But you were doing science A levels.'

'And Art,' she said. 'And the teacher who taught my textiles class at GCSE wrote me a special reference, explaining that even though I hadn't done the subject at A level I was more than capable of doing a degree. At my interview, I wore a dress I'd made and I also took a suit I'd made with me. I talked the interviewers through all the stitching and the cut and the material, so they knew I understood what I was doing. And they offered me an unconditional place.'

He could see the pain in her eyes, and drew her closer. 'So what made you realise you didn't want to be a doctor?'

'My mum.' Claire dragged in a breath. 'She was only thirty-seven when she died, Sean.' Tears filmed her eyes. 'She barely made it past half the proverbial three score years and ten. In the last week of her life, when we were talking she held my hand and told me to follow my dream and do what my heart told me was the right thing.'

Which clearly hadn't been medicine.

Not knowing what to say, he just stroked her hair.

'Even when I was tiny, I used to draw dresses. Those paper dolls—mine were always the best dressed in class. I used to sketch all the time. I wanted to design dresses. Specifically, wedding dresses.'

He had a feeling he knew why she tended to fight with her father, now.

Her next words confirmed it. 'Dad said designers were ten a penny, whereas being a doctor meant I'd have a proper job for life.' She sighed. 'I know he had my best interests at heart. He had a tough upbringing, and he didn't want me ever to struggle with money, the way he did when he was young. But being a doctor was *his* dream, not mine. He said I could still do dressmaking and what have you on the side—but no way would I have had the time, not with the crazy hours that newly qualified doctors work. It was an all or nothing thing.' She grimaced. 'We had a huge fight over it. He said I'd just be wasting a degree if I studied textile design instead, and he gave me an ultimatum. Study medicine, and he'd support me through uni; study textiles, and he was kicking me out until I came to my senses.'

That sounded like the words of a scared man, Sean thought. One who wanted the best for his daughter and didn't know how to get that through to her. And he'd said totally the wrong thing to a teenage girl who'd just lost the person she loved most in the world and wasn't dealing with it very well. Probably because he was in exactly the same boat.

'That's quite an ultimatum,' Sean said, trying to find words that wouldn't make Claire think he was judging her.

'It was pretty bad at the time.' She paused. 'I talked to your mum about it.'

He was surprised. 'My mum?'

Claire nodded. 'She was lovely—she knew I was going off the rails a bit and I'd started drinking to blot out the pain of losing Mum, so she took me under her wing.'

Exactly what Sean would've expected from his mother. And now he knew why she'd been so insistent that he should look after Claire, the night of Ashleigh's eighteenth birthday party. She'd known the full story. And she'd known that she could trust Sean to do the right thing. To look after Claire when she needed it.

Claire smiled grimly. 'The drinking was also the worst thing I could have done in Dad's eyes, because his dad used to drink and gamble. I think that was half the reason why I did it, because I wanted to make him as angry as he made me. But your mum sat me down and told me that my mum would hate to see what I was doing to myself, and she made me see that the way I was behaving really wasn't helping the situation. I told her what Mum said about following my dream, and she asked me what I really wanted to do with my life. I showed her my sketchbooks and she said that my passion for needlework showed, and it'd be a shame to ignore my talents.' She smiled. 'And then she talked to Dad. He still didn't think that designing dresses was a stable career—he wanted me to have what he thought of as a "proper" job.'

'Does he still think that?' Sean asked.

'Oh, yes. And he tells me it, too, every so often,' Claire said, sounding both hurt and exasperated. 'When I left the fashion house where I worked after I graduated, he panicked that I wouldn't be able to make a go of my own business. Especially because there was a recession on. He wanted me to go back to uni instead.'

'And train to be a doctor?'

'Because then I'd definitely have a job for life.' She wrinkled her nose. 'But it's not just about the academic side of things. Sure, I could've done the degree and the post-grad training. But my heart wouldn't have been in it, and that wouldn't be fair to my patients.' She sighed. 'And I had a bit of a cash flow problem last year. I took a hit from a couple of clients whose cheques bounced. I still had to pay my suppliers for the materials and, um...' She wrinkled her nose. 'I could've asked Dad to lend me the money to tide me over, but then he would've given me this huge lecture about taking a bigger deposit from my brides and insisting on cash or a direct transfer to my account. Yet again he would've made me feel that he didn't believe in me and I'm not good enough to make it on my own. So I, um, sold my car. It kept me afloat.'

'And have you changed the way you take money?'

She nodded. 'I admit, I learned that one the hard way. Nowadays I ask for stage payments. But there's no real harm done. And Dad doesn't know about it so I avoided the lecture.' Again, Sean could see the flash of pain in her eyes. 'I just wish Dad believed in me a bit more. Gran and Aunty Lou believe in me. So does Ash.'

'So do I,' Sean said.

At her look of utter surprise, he said softly, 'Ashleigh's wedding dress convinced me. I admit, I had my doubts about you. Especially when you lost her dress. But you came up with a workable solution—and, when the original dress turned up, I could see just how talented you are. Mum was right about you, Claire. Yes, you could've been a perfectly competent doctor, but you would've ignored your talents—and that would've been a waste.'

Her eyes sparkled with tears. 'From you, that's one hell of a compliment. And not one I ever thought I'd hear. Thank you.'

'It's sincerely meant,' he said. 'You did the right thing, following your dreams.'

'I know I did. And I'm happy doing what I do. I'm never going to be rich, but I make enough for what I need—and that's important.' She paused. 'But what about you, Sean? What about your dreams?'

'I'm living them,' he said automatically.

'But supposing Farrell's didn't exist,' she persisted. 'What would you do then?'

'Start up another Farrell's, I guess,' he said.

'So toffee really is your dream?' She didn't sound as if she believed him.

'Of course toffee's my dream. What's wrong with that?' he asked.

'You're the fourth generation to run the business, Sean,' she said softly. 'You have a huge sense of family and heritage and integrity and duty. Even if you didn't really want to do it, you wouldn't walk away from your family business. Ever.'

It shocked him that she could read him so accurately. Nobody else ever had. She wasn't judging him; she was just stating facts. 'I like my job,' he protested. He *did*.

'I'm not saying you don't,' she said softly. 'I'm just asking you, what's your dream?'

'I'm living it,' he said again. Though now she'd made him question that.

It was true that he would never have walked away from the business, even if his parents hadn't been killed. He'd always wanted to be part of Farrell's. It was his heritage.

But, if he was really honest about it, he'd felt such

pressure to keep the business going the same way that his father had always run things. After his parents had died in the crash, he'd needed to keep things stable for everyone who worked in the business, and keeping to the way things had always been done seemed the best way to keep everything on a stable footing.

He'd been so busy keeping the business going. And then, once he'd proved to his staff and his competitors that he was more than capable of running the business well, he'd been so busy making sure that things stayed that way that he just simply hadn't had the time to think about what he wanted.

Just before his parents' accident, he'd been working on some new product ideas. Something that would've been his contribution to the way the family business developed. He'd loved doing the research and development work. But he'd had to shelve it all after the accident, and he'd never had time to go back to his ideas.

Though it was pointless dwelling on might-have-beens. Things were as they were. And the sudden feeling of uncertainty made him antsy.

Sean had intended to ask Claire to stay, that night; but right at that moment he needed some distance between them, to get his equilibrium back. 'I'd better check to see if your clothes are dry.'

They were. So it was easy to suggest making a cold drink while she got dressed. Easier still to hint that it was time for her to go home—particularly as Claire took the hint. He let her walk out of the door without kissing her goodbye.

And he spent the rest of the evening wide awake, miserable and regretting it. She'd pushed him and he'd done what he always did and closed off, not wanting her to get too close.

But her words went round and round in his head. *What's your dream?*

The problem was, you couldn't always follow your dreams. Not if you had responsibilities and other people depended on you.

Everybody has a dream, Sean.

What did he really want?

He sat at his desk, staring out of the window at a garden it was too dark to see. Then he gritted his teeth, turned back to his computer and opened a file.

Dreams were a luxury. And he had a business to run—one that had just managed to survive a takeover bid. Dreams would have to wait.

KATE HARDY

CHAPTER TEN

SEAN SPENT THE next day totally unable to concentrate.

Which was ridiculous because he never, but never, let any of his girlfriends distract him from work.

But Claire Stewart was different, and she got under his skin in a way that nobody ever had before. He definitely wasn't letting her do it, but it was happening all the same—and he really didn't know what to do about it.

Part of him wanted to call her because he wanted to see her; and part of him was running scared because she made him look at things in his life that he'd rather ignore.

And he still couldn't get her words out of his head. *Everybody has a dream, Sean.* Just what was his?

He still hadn't worked out what to say to her by the evening, so he buried himself in work instead. And he noticed that she hadn't called him, either. So did that mean she, too, thought this was turning out to be a seriously bad idea and they ought to end it?

And then, on Tuesday morning, his PA brought him a plain white box.

'What's this?' he asked.

Jen shrugged. 'I have no idea. I was just asked to give it to you.'

There was no note with the box. He frowned. 'Who brought it?'

'A blonde woman. She wouldn't give her name. She said you'd know who it was from,' Jen said.

His heart skipped a beat.

Claire.

But if Claire had actually come to the factory and dropped this off personally, why hadn't she come to see him?

Or maybe she thought he'd refuse to see her. They hadn't exactly had a fight on Sunday evening, but he had to acknowledge that things had been a little bit strained when she'd left. Maybe this was her idea of a parley, the beginning of some kind of truce.

And hadn't she said about not sending him flowers and how you couldn't give chocolates to a confectioner?

'Thank you. I have a pretty good idea who it's from,' he said to Jen, and waited until she'd closed the door behind her before opening the box.

Claire had brought him cake.

Not just cake—the most delectable lemon cake he'd ever eaten in his life.

He gave in and called her business line.

She answered within three rings. 'Dream of a Dress, Claire speaking.'

'Thank you for the cake,' he said.

'Pleasure.'

Her voice was completely neutral, so he couldn't tell her mood. Well, he'd do things her way for once and ask her straight out. 'Why didn't you come in and say hello?'

'Your PA said you were in a meeting, and I didn't really have time to wait until you were done.'

'Fair enough.' He paused. He knew what he needed to say, and he was enough of a man not to shirk it. 'Claire, I owe you an apology.'

'What for?'

'Pushing you away on Sunday night.'

'Uh-huh.'

He sighed, guessing what she wanted him to say. 'I still can't answer your question.'

'Can't or won't?'

'A bit of both, if I'm honest,' he said.

'OK. Are you busy tonight?'

'Why?' he asked.

'I thought we could go and smell some roses.'

Claire-speak for having some fun, he guessed.

'Can you meet me at my place?'

'Sure. Would seven work for you?'

'Fine. Don't eat,' she said, 'because we can probably grab something on the way. Some of the food stalls at Camden Lock will still be open at that time.'

Clearly she intended to take him for a walk somewhere. 'And is this a jeans and running shoes thing?' he checked.

'You can wear your prissiest suit and your smartest shoes—whatever you like, as long as you can walk for half an hour or so and still be comfortable.'

When Sean turned up at her shop at exactly seven o'clock, Claire was wearing a navy summer dress patterned with daisies and flat court shoes. Her hair was tied back with another chiffon scarf—clearly that was Claire's favoured style—but he was pleased that she didn't add her awful khaki cap, this time. Instead, she just donned a pair of dark glasses.

They walked down to Camden Lock, grabbed a burger and shared some polenta fries, then headed along the canalside towards Regent's Park. He'd never really explored the area before, and it was a surprisingly pretty walk; some of the houses were truly gorgeous, and all the while there were birds singing in the trees and the calm presence of the canal.

'I love the walk along here. It's only ten minutes or so between the lock and the park,' she said.

And then Sean discovered that Claire had meant it literally about coming to smell the roses when she took him across Regent's Park to Queen Mary's Garden.

'This place is amazing—it's the biggest collection of roses in London,' she told him.

There were pretty bowers, huge beds filled with all different types of roses, and walking through them was like breathing pure scent; it totally filled his senses.

'This is incredible,' he said. 'I didn't think you meant it literally about smelling the roses.'

'I meant it metaphorically as well—you must know that WH Davies poem, "What is this life if full of care, We have no time to stand and stare,",' she said. 'You have to make time for things like this, Sean, or you miss out on so much.'

He knew she had a point. 'Yeah,' he said softly, and tightened his fingers round hers.

He could just about remember coming to see the roses in Regent's Park as a child, but everything since his parents' death was a blur of work, work and more work.

Six years of blurriness.

Being with Claire had brought everything into sharp focus again. Though Sean wasn't entirely sure he liked what he saw when he looked at his life—and it made him antsy. Claire was definitely dangerous to his peace of mind.

She drew him over to look at the borders of delphiniums, every shade of white and cream and blue through to almost black.

'Now these I *really* love,' she said. 'The colour, the shape, the texture—everything.'

He looked at her. 'So you're a secret gardener?'

'Except doing it properly would take time I don't really have to spare,' she said. 'Though, yes, if had a decent-sized garden I'd plant it as a cottage garden with loads of these and hollyhocks and foxgloves, and tiny little lily-of-the-valley and violets.'

'These ones here are exactly the same colour as your eyes.'

She grinned. 'Careful, Sean. You're waxing a bit poetic.'

Just to make the point, he kissed her.

'Tsk,' she teased. 'Is that the only way you have to shut me up?'

'It worked for Benedick,' he said.

'*Much Ado* is a rom-com—and I thought you said you didn't like rom-coms?'

'I said I didn't mind ones with great dialogue—and dialogue doesn't get any better than Beatrice.' He could see Claire playing Beatrice; he'd noticed that she often had that deliciously acerbic bite to her words.

'And it's a good plot,' she said, 'except Hero ends up with a man who isn't good enough for her. I hate the bit where Claudio shames her on their wedding day, and it always makes me want to yell to her, "Don't do it!" at the end when she marries him.'

'They were different times and different mores, though I do know what you mean,' he said. 'I wouldn't want Ashleigh to marry a weak, selfish man.'

She winced. 'Like Rob Riverton. And I introduced her to him.'

'Not one of your better calls,' Sean said.

'I know.' She looked guilty. 'I did tell her to dump

him because he wasn't good enough for her and he didn't treat her properly.'

A month ago, Sean wouldn't have believed that. Now, he did, because he'd seen for himself that Claire had integrity. 'Claire,' he said, yanked her into his arms and kissed her.

'Was that to shut me up again?' she asked when he broke the kiss.

'No—it was because you're irresistible.'

She clearly didn't know what to say to that, because it silenced her.

They walked back along the canalside to Camden, hand in hand; then he bought them both a glass of wine and they sat outside, enjoying the late evening sunshine before walking back to her flat.

'Do you want to come in?' she asked.

'Is that wise?'

'Probably not, but I'm asking anyway.'

'Probably not,' he agreed, 'but I'm saying yes.'

They sat with the windows open, the curtains open and music playing; there was a jug of iced water on the coffee table, and she'd put frozen slices of lime in the jug. Sean was surprised by how at home he felt here; the room was decorated in very girly colours, compared to his own neutral colour scheme, but he felt as if he belonged.

'It's getting late. I ought to go,' he said softly. 'I have meetings, first thing.'

'You don't have to go,' Claire said. 'You could stay.' She paused. 'If you want to.'

'Are you sure?'

'I'm sure.'

In answer, he closed her curtains and carried her to her bed.

* * *

The next morning, Claire woke before her alarm went off to find herself alone in bed, and Sean's side of the bed was stone cold. She was a bit disappointed that he hadn't even woken her before he left, or put a note on the pillow. Then again, he'd said that he had early meetings. He'd probably left at some unearthly hour and hadn't wanted to disturb her sleep.

At that precise moment he walked in, carrying a tray with two paper cups of coffee and a plate of pastries. 'Breakfast is served, my lady.'

'You went out to buy us breakfast? That's—that's so *lovely*,' she said, sitting up, 'but you really didn't have to. I have fruit and yoghurt in the fridge, plus bread and granola in the cupboard.'

'I noticed a bakery round the corner from yours. I thought croissants might be nice, and I'm running a bit short on time so I bought the coffee rather than making it.'

'That sounds to me like an excuse for having decadent tendencies,' she teased.

He laughed back. 'Maybe.'

He sat on the bed and shared the almond-filled croissants with her. 'You thought I'd gone without saying goodbye, didn't you?'

'Um—well, yes,' she admitted.

'I wouldn't do that to you. I would at least have left you a note.' He finished his coffee and kissed her lightly. 'Sorry. I really *do* have to go now. Can I call you later?'

'I'd like that.' Claire wrapped herself in her robe so she could pad barefoot to the kitchen with him and kiss him goodbye at her front door.

She still couldn't quite get over the fact he'd gone out to buy them a decadent breakfast. And he'd stayed last night. This thing between them was moving so incredibly fast; it scared and exhilarated her at the same time. She guessed it would be the same for Sean. But would it scare him enough to make him push her away again, the way he had the other night? Or would he finally let her in?

They were both busy during the week, but Sean texted her on Friday.

Do you have any appointments over lunch?

Sorry, yes.

And, regretfully, she wasn't playing hard to get. She really did have appointments that she couldn't move.

OK. Are you busy after work?

Yes, but that was something she could move.

Why?

Am trying to be like you and plan a spontaneous date.

She couldn't help laughing. Planning and spontaneity didn't go together.

OK.

Cinema? he suggested.

Depends. Is popcorn on offer?

Could be... he texted back.

Deal. Time and place?

Can pick you up.

She wanted to keep at least some of her independence.

Saves time if I meet you there.

OK. Will check out films and text you where and when.

Claire had expected him to choose some kind of noir movie, but when she got to the cinema and met him with a kiss she discovered that he'd picked a rom-com.

'Is this to indulge me?' she asked.

'I've seen this one before. The structure's good and the acting's good,' he said.

'You're such a film snob,' she teased, but it warmed her that he'd thought of what she'd enjoy rather than imposing his choices on her regardless.

They sat in the back row, holding hands, and Claire enjoyed the film thoroughly. Back at his place afterwards, they were curled in bed together, when Sean said, 'I had a focus group meeting today.'

She remembered the samples he'd given her. 'Did it go how you wanted?'

'Not really,' he said. 'We need a rethink.'

'For what it's worth, I've always thought that your caramel hearts would be great as bridal favours. That's the sort of thing my brides always ask me if I know about, because not everyone likes the traditional sugared almonds.'

'Bridal favours?' he queried.

'Uh-huh—the hearts could be wrapped in silver or

gold foil, and you can offer a choice of organza bags with them in say white, silver or gold, so brides can buy the whole package. They could be ordered direct from your website, or you could offer the special bridal package through selected shops.'

He nodded. 'That's brilliant, Claire. Thank you. I never even considered that sort of thing.'

'Why would you, unless you were connected to a wedding business?' she pointed out.

'I guess not.'

'So why didn't the focus group like the salted caramels? I thought they were fabulous.'

'It's a move too far from the core business. Farrell's has produced hard toffee for generations. We're not really associated with chocolates, apart from the caramel hearts—which were my mum's idea.'

'Are you looking to move away from making toffee, then?'

'Yes and no,' he said. 'What I want to do is look at other sorts of toffee.'

She frowned. 'Am I being dense? Because toffee's—well—toffee.'

'Unless it's in something,' he said. 'Toffee popcorn, like the one you chose tonight at the cinema. Or toffee ice cream.'

'You weren't concentrating on the film, were you?' she asked. 'You were thinking about work.'

'I was thinking about you, actually,' he said. 'But the toffee popcorn did set off a lightbulb in the back of my head.' He wrinkled his nose. 'If I took the business in that direction, it'd mean buying a whole different set of machinery and arranging a whole different set of staff training. I'd need to be sure that the investment would be worth the cost and Farrell's would see a good return on the money.'

'Unless,' she said, 'you collaborated with other manufacturers—ones who already have the factory set-up and the staff. Maybe you could license them to use your toffee.'

'That's a great idea. And I could draw up a shortlist of other family-run businesses whose ideas and ethos are the same as Farrell's. People who'd make good business partners.'

'That's your dream, isn't it?' she asked softly. 'To keep your heritage—but to put your own stamp on it.'

'I guess. Research and development was always my favourite thing,' he admitted. 'I wanted to look at developing different flavours of toffee. Something different from mint, treacle, orange or nut. I was thinking cinnamon or ginger for Christmas, or maybe special seasonal editions of the chocolate hearts—say a strawberries and cream version for summer.'

'That's a great idea,' she said. 'Maybe white chocolate.'

'And different packaging,' he said. 'Something to position Farrell's hearts as the kind of thing you buy as special treats.'

'You could sell them in little boxes as well as big ones,' she said. 'For people who want a treat but don't want a big box.'

He kissed her. 'I'm beginning to think that I should employ you on my R and D team.'

'Now that,' she said, 'really wouldn't work. I'm used to doing things my way and I'd hate to have to go by someone else's rules all the while. Besides, I don't want you bossing me about and I think we'd end up fighting.'

He wrinkled his nose. 'I don't want to fight with you, Claire—I like how things are now.'

'Me, too,' she admitted.

'Make love, not war—that's a great slogan, you know.'

She grinned. 'Just as long as it's not all talk and no action, Mr Farrell.'

He laughed. 'I can take a hint.' And he kissed her until she was dizzy.

CHAPTER ELEVEN

OVER THE NEXT couple of weeks, Claire and Sean grew closer. Claire didn't get to see Sean every evening, but she talked to him every day and found herself really looking forward to the times they did see each other. And even on days when things were frustrating and refused to go right, or she had a client who changed her mind about what she wanted at least twice a day, it wasn't so bad because Claire knew she would be seeing Sean or talking to him later.

And he indulged her by taking her to one of her favourite places—the Victoria and Albert Museum. She took him to see her favourite pieces of clothing, showing him the fabrics, the shapes and the stitching that had inspired some of her own designs. When they stopped for a cold drink in the café, she looked at him.

'Sorry. I rather went into nerd mode. You should have told me to shut up.'

He smiled. 'Actually, I really enjoyed it.'

'But I was lecturing you, making you look at fiddly bits and pieces that probably bored you stupid.'

'You were lit up, Claire. Clothing design is your passion. And it was a privilege to see it,' he said softly. He reached across the table, took her hand and drew it to his lips. 'Don't ever lose that passion.'

He'd accepted her for who she was, Claire thought with sudden shock. The first man she'd ever dated who'd seen who she was, accepted it, and encouraged her to do what she loved.

In turn, Sean gave her a personal guided tour of the toffee factory. 'I'm afraid the white coat and the hair covering are non-negotiable,' he said.

'Health and safety. This is a working factory. And the clothes are about function, not form—just as they should be,' she said.

'I guess.' He took her through the factory, explaining what the various stages were and letting her taste the different products.

'I love the fact you're still using your great-grandparents' recipe for the toffee,' she said. 'And the photographs.' She'd noticed the blown-up photographs from years before lining the walls in the reception area. 'It's lovely to see that connection over the years.'

'A bit like you,' he said, 'and the way you hand-decorate a dress exactly the same as they would've done it two hundred years ago.'

'I guess.'

They were halfway through when Sean's sales manager came over.

'Sean, I'm really sorry to interrupt,' he said, smiling acknowledgement at Claire. 'I'm afraid we've got a bit of a situation.'

'Hey—don't mind me,' Claire said. 'The business comes first. I can do a tour at any time.'

'Thanks,' Sean said. 'What's the problem, Will?'

'I had the press on the phone earlier, talking about the takeover bid,' Will said. 'I explained that it's not happening and Farrell's is carrying on exactly as before, but someone's clearly been spreading doubts among our biggest customers, because I've been fielding phone calls ever since. And one of our customers in particular says he wants to talk to the organ grinder, not the monkey.'

'You're my sales manager,' Sean said. 'Which makes you as much of an organ grinder as I am.'

Will looked awkward. 'Not in Mel Archer's eyes.'

'Ah. *Him.*' Sean grimaced. 'Claire, would you mind if I let Will finish the tour with you?'

'Sure,' she said.

'I'll talk to Archer and explain the situation to him,' Sean said. 'And I'll make it very clear to him that I trust my senior team to do their jobs well and use their initiative.'

'Sorry.'

'It's not your fault,' Sean said. 'I'll see you later, Claire.'

She smiled at him. 'No worries. I'll wait for you in reception.'

'Sorry. It's the monkey rather than the organ grinder for you, too,' Will said.

She smiled. 'Sean says you're an organ grinder. That's good enough for me.'

Will finished taking her round and answered all her questions. Including ones she knew she probably shouldn't ask but couldn't help herself; this was a chance to see another side of Sean.

'So have you worked for Sean for long?' she asked Will.

'Three years,' Will said. 'And he's probably the best manager I've ever worked with. He doesn't micromanage—he trusts you to get on and do your job, though he's always there if things get sticky.'

'Which I guess they would be, in a toffee factory,' Claire said with a smile.

Will laughed. 'Yeah. Pun not actually intended. What I mean is he knows the business inside out. He's there if you need support, and if there's a problem you can't solve he'll have an answer—though what he does is ask you questions to make you think a bit more about it and work it out for yourself.'

So her super-efficient businessman liked to teach people and develop his staff, too. And it was something she knew he wouldn't have told her himself.

From the half of the tour Sean had given her and the insights Will added, Claire realised that maybe Sean really was living his dream; he really did love the factory and his job, and not just because it was his heritage and he felt duty-bound to preserve it for the next generation. Though she rather thought that if he'd had a choice in the matter, he would've worked in the research and development side of the business.

'He's a good man,' she said, meaning it.

When Ashleigh and Luke returned from their honeymoon, they invited Claire over to see the wedding photographs. She arrived bearing champagne and brownies. Sean was there already, and she gave him a cool nod of acknowledgement before cooing over the photographs and choosing the ones she wanted copies of.

A little later, he offered to help her make coffee. 'Have I done something to upset you?' he asked softly when they were alone in Ashleigh's kitchen.

'No.' Clare frowned. 'What makes you think that?'

'Just you seemed a little cool with me tonight.'

'In front of Ash, yes—she expects me to be just on the verge of civil with you. If I'm nice to you, she's going to guess something's going on, and I don't want her to know about this.' Claire took a deep breath. 'She's already asked me a couple of questions, and I told her we came to a kind of truce in Capri—once you realised it wasn't my fault her wedding dress disappeared—and you were one step away from grovelling.'

'You told her I was *grovelling*?'

Claire grinned. 'She just laughed and said grovelling isn't in your vocabulary, and she'd give it a week before we started sniping at each other again.'

He moved closer. 'I'm definitely not grovelling, but I'm not sniping either.' He paused. 'In fact, I'd rather just kiss you.'

'I'd rather that, too,' she said softly, 'but I'm not ready for Ash to know about this yet.'

'So I'm your dirty little secret?'

'For now—and I'm yours,' she said.

At the end of the evening, Sean said, 'Claire, it's raining—I'll give you a lift home to save you getting drenched.'

'This is quite some truce,' Ashleigh said, giving them both a piercing look. 'Though you probably won't make it back to Claire's before the ceasefire ends.'

'I won't fight if she doesn't,' Sean said. 'Claire?'

'No fighting, and thank you very much for the offer of the lift.'

Ashleigh narrowed her eyes at both of them, but didn't say any more.

'Do you have any idea how close you were to breaking our cover?' Claire asked crossly on the way home. 'I'm sure Ash has guessed.'

'What's your problem with anyone knowing about you and me?' Sean asked.

'Because it's still early days. And, actually, unless my calendar's wrong, you'll be dumping me in the next few days anyway.'

'How do you work that out?'

'Because, Sean Farrell, you never date anyone for more than three weeks in a row.'

'I don't dump my girlfriends exactly three weeks in to a relationship,' he said. 'That's a little old and a little unfair.'

'But you dump them,' Claire persisted.

'No, I break up with them nicely and I make them feel it's their decision,' he corrected.

'When it's actually yours.'

He shrugged. 'If it makes them feel better about the situation, what's the problem?'

'You're impossible.'

He laughed. 'Ashleigh said we wouldn't make it back to your place before we started fighting. She was right.'

'I'm not fighting, I'm just making a statement of facts—and don't you dare kiss me to shut me up,' she warned.

'I can't kiss you when I'm driving,' Sean pointed out, 'so that's a rain check.'

'You really are the most exasperating…' Unable to think of a suitable retort, she lapsed into silence.

'Besides,' he said softly, 'you'd be bored to tears with a yes-man or a lapdog.'

'Lapdog?' she asked, not following.

'"When husbands or when lapdogs breathe their last." Alexander Pope,' he explained helpfully.

She rolled her eyes. 'I forgot you did English A level.'

'And dated a couple of English teachers.'

'Would one of those have been the one who made you see a certain rom-com more than once?'

'Yes. At least you haven't done that.'

'You're still impossible,' she grumbled.

'Yup,' he said cheerfully.

'And, excuse me, you just missed the turning to my place.'

'Because we're not going to your place. We're going to mine.'

'But I have a bride coming in first thing tomorrow morning for a final fitting,' she protested.

'I have a washer-dryer, an alarm clock, a spare un-used toothbrush, and I'll run you home after breakfast.'

She sighed. 'You've got an answer for everything.'

'Most things,' he corrected, and she groaned.

'I give up.'

'Good,' he said.

He stripped her very slowly once he'd locked his front door behind them, put her clothes in the laundry, then took her to bed. And he was as good as his word, finding her a spare toothbrush, making her coffee in the morning, making sure her clothes were dried, and taking her home.

She kissed him lingeringly in the car. 'See you later. And thanks for the lift.'

Ashleigh dropped by at lunchtime.

'Well, hello, stranger—long time, no see,' Claire teased. 'What is it, a little over twelve hours?'

'We're having lunch,' Ashleigh said. 'Now.'

'Why does this feel as if you're about to tell me off?' Claire asked.

'Because I am. When did this all happen?'

Claire tried to look innocent. 'When did all what happen?'

'You know perfectly well what I mean. You and my brother. And don't deny it. You're both acting totally out of character round each other.'

'He just gave me a lift home last night,' Claire said,

crossing her fingers under the table. It had been a lot more than that.

'Hmm.' Ashleigh folded her arms and gave Claire a level stare.

Claire gave in. 'Ash, it's early days. And you know Sean; it's probably not going to last.'

'Why didn't you tell me?'

'Because when it all goes wrong I don't want our friendship to be collateral damage.'

Ashleigh hugged her. 'Idiot. Nothing would stop me being friends with you.'

'Sean doesn't want you to be collateral damage, either,' Claire pointed out.

Ashleigh rolled her eyes. 'I won't be, and don't you go overprotective on me like my big brother is—remember I'm older than you.'

'OK,' Claire said meekly.

'I thought something was up when he helped you make coffee, and then when he offered you a lift home…I knew it for sure,' Ashleigh said.

'It's still really, really early days,' Claire warned.

'But it's working,'

'At the moment. We still fight, but it's different now.' Claire smiled. 'Sean's not quite as regimented as I thought he was.'

Ashleigh laughed. 'Not with you around, he won't be.'

'And he's stopped calling me the Mistress of Chaos.'

'Good, because you're not.' Ashleigh hugged her again. 'I can't think of anyone I'd like more as my sister-in-law. I've always thought of you as like my sister anyway.'

'We haven't been together long,' Claire warned, 'so I'm not promising anything.'

'I think,' Ashleigh said, 'that you'll be good for each other.'

'Promise me you won't say anything? Even to Luke?'

'It's a bit too late for Luke,' Ashleigh said, 'but I won't say anything to Sean.'

'Thank you. And you'll be the first to know if things move forward. Or,' Claire said, 'when we break up.'

In the two weeks before the wedding show Claire was crazily busy and had almost no free time for dates. Sean took over and brought in takeaways to make sure she ate in the evenings; he also made her take breaks before her eyes started hurting, and gave her massages when her shoulders ached.

Even though part of Claire thought he was being just a little bit overprotective, she was grateful for the TLC. 'I really appreciate this, Sean.'

'I know, and you'd do the same for me if I had an exhibition,' he pointed out. 'By the way, I'm in talks with a couple of manufacturers about joint projects and licensing. Talking to you and brainstorming stuff like that,' he said, 'really helped me see the way I want the company to go in the future.'

'Following your dreams?'

'Maybe,' he said with a smile, and kissed her.

The week before the wedding show, Claire took Sean to meet her family—her father, her grandmother, Aunt Lou and her cousins. Clearly she'd talked to them about him, Sean thought, because they already seemed to know who he was and lots about him. Then he realised that they knew Ashleigh and his background was the same as hers.

Even though they were warm and welcoming and

treated him as if he were one of them, chatting and laughing and teasing him, he still felt strange. His grandparents would've been older than Claire's and had died when he was in his teens. This was the first time for years that Sean had been in a family situation where he wasn't being the protective big brother and the head of the family, and it made him feel lost, not knowing quite where he was supposed to fit in.

It didn't help that Claire's father grilled him mercilessly about his intentions towards Claire. Sean could understand it—he shared Jacob's opinion of Claire's previous boyfriends, at least the ones that he'd met— but it still grated that he'd be judged alongside them.

And he could also see what Claire meant about her dad not believing in her. Jacob didn't see the point of spending time and money making six sets of wedding clothes that hadn't actually been ordered by clients, and he'd said a couple of times during the evening that he couldn't see how Claire would possibly get a return on her investment. Claire had smiled sweetly and glossed over it, but Sean had seen that little pleat between her brows that only appeared when she was really unhappy about something. Clearly she was hurt by the way her father still didn't believe in her.

Well, maybe he could give Jacob Stewart something to think about. 'I always do trade shows,' he said. 'They're really good for awareness—and it makes new customers consider stocking you when they see the quality of your product.'

'Maybe,' Jacob said.

'I don't know if you saw the dress Claire made for my sister, but it was absolutely amazing. She's really good at what she does. And what gives her the extra edge is that she loves what she does, too. That gives her clients confidence. And it's why they tell all their friends about her. Her referral rate is stunning.'

Jacob said nothing, but raised an eyebrow.

Sean decided not to push it any further—the last thing he wanted was for Jacob to upset Claire any further on the subject and knock her confidence at this late stage—but he had to hide a smile when he saw the fervent thumbs-up that Claire's grandmother and aunt did out of Jacob's viewpoint.

Though he was quiet when he drove Claire home.

'I'm sorry, Sean. I shouldn't have asked you to meet them—it's too early,' she said, guessing why he was quiet and getting it totally wrong. 'It's just, well, they'll all be coming to the wedding show and I thought it'd be better if you met them before rather than spring it on you then.'

'No, it was nice to meet them,' he said. 'I liked them.' He wanted to shake her father, but judged it not the most tactful thing to say.

'They liked you—and Dad approved of you, which has to be a first.'

He couldn't hide his surprise. 'Even though I argued with him?'

'You batted my corner,' she said. 'And I appreciate that. I think he did, too. Dad's just…a bit difficult.'

'He'll come round in the end,' Sean said. 'When he sees your collection on the catwalk, he'll understand.'

'Hardly. He's a guy. So he's not the slightest bit interested in dresses,' Claire said, though to Sean's relief this time she was smiling rather than looking upset. 'I just have to remember not to let it get to me.'

'You're going to be brilliant,' Sean said. 'Come on. Let's go to bed.'

She smiled. 'I thought you'd never ask…'

* * *

Over the next week, Claire worked later and later on last-minute changes to the wedding show outfits, and the only way Sean could get her out of her workroom for dinner was to haul her manually over his shoulder and carry her out of the room.

'You need to eat to keep your strength up, and you can't live off sandwiches for the next week,' he told her, 'or you'll make yourself ill.'

'I guess.' She blinked as she took in the fact that her kitchen was actually being used and something smelled gorgeous. 'Hang on, dinner isn't a takeaway.'

'It's nothing fancy, either,' Sean said dryly, 'but it's home-cooked from scratch and there are proper vegetables.' He gave her a rueful smile. 'And at least you have gadgets that help.'

'My electric steamer. Best gadget ever.' She smiled back and stroked his face. 'Sean, thank you. It's really good of you to do this for me.'

'Any time, and you know you'd do the same if I was the one up to my eyes in preparation for a big event, so it's not a big deal.' He kissed her lightly. 'Sit down, milady, because dinner will be served in about thirty seconds.'

But when he'd dished up and they were eating, he noticed that she was pushing her food around her plate. 'Is my cooking that terrible? You don't have to be polite with me—leave it if you hate it.'

'It's wonderful. I'm just tired.' She made an effort to eat.

He tried to distract her a little. 'So do you have a dream of a dress?'

'Not really,' she said.

'So all these years when you've sketched wedding

dresses, you never once drew the one you wanted for yourself?'

'I guess it would depend when and where I got married—if it was on a beach in the Seychelles I wouldn't pick the same dress, veil or shoes as I'd pick for a tiny country church in the middle of winter in, say, the far north of Scotland.'

'I guess,' he said. 'So which kind of wedding would you prefer?'

'It's all academic,' she said.

He could guess why she wasn't answering him—she was obviously worried he'd think she was hinting and had expectations where he was concerned.

'Is that why the outfits in your wedding collection are so diverse?'

'Yes—four seasonal weddings, one vintage-inspired outfit, and one that's more tailored towards a civil wedding,' she explained.

'That's a good range,' he said. 'It will show people what you can do.'

'I hope so.' For a second she looked really worried and vulnerable.

'Claire, you know your stuff, you're good at what you do and your work is really going to shine at the show.' He reached over to squeeze her hand. 'I believe in you.'

'Thank you, though I wasn't fishing for compliments.'

'I know you weren't, and I was being sincere.'

'Sorry.' She wrinkled her nose. 'Ignore me. It's just a bit of stage fright, or whatever the catwalk equivalent is.'

'Which is totally understandable, given that it's your first show.' He cleared their plates away. 'Let me get you some coffee.'

She gave him a tired smile. 'Sorry, I'm really not pulling my weight in this relationship right now.'

'Claire, you're so busy you barely have time to breathe. I'm not going to give you a hard time about that; I just want to take some of the weight off your shoulders,' he said.

'Then thank you. Coffee would be lovely.'

He made two mugs of coffee and set them on the table. 'This is decaf,' he said, 'because I think you're already going to have enough trouble getting to sleep and the last thing you need is caffeine.'

'I guess.'

And he hoped that what he was about to do would distract her enough to let her fall asleep in his arms tonight and stop worrying quite so much about the wedding show.

He rescued the box he'd stowed in her fridge earlier—a box containing a very important message. He checked behind the door that he hadn't accidentally disturbed the contents of the box and mixed up the order of the lettered chocolates, then brought them out and placed the box on the table in front of her.

She gave him a tired smile. 'Would these be some of your awesome salted caramels? Or are you trying out new stuff on me as your personal focus group?'

'Open the box and see,' he invited.

She did so, and her eyes widened as she read the message. When she looked back at him, he could see the sheen of tears in her eyes. *'Sean.'*

'Hey. They say you should say it with flowers, but I know you like to be different, so I thought I'd say it in chocolate.' He'd iced the letters himself. *I love you Claire.* He paused. 'Or maybe I just need to say it.' He swallowed hard. Funny how his throat felt as if it were filled with sand. 'I've never said this to anyone before. I love you, Claire. I think I probably have for years, but the idea of letting anyone close scared me spitless. You know you asked me what scared me? *That.* Deep down guess I was worried that I'd end up losing my partner like I lost my parents, so it was easier to keep you at a distance.'

'So what changed?' she asked.

'Capri,' he said. 'Seeing the way you just got on with things and sorted out the problems when Ashleigh's dress went missing. And then dancing with you. I really couldn't take my eyes off you—it wasn't just the song. I tried to tell myself that it was just physical attraction, but it's more than that. So very much more.'

'Oh, Sean.' She blinked back the tears.

And now he just couldn't shut up. 'And in these last few weeks, getting to know you, I've seen you for who you really are. You're funny and you're brave and you're bossy, and you think outside the box, and—you know your speed dating question thing, about what you're looking for in a partner? I can answer that, now. I'm looking for *you*, Claire. You're everything I want.' He gave her a wry smile. 'Though my timing's a bit rubbish, given that you're up to your eyes right now.'

'Your timing's perfect,' she said softly. 'You know, I had a huge crush on you when I was fourteen, but you were my best friend's older brother, which made you off limits. And you always made me feel as if I was a nuisance.'

'You probably were, when you were a teenager.'

She laughed. 'Tell it to me straight, why don't you?'

He laughed back. 'You wouldn't have it any other way, and you know it—I love you, Claire.'

'I love you, too, Sean.' She pushed her chair back, came round to his side of the table, wrapped her arms round him and kissed him. 'Over the last few weeks

I've got to know you and you're not quite who I thought you were, either. You're this human dynamo but you also think on your feet. You're not regimented and rule-bound.'

'No?'

'Well, maybe just a little bit—and you do look good in a suit.' She smiled at him. 'Though how I really like you dressed is in faded jeans, and a white shirt with the sleeves rolled up. It makes you much more touchable.'

'Noted,' he said.

He could see that she was so tired, she didn't even have the energy to drink her coffee. So he carried her to bed, cherished her, and let her fall asleep in his arms. He wasn't ready to sleep yet; it was good just to lie in the dark with her in his arms, thinking. How amazing it was that she felt the same way about him. So maybe, just maybe, this was going to work out.

CHAPTER TWELVE

ON THE MORNING of the wedding show, Claire was up before six, bustling around and double-checking things on her list.

Then her mobile phone rang. Sean couldn't tell much from Claire's end of the conversation, but her face had turned white and there was a tiny pleat above her nose that told him something was definitely wrong.

When she ended the call, she blew out a breath. 'Sorry, I'm going to have to neglect you and make a ton of phone calls now.'

'What's happened?'

'That was the modelling agency.' She closed her eyes for a moment. 'It seems that the six male models that I booked through the agency are all really good friends. They went out together for a meal last night, and they've all gone down with food poisoning so they can't do the show.'

'So the agency's going to send you someone else?'

She shook her head. 'All their models are either already booked out or away. So they're very sorry to let me down, but it's due to circumstances beyond their control and they're sure I'll understand, and of course they'll return my fee.'

The sing-song, patronising tone in which she replayed the conversation told Sean just how angry Claire was—and he wasn't surprised. She'd been very badly let down.

'I'll just have to go through my diary and beg a few favours, and hope that I can find six men willing to stand in for the models.' She raked a hand through her hair. 'And I need to look at my list and see where I can cut a few corners, because I'll have to alter their clothes to fit the stand-ins, and...' She shook her head, looking utterly miserable.

He put his arms round her and hugged her. 'You need five. I'll do it.'

She stared at him as if the words hadn't quite sunk in. '*You'll* do it?'

'Well, obviously I don't know the first thing about a catwalk,' he said, 'so someone's going to have to teach me how to do the model walk thing. But everyone's going to be looking at the clothes and not the model in any case, so I guess that probably doesn't matter too much.'

'You'll do it,' she repeated, sounding disbelieving.

'Is it that much of a stretch to see me as a model?' he asked wryly.

'No, it's not that at all. You'd be *fabulous*. It's just that—it's a pretty public thing, standing on a catwalk at a wedding show with everyone staring at you, and it's so far from what you normally do that I thought you'd find it too embarrassing or awkward or...' She tailed off. 'Oh, my God, Sean. You'd really do that for me?'

'Yes,' he said firmly.

'Thank you.' She hugged him fiercely. 'That means I only have to find five.'

'You've already got enough to do. I'll find them for you,' he said. 'I reckon we can count on Luke and Tom, and I have a few others in mind. Just tell me the rough heights and sizes you need, and I'll ring round and sort it out.'

'Your height and build would be perfect, but I can adjust things if I need to—the men's outfits are easier to adjust than the women's, so I guess I'm lucky that it was the male models and not the female ones or the children who had to bail out on me. Sean, are you really sure about this?'

'Really,' he confirmed. 'I'm on Team Claire, remember? Now go hit that shower, I'll have coffee ready by the time you're out, and I'll start ringing round.'

She hugged him. 'Have I told you how wonderful you are? Five minutes ago it felt as if the world had ended, and now...'

'Hey—you'd do the same for me,' he pointed out.

Half an hour later, Sean had it all arranged. Luke and Tom agreed immediately to stand in, plus Tom's partner. Sean called in his best friend and his sales manager from the factory, and they all agreed to meet him and Claire at the wedding show two hours before it started, so Claire could do any last-minute necessary alterations to their outfits. Then he made Claire sit down and eat breakfast, before helping her to load everything into the van she'd hired for the day.

'Sure we've got all the wedding dresses?' he asked before he closed the van doors. 'Though I guess we're going to Earl's Court rather than Capri, so we should be OK.'

'Not funny, Sean.' She narrowed her eyes at him.

He kissed her lightly. 'That was misplaced humour and I apologise. It's all going to be fine, Claire. Just breathe and check your list.'

'Sorry, I'm being unfair and overly grouchy. Ignore

me.' She looked over her list. 'Everything's ticked off and loaded, so we're ready to roll.'

'At least we've got the bumps out of the way this side of the catwalk. It's all going to be fine now.' He kissed her again. 'By the way, I meant to tell you, I've got some extra giveaways for you. Will from the office is bringing them to the show.'

'Giveaways?' Her eyes went wide. 'Oh, no. I completely forgot about giveaways. I meant to order some pens. I've been so focused on the outfits that it totally slipped my mind.'

'You have business cards?'

'Yes.'

'Grab them,' he said, 'and we'll get a production line stuffing them at the show.'

'Stuffing what?' She looked at him blankly.

'My genius girlfriend talked about wedding favours. I had some samples run up, with white organza bags and gold foil on the caramel hearts. The bag is just the right size to put your business card in as well—and don't worry about the pens. Everyone will remember the chocolate.'

'Sean, that's above and beyond.'

'No, it's supporting you,' he corrected, 'and it also works as a test run for me, so we both win. Let's get this show on the road.'

At the wedding show, people were busy setting up exhibition stands and the place was bustling. Claire was busy measuring her new male models and doing alterations; then, when the female models arrived, she filled them in on the situation and got them to teach the men how to walk. Her stand was set up with showbooks of her designs, and her part-time shop assistant Iona was there to field enquiries and take contact details of people who were interested in having a consultation about a wedding dress. Will had brought the organza bags and chocolates with him, so Sean had a production line of people stuffing bags with the chocolates and Claire's business card. He knew how much was riding on this.

And it also worried him. Claire had already had to deal with extra problems that weren't of her making today. If this didn't go to plan, all her hard work would have been for nothing.

What he wanted to do was to make sure that the people she wanted to see her collection actually saw it. She'd already mentioned the names of some of the fashion houses who were going to be there. A little networking might just give them the push they needed to make sure they saw Claire's work.

While Claire was making last-minute fixes to the dresses, Sean slipped away quietly to find the movers and shakers of her world. Claire had just about finished by the time he returned.

'Everything OK?' he asked.

'Yes.' She smiled at him. 'You're amazing and I love you. Now go strut your stuff.'

The dresses all looked breathtaking. He knew how much work had gone into them, along with Claire's heart and soul. Please let the reviewers be kind rather than snarky, he begged silently. Please let her get the kudos she deserved. Please let the fashion houses keep their word and come to see her. Please let them give her a chance.

Claire's hands were shaking visibly. Ashleigh was sitting next to her; she took Claire's hands and held them tightly. 'Breathe. It's going to be just fine.'

'They all look amazing,' Claire's grandmother added.

'You're going to wow the lot of them,' Aunt Lou said, reaching over to pat her shoulder.

Only Jacob was silent, but Claire hadn't really expected anything from her dad; she knew that fashion shows weren't his thing. The fact that he'd actually turned up meant that he was on her side for once—didn't it?

But finally the catwalk segment of the show began. Her collection was on first. The models came down the catwalk, one group at a time: the bride, groom and bridesmaids. Autumn. Winter. Spring. Summer. Sean, looking incredibly gorgeous in morning dress and a top hat with his vintage-inspired bride beside him; her heart skipped a beat when he caught her eye and smiled at her. The contemporary civil wedding.

And then finally, the whole collection of six stood on the stage in a tableau. Claire became aware of music, lights—and was that applause?

'You did it, love,' her grandmother said and hugged her. 'Listen to everyone clapping. They think you're as fantastic as we do.'

'We did it.' Claire was shaking with a mixture of relief and adrenaline. She swallowed hard. 'I need to get back to my stand.'

'Iona can cope for another five minutes,' Aunt Lou said with a smile. 'Just enjoy this bit.'

A woman came over to join them. 'Claire Stewart?' she asked.

Claire looked up. 'Yes.'

'Pia Verdi,' the woman introduced herself, and handed over her business card.

Claire's eyes widened as she took in the name of one of the biggest wedding dress manufacturers in the country.

'I like what I've just seen up there, and I'd like to

talk to you about designing a collection for us,' Pia said. 'Obviously you won't have your diary on you now, but call my PA on Monday morning and we'll set up a meeting.'

'Thank you—I'd really like that,' Claire said.

The one thing she'd been secretly hoping for—her chance in the big league. To design a collection that would be sold internationally and would have her name on it.

She just about managed to keep it together until Sean—who'd clearly changed out of his wedding outfit at top speed—came out. He picked her up and spun her round, and she laughed.

'We did it, Sean.'

'Not me. You're the one who designed those amazing outfits.'

'But you supported me when I needed it. Thank you so, so much.' She handed him the business card and grinned her head off. 'Look who wants to talk to me next week!'

'They're offering you a job?' he asked.

'Better than that—they're asking me to talk to them about designing a collection. So I'll get my name out there, but I still get to do my brides and design one-offs as well. It's the icing on the cake. Everything I wanted. I'm so happy.'

'That's brilliant news.' He hugged her. 'I'm so proud of you, Claire. You deserve this.'

'Thanks.' She beamed at him. 'Though I'd better come down off cloud nine and get back to the stand. It's not fair to leave Iona on her own.'

'I'm so glad Pia Verdi came to see you,' he said.

She frowned as his words sank in. 'Hang on. Are you telling me you know her?'

'Um, not exactly.'

Her eyes narrowed as she looked at him. 'Sean?'

He blew out a breath. 'I just networked a bit while you were sorting stuff out, that's all.'

Claire went cold. 'You *networked*?'

'I just told her that your collection was brilliant and she needed to see it.'

Bile rose in Claire's throat as she realised what had actually happened. So much for thinking that she'd got this on her own merit. That her designs had been good enough to attract the attention of one of the biggest fashion houses.

Because Sean had intervened.

Without him talking to her, Pia Verdi probably wouldn't even have bothered coming to see Claire's collection.

And, although part of Claire knew that he'd done something really nice for her, part of her was horrified. Because what this really meant was that Sean was as overprotective as her father. Whatever Sean had said, he didn't really believe in her: he didn't think that she could make it on her own, and he thought she'd always need a bit of a helping hand. To be looked after.

Stifled.

So what she'd thought was her triumph had turned out to be nothing of the kind.

'You spoke to Pia Verdi,' she repeated. 'You told her to come and see my collection.'

He waved a dismissive hand. 'Claire, it was just a little bit of networking, that's all. You would've done the same for me.'

'No.' She shook her head. 'No, I wouldn't have thought that I needed to interfere. Because I *know* you can do things on your own. I *know* that you'll succeed without having someone to push you and support you. And you...' She blew out a breath. 'You just have to be in control. All the time. That's not what I want.'

'Claire, I—'

'No,' she cut in. 'No. I think you've just clarified something for me. Something important. I can't do this, Sean. I can't be with someone who doesn't consult me and who always plays things by the book—*his* book.' She shook her head. 'I'm sorry. I know you meant well, but...this isn't what I want.' She took a deep breath. There was no going back now. 'It's over.'

'Claire—'

She took a backward step, avoiding his outstretched hand. 'No. Goodbye, Sean.'

She walked away with her head held high. And all the time she was thinking, just how could today have turned from so spectacularly wonderful to so spectacularly terrible? How could it all have gone so wrong?

Even though her heart was breaking, she smiled and smiled at everyone who came to her exhibition stand. She talked about dresses and took notes. She refused help from everyone to pack things away at the end of the show and did it all herself; by then, her anger had burned out to leave nothing but sadness. Sean had taken her at her word and left, which was probably for the best; but her stupid heart still wished that he were there with her.

Well, too late. It was over—and they were too different for it to have worked out long term. So this summer had just been a fling. One day she'd be able to look back on it and remember the good times, but all she could think of now was the bitterness of her disappointment and how she wished he'd been the man she thought he was.

* * *

Stupid, stupid, *stupid*.

Sean hated himself for the way the light had gone from Claire's eyes. Because he'd been the one to cause it. He'd burst her bubble big-time—ruined the exuberance she'd felt at her well-deserved success. He'd meant well—he'd talked to Pia Verdi and the others with the best possible intentions—but now he could see that he'd done completely the wrong thing. He'd taken it all away from Claire, and he'd made her feel as if the bottom had dropped out of her world.

It felt as if the bottom had fallen out of his world, too. He'd lost something so precious. He knew it was all his own fault; and he really wasn't sure he was ever going to be able to fix this.

He definitely couldn't fix it today; he knew he needed to give her time to cool down. But tomorrow he'd call her. Apologise. Really lay his heart on the line—and hope that she'd forgive him and give him a second chance.

CHAPTER THIRTEEN

IT SHOULD HAVE been a night of celebration.

Not wanting to jinx things before the wedding show, Claire hadn't booked a table at a restaurant in advance; though she'd planned to take her family, Sean, Ashleigh and Luke out to dinner that evening, to thank them for all the support they'd given her in the run-up to the show.

But now the food would just taste like ashes; and she didn't want her misery to infect anyone else. So she smiled and smiled and lied her face off to her family and her best friend, pretending that her heart wasn't breaking at all. 'I'm fine. Anyway, I need to get the van back to the hire company, and start sorting out all these enquiries…'

Finally she persuaded them all to stop worrying about her, and left in the van on her own. But, by the time she'd dropped all the outfits back at her shop, delivered the van back to the hirer and caught the tube back to her flat, she felt drained and empty. Dinner was a glass of milk—which was just about all she could face—and she lay alone in her bed, dry-eyed and too miserable to sleep and wishing that things were different.

Had she been unfair to Sean?

Or were her fears—that he'd be overprotective and stifling in the future, and they'd be utterly miserable together—justified?

Claire still hadn't worked it out by the time she got up at six, the next morning. It was ridiculously early for a Sunday, but there was no point in just lying there and brooding. Though she felt like death warmed up after yet another night of not sleeping properly, and it took three cups of coffee with extra sugar before she could function enough to take a shower and wash her hair.

Work seemed to be about the best answer. If she concentrated on sketching a new design, she wouldn't have room in the front of her head to think about what had happened with Sean. And maybe the back of her head would come up with some answers.

She hoped.

She was sketching in her living room when her doorbell rang.

Odd. She wasn't expecting anyone to call. And she hadn't replied to any of the messages on her phone yet, so as far as everyone else was concerned she was probably still asleep, exhausted after the wedding show.

And who would ring her doorbell before half past eight on a Sunday morning, anyway?

She walked downstairs and blinked in surprise when she opened the door.

Sean was standing there—dressed in jeans and a white shirt rather than his normal formal attire—and he was carrying literally an armful of flowers. She could barely see him behind all the blooms and the foliage of delphiniums, stocks, gerberas and roses.

She blinked at him. 'Sean?'

'Can I come in?' he asked.

'I...' Help. What did she say now?

'I'll say what I've got to say on your doorstep, if I have to,' he said. 'But I'd rather talk to you in private.'

She wasn't too sure that she wanted an audience, either. 'Come up,' she said, and stood aside so he could go past and she could close the door behind them.

'Firstly,' he said, 'I wanted to say sorry. And these are just...' He stopped, glanced down at the flowers and then at her. 'I've gone over the top, haven't I?'

'They're gorgeous—though I'm not sure if I have enough vases, glasses and mugs to fit them all in,' she said.

'I just wanted to say sorry. And I kind of thought I needed to make a big gesture, because the words aren't quite enough. And I know you love flowers. And...' His voice trailed off.

'You're carrying an entire English cottage garden there.' She was still hurt that he didn't truly believe in her, but she could see how hard he was trying to start making things right. And as he stood there in the middle of all the flowers, looking completely like a fish out of water...how could she stay angry with him?

'Let's get these gorgeous flowers in water before they start wilting.' She went into the kitchen and found every receptacle she had, and started filling them with water. 'They're lovely. Thank you. Where did you get them?' she asked. 'Covent Garden flower market isn't open on Sundays.'

'Columbia Road market,' he said. 'I looked up where I could get really good fresh flowers first thing on a Sunday morning.'

She thought about it. 'So you carried all these on the tube?'

'Uh-huh.' He gave her a rueful smile. 'I had to get someone to help me at the ticket barrier.'

He'd gone to a real effort for her. And he'd done something that would've made people stare at him—something she knew would've made him feel uncomfortable.

So this apology was sincerely meant. But she still needed to hear the words.

When they'd finished putting the flowers in water—including using the bowl of her kitchen sink—she said, 'Do you want a coffee?'

'No, thanks. I just need to talk to you,' he said. He took a deep breath. 'Claire, I honestly didn't mean to hurt you. I just wanted to help. But I realise now that I handled it totally the wrong way. I interfered instead of supporting you properly and asking you what you needed me to do. I made you feel as if you were hopeless and couldn't do anything on your own—but, Claire, I *do* believe in you. I knew your designs would make any of the fashion houses sit up and take notice. But the wedding show was so busy, I didn't want to take the risk that they wouldn't get time to see your collection and you wouldn't get your chance. That's the only reason I went to talk to Pia Verdi.'

His expression was serious and completely sincere. She knew he meant what he said.

And she also knew that she owed him an apology, too. They were *both* in the wrong.

'I overreacted a bit as well,' she said. 'I'd been working flat out for weeks and, after the way everything had gone wrong from the first…well, I think it just caught me at the wrong time. Now I've had time to think about it, I know your heart was in the right place. You meant well. But yesterday I felt that you were being overprotective and stifling, the way Dad is, because you don't think I can do it on my own. You think that I need looking after all the time.'

'Claire, I'm not your father. I know you can do it on your own,' he said softly. 'And, for the record, I don't think you need looking after. Actually, I think it would drive you bananas.'

'It would.' She took a deep breath. 'I want an equal partnership with someone who'll back me and who'll let me back them.'

'That's what I want, too,' Sean said.

Hope bloomed in her heart. 'Before yesterday—before things went wrong—that's what I thought we had,' she said.

'We did,' he said. 'We *do*.'

She bit her lip. 'I've hurt you as much as you hurt me. I was angry and unfair and ungrateful, I pushed you away, and I'm sorry. And, if I try to think first instead of reacting first in future, do you think we could start again?'

'So Ms Follow-Your-Heart turns into a rulebook devotee?' Sean said. 'No deal. Because I want a partner who thinks outside the box and stops me being regimented.'

'You're not regimented—well, not *all* the time,' she amended.

'Thank you. I think.' He looked at her. 'I can't promise perfection and I can't promise we won't ever fight again, Claire.'

'It wouldn't be normal if we didn't ever fight again,' she pointed out.

'True. I guess we just need to learn to compromise. Do things the middle way instead of both thinking that our way's the only way.' He opened his arms. 'So. You and me. How about it?'

She stepped into his arms. 'Yes.'

'Good.' He kissed her lingeringly. 'And we'll talk more in future. I promise I won't think I know best.'

'And I promise I won't go super-stubborn.'

He laughed. 'Maybe we ought to qualify that and say we'll *try*.'

'Good plan.'

He arched an eyebrow. 'Are you going to admit that planning's good, outside business?'

She laughed. 'That would be a no. Most of the time. Are you going to admit that being spontaneous means you have more fun?'

He grinned. 'Not if I'm hungry and I've just been drenched in a downpour.'

'Compromise,' she said. 'That works for me.'

'Me, too.' He kissed her again. 'And we'll make this work. Together.'

EPILOGUE

Two months later

CLAIRE WAS WORKING on the preliminary sketches for her first collection for Pia Verdi when her phone beeped.

She glanced at the screen. Sean. Probably telling her that he was going to be late home tonight, she thought with a smile. Although they hadn't officially moved in with each other, they'd fallen into a routine of spending weeknights at her place and weekends at his.

V and A. Thirty minutes. Be there.

Was he kidding?

Three tube changes! Takes thirty minutes PLUS walk to station, she typed back.

And of course he'd know she knew this. The Victoria and Albert Museum was her favourite place in London. She'd taken him there several times and always lingered in front of her favourite dress, a red grosgrain and chiffon dress by Chanel. She never, ever tired of seeing that dress.

Forty minutes, then.

Half a minute later, there was another text.

Make it fifty and change into your blue dress. The one with the daisies.

Why?

Tell you when you get here.

She grinned. Sean was clearly in playful mode, so this could be fun. But why did he want to meet her at the museum? And why that dress in particular?

She still didn't have a clue when she actually got to Kensington. She texted him from the museum entrance: Where are you?

Right next to your favourite exhibit.

Easy enough, she thought, and went to find him.

He was standing next to the display case, dressed up to the nines: a beautifully cut dark suit and a white shirt, but for once he wasn't wearing a tie. That little detail was enough to soften the whole package. Just how she liked it.

'OK. I'm here.' She gestured to her outfit. 'Blue dress. Daisies. As requested, Mr Farrell.'

'You look beautiful,' he said.

'Thank you. But I'm still trying to work out why you wanted to meet me here.'

'Because I'm just about to add to your workload.'

She frowned. 'I don't understand.'

He dropped to one knee. 'Claire Stewart, I love you with all my heart. Will you marry me?'

'I…' She stared at him. 'Sean. I can't quite take this in. You're really asking me to marry you?'

'I'm down on one knee and I used the proper form,' he pointed out.

This was the last thing she'd expected on a Thursday afternoon in her favourite museum. 'Sean.'

'I've been thinking about it for the last month. Where else could you ask a wedding dress designer to marry you, except in her favourite place in London? And next to her favourite exhibit, too?'

Now she knew why he'd asked her to wear his favourite dress: to make this just as special for him. And why he'd said he was adding to her workload—because now she'd have a very special wedding dress to design. Her own.

She smiled. 'Sean Farrell, I love you with all my heart, too. And I'd be thrilled to marry you.'

He stood up, swung her round, and kissed her thoroughly. Then he took something from his pocket. 'We need to formalise this.'

She blinked. 'You bought me a ring?'

'Without consulting you? No chance. This is temporary. Go with the flow. *Carpe diem*,' he said, and slid something onto the ring finger of her left hand.

When she looked at it, she burst out laughing. He'd made her a ring out of unused toffee wrappers.

'We'll choose the proper one together,' he said. 'Just as we'll make all our important decisions together.'

'An equal partnership,' she said, and kissed him. 'Perfect.'

* * * * *

VALTIERI'S BRIDE

CAROLINE ANDERSON

CHAPTER ONE

WHAT *on earth* was she doing?

As the taxi pulled up in front of the Jet Centre at London City Airport, he paused, wallet in hand, and stared spellbound across the drop-off point.

Wow. She was *gorgeous*.

Even in the crazy fancy-dress outfit, her beauty shone out like a beacon. Her curves—soft, feminine curves—were in all the right places, and her face was alight with laughter, the skin pale and clear, her cheeks tinged pink by the long blonde curls whipping round her face in the cutting wind. She looked bright and alive and impossibly lovely, and he felt something squeeze in his chest.

Something that had been dormant for a very long time.

As he watched she anchored the curls absently with one hand, the other gesturing expressively as she smiled and talked to the man she'd stopped at the entrance. She was obviously selling something. Goodness knows what, he couldn't read the piece of card she was brandishing from this distance, but the man laughed and raised a hand in refusal and backed away, entering the building with a chuckle.

Her smile fading, she turned to her companion, more sensibly dressed in jeans and a little jacket. Massimo flicked his eyes over her, but she didn't hold his attention. Not like the blonde, and he found his eyes drawn back to her against his will.

Dio, she was exquisite. By rights she should have looked an utter tramp but somehow, even in the tacky low-cut dress and a gaudy plastic tiara, she was, quite simply, riveting. There was something about her that transcended all of that, and he felt himself inexplicably drawn to her.

He paid the taxi driver, hoisted his flight bag over his shoulder and headed for the entrance. She was busy again, talking to another man, and as the doors opened he caught her eye and she flashed a hopeful smile at him.

He didn't have time to pause, whatever she was selling, he thought regretfully, but the smile hit him in the solar plexus, and he set his bag down on the floor by the desk once he was inside, momentarily winded.

'Morning, Mr Valtieri. Welcome back to the Jet Centre. The rest of your party have arrived.'

'Thank you.' He cleared his throat and glanced over his shoulder at the woman. 'Is that some kind of publicity stunt?'

The official gave a quiet, mildly exasperated sigh and smiled wryly.

'No, sir. I understand she's trying to get a flight to Italy.'

Massimo felt his right eyebrow hike. 'In a *wedding dress*?'

He gave a slight chuckle. 'Apparently so. Some competition to win a wedding.'

He felt a curious sense of disappointment. Not that it made the slightest bit of difference that she was getting married; she was nothing to him and never would be, but nevertheless...

'We asked her to leave the building, but short of escorting her right back to the main road, there's little more we can do to get rid of her and she seems harmless enough. Our clients seem to be finding her quite entertaining, anyway.'

He could understand that. He was entertained himself—mesmerised, if he was honest. And intrigued—

'Whereabouts in Italy?' he asked casually, although the tightness in his gut was far from casual.

'I think I heard her mention Siena—but, Mr Valtieri, you really don't want to get involved,' he warned, looking troubled. 'I think she's a little…'

'Crazy?' he said drily, and the man's mouth twitched.

'Your word, sir, not mine.'

As they watched, the other man walked away and she gave her companion a wry little smile. She said something, shrugged her slender shoulders in that ridiculous meringue of a dress, then rubbed her arms briskly. She must be freezing! September was a strange month, and today there wasn't a trace of sunshine and a biting wind was whipping up the Thames estuary.

No! It was none of his business if she hadn't had the sense to dress for the weather, he told himself firmly, but then he saw another man approach the doors, saw the woman straighten her spine and go up to him, her face wreathed in smiles as she launched into a fresh charm offensive, and he felt his gut clench.

He knew the man slightly, more by reputation than anything else, and he was absolutely the last person this enchanting and slightly eccentric young woman needed to get involved with. And he would be flying to his private airfield, about an hour's drive from Siena. Close enough, if you were desperate…

He couldn't let it happen. He had more than enough on his conscience.

The doors parted with a hiss as he strode up to them, and he gave the other man a look he had no trouble reading. He told him—in Italian, and succinctly—to back off, and Nico shrugged and took his advice, smiling regretfully at the woman before moving away from her, and Massimo gave him a curt nod and turned to the woman, meeting her eyes again—vivid, startling blue eyes that didn't look at all happy with what he'd just done. There was no smile this time, just those eyes like blue ice-chips skewering him as he stood there.

Stunning eyes, framed by long, dark lashes. Her mouth, even without the smile, was soft and full and kissable— No! He sucked in a breath, and found himself drawing a delicate and haunting fragrance into his lungs.

It rocked him for a second, took away his senses, and when they came back they *all* came back, slamming into him with the force of an express train and leaving him wanting in a way he hadn't wanted for years. Maybe ever—

'What did you *say* to him?' Lydia asked furiously, hardly able to believe the way he'd dismissed that man with a few choice words—not that she'd understood one of them, of course, but there was more to language than vocabulary and he'd been pretty explicit, she was sure. But she'd been so close to success and she was really, really cross and frustrated now. 'He'd just offered me a seat in his plane!'

'Believe me, you don't want to go on his plane.'

'Believe me, I do!' she retorted, but he shook his head.

'No. I'm sorry, I can't let you do it, it just isn't safe,' he said, a little crisply, and she dropped her head back and gave a sharp sigh.

Damn. He must be airport security, and a higher authority than the nice young man who'd shifted them outside. She sensed there'd be no arguing with him. There was a quiet implacability about him that reminded her of her father, and she knew when she was beaten. She met his eyes again, and tried not to notice that they were the colour of dark, bitter chocolate, warm and rich and really rather gorgeous.

And unyielding.

She gave up.

'I would have been perfectly safe, I've got a minder and I'm no threat to anyone and nobody's complained, as far as I know, but you can call the dogs off, I'm going.'

To her surprise he smiled, those amazing eyes softening and turning her bones to mush.

'Relax, I'm nothing to do with Security, I just have a social conscience. I believe you need to go to Siena?'

Siena? Nobody, she'd discovered, was flying to Siena but it seemed, incredibly, that he might be, or else why would he be asking? She stifled the little flicker of hope. 'I thought you said it wasn't safe?'

'It wasn't safe with *Nico*.'

'And it's safe with you?'

'Safer. My pilot won't have been drinking, and I—' He broke off, and watched her eyes widen as her mind filled in the blanks.

'And you?' she prompted a little warily, when he left it hanging there.

He sighed sharply and raked a hand through his hair, rumpling the dark strands threaded with silver at the temples. He seemed impatient, as if he was helping her against his better judgement.

'He has a—reputation,' he said finally.

She dragged her eyes off his hair. It had flopped forwards, and her fingers itched to smooth it back, to feel the texture…

'And you don't?'

'Let's just say that I respect women.' His mouth flickered in a wry smile. 'If you want a reference, my lawyer and doctor brothers would probably vouch for me, as would my three sisters—failing that, you could phone Carlotta. She's worked for the family for hundreds of years, and she delivered me and looks after my children.'

He had children? She glanced down and clocked the wedding ring on his finger, and with a sigh of relief, she thrust a laminated sheet at him and dug out her smile again. This time, it was far easier, and she felt a flicker of excitement burst into life.

'It's a competition to win a wedding at a hotel near Siena. There are two of us in the final leg, and I have to get to the hotel first to win the prize. This is Claire, she's from the radio station doing the publicity.'

Massimo gave Claire a cursory smile. He wasn't in the least interested in Claire. She was obviously the minder, and pretty enough, but this woman with the crazy outfit and sassy mouth…

He scanned the sheet, scanned it again, shook his head in disbelief and handed it back, frankly appalled. 'You must be mad. You have only a hundred pounds, a wedding dress and a passport, and you have to race to Siena to win this wedding? What on *earth* is your fiancé thinking of to let you do it?'

'Not my fiancé. I don't have a fiancé, and if I did, I wouldn't need his permission,' she said crisply, those eyes turning to ice again. 'It's for my sister. She had an accident, and they'd planned—oh, it doesn't matter. Either you can help me or you can't, and if you can't, the clock's ticking and I really have to get on.'

She didn't have a fiancé? 'I can help you,' he said before he could let himself think about it, and he thrust out his hand. 'Massimo Valtieri. If you're ready to go, I can give you a lift to Siena now.'

He pronounced it Mah-*see*-mo, long and slow and drawn out, his Italian accent coming over loud and clear as he said his name, and she felt a shiver of something primeval down her spine. Or maybe it was just the cold. She smiled at her self-appointed knight in shining armour and held out her hand.

'I'm Lydia Fletcher—and if you can get us there before the others, I'll love you forever.'

His warm, strong and surprisingly slightly calloused fingers closed firmly round hers, and she felt the world shift a little under her feet. And not just hers, apparently. She saw the shockwave hit his eyes, felt the recognition of something momentous passing between them, and in that crazy and insane instant she wondered if anything would ever be the same again.

The plane was small but, as the saying goes, perfectly formed.

Very perfectly, as far as she was concerned. It had comfortable seats, lots of legroom, a sober pilot and a flight plan that without doubt would win her sister the wedding of her dreams.

Lydia could hardly believe her luck.

She buckled herself in, grabbed Claire's hand and hung on tight as the plane taxied to the end of the runway. 'We did it. We got a flight straight there!' she whispered, and Claire's face lit up with her smile, her eyes sparkling.

'I know. Amazing! We're going to do it. We can't fail. I just know you're going to win!'

The engines roared, the small plane shuddering, and then it was off like a slingshot, the force of their acceleration pushing her back hard into the leather seat as the jet tipped and climbed. The Thames was flying past, dropping rapidly below them as they rose into the air over London, and then they were heading out over the Thames estuary towards France, levelling off, and the seat belt light went out.

'Oh, this is so exciting! I'm going to update the diary,' Claire said, pulling out her little notebook computer, and Lydia turned her head and met Massimo's eyes across the narrow aisle.

He unclipped his seat belt and shifted his body so he was

facing her, his eyes scanning her face. His mouth tipped into a smile, and her stomach turned over—from the steep ascent, or from the warmth of that liquid-chocolate gaze?

'All right?'

'Amazing.' She smiled back, her mouth curving involuntarily in response to his, then turning down as she pulled a face. 'I don't know how to thank you. I'm so sorry I was rude.'

His mouth twitched. 'Don't worry. You weren't nearly as rude to me as I was to Nico.'

'What *did* you say to him?' she asked curiously, and he gave a soft laugh.

'I'm not sure it would translate. Certainly not in mixed company.'

'I think I got the gist—'

'I hope not!'

She gave a little laugh. 'Probably not. I don't know any street Italian—well, no Italian at all, really. And I feel awful now for biting your head off, but…well, it means a lot to me, to win this wedding.'

'Yes, I gather. You were telling me about your sister?' he said.

'Jennifer. She had an accident a few months ago and she was in a wheelchair, but she's getting better, she's on crutches now, but her fiancé had to give up his job to help look after her. They're living with my parents and Andy's working with Dad at the moment for their keep. My parents have got a farm—well, not really a farm, more of a smallholding, really, but they get by, and they could always have the wedding there. There's a vegetable packing barn they could dress up for the wedding reception, but—well, my grandmother lived in Italy for a while and Jen's always dreamed of getting married there, and now they haven't got enough money even for a glass of cheap bubbly and a few sandwiches. So when I heard about this competition I just jumped at it, but I never in my wildest dreams imagined we'd get this far, never mind get a flight to exactly the right place. I'm just so grateful I don't know where to start.'

She was gabbling. She stopped, snapped her mouth shut and gave him a rueful grin. 'Sorry. I always talk a lot when the adrenaline's running.'

He smiled and leant back, utterly charmed by her. More than charmed...

'Relax. I have three sisters and two daughters, so I'm quite used to it, I've had a lot of practice.'

'Gosh, it sounds like it. And you've got two brothers as well?'

'*Si*. Luca's the doctor and he's married to an English girl called Isabelle, and Gio's the lawyer. I also have a son, and two parents, and a million aunts and uncles and cousins.'

'So what do you do?' she asked, irresistibly curious, and he gave her a slightly lopsided grin.

'You could say I'm a farmer, too. We grow grapes and olives and we make cheese.'

She glanced around at the plane. 'You must make a heck of a lot of cheese,' she said drily, and he chuckled, soft and low under his breath, just loud enough for her to hear.

The slight huff of his breath made an errant curl drift against her cheek, and it was almost as if his fingertips had brushed lightly against her skin.

'Not that much,' he said, his eyes still smiling. 'Mostly we concentrate on our wine and olive oil—Tuscan olive oil is sharper, tangier than the oil from southern Italy because we harvest the olives younger to avoid the frosts, and it gives it a distinctive and rich peppery flavour. But again, we don't make a huge amount, we concentrate on quality and aim for the boutique market with limited editions of certified, artisan products. That's what I was doing in England—I've been at a trade fair pushing our oil and wine to restaurateurs and gourmet delicatessens.'

She sat up straighter. 'Really? Did you take samples with you?'

He laughed. 'Of course. How else can I convince people that our products are the best? But the timing was bad, because we're about to harvest the grapes and I'm needed at home. That's why we chartered the plane, to save time.'

Chartered. So it wasn't his. That made him more approachable, somehow and, if it was possible, even more attractive. As did the fact that he was a farmer. She knew about farming, about aiming for a niche market and going for quality rather than quantity. It was how she'd been brought up. She relaxed, hitched one foot up under her and hugged her knee under the voluminous skirt.

'So, these samples—do you have any on the plane that I could try?'

'Sorry, we're out of wine,' he said, but then she laughed and shook her head.

'That's not what I meant, although I'm sure it's very good. I was talking about the olive oil. Professional interest.'

'You grow olives on your farm in England?' he asked incredulously, and she laughed again, tightening his gut and sending need arrowing south. It shocked him slightly, and he forced himself to concentrate.

'No. Of course not. I've been living in a flat with a pot of basil on the window sill until recently! But I love food.'

'You mentioned a professional interest.'

She nodded. 'I'm a—' She was going to say chef, but could you be a chef if you didn't have a restaurant? If your kitchen had been taken away from you and you had nothing left of your promising career? 'I cook,' she said, and he got up and went to the rear of the plane and returned with a bottle of oil.

'Here.'

He opened it and held it out to her, and she sniffed it slowly, drawing the sharp, fruity scent down into her lungs. 'Oh, that's gorgeous. May I?'

And taking it from him, she tipped a tiny pool into her hand and dipped her finger into it, sucking the tip and making an appreciative noise. Heat slammed through him, and he recorked the bottle and put it away to give him something to do while he reassembled his brain.

He never, *never* reacted to a woman like this! What on earth was he thinking of? Apart from the obvious, but he didn't want to think about that. He hadn't looked at a woman in that way for years, hadn't thought about sex in he didn't know how long. So why now, why this woman?

She wiped up the last drop, sucking her finger again and then licking her palm, leaving a fine sheen of oil on her lips that he really, really badly want to kiss away.

'Oh, that is so good,' she said, rubbing her hands together to remove the last trace. 'It's a shame we don't have any bread or balsamic vinegar for dunking.'

He pulled a business card out of his top pocket and handed it to her, pulling his mind back into order and his eyes out of her cleavage. 'Email me your address when you get home, I'll send you some of our wine and oil, and also a traditional *aceto balsamico* made by my cousin in Modena. They only make a little, but it's the best I've ever tasted. We took some with us, but I haven't got any of that left, either.'

'Wow. Well, if it's as good as the olive oil, it must be fabulous!'

'It is. We're really proud of it in the family. It's nearly as good as our olive oil and wine.'

She laughed, as she was meant to, tucking the card into her bag, then she tipped her head on one side. 'Is it a family business?'

He nodded. 'Yes, most definitely. We've been there for

more than three hundred years. We're very lucky. The soil is perfect, the slopes are all in the right direction, and if we can't grow one thing on any particular slope, we grow another, or use it for pasture. And then there are the chestnut woods. We export a lot of canned chestnuts, both whole and puréed.'

'And your wife?' she asked, her curiosity getting the better of her. 'Does she help with the business, or do you keep her too busy producing children for you?'

There was a heartbeat of silence before his eyes clouded, and his smile twisted a little as he looked away. 'Angelina died five years ago,' he said softly, and she felt a wave of regret that she'd blundered in and brought his grief to life when they'd been having a sensible and intelligent conversation about something she was genuinely interested in.

She reached across the aisle and touched his arm gently. 'I'm so sorry. I wouldn't have brought it up if...'

'Don't apologise. It's not your fault. Anyway, five years is a long time.'

Long enough that, when confronted by a vivacious, dynamic and delightful woman with beautiful, generous curves and a low-cut dress that gave him a more than adequate view of those curves, he'd almost forgotten his wife...

Guilt lanced through him, and he pulled out his wallet and showed her the photos—him and Angelina on their wedding day, and one with the girls clustered around her and the baby in her arms, all of them laughing. He loved that one. It was the last photograph he had of her, and one of the best. He carried it everywhere.

She looked at them, her lips slightly parted, and he could see the sheen of tears in her eyes.

'You must miss her so much. Your poor children.'

'It's not so bad now, but they missed her at first,' he said gruffly. And he'd missed her. He'd missed her every single day, but missing her didn't bring her back, and he'd buried himself in work.

He was still burying himself in work.

Wasn't he?

Not effectively. Not any more, apparently, because suddenly he was beginning to think about things he hadn't thought about for years, and he wasn't ready for that. He couldn't deal with it, couldn't think about it. Not now. He had work to do, work that couldn't wait. Work he should be doing now.

He put the wallet away and excused himself, moving to sit with the others and discuss how to follow up the contacts they'd made and where they went from here with their marketing strategy, with his back firmly to Lydia and that ridiculous wedding dress that was threatening to tip him over the brink.

Lydia stared at his back, regret forming a lump in her throat.

She'd done it again. Opened her mouth and jumped in with both feet. She was good at that, gifted almost. And now he'd pulled away from her, and must be regretting the impulse that had made him offer her and Claire a lift to Italy.

She wanted to apologise, to take back her stupid and trite and intrusive question about his wife—Angelina, she thought, remembering the way he'd said her name, the way he'd almost tasted it as he said it, no doubt savouring the precious memories. But life didn't work like that.

Like feathers from a burst cushion, it simply wasn't possible to gather the words up and stuff them back in without trace. She just needed to move on from the embarrassing lapse, to keep out of his personal life and take his offer of a lift at face value.

And stop thinking about those incredible, warm chocolate eyes…

'I can't believe he's taking us right to Siena!' Claire said quietly, her eyes sparkling with delight. 'Jo will be so miffed when we get there first, she was so confident!'

Lydia dredged up her smile again, not hard when she thought about Jen and how deliriously happy she'd be to have her Tuscan wedding. 'I can't believe it, either. Amazing.'

Claire tilted her head on one side. 'What was he showing you? He looked sort of sad.'

She felt her smile slip. 'Photos of his wife. She died five years ago. They've got three little children—ten, seven and five, I think he said. Something like that.'

'Gosh. So the little one must have been tiny—did she die giving birth?'

'No. No, she can't have done. There was a photo of her with two little girls and a baby in her arms, so no. But it must have been soon after.'

'How awful. Fancy never knowing your mother. I'd die if I didn't have my mum to ring up and tell about stuff.'

Lydia nodded. She adored her mother, phoned her all the time, shared everything with her and Jen. What would it have been like never to have known her?

Tears welled in her eyes again, and she brushed them away crossly, but then she felt a light touch on her arm and looked up, and he was staring down at her, his face concerned.

He frowned and reached out a hand, touching the moisture on her cheek with a gentle fingertip.

'Lydia?'

She shook her head. 'I'm fine. Ignore me, I'm a sentimental idiot.'

He dropped to his haunches and took her hand, and she had a sudden and overwhelming urge to cry in earnest. 'I'm sorry. I didn't mean to distress you. You don't need to cry for us.'

She shook her head and sniffed again. 'I'm not. Not really.

I was thinking about my mother—about how I'd miss her—and I'm twenty-eight, not five.'

He nodded. 'Yes. It's very hard.' His mouth quirked in a fleeting smile. 'I'm sorry, I've neglected you. Can I get you a drink? Tea? Coffee? Water? Something stronger?'

'It's a bit early for stronger,' she said, trying for a light note, and he smiled again, more warmly this time, and straightened up.

'Nico would have been on the second bottle of champagne by now,' he said, and she felt a wave of relief that he'd saved her from what sounded more and more like a dangerous mistake.

'Fizzy water would be nice, if you have any?' she said, and he nodded.

'Claire?'

'That would be lovely. Thank you.'

He moved away, and she let her breath out slowly. She hadn't really registered, until he'd crouched beside her, just how big he was. Not bulky, not in any way, but he'd shed his jacket and rolled up his shirtsleeves, and she'd been treated to the broad shoulders and solid chest at close range, and then his narrow hips and lean waist and those long, strong legs as he'd straightened up.

His hands, appearing in her line of sight again, were clamped round two tall glasses beaded with moisture and fizzing gently. Large hands, strong and capable, no-nonsense.

Safe, sure hands that had held hers and warmed her to the core.

Her breasts tingled unexpectedly, and she took the glass from him and tried not to drop it. 'Thank you.'

'*Prego*, you're welcome. Are you hungry? We have fruit and pastries, too.'

'No. No, I'm much too excited to eat now,' she confessed,

sipping the water and hoping the cool liquid would slake the heat rising up inside her.

Crazy! He was totally uninterested in her, and even if he wasn't, she wasn't in the market for any more complications in her life. Her relationship with Russell had been fraught with complications, and the end of it had been a revelation. There was no way she was jumping back into that pond any time soon. The last frog she'd kissed had turned into a king-sized toad.

'How long before we land?' she asked, and he checked his watch, treating her to a bronzed, muscular forearm and strong-boned wrist lightly scattered with dark hair. She stared at it and swallowed. How ridiculous that an arm could be so sexy.

'Just over an hour. Excuse me, we have work to do, but please, if you need anything, just ask.'

He turned back to his colleagues, sitting down and flexing his broad shoulders, and Lydia felt her gut clench. She'd never, *never* felt like that about anyone before, and she couldn't believe she was reacting to him that way. It must just be the adrenaline.

One more hour to get through before they were there and they could thank him and get away—hopefully before she disgraced herself. The poor man was still grieving for his wife. What was she thinking about?

Ridiculous! She'd known him, what, less than two hours altogether? Scarcely more than one. And she'd already put her foot firmly in it.

Vowing not to say another thing, she settled back in her seat and looked out of the window at the mountains.

They must be the Alps, she realised, fascinated by the jagged peaks and plunging valleys, and then the mountains fell away behind them and they were moving over a chequered landscape of forests and small, neat fields. They were curiously ordered and disciplined, serried ranks of what must be olive trees and grape vines, she guessed, planted with geometric precision, the pattern of the fields interlaced with narrow winding roads lined with avenues of tall, slender cypress trees.

Tuscany, she thought with a shiver of excitement.

The seat belt light came on, and Massimo returned to his seat across the aisle from her as the plane started its descent.

'Not long now,' he said, flashing her a smile. And then they were there, a perfect touchdown on Tuscan soil with the prize almost in reach.

Jen was going to get her wedding. Just a few more minutes…

They taxied to a stop outside the airport building, and after a moment the steps were wheeled out to them and the door was opened.

'We're really here!' she said to Claire, and Claire's eyes were sparkling as she got to her feet.

'I know. I can't believe it!'

They were standing at the top of the steps now, and Massimo smiled and gestured to them. 'After you. Do you have the address of the hotel? I'll drive you there.'

'Are you sure?'

'I'd hate you not to win after all this,' he said with a grin.

'Wow, thank you, that's really kind of you!' Lydia said, reaching for her skirts as she took another step.

It happened in slow motion.

One moment she was there beside him, the next the steps had disappeared from under her feet and she was falling, tumbling end over end, hitting what seemed like every step until finally her head reached the tarmac and she crumpled on the ground in a heap.

Her scream was cut off abruptly, and Massimo hurled himself down the steps to her side, his heart racing. No! Please, she couldn't be dead...

She wasn't. He could feel a pulse in her neck, and he let his breath out on a long, ragged sigh and sat back on his heels to assess her.

Stay calm, he told himself. She's alive. She'll be all right.

But he wouldn't really believe it until she stirred, and even then...

'Is she all right?'

He glanced up at Claire, kneeling on the other side of her, her face chalk white with fear.

'I think so,' he said, but he didn't think any such thing. Fear was coursing through him, bringing bile rising to his throat. Why wasn't she moving? This couldn't be happening again.

Lydia moaned. Warm, hard fingers had searched for a pulse in her neck, and as she slowly came to, she heard him snap out something in Italian while she lay there, shocked and a little stunned, wondering if it was a good idea to open her eyes. Maybe not yet.

'Lydia? Lydia, talk to me! Open your eyes.'

Her eyes opened slowly and she tried to sit up, but he pressed a hand to her shoulder.

'Stay still. You might have a neck injury. Where do you hurt?'

Where didn't she? She turned her head and winced. 'Ow... my head, for a start. What happened? Did I trip? Oh, I can't believe I was so stupid!'

'You fell down the steps.'

'I know that—ouch.' She felt her head, and her hand came away bloodied and sticky. She stared at it. 'I've cut myself,' she said, and everything began to swim.

'It's OK, Lydia. You'll be OK,' Claire said, but her face

was worried and suddenly everything began to hurt a whole lot more.

Massimo tucked his jacket gently beside her head to support it, just in case she had a neck injury. He wasn't taking any chances on that, but it was the head injury that was worrying him the most, the graze on her forehead, just under her hair. How hard had she hit it? Hard enough to...

It was bleeding faster now, he realised with a wave of dread, a red streak appearing as she shifted slightly, and he stayed beside her on his knees, holding her hand and talking to her comfortingly in between snapping out instructions.

She heard the words '*ambulanza*' and '*ospedale*', and tried to move, wincing and whimpering with pain, but he held her still.

'Don't move. The ambulance is coming to take you to hospital.'

'I don't need to go to hospital, I'm fine, we need to get to the hotel!'

'No,' Massimo and Claire said in unison.

'But the competition.'

'It doesn't matter,' he said flatly. 'You're hurt. You have to be checked out.'

'I'll go later.'

'No.' His voice was implacable, hard and cold and somehow strange, and Lydia looked at him and saw his skin was colourless and grey, his mouth pinched, his eyes veiled.

He obviously couldn't stand the sight of blood, Lydia realised, and reached out her other hand to Claire.

She took it, then looked at Massimo. 'I'll look after her,' she said. 'You go, you've got lots to do. We'll be all right.'

His eyes never left Lydia's.

'No. I'll stay with you,' he insisted, but he moved out of the way to give her space.

She looked so frail suddenly, lying there streaked with

blood, the puffy layers of the dress rising up around her legs and making her look like a broken china doll.

Dio, he felt sick just looking at her, and her face swam, another face drifting over it. He shut his eyes tight, squeezing out the images of his wife, but they refused to fade.

Lydia tried to struggle up again. 'I want to go to the hotel,' she said to Claire, and his eyes snapped open again.

'No way.'

'He's right. Don't be silly. You just lie there and we'll get you checked out, then we'll go. There's still plenty of time.'

But there might not be, she realised, as she lay there on the tarmac in her ridiculous charity shop wedding dress with blood seeping from her head wound, and as the minutes ticked by her joy slid slowly away…

CHAPTER TWO

THE ambulance came, and Claire went with Lydia.

He wanted to go with her himself, he felt he ought to, felt the weight of guilt and worry like an elephant on his chest, but it wasn't his place to accompany her, so Claire went, and he followed in his car, having sent the rest of the team on with a message to his family that he'd been held up but would be with them as soon as he could.

He rang Luca on the way, in case he was there at the hospital in Siena that day as he sometimes was, and his phone was answered instantly.

'Massimo, welcome home. Good flight?'

He nearly laughed. 'No. Where are you? Which hospital?'

'Siena. Why?'

He did laugh then. Or was it a sob of relief? 'I'm on my way there. I gave two girls a lift in the plane, and one of them fell down the steps as we were disembarking. I'm following the ambulance. Luca, she's got a head injury,' he added, his heart pounding with dread, and he heard his brother suck in his breath.

'I'll meet you in the emergency department. She'll be all right, Massimo. We'll take care of her.'

He grunted agreement, switched off the phone and followed the ambulance, focusing on facts and crushing his fear and guilt down. It couldn't happen again. Lightning didn't

strike twice, he told himself, and forced himself to follow the
ambulance at a sensible distance while trying desperately to
put Angelina firmly out of his mind...

Luca was waiting for him at the entrance.

He took the car away to park it and Massimo hovered by
the ambulance as they unloaded Lydia and whisked her inside, Claire holding her hand and reassuring her. It didn't
sound as if it was working, because she kept fretting about
the competition and insisting she was all right when anyone
could see she was far from all right.

She was taken away, Claire with her, and he stayed in the
waiting area, pacing restlessly and driving himself mad with
his imagination of what was happening beyond the doors. His
brother reappeared moments later and handed him the keys,
giving him a keen look.

'You all right?'

Hardly. 'I'm fine,' he said, his voice tight.

'So how do you know this woman?' Luca asked, and he
filled him in quickly with the bare bones of the accident.

'Oh—she's wearing a wedding dress,' he warned. 'It's a
competition, a race to win a wedding.'

A race she'd lost. If only he'd taken her arm, or gone in
front, she would have fallen against him, he could have saved
her...

'Luca, don't let her die,' he said urgently, fear clawing at
him.

'She won't die,' Luca promised, although how he could
say that without knowing—well, he couldn't. It was just a
platitude, Massimo knew that.

'Let me know how she is.'

Luca nodded and went off to investigate, leaving him there
to wait, but he felt bile rise in his throat and got abruptly to
his feet, pacing restlessly again. How long could it take?

Hours, apparently, or at least it felt like it.

Luca reappeared with Claire.

'They're taking X-rays of her leg now but it looks like a sprained ankle. She's just a little concussed and bruised from her fall, but the head injury doesn't look serious,' he said.

'Nor did Angelina's,' he said, switching to Italian.

'She's not Angelina, Massimo. She's not going to die of this.'

'Are you sure?'

'Yes. Yes, I'm sure. She's had a scan. She's fine.'

It should have reassured him, but Massimo felt his heart still slamming against his ribs, the memories crowding him again.

'She's all right,' Luca said quietly. 'This isn't the same.'

He nodded, but he just wanted to get out, to be away from the hospital in the fresh air. Not going to happen. He couldn't leave Lydia, no matter how much he wanted to get away. And he could never get away from Angelina...

Luca took him to her.

She was lying on a trolley, and there was blood streaked all over the front of the hideous dress, but at least they'd taken her off the spinal board. 'How are you?' he asked, knowing the answer but having to ask anyway, and she turned her head and met his eyes, her own clouded with worry and pain.

'I'm fine, they just want to watch me for a while. I've got some bumps and bruises, but nothing's broken, I'm just sore and cross with myself and I want to go to the hotel and they won't let me leave yet. I'm so sorry, Massimo, I've got Claire, you don't need to wait here with me. It could be ages.'

'I do.' He didn't explain, didn't tell her what she didn't need to know, what could only worry her. But he hadn't taken Angelina's head injury seriously. He'd assumed it was nothing. He hadn't watched her, sat with her, checked her every few minutes. If he had—well, he hadn't, but he was damned if he was leaving Lydia alone for a moment until he was sure she was all right.

Luca went back to work, and while the doctors checked her over again and strapped her ankle, Massimo found some coffee for him and Claire and they sat and drank it. Not a good idea. The caffeine shot was the last thing his racing pulse needed.

'I need to make a call,' Claire told him. 'If I go just outside, can you come and get me if there's any news?'

He nodded, watching her leave. She was probably phoning the radio station to tell them about Lydia's accident. And she'd been so close to winning...

She came back, a wan smile on her face. 'Jo's there.'

'Jo?'

'The other contestant. Lydia's lost the race. She's going to be so upset. I can't tell her yet.'

'I think you should. She might stop fretting if it's too late, let herself relax and get better.'

Claire gave a tiny, slightly hysterical laugh. 'You don't know her very well, do you?'

He smiled ruefully. 'No. No, I don't.' And it was ridiculous that he minded the fact.

Lydia looked up as they went back in, and she scanned Claire's face.

'Did you ring the radio station?'

'Yes.'

'Has...' She could hardly bring herself to ask the question, but she took another breath and tried again. 'Has Jo got there yet?' she asked, and then held her breath. It was possible she'd been unlucky, that she hadn't managed to get a flight, that any one of a hundred things could have happened.

They hadn't. She could see it in Claire's eyes, she didn't

need to be told that Jo and Kate, her minder, were already there, and she felt the bitter sting of tears scald her eyes.

'She's there, isn't she?' she asked, just because she needed confirmation.

Claire nodded, and Lydia turned her head away, shutting her eyes against the tears. She was so, *so* cross with herself. They'd been so close to winning, and if she'd only been more careful, gathered up the stupid dress so she could see the steps.

She swallowed hard and looked back up at Claire's worried face. 'Tell her well done for me when you see her.'

'I will, but you'll see her, too. We've got rooms in the hotel for the night. I'll ring them now, let them know what's happening. We can go there when they discharge you.'

'No, I could be ages. Why don't you go, have a shower and something to eat, see the others and I'll get them to ring you if there's any change. Or better still, if you give me back my phone and my purse, I can call you and let you know when I'm leaving, and I'll just get a taxi.'

'I can't leave you alone!'

'She won't be alone, I'll stay with her. I'm staying anyway, whether you're here or not,' Massimo said firmly, and Lydia felt a curious sense of relief. Relief, and guilt.

And she could see the same emotions in Claire's face. She was dithering, chewing her lip in hesitation, and Lydia took her hand and squeezed it.

'There, you see? And his brother works here, so he'll be able to pull strings. It's fine, Claire. Just go. I'll see you later.' And she could get rid of Massimo once Claire had gone…

Claire gave in, reluctantly. 'OK, if you insist. Here, your things. I'll put them in your bag. Where is it?'

'I have no idea. Is it under the bed?'

'No. I haven't seen it.'

'It must have been left on the ground at the airport,' Massimo said. 'My men will have picked it up.'

'Can you check? My passport's in it.'

'*Si.*' He left them briefly, and when he came back he confirmed it had been taken by the others. 'I'll make sure you get it tonight,' he promised.

'Thanks. Right, Claire, you go. I'm fine.'

'You will call me and let me know what's going on as soon as you have any news?'

'Yes, I promise.'

Claire gave in, hugging Lydia a little tearfully before she left them.

Lydia swallowed. Damn. She was going to join in.

'Hey, it's all right. You'll be OK.'

His voice was gentle, reassuring, and his touch on her cheek was oddly comforting. Her eyes filled again.

'I'm causing everyone so much trouble.'

'That's life. Don't worry about it. Are you going to tell your family?'

Oh, cripes. She ought to phone Jen, but she couldn't. Not now. She didn't think she could talk to her just yet.

'Maybe later. I just feel so sleepy.'

'So rest. I'll sit with you.'

Sit with her and watch her. Do what he should have done years ago.

She shut her eyes, just for a moment, but when she opened them again he'd moved from her side. She felt a moment of panic, but then she saw him. He was standing a few feet away reading a poster about head injuries, his hands rammed in his pockets, tension radiating off him.

Funny, she'd thought it was because of the blood, but there was no sign of blood now apart from a dried streak on her dress. Maybe it was hospitals generally. Had Angelina been ill for a long time?

Or maybe hospitals just brought him out in hives. She could understand that. After Jen's accident, she felt the same herself, and yet he was still here, still apparently labouring under some misguided sense of obligation.

He turned his head, saw she was awake and came back to her side, his dark eyes searching hers.

'Are you all right?'

She nodded. 'My head's feeling clearer now. I need to ring Jen,' she said quietly, and he sighed and cupped her cheek, his thumb smoothing away a tear she hadn't realised she'd shed.

'I'm sorry, *cara*. I know how much it meant to you to win this for your sister.'

'It doesn't matter,' she said dismissively, although of course it would to Jen. 'It was just a crazy idea. They can get married at home, it's really not an issue. I really didn't think I'd win anyway, so we haven't lost anything.'

'Claire said Jo's been there for ages. She would probably have beaten you to it anyway,' he said. 'She must have got away very fast.'

She didn't believe it. He was only trying to make it better, to take the sting out of it, but before she had time to argue the doctor came back in, checked her over and delivered her verdict.

Massimo translated.

'You're fine, you need to rest for a few days before you fly home, and you need watching overnight, but you're free to go.'

She thanked the doctor, struggled up and swung her legs over the edge of the trolley, and paused for a moment, her head swimming.

'All right?'

'I'm fine. I need to call a taxi to take me to the hotel.'

'I'll give you a lift.'

'I can't take you out of your way! I've put you to enough trouble as it is. I can get a taxi. I'll be fine.'

But as she slid off the edge of the trolley and straightened up, Massimo caught the sheen of tears in her eyes.

Whatever she'd said, the loss of this prize was tearing her apart for her sister, and he felt guilt wash over him yet again. Logically, he knew he had no obligation to her, no duty that extended any further than simply flying her to Siena as he'd promised. But somehow, somewhere along the way, things had changed and he could no more have left her there at the door of the hospital than he could have left one of his children. And they were waiting for him, had been waiting for him far too long, and guilt tugged at him again.

'Ouch!'

'You can't walk on that ankle. Stay here.'

She stayed, wishing her flight bag was still with her instead of having been whisked away by his team. She could have done with changing out of the dress, but her comfy jeans and soft cotton top were in her bag, and she wanted to cry with frustration and disappointment and pain.

'Here.'

He'd brought a wheelchair, and she eyed it doubtfully.

'I don't know if the dress will fit in it. Horrible thing! I'm going to burn it just as soon as I get it off.'

'Good idea,' he said drily, and they exchanged a smile.

He squashed it in around her, and wheeled her towards the exit. Then he stopped the chair by the door and looked down at her.

'Do you really want to go to the hotel?' he asked.

She tipped her head back to look at him, but it hurt, and she let her breath out in a gusty sigh. 'I don't have a choice. I need a bed for the night, and I can't afford anywhere else.'

He moved so she could see him, crouching down beside her. 'You do have a choice. You can't fly for a few days, and you don't want to stay in a strange hotel on your own for all that time. And anyway, you don't have your bag, so why don't you come back with me?' he said, the guilt about his children growing now and the solution to both problems suddenly blindingly obvious.

'I need to get home to see my children, they've been patient long enough, and you can clean up there and change into your own comfortable clothes and have something to eat and a good night's sleep. Carlotta will look after you.'

Carlotta? Lydia scanned their earlier conversations and came up with the name. She was the woman who looked after his children, who'd worked for them for a hundred years, as he'd put it, and had delivered him.

Carlotta sounded good.

'That's such an imposition. Are you sure you don't mind?'

'I'm sure. It's by far the easiest thing for me. The hotel's the other way, and it would save me a lot of time I don't really have, especially by the time I've dropped your bag over there. And you don't honestly want to be there on your own for days, do you?'

Guilt swamped her, heaped on the disappointment and the worry about Jen, and she felt crushed under the weight of it all. She felt her spine sag, and shook her head. 'I'm so sorry. I've wasted your entire day. If you hadn't given me a lift…'

'Don't go there. What ifs are a waste of time. Yes or no?'

'Yes, please,' she said fervently. 'That would be really kind.'

'Don't mention it. I feel it's all my fault anyway.'

'Rubbish. Of course it's not your fault. You've done so much already, and I don't think I've even thanked you.'

'You have. You were doing that when you fell down the steps.'

'Was I?' She gave him a wry grin, and turned to look up

at him as they arrived at the car, resting her hand on his arm lightly to reassure him. 'It's really not your fault, you know.'

'I know. You missed your step. I know this. I still...'

He was still haunted, because of the head injury, images of Angelina crowding in on him. Angelina falling, Angelina with a headache, Angelina slumped over the kitchen table with one side of her face collapsed. Angelina linked up to a life support machine...

'Massimo?'

'I'm all right,' he said gruffly, and pressing the remote, he opened the door for her and settled her in, then returned the wheelchair and slid into the driver's seat beside her. 'Are you OK?'

'I'm fine.'

'Good. Let's go.'

She phoned Claire and told her what was happening, assured her she would be all right and promised to phone her the next day, then put the phone down in her lap and rested her head back.

Under normal circumstances, she thought numbly, she'd be wallowing in the luxury of his butter-soft leather, beautifully supportive car seats, or taking in the picture-postcard countryside of Tuscany as the car wove and swooped along the narrow winding roads.

As it was she gazed blankly at it all, knowing that she'd have to phone Jen, knowing she should have done it sooner, that her sister would be on tenterhooks, but she didn't have the strength to crush her hopes and dreams.

'Have you told your sister yet?' he asked, as if he'd read her mind.

She shook her head. 'No. I don't know what to say. If I hadn't fallen, we would have won. Easily. It was just so stupid, so clumsy.'

He sighed, his hand reaching out and closing over hers briefly, the warmth of it oddly comforting in a disturbing way. 'I'm sorry. Not because I feel it was my fault, because I know it wasn't, really, but because I know how it feels to let someone down, to have everyone's hopes and dreams resting on your shoulders, to have to carry the responsibility for someone else's happiness.'

She turned towards him, inhibited by the awful, scratchy dress that she couldn't wait to get out of, and studied his profile.

Strong. Clean cut, although no longer clean-shaven, the dark stubble that shadowed his jaw making her hand itch to feel the texture of it against her palm. In the dusk of early evening his olive skin was darker, somehow exotic, and with a little shiver she realised she didn't know him at all. He could be taking her anywhere.

She closed her eyes and told herself not to be ridiculous. He'd followed them to the hospital, got his brother in on the act, a brother she'd heard referred to as *il professore*, and now he was taking her to his family home, to his children, his parents, the woman who'd delivered him all those years ago. Forty years? Maybe. Maybe more, maybe less, but give or take.

Someone who'd stayed with the family for all that time, who surely wouldn't still be there if they were nasty people?

'What's wrong?'

She shrugged, too honest to lie. 'I was just thinking, I don't know you. You could be anyone. After all, I was going in the plane with Nico, and you've pointed out in no uncertain terms that that wouldn't have been a good idea, and I just don't think I'm a very good judge of character.'

'Are you saying you don't trust me?'

She found herself smiling. 'Curiously, I do, or I wouldn't be here with you.'

He flashed her a look, and his mouth tipped into a wry grin. 'Well, thanks.'

'Sorry. It wasn't meant to sound patronising. It's just been a bit of a whirlwind today, and I'm not really firing on all cylinders.'

'I'm sure you're not. Don't worry, you're safe with me, I promise, and we're nearly there. You can have a long lazy shower, or lie in the bath, or have a swim. Whatever you choose.'

'So long as I can get out of this horrible dress, I'll be happy.'

He laughed, the sound filling the car and making something deep inside her shift.

'Good. Stand by to be happy very soon.'

He turned off the road onto a curving gravelled track lined by cypress trees, winding away towards what looked like a huge stone fortress. She sat up straighter. 'What's that building?'

'The house.'

'House?' She felt her jaw drop, and shut her mouth quickly. That was their *house*?

'So…is this your land?'

'*Si.*'

She stared around her, but the light was fading and it was hard to tell what she was looking at. But the massive edifice ahead of them was outlined against the sunset, and as they drew closer she could see lights twinkling in the windows.

They climbed the hill, driving through a massive archway and pulling up in front of a set of sweeping steps. Security lights came on as they stopped, and she could see the steps were flanked by huge terracotta pots with what looked like olive trees in them. The steps rose majestically up to the biggest set of double doors she'd ever seen in her life. Strong doors, doors that would keep you safe against all invaders.

She had to catch her jaw again, and for once in her life she was lost for words. She'd thought, foolishly, it seemed, that it might shrink as they got closer, but it hadn't. If anything it had grown, and she realised it truly was a fortress.

An ancient, impressive and no doubt historically significant fortress. And it was his family home?

She thought of their modest farmhouse, the place she called home, and felt the sudden almost overwhelming urge to laugh. What on earth did he think of her, all tarted up in her ludicrous charity shop wedding dress and capering about outside the airport begging a lift from any old stranger?

'Lydia?'

He was standing by her, the door open, and she gathered up the dress and her purse and phone and squirmed off the seat and out of the car, balancing on her good leg and eyeing the steps dubiously.

How on earth—?

No problem, apparently. He shut the car door, and then to her surprise he scooped her up into his arms.

She gave a little shriek and wrapped her arms around his neck, so that her nose was pressed close to his throat in the open neck of his shirt. Oh, God. He smelt of lemons and musk and warm, virile male, and she could feel the beat of his heart against her side.

Or was it her own? She didn't know. It could have been either.

He glanced down at her, concerned that he might be hurting her. There was a little frown creasing the soft skin between her brows, and he had the crazy urge to kiss it away. He almost did, but stopped himself in time.

She was a stranger, nothing more, and he tried to ignore the feel of her against his chest, the fullness of her breasts pressing into his ribs and making his heart pound like a drum. She had her head tucked close to his shoulder, and he could feel the whisper of her breath against his skin. Under the antiseptic her hair smelled of fresh fruit and summer flowers, and he wanted to bury his face in it and breathe in.

He daren't look down again, though. She'd wrapped her arms around his neck and the front of the dress was gaping slightly, the soft swell of those beautiful breasts tempting him almost beyond endurance.

Crazy. Stupid. Whatever was the matter with him? He gritted his teeth, shifted her a little closer and turned towards the steps.

Lydia felt his body tense, saw his jaw tighten and she wondered why. She didn't have time to work it out, though, even if she could, because as he headed towards the house three children came tumbling down the steps and came to a sliding halt in front of them, their mouths open, their faces shocked.

'Pàpa?'

The eldest, a thin, gangly girl with a riot of dark curls and her father's beautiful eyes, stared from one of them to the other, and the look on her face was pure horror.

'I think you'd better explain to your children that I am *not* your new wife,' she said drily, and the girl glanced back at her and then up at her father again.

'Pàpa?'

He was miles away, caught up in a fairy-tale fantasy of carrying this beautiful woman over the threshold and then peeling away the layers of her bridal gown...

'Massimo? I think you need to explain to the children,' Lydia said softly, watching his face at close range. There was a tic in his jaw, the muscle jumping. Had he carried Angelina up these steps?

'It's all right, Francesca,' he said in English, struggling to find his voice. 'This is Miss Fletcher. I met her today at the airport, and she's had an accident and has to rest for a few days, so I've brought her here. Say hello.'

She frowned and asked something in Italian, and he smiled a little grimly and shook his head. 'No. We are *not* married. Say hello to Miss Fletcher, *cara*.'

'Hello, Miss Fletcher,' Francesca said in careful English, her smile wary but her shoulders relaxing a little, and Lydia smiled back at her. She felt a little awkward, gathered up in his arms against that hard, broad chest with the scent of his body doing extraordinary things to her heart, but there was nothing she could do about it except smile and hope his arms didn't break.

'Hello, Francesca. Thank you for speaking English so I can understand you.'

'That's OK. We have to speak English to Auntie Isabelle. This is Lavinia, and this is Antonino. Say hello,' she prompted.

Lydia looked at the other two, clustered round their sister. Lavinia was the next in line, with the same dark, glorious curls but mischief dancing in her eyes, and Antonino, leaning against Francesca and squiggling the toe of his shoe on the gravel, was the youngest. The baby in the photo, the little one who must have lost his mother before he ever really knew her.

Her heart ached for them all, and she felt a welling in her chest and crushed it as she smiled at them.

'Hello, Lavinia, hello, Antonino. It's nice to meet you,' she said, and they replied politely, Lavinia openly studying her, her eyes brimming over with questions.

'And this is Carlotta,' Massimo said, and she lifted her head and met searching, wise eyes in a wizened face. He spoke rapidly to her in Italian, explaining her ridiculous fancy-dress outfit no doubt, and she saw the moment he told her that they'd lost the competition, because Carlotta's face softened and she looked at Lydia and shook her head.

'Sorry,' she said, lifting her hands. 'So sorry for you. Come, I help you change and you will be happier, *si*?'

'Si,' she said with a wry chuckle, and Massimo shifted her more firmly against his chest and followed Carlotta puffing and wheezing up the steps.

The children were tugging at him and questioning him in Italian, and he was laughing and answering them as fast as he could. Bless their little hearts, she could see they were hanging on his every word.

He was the centre of their world, and they'd missed him, and she'd kept him away from them all these hours when they must have been desperate to have him back. She felt another shaft of guilt, but Carlotta was leading the way through the big double doors, and she looked away from the children and gasped softly.

They were in a cloistered courtyard, with a broad covered walkway surrounding the open central area that must cast a welcome shade in the heat of the day, but now in the evening it was softly lit and she could see more of the huge pots of olive trees set on the old stone paving in the centre, and on the low wall that divided the courtyard from the cloistered walkway geraniums tumbled over the edge, bringing colour and scent to the evening air.

But that wasn't what had caught her attention. It was the frescoed walls, the ancient faded murals under the shelter of the cloisters that took her breath away.

He didn't pause, though, or give her time to take in the beautiful paintings, but carried her through one of the several doors set in the walls, then along a short hallway and into a bedroom.

He set her gently on the bed, and she felt oddly bereft as he straightened up and moved away.

'I'll be in the kitchen with the children. Carlotta will tell me when you're ready and I'll come and get you.'

'Thank you.'

He smiled fleetingly and went out, the children's clamouring voices receding as he walked away, and Carlotta closed the door.

'Your bath,' she said, pushing open another door, and she saw a room lined with pale travertine marble, the white suite simple and yet luxurious. And the bath—she could stick her bandaged leg up on the side and just wallow. Pure luxury.

'Thank you.' She couldn't wait. All she wanted was to get out of the dress and into water. But the zip...

'I help you,' Carlotta said, and as the zip slid down, she was freed from the scratchy fabric at last. A bit too freed. She clutched at the top as it threatened to drift away and smiled at Carlotta.

'I can manage now,' she said, and Carlotta nodded.

'I get your bag.'

She went out, and Lydia closed the bedroom door behind her, leaning back against it and looking around again.

It was much simpler than the imposing and impressive entrance, she saw with relief. Against expectations it wasn't vast, but it was pristine, the bed made up with sparkling white linen, the rug on the floor soft underfoot, and the view from the French window would be amazing in daylight.

She limped gingerly over to the window and stared out, pressing her face against the glass. The doors opened onto what looked like a terrace, and beyond—gosh, the view must be utterly breathtaking, she imagined, because even at dusk it was extraordinary, the twinkling lights of villages and scattered houses sparkling in the twilight.

Moving away from the window, she glanced around her, taking in her surroundings in more detail. The floor was tiled, the ceiling beamed, with chestnut perhaps? Probably, with terracotta tiles between the beams. Sturdy, simple and homely—which was crazy, considering the scale of the place and the grandeur of the entrance! But it seemed more like a farm now, curiously, less of a fortress, and much less threatening.

And that established, she let go of the awful dress, kicked it away from her legs, bundled it up in a ball and hopped into the bathroom.

The water was calling her. Studying the architecture could wait.

CHAPTER THREE

WHAT was that noise?

Lydia lifted her head, water streaming off her hair as she surfaced to investigate.

'Signorina? Signorina!'

Carlotta's voice was desperate as she rattled the handle on the bathroom door, and Lydia felt a stab of alarm.

'What is it?' she asked, sitting up with a splash and sluicing the water from her hair with her hands.

'Oh, *signorina*! You are all right?'

She closed her eyes and twisted her hair into a rope, squeezing out the rest of the water and suppressing a sigh. 'I'm fine. I'm OK, really. I won't be long.'

'I wait, I help you.'

'No, really, there's no need. I'll be all right.'

'But Massimo say I no leave you!' she protested, clearly worried for some reason, but Lydia assured her again that she was fine.

'OK,' she said after a moment, sounding dubious. 'I leave your bag here. You call me for help?'

'I will. Thank you. *Grazie.*'

'*Prego.*'

She heard the bedroom door close, and rested her head back down on the bath with a sigh. The woman was kindness itself, but Lydia just wanted to be left alone. Her head ached, her ankle throbbed, she had a million bruises all over her body and she still had to phone her sister.

The phone rang, almost as if she'd triggered it with her thoughts, and she could tell by the ringtone it was Jen.

Oh, rats. She must have heard the news.

There was no getting round it, so she struggled awkwardly out of the bath and hobbled back to the bed, swathed in the biggest towel she'd ever seen, and dug out her phone and rang Jen back.

'What's going on? They said you'd had an accident! I've been trying to phone you for ages but you haven't been answering! Are you all right? We've been frantic!'

'Sorry, Jen, I was in the bath. I'm fine, really, it was just a little slip on the steps of a plane and I've twisted my ankle. Nothing serious.'

Well, she hoped it wasn't. She crossed her fingers, just to be on the safe side, and filled in a few more details. She didn't tell her the truth, just that Jo had got there first.

'I'm so sorry, we really tried, but we probably wouldn't have made it even without the accident.'

There was a heartbeat of hesitation, then Jen said, 'Don't worry, it really doesn't matter and it's not important. I just need you to be all right. And don't go blaming yourself, it's not your fault.'

Why did *everyone* say that? It *was* her fault. If she'd looked where she was going, taken a bit more care, Jen and Andy would have been having the wedding of their dreams in a few months' time. As it was, well, as it was they wouldn't, but she wasn't going to give Jen anything to beat herself up about, so she told her she was fine, just a little twinge—and nothing at all about the head injury.

'Actually, since I'm over here, I thought I'd stay on for a few days. I've found a farm where I can get bed and breakfast, and I'm going to have a little holiday.'

Well, it wasn't entirely a lie. It *was* a farm, she had a bed, and she was sure they wouldn't make her starve while she recovered.

'You do that. It sounds lovely,' Jen said wistfully, and Lydia screwed her face up and bit her lip.

Damn. She'd been so close, and the disappointment that Jen was trying so hard to disguise was ripping Lydia apart.

Ending the call with a promise to ring when she was coming home, she dug her clean clothes out of the flight bag and pulled her jeans on carefully over her swollen, throbbing ankle. The soft, worn fabric of the jeans and the T-shirt were comforting against her skin, chafed from her fall as well as the boning and beading in the dress, and she looked around for the offending article. It was gone. Taken away by Carlotta? She hoped she hadn't thrown it out. She wanted the pleasure of that for herself.

She put her trainers on, managing to squeeze her bandaged foot in with care, and hobbled out of her room in search of the others, but the corridor outside didn't seem to lead anywhere except her room, a little sitting room and a room that looked like an office, so she went back through the door to the beautiful cloistered courtyard and looked around for any clues.

There were none.

So now what? She couldn't just stand there and yell, nor could she go round the courtyard systematically opening all the doors. Not that there were that many, but even so.

She was sitting there on the low wall around the central courtyard, studying the beautiful frescoes and trying to work out what to do if nobody showed up, when the door nearest to her opened and Massimo appeared. He'd showered and changed out of the suit into jeans and a soft white linen shirt stark against his olive skin, the cuffs rolled back to reveal those tanned forearms which had nearly been her undoing on the plane, and her heart gave a tiny lurch.

Stupid.

He caught sight of her and smiled, and her heart did another little jiggle as he walked towards her.

'Lydia, I was just coming to see if you were all right. I'm sorry, I should have come back quicker. How are you? How's the head?'

'Fine,' she said with a rueful smile. 'I'm just a bit lost. I didn't want to go round opening all the doors, it seemed rude.'

'You should have shouted. I would have heard you.'

'I'm not in the habit of yelling for help,' she said drily, and he chuckled and came over to her side.

'Let me help you now,' he said, and offered her his arm. 'It's not far, hang on and hop, or would you rather I carried you?'

'I'll hop,' she said hastily, not sure she could cope with being snuggled up to that broad, solid chest again, with the feel of his arms strong and safe under her. 'I don't want to break you.'

He laughed at that. 'I don't think you'll break me. Did you find everything you needed? How's your room?'

She slipped her arm through his, conscious of the smell of him again, refreshed now by his shower and overlaid with soap and more of the citrusy cologne that had been haunting her nostrils all day. She wanted to press her nose to his chest, to breathe him in, to absorb the warmth and scent and maleness of him.

Not appropriate. She forced herself to concentrate.

'Lovely. The bath was utter bliss. I can't tell you how wonderful it was to get out of that awful dress. I hope Carlotta hasn't burned it, I want to do it myself.'

He laughed again, a warm, rich sound that echoed round the courtyard, and scanned her body with his eyes. 'It really didn't do you justice,' he said softly, and in the gentle light she thought she caught a glimpse of whatever it was she'd seen in his eyes at the airport.

But then it was gone, and he was opening the door and ushering her through to a big, brightly lit kitchen. Carlotta was busy at the stove, and the children were seated at a large table in the middle of the room, Antonino kneeling up and leaning over to interfere with what Lavinia was doing.

She pushed him aside crossly, and Massimo intervened before a fight could break out, diffusing it swiftly by splitting them up. While he was busy, Carlotta came and helped her to the table. She smiled at her gratefully.

'I'm sorry to put you to so much trouble.'

'Is no trouble,' she said. 'Sit, sit. Is ready.'

She sniffed, and smiled. 'It smells wonderful.'

'*Buono.* You eat, then you feel better. Sit!'

She flapped her apron at Lydia, and she sat obediently at the last place laid at the long table. It was opposite Francesca, and Massimo was at the end of the table on her right, bracketed by the two younger ones who'd been split up to stop them squabbling.

They were fractious—overtired, she thought guiltily, and missing their father. But Francesca was watching her warily. She smiled at the girl apologetically.

'I'm sorry I kept your father away from you for so long. He's been so kind and helpful.'

'He is. He helps everybody. Are you better now?'

'I'm all right. I've just got a bit of a headache but I don't think it's much more than that. I was so stupid. I tripped over the hem of my dress and fell down the steps of the plane and hit my head.'

Behind her, there was a clatter, and Francesca went chalk white, her eyes huge with horror and distress.

'*Scusami,*' she mumbled, and pushing back her chair, she

ran from the room, her father following, his chair crashing over as he leapt to his feet.

'Francesca!' He reached the door before it closed, and she could hear his voice calling as he ran after her. Horrified, uncertain what she'd done, she turned to Carlotta and found her with her apron pressed to her face, her eyes above it creased with distress.

'What did I say?' she whispered, conscious of the little ones, but Carlotta just shook her head and picked up the pan and thrust it in the sink.

'Is nothing. Here, eat. Antonino!'

He sat down, and Lavinia put away the book he'd been trying to tug away from her, and Carlotta picked up Massimo's overturned chair and ladled food out onto all their plates.

There was fresh bread drizzled with olive oil, and a thick, rich stew of beans and sausage and gloriously red tomatoes. It smelt wonderful, tasted amazing, but Lydia could scarcely eat it. The children were eating. Whatever it was she'd said or done had gone right over their heads, but something had driven Francesca from the room, and her father after her.

The same something that had made Massimo go pale at the airport, as he'd knelt on the tarmac at her side? The same something that had made him stand, rigid with tension, staring grimly at a poster when he thought she was asleep in the room at the hospital?

She pushed back her chair and hopped over to the sink, where Carlotta was scrubbing furiously at a pot. 'I'm sorry, I can't eat. Carlotta, what did I say?' she asked under her breath, and those old, wise eyes that had seen so much met hers, and she shook her head, twisting her hands in the dishcloth and biting her lips.

She put the pot on the draining board, and Lydia automatically picked up a tea towel and dried it, her hip propped against the edge of the sink unit as she balanced on her good leg. Another pot followed, and another, and finally Carlotta stopped scouring the pots as if they were lined with demons and her hands came to rest.

She hobbled over to the children, cleared up their plates, gave them pudding and then gathered them up like a mother hen.

'Wait here. Eat. He will come back.'

They left her there in the kitchen, their footsteps echoing along a corridor and up stairs, and Lydia sank down at the table and stared blankly at the far wall, going over and over her words in her head and getting nowhere.

Carlotta appeared again and put Francesca's supper in a microwave.

'Is she coming down again? I want to apologise for upsetting her.'

'No. Is all right, *signorina*. Her *pàpa* look after her.' And lifting the plate out of the microwave, she carried it out of the room on a tray, leaving Lydia alone again.

She poked at her food, but it was cold now, the beans congealing in the sauce, and she ripped up a bit of bread and dabbed it absently in the stew. What had she said, that had caused such distress?

She had no idea, but she couldn't leave the kitchen without finding out, and there was still a pile of washing up to do. She didn't know where anything lived, but the table was big enough to put it all on, and there was a dishwasher sitting there empty.

Well, if she could do nothing else while she waited, she could do that, she told herself, and pushing up her sleeves, she hopped over to the dishwasher and set about clearing up the kitchen.

He had to go down to her—to explain, or apologise properly, at the very least.

His stomach growled, but he ignored it. He couldn't eat,

not while his daughter was just settling into sleep at last, her sobs fading quietly away into the night.

He closed his eyes. Talking to Lydia, dredging it all up again, was the last thing he wanted to do, the very last, but he had no choice. Leaning over Francesca, he pressed a kiss lightly against her cheek, and straightened. She was sleeping peacefully now; he could leave her.

Leave her, and go and find Lydia, if she hadn't had the sense to pack up her things and leave. It seemed unlikely, but he couldn't blame her.

He found her in the kitchen, sitting with Carlotta over a cup of coffee, the kitchen sparkling. He stared at them, then at the kitchen. Carlotta had been upstairs until a short while ago, settling the others, and the kitchen had been in chaos, so how?

'She's OK now,' he said in Italian. 'Why don't you go to bed, Carlotta? You look exhausted and Roberto's worried about you.'

She nodded and got slowly to her feet, then rested her hand on Lydia's shoulder and patted it before leaving her side. 'I *am* tired,' she said to him in Italian, 'but you need to speak to Lydia. I couldn't leave her. She's a good girl, Massimo. Look at my kitchen! A good, kind girl, and she's unhappy. Worried.'

He sighed. 'I know. Did you explain?'

'No. It's not my place, but be gentle with her—and yourself.' And with that pointed remark, she left them alone together.

Lydia looked up at him and searched his eyes. 'What did she say to you?'

He gave her a fleeting smile. 'She told me you were a good, kind girl. And she told me to be gentle with you.'

Her eyes filled, and she looked away. 'I don't know what I said, but I'm so, so sorry.'

His conscience pricked him. He should have warned her. He sighed and scrubbed a hand through his hair.

'No. I should be apologising, not you. Forgive us, we aren't normally this rude to visitors. Francesca was upset.'

'I know that. Obviously I made it happen. What I don't know is why,' she said, looking up at him again with grief-stricken eyes.

He reached for a mug, changed his mind and poured himself a glass of wine. 'Can I tempt you?'

'Is it one of yours?'

'No. It's a neighbour's, but it's good. We could take it outside. I don't know if it's wise, though, with your head injury.'

'I'll take the risk,' she said. 'And then will you tell me what I said?'

'You know what you said. What you don't know is what it meant,' he said enigmatically, and picking up both glasses of wine, he headed for the door, glancing back over his shoulder at her. 'Can you manage, or should I carry you?'

Carry her? With her face pressed up against that taunting aftershave, and the feel of his strong, muscled arms around her legs? 'I can manage,' she said hastily, and pushing back her chair, she got to her feet and limped after him out into the still, quiet night.

She could hear the soft chirr of insects, the sound of a motorbike somewhere in the valley below, and then she saw a single headlight slicing through the night, weaving and turning as it followed the snaking road along the valley bottom and disappeared.

He led her to a bench at the edge of the terrace. The ground fell away below them so it felt as if they were perched on the edge of the world, and when she was seated he handed her the glass and sat beside her, his elbows propped on his knees, his own glass dangling from his fingers as he stared out over the velvet blackness.

For a while neither of them said anything, but then the tension got to her and she broke the silence.

'Please tell me.'

He sucked in his breath, looking down, staring into his glass as he slowly swirled the wine before lifting it to his lips.

'Massimo?' she prompted, and he turned his head and met her eyes. Even in the moonlight, she could see the pain etched into his face, and her heart began to thud slowly.

'Angelina died of a brain haemorrhage following a fall,' he began, his voice expressionless. 'Nothing serious, nothing much at all, just a bit of a bump. She'd fallen down the stairs and hit her head on the wall. We all thought she was all right, but she had a bit of a headache later in the day, and we went to bed early. I woke in the night and she was missing, and I found her in the kitchen, slumped over the table, and one side of her face had collapsed.'

Lydia closed her eyes and swallowed hard as the nausea threatened to choke her. What had she *done*? Not just by saying what she had at the table—the same table? But by bringing this on all of them, on Claire, on him, on the children—most especially little Francesca, her eyes wide with pain and shock, fleeing from the table. The image would stay with her forever.

'It wasn't your fault,' he said gently. 'You weren't to know. I probably should have told you—warned you not to talk about it in that way, and why. I let you walk right into it.'

She turned back to him, searching his face in the shadows. She'd known something was wrong when he was bending over her on the tarmac, and again later, staring at the poster. And yet he'd said nothing.

'Why didn't you *tell* me? I knew something was wrong, something else, something more. Luca seemed much more worried than my condition warranted, even I knew that, and he kept looking at you anxiously. I thought he was worried about me, but then I realised it was you he was worried about. I just didn't know why. You should have told me.'

'How could I? You had a head injury. How could I say to you, "I'm sorry, I'm finding this a bit hard to deal with, my wife died of the same thing and I'm a bit worried I might lose you, too." How could I say that?'

He'd been worried he could lose her?

No. Of course he hadn't meant that, he didn't know her. He meant he was worried she might be about to die, too. Nothing more than that.

'You should have left us there instead of staying and getting distressed. I had no business tangling you all up in this mess—oh, Massimo, I'm so sorry.'

She broke off, clamping her teeth hard to stop her eyes from welling over, but his warm hand on her shoulder was the last straw, and she felt the hot, wet slide of a tear down her cheek.

'*Cara*, no. Don't cry for us. It was a long time ago.'

'But it still hurts you, and it'll hurt you forever,' she said unevenly.

'No, it just brought the memories back. We're all right, really. We're getting there. Francesca's the oldest, she remembers Angelina the most clearly, and she's the one who bears the brunt of the loss, because when I'm not there the little ones turn to her. She has to be mother to them, and she's been so strong, but she's just a little girl herself.'

He broke off, his jaw working, and she laid her hand gently against it and sighed.

'I'm so sorry. It must have been dreadful for you all.'

'It was. They took her to hospital, and she died later that day—she was on life support and they tested her brain but there was nothing. No activity at all. They turned off the machine, and I came home and told the children that their mother was gone. That was the hardest thing I've ever had to do in my life.'

His voice broke off again, turning away this time, and Lydia closed her eyes and swallowed the anguished response. There was nothing she could say that wouldn't be trite or meaningless, and so she stayed silent, and after a moment he let out a long, slow breath and sat back against the bench.

'So, now you know,' he said, his voice low and oddly flat.

Wordlessly, she reached out and touched his hand, and he turned it, his fingers threading through hers and holding on tight.

They stayed like that for an age, their hands lying linked between them as they sipped their wine, and then he turned to her in the dim light and searched her face. He'd taken comfort from her touch, felt the warmth of her generous spirit seeping into him, easing the ache which had been a part of him for so long.

How could she do that with just a touch?

No words. Words were too hard, would have been trite. Did she know that?

Yes. He could see that she did, that this woman who talked too much actually knew the value of silence.

He lifted her hand and pressed it to his lips, then smiled at her sadly. 'Did you eat anything?'

She shook her head. 'No. Not really.'

'Nor did I. Shall we see what we can find? It's a very, very long time since breakfast.'

It wasn't exactly *haute cuisine*, but the simple fare of olive bread and ham and cheese with sweetly scented baby plum tomatoes and a bowl of olive oil and balsamic vinegar just hit the spot.

He poured them another glass of wine, but it didn't seem like a good idea and so she gave him the second half and he found some sparkling water for her. She realised she'd thought nothing of handing him her glass of wine for him to finish, and he'd taken it without hesitation and drunk from it without turning a hair.

How odd, when they'd only met a scant twelve hours ago. Thirteen hours and a few minutes, to be more exact.

It seemed more like a lifetime since she'd watched him getting out of the taxi, wondered if he'd be The One to make it happen. The guy she'd been talking to was funny and seemed nice enough, but he wasn't about to give her a lift and she knew that. But Massimo had looked at her as he'd gone into the Jet Centre foyer, his eyes meeting hers and locking...

She glanced up, and found him watching her with a frown.

'Why are you frowning?' she asked, and his mouth kicked up a fraction in one corner, the frown ironed out with a deliberate effort.

'No reason. How's your head now?'

She shrugged. 'OK. It just feels as if I fell over my feet and spent the day hanging about in a hospital.' It was rather worse than that, but he didn't need to know about every ache and pain. The list was endless.

She reached out and covered his hand. 'Massimo, I'm all right,' she said softly, and the little frown came back.

'Sorry. It's just a reflex. I look after people—it's part of my job description. Everyone comes to me with their problems.'

She smiled at him, remembering her conversation with Francesca.

'I'm sorry I kept your father away from you for so long. He's been so kind and helpful.'

'He is. He helps everybody.'

'You're just a fixer, aren't you? You fix everything for everybody all the time, and you hate it when things can't be fixed.'

His frown deepened for a moment, and then he gave a wry laugh and pulled his hand away, swirling the wine in her glass before draining it. 'Is it so obvious?'

She felt her lips twitch. 'Only if you're on the receiving end. Don't get me wrong, I'm massively grateful and just so sorry I've dragged you into this awful mess and upset everyone. I'm more than happy you're a fixer, because goodness only knows I seemed to need one today. I think I need a guardian angel, actually. I just have such a gift for getting into a mess and dragging everybody with me.'

She broke off, and he tipped his head on one side and that little crease between his eyebrows returned fleetingly. 'A gift?'

She sighed. 'Jen's accident was sort of my fault.'

He sat back, his eyes searching hers. 'Tell me,' he said softly, so she did.

She told him about Russell, about their trip to her parents' farm for the weekend, because Jen and Andy were going to be there as well and she hadn't seen them for a while. And she'd shown him the farm, and he'd seen the quad bike, and suggested they went out on it so she could show him all the fields.

'I didn't want to go with him. He was a crazy driver, and I knew he'd want to go too fast, so I said no, but then Jen offered to show him round. She wanted to get him alone, to threaten him with death if he hurt me, but he hurt her instead. He went far too fast, and she told him to stop but he thought she was just being chicken and she wasn't, she knew about the fallen tree hidden in the long grass, and then they hit it and the quad bike cartwheeled through the air and landed on her.'

He winced and closed his eyes briefly. 'And she ended up in a wheelchair?'

'Not for a few weeks. She had a fractured spine, and she

was in a special bed for a while. It wasn't displaced, the spinal cord wasn't severed but it was badly bruised and it took a long time to recover and for the bones to heal. She's getting better now, she's starting to walk again, but she lost her job and so did Andy, so he could look after her. He took away everything from them, and if I'd gone with him, if it had been me, then I might have been able to stop him.'

'You really think so? He sounds like an idiot.'

'He is an idiot,' she said tiredly. 'He's an idiot, and he was my boss, so I lost my job, too.'

'He sacked you?'

She gave him a withering look. 'I walked...and then his business folded without me, and he threatened to sue me if I didn't go back. I told him to take a flying hike.'

'What business was he in?'

'He had a restaurant. I was his chef.'

Hence the tidy kitchen, he realised. She was used to working in a kitchen, used to bringing order to chaos, used to the utensils and the work space and the arrangement of them that always to him defied logic. And his restaurant had folded without her?

'You told me you were a cook,' he rebuked her mildly. 'I didn't realise you were a chef.'

She quirked an eyebrow at him mockingly. 'You told me you were a farmer and you live in a flipping fortress! I think that trumps it,' she said drily, and he laughed and lifted his glass to her.

'Touché,' he said softly, and her heart turned over at the wry warmth in his eyes. 'I'm sorry,' he went on. 'Sorry about this man who clearly didn't deserve you, sorry about your sister, sorry about your job. What a mess. And all because he was a fool.'

'Absolutely.'

'Tell me more about him.'

'Like what?'

'Like why your sister felt she needed to warn him not to hurt you. Had you been hurt before?'

'No, but she didn't really like him. He wasn't always a nice man, and he took advantage of me—made me work ridiculous hours, treated me like a servant at times and yet he could be a charmer, too. He was happy enough to talk me into his bed once he realised I was a good chef—sorry, you really didn't need to know that.'

He smiled slightly. 'Maybe you needed to say it,' he suggested, and her laugh was a little brittle.

'There are so many things I could tell you about him. I said I was a lousy judge of character. I think he had a lot in common with Nico, perhaps.'

He frowned. 'Nico?'

'The guy at the airport?'

'Yes, I know who you mean. In what way? Was he a drinker?'

'Yes. Definitely. But not just a drinker. He was a nasty drunk, especially towards the end of our relationship. He seemed to change. Got arrogant. He used to be quite charming at first, but it was just a front. He—well, let's just say he didn't respect women either.'

His mouth tightened. 'I'm sorry. You shouldn't have had to tolerate that.'

'No, I shouldn't. So—tell me about your house,' she said, changing the subject to give them both a bit of a break. She reached out and tore off another strip of bread, dunking it in the oil that she couldn't get enough of, and looked up to see a strange look on his face. Almost—tender?

Nonsense. She was being silly. 'Well, come on, then,' she mumbled round the bread, and he smiled, the strange look disappearing as if she'd imagined it.

'It's very old. We're not sure of the origins. It seems it

might have been a Medici villa, but the history is a little cloudy. It was built at the time of the Florentine invasion.'

'So how come your family ended up with it?'

His mouth twitched. 'One of our ancestors took possession of it at the end of the seventeenth century.'

That made her laugh. 'Took possession?'

The twitch again, and a wicked twinkle in his eye. 'We're not quite sure how he acquired it, but it's been in the family ever since. He's the one who renamed the villa *Palazzo Valtieri.*'

Palazzo? She nearly laughed at that. Not just a fortress, then, but a proper, full-on palace. Oh, boy.

'I'll show you round it tomorrow. It's beautiful. Some of the frescoes are amazing, and the formal rooms in the part my parents live in are fantastic.'

'Your parents live here?' she asked, puzzled, because there'd been no mention of them. Not that they'd really had time, but—

'*Si.* It's a family business. They're away at the moment, snatching a few days with my sister Carla and her new baby before the harvest starts, but they'll be back the day after tomorrow.'

'So how many rooms are there?'

He laughed. 'I have no idea. I've never counted them, I'm too busy trying not to let it fall down. It's crumbling as fast as we can patch it up, but so long as we can cheat time, that's fine. It's quite interesting.'

'I'm sure it is. And now it's your turn to run it?'

His mouth tugged down at the corners, but there was a smile in his eyes. '*Si.* For my sins. My father keeps trying to interfere, but he's supposed to be retired. He doesn't understand that, though.'

'No. It must be hard to hand it over. My father wouldn't be able to do it. And the harvest is just starting?'

He nodded. 'The grape harvest is first, followed by the chestnuts and the olives. It's relentless now until the end of November, so you can see why I was in a hurry to get back.'

'And I held you up.'

'*Cara*, accidents happen. Don't think about it any more.' He pushed back his chair. 'I think it's time you went to bed. It's after midnight.'

Was it? When had that happened? When they were outside, sitting in the quiet of the night and watching the twinkling lights in the villages? Or now, sitting here eating bread and cheese and olive oil, drinking wine and staring into each other's eyes like lovers?

She nodded and pushed back her chair, and he tucked her arm in his so she could feel the solid muscle of his forearm under her hand, and she hung on him and hopped and hobbled her way to her room.

'Ring me if you need anything. You have my mobile number on my card. I gave it to you on the plane. Do you still have it?'

'Yes—but I won't need you.'

Well, not for anything she'd dream of asking him for…

His brows tugged together. 'Just humour me, OK? If you feel unwell in the night, or want anything, ring me and I'll come down. I'm not far away. And please, don't lock your door.'

'Massimo, I'm feeling all right. My headache's gone, and I feel OK now. You don't need to worry.'

'You can't be too careful,' he said, and she could see a tiny frown between his brows, as if he was still waiting for something awful to happen to her.

They reached her room and he paused at the door, staring down into her eyes and hesitating for the longest moment. And then, just when she thought he was going to kiss her, he stepped back.

'Call me if you need me. If you need anything at all.'

'I will.'

'Good. *Buonanotte*, Lydia,' he murmured softly, and turned and walked away.

CHAPTER FOUR

WHAT was she *thinking* about?

Of course he hadn't been about to kiss her! That bump on the head had obviously been more serious than she'd realised. Maybe a blast of fresh air would help her think clearly?

She opened the French doors onto the terrace and stood there for a moment, letting the night air cool her heated cheeks. She'd been so carried along on the moment, so lured by his natural and easy charm that she'd let herself think all sorts of stupid things.

Of course he wasn't interested in her. Why would he be? She'd been nothing but a thorn in his side since the moment he'd set eyes on her. And even if he hadn't, she wasn't interested! Well, that was a lie, of course she was interested, or she wouldn't even be thinking about it, but there was no way it was going anywhere.

Not after the debacle with Russell. She was sworn off men now for life, or at least for a good five years. And so far, it hadn't been much more than five months!

Leaving the doors open, she limped back to the bed and pulled her pyjamas out of her flight bag, eyeing them dubiously. The skimpy top and little shorts she'd brought for their weightlessness had seemed fine when she was going to be sharing a hotel room with Claire, but here, in this ancient historic house—*palazzo*, even, for heaven's sake! She wondered what on earth he'd make of them.

Nothing. Nothing at all, because he wasn't going to see her in her nightclothes! Cross with herself, her head aching and her ankle throbbing and her bruises giving her a fair amount of grief as well, she changed into the almost-pyjamas, cleaned her teeth and crawled into bed.

Oh, bliss. The pillows were cloud-soft, the down quilt light and yet snuggly, and the breeze from the doors was drifting across her face, bringing with it the scents of sage and lavender and night-scented stocks.

Exhausted, weary beyond belief, she closed her eyes with a little sigh and drifted off to sleep...

Her doors were open.

He hesitated, standing outside on the terrace, questioning his motives.

Did he *really* think she needed checking in the night? Or was he simply indulging his—what? Curiosity? Fantasy? Or, perhaps...need?

He groaned softly. There was no doubt that he *needed* her, needed the warmth of her touch, the laughter in her eyes, the endless chatter and the brilliance of her smile.

The silence, when she'd simply held his hand and offered comfort.

Thinking about that moment brought a lump to his throat, and he swallowed hard. He hadn't allowed himself to need a woman for years, but Lydia had got under his skin, penetrated his defences with her simple kindness, and he wanted her in a way that troubled him greatly, because it was more than just physical.

And he really wasn't sure he was ready for that—would ever be ready for that again. But the need...

He'd just check on her, just to be on the safe side. He couldn't let her lie there alone all night.

Not like Angelina.

Guilt crashed over him again, driving out the need and leaving sorrow in its wake. Focused now, he went into her room, his bare feet silent on the tiled floor, and gave his eyes a moment to adjust to the light.

Had she sensed him? Maybe, because she sighed and shifted, the soft, contented sound drifting to him on the night air. When had he last heard a woman sigh softly in her sleep?

Too long ago to remember, too soon to forget.

It would be so easy to reach out his hand, to touch her. To take her in his arms, warm and sleepy, and make love to her.

Easy, and yet impossibly wrong. What was it about her that made him feel like this, that made him think things he hadn't thought in years? Not since he'd lost Angelina.

He stood over her, staring at her in the moonlight, the thought of his wife reminding him of why he was here. Not to watch Lydia sleep, like some kind of voyeur, but to keep her safe. He focused on her face. It was peaceful, both sides the same, just as it had been when he'd left her for the night, and she was breathing slowly and evenly. As he watched she moved her arms, pushing the covers lower. Both arms, both working.

He swallowed. She was fine, just as she'd told him, he realised in relief. He could go to bed now, relax.

But it was too late. He'd seen her sleeping, heard that soft, feminine sigh and the damage was done. His body, so long denied, had come screaming back to life, and he wouldn't sleep now.

Moving carefully so as not to disturb her, he made his way back to the French doors and out onto the terrace. Propping his hands on his hips, he dropped his head back and sucked in a lungful of cool night air, then let it out slowly before dragging his hand over his face.

He'd swim. Maybe that would take the heat out of his blood. And if it was foolish to swim alone, if he'd told the children a thousand times that no one should ever do it—well, tonight was different.

Everything about tonight seemed different.

He crossed the upper terrace, padded silently down the worn stone steps to the level below and rolled back the thermal cover on the pool. The water was warm, steaming billowing from the surface in the cool night air, and stripping off his clothes, he dived smoothly in.

Something had woken her.

She opened her eyes a fraction, peeping through the slit between her eyelids, but she could see nothing.

She could hear something, though. Not loud, just a little, rhythmic splash—like someone swimming?

She threw off the covers and sat up, wincing a little as her head pounded and the bruises twinged with the movement. She fingered the egg on her head, and sighed. *Idiot*. First thing in the morning she was going to track down that dress and burn the blasted thing.

She inched to the edge of the bed, and stood up slowly, her ankle protesting as she put weight through it. Not as badly as yesterday, though, she thought, and limped out onto the terrace to listen for the noise.

Yes. Definitely someone swimming. And it seemed to be coming from straight ahead. As she felt her way cautiously across the stone slabs and then the grass, she realised that this was the terrace they'd sat on last night, or at least a part of it. They'd been further over, to her left, and straight ahead of her were railings, the top edge gleaming in the moonlight.

She made her way slowly to them and looked down, and

there he was. Well, there someone was, slicing through the water with strong, bold strokes, up and down, up and down, length after length through the swirling steam that rose from the surface of the pool.

Exorcising demons?

Then finally he slowed, rolled to his back and floated spread-eagled on the surface. She could barely make him out because the steam clouded the air in the moonlight, but she knew instinctively it was him.

And as if he'd sensed her, he turned his head and as the veil of mist was drawn back for an instant, their eyes met in the night. Slowly, with no sense of urgency, he swam to the side, folded his arms and rested on them, looking up at her.

'You're awake.'

'Something woke me, then I heard the splashing. Is it sensible to swim on your own in the dark?'

He laughed softly. 'You could always come in. Then I wouldn't be alone.'

'I haven't got any swimming things.'

'Ah. Well, that's probably not very wise then because neither have I.'

She sucked in her breath softly, and closed her eyes, suddenly embarrassed. Amongst other things. 'I'm sorry. I didn't realise. I'll go away.'

'Don't worry, I'm finished. Just close your eyes for a second so I don't offend you while I get out.'

She heard the laughter in his voice, then the sound of him vaulting out of the pool. Her eyes flew open, and she saw him straighten up, water sluicing off his back as he walked calmly to a sun lounger and picked up an abandoned towel. He dried himself briskly as she watched, unable to look away, mesmerised by those broad shoulders that tapered down to lean hips and powerful legs.

In the magical silver light of the moon, the taut, firm globes of his buttocks, paler than the rest of him, could have been carved from marble, like one of the statues that seemed to litter the whole of Italy. Except they'd be warm, of course, alive...

Her mouth dry, she snapped her eyes shut again and made herself breath. In, out, in, out, nice and slowly, slowing down, calmer.

'Would you like a drink?'

She jumped and gave a tiny shriek. 'Don't creep up on people like that!' she whispered fiercely, and rested her hand against the pounding heart beneath her chest.

Yikes. Her all but bare chest, in the crazily insubstantial pyjamas...

'I'm not really dressed for entertaining,' she mumbled, which was ridiculous because the scanty towel twisted round his hips left very little to the imagination.

His fingers, cool and damp, appeared under her chin, tilting her head up so she could see his face instead of just that tantalising towel. His eyes were laughing.

'That makes two of us. I tell you what, I'll go and put the kettle on and pull on my clothes, and you go and find something a little less...'

'Revealing?'

His smile grew crooked. 'I was going to say alluring.'

Alluring. Right.

'I'll get dressed,' she said hastily, and limped rather faster than was sensible back towards her room, shutting the doors firmly behind her.

He watched her hobble away, his eyes tracking her progress across the terrace in the skimpiest of pyjamas, the long slender legs that had been hidden until now revealed by those tiny shorts in a way that did nothing for his peace of mind.

Or the state of his body. He swallowed hard and tightened his grip on the towel.

So much for the swimming cooling him down, he thought wryly, and went into the kitchen through the side door, rubbed himself briskly down with the towel again and pulled on his clothes, then switched on the kettle. Would she be able to find him? Would she even know which way to go?

Yes. She was there, in the doorway, looking deliciously rumpled and sleepy and a little uncertain. She'd pulled on her jeans and the T-shirt she'd been wearing last night, and her unfettered breasts had been confined to a bra. Pity, he thought, and then chided himself. She was a guest in his house, she was injured, and all he could do was lust after her. He should be ashamed of himself.

'Tea, coffee or something else? I expect there are some herbal teabags or something like that.'

'Camomile?' she asked hopefully.

Something to calm her down, because her host, standing there in bare feet, a damp T-shirt clinging to the moisture on his chest and a pair of jeans that should have had a health warning on them hanging on his lean hips was doing nothing for her equilibrium.

Not now she knew what was underneath those clothes.

He poured boiling water into a cup for her, then stuck another cup under the coffee maker and pressed a button. The sound of the grinding beans was loud in the silence, but not loud enough to drown out the sound of her heartbeat.

She should have stayed in her room, kept out of his way.

'Here, I don't know how long you want to keep the teabag in.'

He put the mug down on the table and turned back to the coffee maker, and as she stirred the teabag round absently she watched him. His hands were deft, his movements precise as he spooned sugar and stirred in a splash of milk.

'Won't that keep you awake?' she asked, but he just laughed softly.

'It's not a problem, I'm up now for the day. After I've drunk this I'll go and tackle some work in my office, and then I'll have breakfast with the children before I go out and check the grapes in each field to see if they're ripe.'

'Has the harvest started?'

'La vendemmia?' He shook his head. 'No. If the grapes are ripe, it starts tomorrow. We'll spend the rest of the day making sure we're ready, because once it starts, we don't stop till it's finished. But today—today should be pretty routine.'

So he might have time to show her round...

'Want to come with me and see what we do? If you're interested, of course. Don't feel you have to.'

If she was interested? She nearly laughed. *The farm*, she told herself firmly. He was talking about the *farm*.

'That would be great, if I won't be in your way?'

'No, of course not. It might be dull, though, and once I leave the house I won't be back for hours. I don't know if you're feeling up to it.'

Was he trying to get out of it? Retracting his invitation, thinking better of having her hanging around him all day like a stray kitten that wouldn't leave him alone?

'I can't walk far,' she said, giving him a get-out clause, but he shook his head.

'No, you don't have to. We'll take the car, and if you don't feel well I can always bring you back, it's not a problem.'

That didn't sound as if he was trying to get out of it, and she was genuinely interested.

'It sounds great. What time do you want to leave?'

'Breakfast is at seven. We'll go straight afterwards.'

It was fascinating.

He knew every inch of his land, every nook and cranny,

every slope, every vine, almost, and as he stood on the edge of a little escarpment pointing things out to her, his feet planted firmly in the soil, she thought she'd never seen anyone who belonged so utterly to their home.

He looked as if he'd grown from the very soil beneath his feet, his roots stretching down into it for three hundred years. It was a part of him, and he was a part of it, the latest guardian in its history, and it was clear that he took the privilege incredibly seriously.

As they drove round the huge, sprawling estate to check the ripeness of the grapes on all the slopes, he told her about each of the grape varieties which grew on the different soils and orientations, lifting handfuls of the soil so she could see the texture, sifting it through his fingers as he talked about moisture content and pH levels and how it varied from field to field, and all the time his fingers were caressing the soil like a lover.

He mesmerised her.

Then he dropped the soil, brushed off his hands and gave her a wry smile.

'I'm boring you to death. Come on, it's time for lunch.'

He helped her back to the car, frowning as she trod on some uneven ground and gave a little cry as her ankle twisted.

'I'm sorry, it's too rough for you. Here.' And without hesitating he scooped her off her feet and set her back on the passenger seat, shut the door and went round and slid in behind the wheel.

He must have been mad to bring her out here on the rough ground in the heat of the day, with a head injury and a sprained ankle. He hadn't been thinking clearly, what with the upset of yesterday and Francesca's scene at the table and then the utter distraction of her pyjamas—even if he'd been intending to go back to bed, there was no way he would have slept. In fact, he doubted if he'd ever sleep again!

He put her in the car, drove back to the villa and left her there with Carlotta. He'd been meaning to show her round the house, but frankly, even another moment in her company was too dangerous to contemplate at the moment.

He made a work-related excuse, and escaped.

He had a lot to do, he'd told her as he'd hurried off, because *la vendemmia* would start the following day.

So much for her tour of the house, she thought, but maybe it was as well to keep a bit of distance, because her feelings for him were beginning to confuse her.

Roberto brought the children home from school at the end of the afternoon, and she heard them splashing in the pool. She'd been contemplating the water herself, but without a suit it wasn't a goer, so she'd contented herself with sitting in the sun for a while and relaxing.

She went over to the railings and looked down, and saw all three of them in the water, with Carlotta and Roberto sitting in the shade watching them and keeping order. Carlotta glanced up at her and waved her down, and she limped down the steps and joined them.

It looked so inviting. Was her face a giveaway? Maybe, because Carlotta got to her feet and went to a door set in the wall of the terrace, under the steps. She emerged with a sleek black one-piece and offered it to her. 'Swim?' she said, encouragingly.

It was so, so tempting, and the children didn't seem to mind. Lavinia swam to the edge and grinned at her, and Antonino threw a ball at her and missed, and then giggled because she threw it back and bounced it lightly off his head. Only Francesca kept her distance, and she could understand why. It was the first time she'd seen her since supper last night, and maybe now she'd find a chance to apologise.

She changed in the cubicle Carlotta had taken the costume

from, and sat on the edge of the pool to take off her elastic ankle support.

'Ow. It looks sore.'

She glanced up, and saw Francesca watching her warily, her face troubled.

'I'm all right,' she assured her with a smile. 'I was really stupid to fall like that. I'm so sorry I upset you last night.'

She shrugged, and returned the smile with a tentative one of her own. 'Is OK. I was just tired, and *Pàpa* had been away for days, and—I'm OK. Sometimes, I just remember...'

She nodded, trying to understand what it must be like to be ten and motherless, and coming up with nothing even close, she was sure.

'I'm sorry.' She slipped into the water next to Francesca, and reached out and touched her shoulder gently. Then she smiled at her. 'I wonder, would you teach me some words of Italian?'

'Sure. What?'

'Just basic things. Sorry. Thank you. Hello, goodbye—just things like that.'

'Of course. Swim first, then I teach you.'

And she smiled, a dazzling, pretty smile like the smile of her mother in the photograph, and it nearly broke Lydia's heart.

He came into the kitchen as she was sitting there with the children, Francesca patiently coaching her.

'No! *Mee dees-pya-che,*' said Francesca, and Lydia repeated it, stretching the vowels.

'That's good. *Ciao, bambini!*'

'*Ciao, Pàpa!*' the children chorused, and he came over and sat down with them.

'I'm teaching Lydia *Italiano,*' Francesca told him, grinning at him.

He smiled back, his eyes indulgent. *'Mia bella ragazza,'* he said softly, and her smile widened, a soft blush colouring her cheeks.

'So what do you know?' he asked Lydia, and she laughed ruefully.

'Mi dispiace—I thought sorry was a word I ought to master pretty early on, with my track record,' she said drily, and he chuckled.

'Anything else?'

'Grazie mille—I seem to need that a lot, too! And *per favore*, because it's rude not to say please. And *prego*, just in case I ever get the chance to do something that someone thanks me for. And that's it, so far, but I think it's the most critical ones.'

He laughed. 'It's a good start. Right, children, bedtime. Say goodnight.'

'Buonanotte, Lydia,' they chorused, and she smiled at them and said, *'Buonanotte,'* back.

And then she looked at Francesca, and added, *'Grazie mille*, Francesca,' her eyes soft, and Francesca smiled back.

'Prego. We do more tomorrow?'

'Si.'

She grinned, and then out of the blue she came over to Lydia and kissed her on both cheeks. 'Goodnight.'

'Goodnight, Francesca.'

He ushered them away, although Francesca didn't really need to go to bed this early, but she'd lost sleep the night before and she was always happy to lie in bed and read.

He chivvied them through the bathroom, checked their teeth, redid Antonino's and then tucked them up. As he bent to kiss Francesca goodnight, she slid her arms round his neck and hugged him. 'I like Lydia,' she said. 'She's nice.'

'She is nice,' he said. 'Thank you for helping her.'

'It's OK. How long is she staying?'

'I don't know. A few days, just until she's better. You go to sleep, now.'

He turned off her top light, leaving the bedside light on so she could read for a while, and went back down to the kitchen.

Lydia was sitting there studying an English-Italian dictionary that Francesca must have lent her, and he poured two glasses of wine and sat down opposite her.

'She's a lovely girl.'

'She is. She's very like her mother. Kind. Generous.'

Lydia nodded. 'I'm really sorry you lost her.'

He smiled, but said nothing. What was there to say? Nothing he hadn't said before.

'So, the harvest starts tomorrow,' Lydia said after a moment.

'*Si.* You should come down. Carlotta brings lunch for everyone at around twelve-thirty. Come with her, I'll show you what we do.'

Massimo left before dawn the following morning, and she found Carlotta up to her eyes in the kitchen.

'How many people are you feeding?' she asked.

Carlotta's face crunched up thoughtfully, and she said something in Italian which was meaningless, then held up her outspread hands and flashed them six times. Sixty. *Sixty?*

'Wow! That's a lot of work.'

'*Si.* Is lot of work.'

She looked tired at the very thought, and Lydia frowned slightly and began to help without waiting to be asked. They loaded the food into a truck at twelve, and Roberto, Carlotta's husband, drove them down to the centre of operations.

They followed the route she'd travelled with Massimo the day before, bumping along the gravelled road to a group of buildings. It was a hive of activity, small tractors and pickup trucks in convoy bringing in the grapes, a tractor and trailer with men and women crowded on the back laughing and joking, their spirits high.

Massimo met them there, and helped her down out of the truck with a smile. 'Come, I'll show you round,' he said, and led her to the production line.

Around the tractors laden with baskets of grapes, the air was alive with the hum of bees. Everyone was covered in sticky purple grape juice, the air heavy with sweat and the sweet scent of freshly pressed grapes, and over the sound of excited voices she could hear the noise of the motors powering the pumps and the pressing machines.

'It's fascinating,' she yelled, and he nodded.

'It is. You can stay, if you like, see what we do with the grapes.'

'Do you need me underfoot?' she asked, and his mouth quirked.

'I'm sure I'll manage. You ask intelligent questions. I can live with that.'

His words made her oddly happy, and she smiled. 'Thank you. They seem to be enjoying themselves,' she added, gesturing to the laughing workers, and he grinned.

'Why wouldn't they be? We all love the harvest. And anyway, it's lunchtime,' he said pragmatically as the machines fell silent, and she laughed.

'So it is. I'm starving.'

The lunch was just a cold spread of bread and cheese and ham and tomatoes, much like their impromptu supper in the middle of the first night, and the exhausted and hungry workers fell on it like locusts.

'Carlotta told me there are about sixty people to feed. Does she do this every day?'

'Yes—and an evening meal for everyone. It's too much for her, but she won't let anyone else take over, she insists on

being in charge and she's so fussy about who she'll allow in
her kitchen it's not easy to get help that she'll accept.'

She nodded. She could understand that. She'd learned the
art of delegation, but you still had to have a handle on everything that was happening in the kitchen and that took energy
and physical resources that Carlotta probably didn't have any
more.

'How old is she?'

Massimo laughed. 'It's a state secret and more than my
life's worth to reveal it. Roberto's eighty-two. She tells me
it's none of my business, which makes it difficult as she's on
the payroll, so I had to prise it out of Roberto. Let's just say
there's not much between them.'

That made her chuckle, but it also made her think. Carlotta
hadn't minded her helping out in the kitchen this morning, or
the other night—in fact, she'd almost seemed grateful. Maybe
she'd see if she could help that afternoon. 'I think I'll head
back with them,' she told him. 'It's a bit hot out here for me
now anyway, and I could do with putting my foot up for a
while.'

It wasn't a lie, none of it, but she had no intention of putting her foot up if Carlotta would let her help. And it would
be a way to repay them for all the trouble she'd caused.

It was an amazing amount of work.

It would have been a lot for a team. For Carlotta, whose
age was unknown but somewhere in the ballpark of eighty-
plus, it was ridiculous. She had just the one helper, Maria,
who sighed with relief when Lydia offered her assistance.

So did Carlotta.

Oh, she made a fuss, protested a little, but more on the lines
of 'Oh, you don't really want to,' rather than, 'No, thank you,
I don't need your help.'

So she rolled up her sleeves and pitched in, peeling and

chopping a huge pile of vegetables. Carlotta was in charge of browning the diced chicken, seasoning the tomato-based sauce, tasting.

That was fine. This was her show. Lydia was just going along for the ride, and making up for the disaster of her first evening here, but by the time they were finished and ready to serve it on trestle tables under the cherry trees, her ankle was paying for it.

She stood on one leg like a stork, her sore foot hooked round her other calf, wishing she could sit down and yet knowing she was needed as they dished up to the hungry hordes.

They still looked happy, she thought. Happy and dirty and smelly and as if they'd had a good day, and there was a good deal of teasing and flirting going on, some of it in her direction.

She smiled back, dished up and wondered where Massimo was. She found herself scanning the crowd for him, and told herself not to be silly. He'd be with the children, not here, not eating with the workers.

She was wrong. A few minutes later, when the queue was thinning out and she was at the end of her tether, she felt a light touch on her waist.

'You should be resting. I'll take over.'

And his firm hands eased her aside, took the ladle from her hand and carried on.

'You don't need to do that. You've been working all day.'

'So have you, I gather, and you're hurt. Have you eaten?'

'No. I was waiting till we'd finished.'

He ladled sauce onto the last plate and turned to her. 'We're finished. Grab two plates, we'll go and eat. And you can put your foot up. You told me you were going to do that and I hear you've been standing all day.'

They sat at the end of a trestle, so she was squashed between a young girl from one of the villages and her host, and the air was heady with the scent of sweat and grape juice and the rich tomato and basil sauce.

He shaved cheese over her pasta, his arm brushing hers as he held it over her plate, and the soft chafe of hair against her skin made her nerve-endings dance.

'So, is it a good harvest?' she asked, and he grinned.

'Very good. Maybe the best I can remember. It'll be a vintage year for our Brunello.'

'Brunello? I thought that was only from Montalcino?'

'It is. Part of the estate is in the Montalcino territory. It's very strictly regulated, but it's a very important part of our revenue.'

'I'm sure.' She was. During the course of her training and apprenticeships she'd learned a lot about wines, and she knew that Brunellos were always expensive, some of them extremely so. Expensive, and exclusive. Definitely niche market.

Her father would be interested. He'd like Massimo, she realised. They had a lot in common, in so many ways, for all the gulf between them.

Deep in thought, she ate the hearty meal, swiped the last off the sauce from her plate with a chunk of bread and licked her lips, glancing up to see him watching her with a smile on his face.

'What?'

'You. You really appreciate food.'

'I do. Carlotta's a good cook. That was delicious.'

'Are you making notes?'

She laughed. 'Only mental ones.'

He glanced over her head, and a smile touched his face. 'My parents are back. They're looking forward to meeting you.'

Really? Like this, covered in tomato sauce and reeking of

chopped onions? She probably had an orange tide-line round her mouth, and her hair was dragged back into an elastic band, and—

'Mamma, *Pàpa*, this is Lydia.'

She scrambled to her feet, wincing as her sore ankle took her weight, and looked up into the eyes of an elegant, beautiful, immaculately groomed woman with clear, searching eyes.

'Lydia. How nice to meet you. Welcome to our home. I'm Elisa Valtieri, and this is my husband, Vittorio.'

'Hello. It's lovely to meet you, too.' Even if she did look a fright.

She shook their hands, Elisa's warm and gentle, Vittorio's rougher, his fingers strong and hard, a hand that wasn't afraid of work. He was an older version of his son, and his eyes were kind. He reminded her of her father.

'My son tells me you've had an accident?' Elisa said, her eyes concerned.

'Yes, I was really stupid, and he's been unbelievably kind.'

'And so, I think, have you. Carlotta is singing your praises.'

'Oh.' She felt herself colour, and laughed a little awkwardly. 'I didn't have anything else to do.'

'Except rest,' Massimo said drily, but his smile was gentle and warmed her right down to her toes.

And then she glanced back and found his mother looking at her, curiosity and interest in those lively brown eyes, and she excused herself, mumbling some comment about them having a lot to catch up on, and hobbled quickly back to Carlotta to see if there was anything she could do to help.

Anything, other than stand there while his mother eyed her speculatively, her eyes asking questions Lydia had no intention of answering.

If she even knew the answers...

CHAPTER FIVE

'You ran away.'

She was sitting outside her room on a bench with her foot up, flicking through a magazine she'd found, and she looked up guiltily into his thoughtful eyes.

'I had to help Carlotta.'

'And it was easier than dealing with my mother,' he said softly, a fleeting smile in his eyes. 'I'm sorry, she can be a little…'

'A little…?'

He grinned slightly crookedly. 'She doesn't like me being on my own. Every time I speak to a woman under fifty, her radar picks it up. She's been interrogating me for the last three hours.'

Lydia laughed, and she put the magazine down, swung her foot to the ground and patted the bench. 'Want to hide here for a while?'

His mouth twitched. 'How did you guess? Give me a moment.'

He vanished, then reappeared with a bottle of wine and two glasses. 'Prosecco?'

'Lovely. Thanks.' She took a glass from him, sniffing the bubbles and wrinkling her nose as she sipped. 'Mmm, that's really nice. So, how was the baby?'

'Beautiful, perfect, amazing, the best baby in the world—

oh, apart from all their other grandchildren. This is the sixth, and Luca and Isabelle are about to make it seven. Their second is due any time now.'

'Wow. Lots of babies.'

'Yes, and she loves it. Nothing makes her happier. Luca and Isabelle and my brother Gio are coming over tomorrow for dinner with some neighbours, by the way. I'd like you to join us, if you can tolerate it.'

She stared at him. 'Really? I'm only here by default, and I feel such a fraud. I really ought to go home.'

'How's your head now?'

She pulled a face. 'Better. I'm still getting the odd headache, but nothing to worry about. It's my ankle and the other bruises and scrapes that are sorest. I think I hit every step.'

He frowned. 'I'm sorry. I didn't really think about the things I can't see.'

Well, that was a lie. He thought about them all the time, but there was no way he was confessing that to Lydia. 'So—will you join us?'

She bit her lip, worrying it for a moment with her teeth, which made him want to kiss her just to stop her hurting that soft, full mouth that had been taunting him for days. *Dio*, the whole damn woman had been taunting him for days—

'Can I think about it?'

A kiss? No. No! Not a kiss!

'Of course,' he said, finally managing to unravel his tongue long enough to speak. 'Of course you may. It won't be anything impressive, Carlotta's got enough to do as it is, but my mother wanted to see Isabelle and Luca before the baby comes, and Gio's coming, and so my mother's invited Anita and her parents, and so it gets bigger—you know how it is.'

She laughed softly. 'I can imagine. Who's Anita?'

'The daughter of our neighbours. She and Gio had a thing a

while back, and my mother keeps trying to get them together again. Can't see it working, really, but she likes to try.'

'And how do they feel?'

He laughed abruptly. 'I wouldn't dare ask Gio. He has a fairly bitter and twisted attitude to love. Comes from being a lawyer, I suppose. His first line of defence is always a pre-nuptial agreement.'

She raised an eyebrow. 'Trust issues, then. I can understand that. I have a few of my own after Russell.'

'I'm sure. People like that can take away something precious, a sort of innocence, a naivety, and once it's gone you can never get it back. Although I have no idea what happened to Gio. He won't talk about it.'

'What about Anita? What's she like?'

His low chuckle made her smile. 'Anita's a wedding planner. What do you think?'

'I think she might like to plan her own?'

'Indeed. But Gio can't see what's under his nose, even if Mamma keeps putting her there.' He tipped his head on one side. 'It could be an interesting evening. And if you're there, it might take the heat off Gio, so he'll probably be so busy being grateful he'll forget to quiz me about you, so it could be better all round!'

She started to laugh at that, and he joined in with another chuckle and topped up her glass.

'Here's to families and their politics and complications,' he said drily, and touched his glass to hers.

'Amen to that,' she said, remembering guiltily that she'd meant to phone Jen again. 'I heard from Claire, by the way—she's back home safely, and she said Jo's ecstatic about winning.'

'How's your sister about it?'

She pulled a face. 'I'm not sure. She was putting on a brave face, but I think she's gutted. I know none of us expected me to win but, you know, it would have been so nice.'

He nodded. 'I'm sorry.'

'Don't be. You've done more than enough.' She drained her glass and handed it to him. 'I'm going to turn in. I need to rest my leg properly, and tomorrow I need to think about arranging a flight back home.'

'For tomorrow?' He sounded startled, and she shook her head.

'No. I thought maybe the next day? I probably ought to phone the hospital and get the go-ahead to fly.'

'I can take you there if you want a check-up.'

'You've got so much to do.'

'Nothing that's more important,' he said, and although it wasn't true, she knew that for him there was nothing more important than making sure there wasn't another Angelina.

'I'll see what they say,' she compromised. There was always the bus, surely? She'd ask Carlotta in the morning.

She got to her feet, and he stood up and took her hand, tucking it in the crook of his arm and helping her to the French doors. Quite unnecessarily, since she'd been hobbling around without help since the second day, really, but it was still nice to feel the strength of his arm beneath her hand, the muscles warm and hard beneath the fine fabric of his shirt.

Silk and linen, she thought, sampling the texture with her fingertips, savouring it.

He hesitated at the door, and then just when she thought he was going to walk away, he lowered his head and touched his lips to hers, sending rivers of ice and fire dancing over her skin.

It was a slow kiss, lingering, thoughtful, their mouths the only point of contact, but then the velvet stroke of his tongue against her lips made her gasp softly and part them for him, and everything changed.

He gave a muffled groan and deepened the kiss, searching the secret recesses of her mouth, his tongue finding hers and dancing with it, retreating, tangling, coaxing until she thought her legs would collapse.

Then he eased away, breaking the contact so slowly so that for a tiny second their lips still clung.

'*Buonanotte*, Lydia,' he murmured unevenly, his breath warm against her mouth, and then straightening slowly, he took a step back and turned briskly away, gathering up the glasses and the bottle as he went without a backwards glance.

She watched him go, then closed the curtains and undressed, leaving the doors open. The night was warm still, the light breeze welcome, and she lay there in the darkness, her fingertips tracing her lips, and thought about his kiss...

He must have been mad to kiss her!

Crazy. Insane. If he hadn't walked away, he would have taken her right there, standing on the terrace in full view of anyone who walked past.

He headed for the stairs, but then hesitated. He wouldn't sleep—but what else could he do? His office was next to her room, and he didn't trust himself that close to her. The pool, his first choice of distraction for the sheer physical exertion it offered, was too close to her room, and she slept with her doors open. She'd hear him, come and investigate, and...

So not the pool, then.

Letting out a long, weary sigh, he headed slowly up the stairs to his room, and sat on the bed, staring at the photograph of Angelina on his bedside table.

He'd loved her—really, deeply and enduringly loved her. But she was gone, and now, as he looked at her face, another face seemed superimposed on it, a face with laughing eyes and a soft, full bottom lip that he could still taste.

He groaned and fell back against the pillows, staring up

at the ceiling. The day after tomorrow, she'd be gone, he told himself, and then had to deal with the strange and unsettling sense of loss he felt at the thought that he was about to lose her.

She didn't sleep well.

Her dreams had been vivid and unsettling, and as soon as she heard signs of life, she got up, showered and put on her rinsed-out underwear, and then sat down on the edge of the bed and sighed thoughtfully as she studied her clothes.

She couldn't join them for dinner—not if their neighbours were coming. She'd seen Elisa, seen the expensive and elegant clothes she'd worn for travelling back home from her daughter's house, and the only things she had with her were the jeans and top she'd been wearing now for two days, including all the cooking she'd done yesterday.

No way could she wear them to dinner, even if she'd earn Gio's undying gratitude and give Elisa something else to think about! She put the clothes on, simply because she had absolutely no choice apart from the wedding dress Carlotta had stuffed in a bag for her and which she yet had to burn, and went outside and round the corner to the kitchen.

Carlotta was there, already making headway on the lunch preparations, and the children were sitting at the table eating breakfast. For a slightly crazy moment, she wondered if they could tell what she'd been dreaming about, if the fact that she'd kissed their father was written all over her face.

She said good morning to them, in her best Italian learned yesterday from Francesca, asked them how they were and then went over to Carlotta. '*Buongiorno*, Carlotta,' she said softly, and Carlotta blushed and smiled at her and patted her cheek.

'*Buongiorno, signorina,*' she said. 'Did you have good sleep?'

'Very good,' she said, trying not to think of the dreams and blushing slightly anyway. 'What can I do to help you?'

'No, no, you sit. I can do it.'

'You know I can't do that,' she chided softly. She stuck a mug under the coffee machine, pressed the button and waited, then added milk and went back to Carlotta, sipping the hot, fragrant brew gratefully. 'Oh, that's lovely. Right. What shall I do first?'

Carlotta gave in. 'We need to cut the meat, and the bread, and—'

'Just like yesterday?'

'*Si.*'

'So I'll do that, and you can make preparations for tonight. I know you have dinner to cook for the family as well as for the workers.'

Her brow creased, looking troubled, and Lydia could tell she was worried. Exhausted, more like. 'Look, let me do this, and maybe I can give you a hand with that, too?' she offered, but that was a step too far. Carlotta straightened her gnarled old spine and plodded to the fridge.

'I do it,' she said firmly, and so Lydia gave in and concentrated on preparing lunch for sixty people in the shortest possible time, so she could move on to cooking the pasta sauce for the evening shift with Maria. At least that way Carlotta would be free to concentrate on dinner.

Massimo found her in the kitchen at six, in the throes of draining gnocci for the workers, and she nearly dropped the pan. Crazy. Ridiculous, but the sight of him made her heart pound and she felt like a gangly teenager, awkward and confused because of the kiss.

'Are you in here again?' he asked, taking the other side of the huge pan and helping her tip it into the enormous strainer.

'Looks like me,' she said with a forced grin, but he just

frowned and avoided her eyes, as if he, too, was feeling awkward and uncomfortable about the kiss.

'Did you speak to the hospital?' he asked, and she realised he would be glad to get rid of her. She'd been nothing but trouble for him, and she was unsettling the carefully constructed and safe status quo he'd created around them all.

'Yes. I'm fine to travel,' she said, although it wasn't quite true. They'd said they needed to examine her, and when she'd said she was too busy, they'd fussed a bit but what could they do? So she'd booked a flight. 'I've got a seat on a plane at three tomorrow afternoon from Pisa,' she told him, and he frowned again.

'Really? You didn't have to go so soon,' he said, confusing her even more.

'It's not soon. It'll be five days—that's what they said, and I've been under your feet long enough.'

And any longer, she realised, and things were going to happen between them. There was such a pull every time she was with him, and that kiss last night—

She thrust the big pot at him. 'Here, carry the *gnocci* outside for me. I'll bring the sauce.'

He followed her, set the food down for the workers and stood at her side, dishing up.

'So can I persuade you to join us for dinner?' he asked, but she shook her head.

'I've got nothing to wear,' she said, feeling safe because he couldn't argue with that, but she was wrong.

'You're about the same size as Serena. I'm sure she wouldn't mind if you borrowed something from her wardrobe. She always leaves something here. Carlotta will show you.'

'Carlotta's trying to prepare a meal for ten people this evening, Massimo. She doesn't have time to worry about clothes for me.'

'Then I'll take you,' he said, and the moment the serving was finishing, he hustled her back into the house before she could argue.

He was right. She and Serena were about the same size, something she already knew because she'd borrowed her costume to swim in, and she found a pair of black trousers that were the right length with her flat black pumps, and a pretty top that wasn't in the first flush of youth but was nice enough.

She didn't want to take anything too special, but she didn't think Serena would mind if she borrowed that one, and it was good enough, surely, for an interloper?

She went back to the kitchen, still in her jeans and T-shirt, and found Carlotta sitting at the table with her head on her arms, and Roberto beside her wringing his hands.

'Carlotta?'

'She is tired, *signorina*,' he explained worriedly. 'Signora Valtieri has many people for dinner, and my Carlotta…'

'I'll do it,' she said quickly, sitting down and taking Carlotta's hands in hers. 'Carlotta, tell me what you were going to cook them, and I'll do it.'

'But Massimo said…'

'Never mind what he said. I can cook and be there at the same time. Don't worry about me. We can make it easy. Just tell me what you're cooking, and Roberto can help me find things. We'll manage, and nobody need ever know.'

Her eyes filled with tears, and Lydia pulled a tissue out of a box and shoved it in her hand. 'Come on, stop that, it's all right. We've got cooking to do.'

Well, it wasn't her greatest meal ever, she thought as she sat with the others and Roberto waited on them, but it certainly didn't let Carlotta down, and from the compliments going back to the kitchen via Roberto, she knew Carlotta would be feeling much less worried.

As for her, in her borrowed top and trousers, she felt under-dressed and overawed—not so much by the company as by the amazing dining room itself. Like her room and the kitchen, it opened to the terrace, but in the centre, with two pairs of double doors flung wide so they could hear the tweeting and twittering of the swallows swooping past the windows.

But it was the walls which stunned her. Murals again, like the ones in the cloistered walkway around the courtyard, but this time all over the ornate vaulted ceiling as well.

'Beautiful, isn't it?' Gio said quietly. 'I never get tired of looking at this ceiling. And it's a good way to avoid my mother's attention.'

She nearly laughed at that. He was funny—very funny, very quick, very witty, very dry. A typical lawyer, she thought, used to brandishing his tongue in court like a rapier, slashing through the opposition. He would be formidable, she realised, and she didn't envy the woman who was so clearly still in love with him.

Anita was lovely, though. Strikingly beautiful, but warm and funny and kind, and Lydia wondered if she realised just how often Gio glanced at her when she'd looked away.

Elisa did, she was sure of it.

And then she met Massimo's eyes, and realised he was studying her thoughtfully.

'Excuse me, I have to go and do something in the kitchen,' she murmured. 'Carlotta very kindly let me experiment with the dessert, and I need to put the finishing touches to it.'

She bolted, running along the corridor and arriving in the kitchen just as Carlotta had put out the bowls.

'Roberto say you tell them I cook everything!' she said, wringing her hands and hugging her.

Lydia hugged her back. 'You did, really. I just helped you. You told me exactly what to do.'

'You *know* what to do. You such good *cuoca*—good cook. Look at this! So easy—so beautiful. *Bellisima!*'

She spread her hands wide, and Lydia looked. Five to a tray, there were ten individual gleaming white bowls, each containing glorious red and black frozen berries fogged with icy dew, and in the pan on the stove Roberto was gently heating the white chocolate sauce. Sickly sweet, immensely sticky and a perfect complement to the sharp berries, it was her favourite no-frills emergency pud, and she took the pan from Roberto, poured a swirl around the edge of each plate and then they grabbed a tray each and went back to the dining room.

'I hope you like it,' she said brightly. 'If not, please don't blame Carlotta, I made her let me try it!'

Elisa frowned slightly, but Massimo just gave her a level look, and as she set the plate down in front of him, he murmured, 'Liar,' softly, so only she could hear.

She flashed him a smile and went back to her place, between Gio and Anita's father, and opposite Isabelle. 'So, tell me, what's it like living in Tuscany full-time?' she asked Isabelle, although she could see that she was blissfully contented and the answer was going to be biased.

'Wonderful,' Isabelle said, leaning her head against Luca's shoulder and smiling up at him. 'The family couldn't have been kinder.'

'That's not true. I tried to warn you off,' Gio said, and Luca laughed.

'You try and warn everybody off,' he said frankly, 'but luckily for me she didn't listen to you. Lydia, this dessert is amazing. Try it, *cara.*'

He held a spoonful up to Isabelle's lips, and Lydia felt a lump rise in her throat. Their love was so open and uncomplicated and genuine, so unlike the relationship she'd had with Russell. Isabelle and Luca were like Jen and Andy, unashamedly devoted to each other, and she wondered with a little ache what it must feel like to be the centre of someone's world, to be so clearly and deeply loved. *That* would be amazing.

She glanced across the table, and found Massimo watching her, his eyes thoughtful. He lifted his spoon to her in salute.

'Amazing, indeed.'

She blinked. He was talking about the dessert, not about love. Nothing to do with love, or with her, or him, or the two of them, or that kiss last night.

'Thank you,' she said, a little breathlessly, and turned her attention to the sickly, sticky white chocolate sauce. If she glued her tongue up enough with that, maybe it would keep it out of trouble.

'So how much of that was you, and how much was Carlotta?'

It was midnight, and everyone else had left or gone to bed. They were alone in the kitchen, putting away the last of the serving dishes that she'd just washed by hand, and Massimo was making her a cup of camomile tea.

'Honestly? I gave her a hand.'

'And the dessert?'

'Massimo, she was tired. She had all the ingredients for my quick fix, so I just improvised.'

'Hmm,' he said, but he left it at that, to her relief. She sensed he didn't believe her, but he had no proof, and Carlotta had been so distraught.

'Right, we're done here,' he said briskly. 'Let's go outside and sit and drink this.'

They went on her bench, outside her room, and sat in companionable silence drinking their tea. At least, it started out companionable, and then last night's kiss intruded, and she felt the tension creep in, making the air seem to fizz with the sparks that passed between them.

'You don't have to go tomorrow, you know,' he said, breaking the silence after it had stretched out into the hereafter.

'I do. I've bought a ticket.'

'I'll buy you another one. Wait a few more days.'

'Why? So I can finish falling for you? That's not a good idea, Massimo.'

He laughed softly, and she thought it was the saddest sound she'd ever heard. 'No. Probably not. I have nothing to offer you, Lydia. I wish I did.'

'I don't want anything.'

'That's not quite true. We both want something. It's just not wise.'

'Is it ever?'

'I don't know. Not for us, I don't think. We've both been hurt enough by the things that have happened, and I don't know about you but I'm not ready to try again. I have so many demands on me, so many calls on my time, so much *duty*.'

She put her cup down very carefully and turned to face him. 'We could just take tonight as it comes,' she said quietly, her heart in her mouth. 'No strings, just one night. No duty, no demands. Just a little time out from reality, for both of us.'

The silence was broken only by the beating of her heart, the roaring in her ears so loud that she could scarcely hear herself think. For an age he sat motionless, then he lifted a hand and touched her cheek.

'Why, *cara*? Why tonight?'

'Because it's our last chance?'

'Why me?'

'I don't know. It just seems right.'

Again he hesitated, then he took her hand and pressed it to his lips. 'Give me ten minutes. I need to check the children.'

She nodded, her mouth dry, and he brushed her lips with his and left her there, her fingers resting on the damp, tingling skin as if to hold the kiss in place.

Ten minutes, she thought. Ten minutes, and my life will change forever.

He didn't come back.

She gave up after half an hour, and went to bed alone, humiliated and disappointed. How stupid, to proposition a man so far out of her league. He was probably still laughing at her in his room.

He wasn't. There was a soft knock on the door, and he walked in off the terrace. 'Lydia? I'm sorry I was so long. Are you still awake?'

She propped herself up on one elbow, trying to read his face, but his back was to the moonlight. 'Yes. What happened? I'd given up on you.'

'Antonino woke. He had a nightmare. He's all right now, but I didn't want to leave him till he was settled.'

He sat on the edge of the bed, his eyes shadowed in the darkness, and she reached for the bedside light. He caught her hand. 'No. Leave it off. Let's just have the moonlight.'

He opened the curtains wide, but closed the doors—for privacy? She didn't know, but she was grateful that he had because she felt suddenly vulnerable as he stripped off his clothes and turned back the covers, lying down beside her and taking her into his arms.

The shock of that first contact took their breath away, and he rested his head against hers and gave a shuddering sigh. 'Oh, Lydia, *cara*, you feel so good,' he murmured, and then after that she couldn't understand anything he said, because his voice deepened, the words slurred and incoherent. He was speaking Italian, she realised at last, his breath trembling over her body with every groaning sigh as his hands cupped and moulded her.

She arched against him, her body aching for him, a need like no need she'd ever felt swamping her common sense and turning her to jelly. She ran her hands over him, learning his contours, the feel of his skin like hot silk over the taut, corded muscles beneath, and then she tasted him, her tongue testing the salt of his skin, breathing in the warm musk and the lingering trace of cologne.

He seemed to be everywhere, his hands and mouth caressing every part of her, their legs tangling as his mouth returned to hers and he kissed her as if he'd die without her.

'Please,' she whispered, her voice shaking with need, and he paused, fumbling for something on the bedside table.

Taking care of her, she realised, something she'd utterly forgotten, but not him. He'd remembered, and made sure that she was safe with him.

No strings. No repercussions.

Then he reached for her, taking her into his arms, and as he moved over her she stopped thinking altogether and just *felt*.

He woke to the touch of her hand on his chest, lying lightly over his heart.

She was asleep, her head lying on his shoulder, her body silvered by the moonlight. He shifted carefully, and she sighed and let him go, so he could lever himself up and look down at her.

There was a dark stain over one hipbone. He hadn't noticed it last night, but now he did. A bruise, from her fall. And there was another, on her shoulder, and one on her thigh, high up on the side. He kissed them all, tracing the outline with his lips, kissing them better like the bruises of a child.

It worked, his brother Luca told him, because the caress

released endorphins, feel-good hormones, and so you really could kiss someone better, but only surely if they were awake—

'Massimo?'

He turned his head and met her eyes. 'You're hurt all over.'

'I'm all right now.'

She smiled, reaching up and cradling his jaw in her hand, and he turned his face into her hand and kissed her palm, his tongue stroking softly over the sensitive skin.

'What time is it?'

He glanced at his watch and sighed. 'Two. Just after.'

Two. Her flight was in thirteen hours.

She swallowed hard and drew his face down to hers. 'Make love to me again,' she whispered.

How could he refuse? How could he walk away from her, even though it was madness?

Time out, she'd said, from reality. He needed that so badly, and he wasn't strong enough to resist.

Thirteen hours, he thought, and as he took her in his arms again, his heart squeezed in his chest.

Saying goodbye to the children and Carlotta and Roberto was hard. Saying goodbye to Massimo was agony.

He'd parked at the airport, in the short stay carpark, and they'd had lunch in the café, sitting outside under the trailing pergola. She positioned herself in the sun, but it didn't seem to be able to warm her, because she was cold inside, her heart aching.

'Thank you for everything you've done for me,' she said, trying hard not to cry, but it was difficult and she felt a tear escape and slither down her cheek.

'Oh, *bella*.' He sighed, and reaching out his hand, he brushed it gently away. 'No tears. Please, no tears.'

'Happy tears,' she lied. 'I've had a wonderful time.'

He nodded, but his eyes didn't look happy, and she was sure hers didn't. She tried to smile.

'Give my love to the children, and thank Francesca again for my Italian lessons.'

He smiled, his mouth turning down at the corners ruefully. 'They'll miss you. They had fun with you.'

'They'll forget me,' she reassured him. 'Children move on very quickly.'

But maybe not if they'd been hurt in the past, he thought, and wondered if this had been so safe after all, so without consequences, without repercussions.

Maybe not.

He left her at the departures gate, standing there with his arms round her while she hugged him tight. She let him go, looked up, her eyes sparkling with tears.

'Take care,' she said, and he nodded.

'You, too. Safe journey.'

And without waiting to see her go through the gate, he walked away, emotions raging through him.

Madness. He'd thought he could handle it, but—

He'd got her address from her, so he could send her a crate of wine and oil.

That was all, he told himself. Nothing more. He certainly wasn't going to contact her, or see her again—

He sucked in a breath, surprised by the sharp stab of loss. Ships in the night, he told himself more firmly. They'd had a good time but now it was over, she was gone and he could get on with his life.

How hard could it be?

CHAPTER SIX

'WHY don't you just go and see her?'

Massimo looked up from the baby in his arms and forced himself to meet his brother's eyes.

'I don't know what you mean.'

'Of course you do. You've been like a grizzly bear for the last two weeks, and even your own children are avoiding you.'

He frowned. Were they? He hadn't noticed, he realised in horror, and winced at the wave of guilt. But…

'It's not a crime to want her, you know,' Luca said softly.

'It's not that simple.'

'Of course not. Love never is.'

His head jerked up again. 'Who's talking about love?' he snapped, and Luca just raised an eyebrow silently.

'I'm *not* in love with her.'

'If you say so.'

He opened his mouth to say, 'I do say so,' and shut it smartly. 'I've just been busy,' he said instead, making excuses. 'Carlotta's been ill, and I've been trying to juggle looking after the children in the evenings and getting them ready for school without neglecting all the work of the grape harvest.'

'But that's over now—at least the critical bit. And you're wrong, you know, Carlotta isn't ill, she's old and tired and she needs to stop working before she becomes ill.'

Massimo laughed out loud at that, startling his new nephew

and making him cry. He shushed him automatically, soothing the fractious baby, and then looked up at Luca again. 'I'll let you tell her that.'

'I have done. She won't listen because she thinks she's indispensable and she doesn't want to let anybody down. And she's going to kill herself unless someone does something to stop her.'

And then it dawned on him. Just the germ of an idea, but if it worked...

He got to his feet, wanting to get started, now that the thought had germinated. He didn't know why he hadn't thought of it before, except he'd been deliberately putting it—her—out of his mind.

'I think I'll take a few days off,' he said casually. 'I could do with a break. I'll take the car and leave the children here. Mamma can look after them. It'll keep her off Gio's back for a while and they can play with little Annamaria while Isabelle rests.'

Luca took the baby from him and smiled knowingly.

'Give her my love.'

He frowned. 'Who? I don't know what you're talking about. This is a business trip. I have some trade samples to deliver.'

His brother laughed and shut the door behind him.

'Do you know anyone with a posh left-hand-drive Mercedes with a foreign number plate?'

Lydia's head jerked up. She did—but he wouldn't be here. There was no way he'd be here, and certainly not without warning—

'Tall, dark-haired, uber-sexy. Wow, in fact. Very, *very* wow!'

Her mouth dried, her heart thundering. No. Surely not—not when she was just getting over him—

'Let me see.'

She leant over Jen's shoulder and peeped through the doorway, and her heart, already racing, somersaulted in her chest. Over him? Not a chance. She'd been fooling herself for over two weeks, convincing herself she didn't care about him, it had just been a holiday romance, and one sight of him and all of it had come slamming back. She backed away, one hand on her heart, trying to stop it vaulting out through her ribs, the other over her mouth holding back the chaotic emotions that were threatening to erupt.

'It's him, isn't it? Your farmer guy. You never said he was that hot!'

No, she hadn't. She'd said very little about him because she'd been desperately trying to forget him and avoid the inevitable interrogation if she so much as hinted at a relationship. But—farmer? Try millionaire. More than that. Try serious landowner, old-money, from one of Italy's most well-known and respected families. Not a huge brand name, but big enough, she'd discovered when she'd checked on the internet in a moment of weakness and aching, pathetic need.

And try lover—just for one night, but the most magical, memorable and relived night of her life.

She looked down at herself and gave a tiny, desperate scream. She was cleaning tack—old, tatty tack from an even older, tattier pony who'd finally met his maker, and they were going to sell it. Not for much, but the saddle was good enough to raise a couple of hundred pounds towards Jen's wedding.

'He's looking around.'

So was she—for a way to escape from the tack room and back to the house without being seen, so she could clean up and at least look slightly less disreputable, but there was no other way out, and...

'He's seen me. He's coming over. Hi, there. Can I help?'

'I hope so. I'm looking for Lydia Fletcher.'

His voice made her heart thud even harder, and she backed into the shadows, clutching the filthy, soapy rag in a desperate fist.

'She's here,' Jen said, dumping her in it and flashing him her most charming smile. 'I'm her sister, Jen—and she's rather grubby, so she probably doesn't want you to see her like that, so why don't I take you over to the house and make you a cup of tea—'

'I don't mind if she's grubby. She's seen me looking worse, I'm sure.'

And before Jen could usher him away, he stepped past her into the tack room, sucking all the air out of it in that simple movement.

'Ciao, bella,' he said softly, a smile lurking in his eyes, and she felt all her resolve melt away to nothing.

'Ciao,' she echoed, and then toughened up. 'I didn't expect to see you again.'

She peered past him at Jen, hovering in the doorway. 'Why don't you go and put the kettle on?' she said firmly.

With a tiny, knowing smile, Jen took a step away, then mouthed, 'Be nice!'

Nice? She had no intention of being anything but nice, but she also had absolutely no intention of being anything more accommodating. He'd been so clear about not wanting a relationship, and she'd thought she could handle their night together, thought she could walk away. Well, she wasn't letting him in again, because she'd never get over it a second time.

'You could have warned me you were coming,' she said when Jen had gone, her crutches scrunching in the gravel. 'And don't tell me you lost my phone number, because it was on the same piece of paper as my address, which you clearly have or you wouldn't be here.'

'I haven't lost it. I didn't want to give you the chance to avoid me.'

'You thought I would?'

'I thought you might want to, and I didn't want you to run away without hearing me out.' He looked around, studying the dusty room with the saddle racks screwed to the old beams, the saddle horse in the middle of the room with Bruno's saddle on it, half-cleaned, the hook dangling from the ceiling with his bridle and stirrup leathers hanging from it, still covered in mould and dust and old grease.

Just like her, really, smeared in soapy filth and not in any way dressed to impress.

'Evocative smell.' He fingered the saddle flap, rubbing his fingertips together and sniffing them. 'It takes me back. I had a friend with horses when I was at boarding school over here, and I stayed with him sometimes. We used to have to clean the tack after we rode.'

He smiled, as if it was a good memory, and then he lifted his hand and touched a finger to her cheek. 'You've got dirt on your face.'

'I'm sure. And don't you dare spit on a tissue and rub it off.'

He chuckled, and shifting an old riding hat, he sat down on a rickety chair and crossed one foot over the other knee, his hands resting casually on his ankle as if he really didn't care how dirty the chair was.

'Well, don't let me stop you. You need to finish what you're doing—at least the saddle.'

She did. It was half-done, and she couldn't leave it like that or it would mark. She scrunched the rag in her fingers and nodded. 'If you don't mind.'

'Of course not. I didn't know you had a horse,' he added, after a slight pause.

'We don't—not any more.'

His eyes narrowed, and he leant forwards. 'Lydia?' he said

softly, and she sniffed and turned away, reaching for the saddle soap.

'He died,' she said flatly. 'We don't need the tack, so I'm going to sell it. It's a crime to let it rot out here when someone could be using it.'

'I'm sorry.'

'Don't be. He was ancient.'

'But you loved him.'

'Of course. That's what life's all about, isn't it? Loving things and losing them?' She put the rag down and turned back to him, her heart aching so badly that she was ready to howl her eyes out. 'Massimo, why are you here?'

'I promised you some olive oil and wine and balsamic vinegar.'

She blinked, and stared at him, dumbfounded. 'You drove all this way to deliver me *olive oil*? That's ridiculous. Why are you really here, in the middle of harvest? And what was that about not wanting me to run away before hearing you out?'

He smiled slowly—reluctantly. 'OK. I have a proposition for you. Finish the saddle, and I'll tell you.'

'Tell me now.'

'I'll tell you while you finish,' he compromised, so she picked up the rag again and reapplied it to the saddle, putting on rather more saddle soap than was necessary. He watched her, watched the fierce way she rubbed the leather, the pucker in her brow as she waited for him to speak.

'So?' she prompted, her patience running out.

'So—I think Carlotta is unwell. Luca says not, and he's the doctor. He says she's just old, and tired, and needs to stop before she kills herself.'

'I agree. She's been too old for years, probably, but I don't suppose she'll listen if you tell her that.'

'No. She won't. And the trouble is she won't allow anyone else in her kitchen.' He paused for a heartbeat. 'Anyone except *you.*'

She dropped the rag and spun round. 'Me!' she squeaked, and then swallowed hard. 'I—I don't understand! What have I got to do with anything?'

'We need someone to feed everybody for the harvest. After that, we'll need someone as a housekeeper. Carlotta won't give that up until she's dead, but we can get her local help, and draft in caterers for events like big dinner parties and so on. But for the harvest, we need someone she trusts who can cater for sixty people twice a day without getting in a flap— someone who knows what they're doing, who understands what's required and who's available.'

'I'm not available,' she said instantly, and he felt a sharp stab of disappointment.

'You have another job?'

She shook her head. 'No, not really, but I'm helping with the farm, and doing the odd bit of outside catering, a bit of relief work in the pub. Nothing much, but I'm trying to get my career back on track and I can't do that if I'm gallivanting about all over Tuscany, however much I want to help you out. I have to earn a living—'

'You haven't heard my proposition yet.'

She stared at him, trying to work out what he was getting at. What he was offering. She wasn't sure she wanted to know, because she had a feeling it would involve a lot of heartache, but—

'What proposition? I thought that was your proposition?'

'You come back with me, work for the harvest and I'll give your sister her wedding.'

She stared at him, confused. She couldn't have heard him right. 'I don't understand,' she said, finding her voice at last.

'It's not hard. The hotel was offering the ceremony, a reception for—what, fifty people?—a room for their wedding night, accommodation for the night before for the bridal party, a food and drink package—anything I've missed?'

She shook her head. 'Flowers, maybe?'

'OK. Well, we can offer all that. There's a chapel where they can marry, if they're Catholic, or they could have a blessing there and marry in the Town Hall, or whatever they wanted, and we'll give them a marquee with tables and chairs and a dance floor, and food and wine for the guests. And flowers. And if they don't want to stay in the guest wing of the villa, there's a lodge in the woods they can have the use of for their honeymoon.'

Her jaw dropped, and her eyes suddenly filled with tears. 'That's ridiculously generous! Why would you do this for them?'

'Because if I hadn't distracted you on the steps, you wouldn't have fallen, and your sister would have had her wedding.'

'No! Massimo, it wasn't your fault! I don't need your guilt as well as my own! This is not your problem.'

'Nevertheless, you would have won if you hadn't fallen, and yet when I took you back to my home that night you just waded in and helped Carlotta, even though you were hurt and disappointed. You didn't need to do that, but you saw she was struggling, and you put your own worries and injuries out of your mind and just quietly got on with it, even though you were much more sore than you let on.'

'What makes you say that?'

He smiled tenderly. 'I saw the bruises, cara. All over your body.'

She blushed furiously, stooping to pick the rag up off the floor, but it was covered in dust and she put it down again. The saddle was already soaped to death.

'And that dinner party—I know quite well that all of those dishes were yours. Carlotta doesn't cook like that, and yet you left an old woman her pride, and for that alone, I would give you this wedding for your sister.'

The tears spilled down her cheeks, and she scrubbed them away with the backs of her hands. Not a good idea, she realised instantly, when they were covered in soapy filth, but he was there in front of her, a tissue in his hand, wiping the tears away and the smears of dirt with them.

'Silly girl, there's no need to cry,' he tutted softly, and she pushed his hand away.

'Well, of course I'm crying, you idiot!' she sniffed, swallowing the tears. 'You're being ridiculously generous. But I can't possibly accept.'

'Why not? We need you—and that is real and genuine. I knew you'd refuse the wedding if I just offered it, but we really need help with the harvest, and it's the only way Carlotta will allow us to help her. If we do nothing, she'll work herself to death, but she'll be devastated if we bring in a total stranger to help out.'

'I was a total stranger,' she reminded him.

He gave that tender smile again, the one that had unravelled her before. 'Yes—but now you're a friend, and I'm asking you, as a friend, to help her.'

She swallowed. 'And in return you'll give Jen this amazing wedding?'

'*Si.*'

'And what about us?'

Something troubled flickered in his eyes for a second until the shutters came down. 'What about us?'

'We agreed it was just for one night.'

'Yes, we did. No strings. A little time out from reality.'

'And it stays that way?'

He inclined his head. '*Si.* It stays that way. It has to.'

Did it? She felt—what? Regret? Relief? A curious mixture of both, probably, although if she was honest she might have been hoping…

'Can I think about it?'

'Not for long. I have to return first thing tomorrow morning. I would like to take you with me.'

She nodded. 'Right. Um. I need to finish this—what are you *doing*?'

He'd taken off his jacket, slung it over the back of the chair and was rolling up his sleeves. 'Helping,' he said, and taking a clean rag from the pile, he buffed the saddle to a lovely, soft sheen. 'There. What else?'

It took them half an hour to clean the rest of Bruno's tack, and then she led him back to the house and showed him where he could wash his hands in the scullery sink.

'Don't mention any of this to Jen, not until I've made up my mind,' she warned softly, and he nodded.

Her sister was in the kitchen, and she pointed her in the direction of the kettle and ran upstairs to shower. Ten minutes later, she was back down in the kitchen with her hair in soggy rats' tails and her face pink and shiny from the steam, but at least she was clean.

He glanced up at her and got to his feet with a smile. 'Better now?'

'Cleaner,' she said wryly. 'Is Jen looking after you?'

Jen was, she could see that. The teapot was on the table, and the packet of biscuits they'd been saving for visitors was largely demolished.

'She's been telling me all about you,' he said, making her panic, but Jen just grinned and helped herself to another biscuit.

'I've invited him to stay the night,' she said airily, dunking it in her tea while Lydia tried not to panic yet again.

'I haven't said yes,' he told her, his eyes laughing as he

registered her reaction. 'There's a pub in the village with a sign saying they do rooms. I thought I might stay there.'

'You can't stay there. The pub's awful!' she said without thinking, and then could have kicked herself, because realistically there was nowhere else for miles.

She heard the door open, and the dogs came running in, tails wagging, straight up to him to check him out, and her mother was hard on their heels.

'Darling? Oh!'

She stopped in the doorway, searched his face as he straightened up from patting the dogs, and started to smile. 'Hello. I'm Maggie Fletcher, Lydia's mother, and I'm guessing from the number plate on your car you must be her Italian knight in shining armour.'

He laughed and held out his hand. 'Massimo Valtieri—but I'm not sure I'm any kind of a knight.'

'Well, you rescued my daughter, so I'm very grateful to you.'

'She hurt herself leaving my plane,' he pointed out, 'so really you should be throwing me out, not thanking me!'

'Well, I'll thank you anyway, for trying to get her there in time to win the competition. I always said it was a crazy idea.'

'Me, too.' He smiled, and Lydia ground her teeth. The last thing she needed was him cosying up to her mother, but it got worse.

'I promised her some produce from the estate, and I thought, as I had a few days when I could get away, I'd deliver it in person. I'll bring it in, if I may?'

'Of course! How very kind of you.'

It wasn't kind. It was an excuse to bribe her into going back there to feed the troops by dangling a carrot in front of her that he knew perfectly well she'd be unable to resist. Two carrots, really, because as well as Jen's wedding, which was giving her the world's biggest guilt trip, there was the problem of the aging and devoted Carlotta, who'd become her friend.

'I'll help you,' she said hastily, following him out to the car so she could get him alone for a moment.

He was one step ahead of her, though, she realised, because as he popped the boot open, he turned to her, his face serious. 'Before you say anything, I'm not going to mention it to your family. This is entirely your decision, and if you decline, I won't say any more about it.'

Well, damn. He wasn't even going to *try* to talk her into it! Which, she thought with a surge of disappointment, could only mean that he really wasn't interested in picking up their relationship, and was going to leave it as it stood, as he'd said, with just that one night between them.

Not that she wanted him to do anything else. She really didn't want to get involved with another man, not after the hatchet job Russell had done on her self-esteem, and not when she was trying to resurrect her devastated career, but...

'Here. This is a case of our olive oils. There are three types, different varietals, and they're quite distinctive. Then this is a case of our wines—including a couple of bottles of vintage Brunello. You really need to save them for an important occasion, they're quite special. There's a nice *vinsanto* dessert wine in there, as well. And this is the *aceto balsamico* I promised you, from my cousin in Modena.'

While she was still standing there open-mouthed, he reached into a cool box and pulled out a leg of lamb and a whole Pecorino cheese.

'Something for your mother's larder,' he said with a smile, and without any warning she burst into tears.

'Hey,' he said softly, and wrapping his arms around her, he drew her up against his chest. He could feel the shudders running through her, and he cradled her against his heart and rocked her, shushing her gently. 'Lydia, please, *cara*, don't cry.'

'I'm not,' she lied, bunching her fists in his shirt and burrowing into his chest, and he chuckled and hugged her.

'I don't think that's quite true,' he murmured. 'Come on, it's just a few things.'

'It's nothing to do with the things,' she choked out. Her fist hit him squarely in the chest. 'I didn't think I'd ever see you again, and I was trying to move on, and then you just come back into my life and drop this bombshell on me about the wedding, and of all the times to choose, when I'm already...'

Realisation dawned, and he stroked her hair, gentling her. 'Oh, *cara*, I'm sorry. When did he die, the pony?'

She sniffed hard and tried to pull away, but he wouldn't let her, he just held her tight, and after a moment she went still, unyielding but resigned. 'Last week,' she said, her voice clogged with tears. 'We found him dead in the field.'

'And you haven't cried,' he said.

She gave up fighting and let her head rest against his chest. 'No. But he was old.'

'We lost our dog last year. She was very, very old, and she'd been getting steadily worse. After she died, I didn't cry for weeks, and then one day it suddenly hit me and I disintegrated. Luca said he thought it was to do with Angelina. Sometimes grief is like that. We can't acknowledge it for the things that really hurt, and then something else comes along, and it's safe then to let go, to let out the hurt that you can't face.'

She lifted her head and looked up at him through her tears.

'But I don't hurt.'

'Don't you? Even after Russell treated you the way he did? For God's sake, Lydia, he was supposed to be your lover, and yet when he'd crippled your sister, his only reaction was anger that you'd left him and his business was suffering! What kind of a man is that? Of course you're hurting.'

She stared at him, hearing her feelings put into words somehow making sense of them all at last. She eased away from him, needing a little space, her emotions settling now.

'You know I can't say no, don't you? To your proposition?'

His mouth quirked slightly and he nodded slowly and let her go. 'Yes. I do know, and I realise it's unfair to ask this of you, but—I need help for Carlotta, and you need the wedding. This way, we both win.'

Or lose, depending on whether or not he could keep his heart intact, seeing her every day, working alongside her, knowing she'd be just there in the room beside his office, taunting him even in her sleep.

She met his eyes, her own troubled. 'I don't want an affair. I can't do it. One night was dangerous enough. I'm not ready, and I don't want to hurt your children.'

He nodded. 'I know. And I agree. If I wanted an affair, it would be with a woman my children would never meet, someone they wouldn't lose their hearts to. But I would like to be your friend, Lydia. I don't know if that could work but I would like to try.'

No. It couldn't work. It was impossible, because she was already more than half in love with him, but—Jen needed her wedding, and she'd already had it snatched away from her once. This was another chance, equally as crazy, equally as dangerous, if not more so.

It was a chance she had to take.

'OK, I'll do it,' she said, without giving herself any further time to think, and his shoulders dropped slightly and he smiled.

'*Grazie, cara. Grazie mille.* And I know you aren't doing it for me, but for your sister and also for Carlotta, and for that, I thank you even more.'

He hugged her—just a gentle, affectionate hug between friends, or so he told himself as she slid her arms round him and hugged him back, but the feel of her in his arms, the soft pressure of her breasts, the smell of her shampoo and the warmth of her body against his all told him he was lying.

He was in this right up to his neck, and if he couldn't hold it together for the next two months—but he had to. There was no choice. Neither of them was ready for this.

He let her go, stepped back and dumped the lamb and the cheese in her arms. 'Let's go back in.'

'Talk to me about your dream wedding,' he said to Jen, after they'd taken all the things in from the car.

Her smile tugged his heartstrings. 'I don't dream about my wedding. The last time I did that, it turned into a nightmare for Lydia, so I'm keeping my feet firmly on the ground from now on, and we're going to do something very simple and quiet from here, and it'll be fine.'

'What if I was to offer you the *palazzo* as a venue?' he suggested, and Jen's jaw dropped.

'What?' she said, and then shook her head. 'I'm sorry, I don't understand.'

'The same deal as the hotel.'

She stared, looking from Lydia to Massimo and back again, and shook her head once more. 'I don't...'

'They need me,' Lydia explained. 'Carlotta's not well, and if I cook for the harvest season, you can have your wedding. I don't have another job yet, and it's good experience and an interesting place to work, so I thought it might be a good idea.'

'I've brought a DVD of my brother's wedding so you can see the setting. It might help you to decide.'

He handed it to her, and she handed it straight back.

'There's a catch,' she said, her voice strained. 'Lydia?'

'No catch. I work, you get the wedding.'

'But—that's so generous!'

'Nonsense. We'd have to pay a caterer to do the job, and it would cost easily as much.'

'But—Lydia, what about you? You were looking for another job, and you were talking about setting up an outside catering business. How can you do that if you're out of the country? No, I can't let you do it!'

'Tough, kid,' she said firmly, squashing her tears again. Heavens, she never cried, and this man was turning her into a fountain! 'I'm not doing it just for you, anyway. This is a job—a real job, believe me. And you know what I'm like. I'd love to know more about Italian food—real, proper country food—and this is my chance, so don't go getting all soppy on me, all right? My catering business will keep. Just say thank you and shut up.'

'Thank you and shut up,' she said meekly, and then burst into tears.

Lydia cooked the leg of lamb for supper and served it with rosemary roast potatoes and a redcurrant *jus*, and carrots and runner beans from the garden, and they all sat round at the battered old kitchen table with the dogs at their feet and opened one of the bottles of Brunello.

'It seems wrong, drinking it in here,' she said apologetically, 'but Andy's doing the accounts on the dining table at the moment and it's swamped.'

'It's not about the room, it's about the flavour. Just try it,' he said, watching her closely.

So she swirled it, sniffed it, rolled it round on her tongue and gave a glorious sigh. 'That is *the* most gorgeous wine I have ever tasted,' she told him, and he inclined his head and smiled.

'Thank you. We're very proud of it, and it's a perfect complement to the lamb. It's beautifully cooked. Well done.'

'Thank you. Thank you for trusting me with it.' She smiled back, suddenly ridiculously happy, and then the men started to talk about farming, and Jen quizzed her about the *palazzo*, because she'd hardly said anything about it since she'd come home.

'It sounds amazing,' Jen said, wide-eyed. 'We'll have to look at that video.'

'You will. It's great. The frescoes are incredible, and the view is to die for, especially at night, when all you can see is the twinkling lights in the distance. It's just gorgeous, and really peaceful. I know it'll sound ridiculous, but it reminded me of home, in a way.'

'I don't think that's ridiculous,' Massimo said, cutting in with a smile. 'It's a home, that's all, just in a beautiful setting, and that's what you have here—a warm and loving family home in a peaceful setting. I'm flattered that you felt like that about mine.'

The conversation drifted on, with him telling them more about the farm, about the harvest and the soil and the weather patterns, and she could have sat there for hours just listening to his voice, but she had so much to do before they left in the morning, not least gathering together her clothes, so she left them all talking and went up to her room.

Bearing in mind she'd be flying back after the harvest was over, she tried to be sensible about the amount she took, but she'd need winter clothes as well as lighter garments, and walking boots so she could explore the countryside, and something respectable in case he sprang another dinner on her—

'You look lost.'

She looked up from her suitcase and sighed. 'I don't know what to take.'

'Your passport?'

'Got that,' she said, waggling it at him with a smile. 'It's clothes. I want enough, but not too much. I don't know what the weather will be like.'

'It can get cold. Bring warm things for later, but don't worry. You can buy anything you don't have.'

'I'm trying to stick to a sensible baggage allowance for when I come back.'

'Don't bother. I'll pay the excess. Just bring what you need.'

'What time are we leaving?'

'Seven.'

'Seven?' she squeaked, and he laughed.

'That's a concession. I would have left at five, or maybe six.'

'I'll be ready whenever you tell me. Have you been shown to your room?'

'*Si.* And the bathroom is opposite?'

'Yes. I'm sorry it doesn't have an *en suite* bathroom—'

'Lydia, stop apologising for your home,' he said gently. 'I'm perfectly capable of crossing a corridor. I'll see you at six for breakfast, OK?'

'OK,' she said, and for a heartbeat she wondered if he'd kiss her goodnight.

He didn't, and she spent a good half-hour trying to convince herself she was glad.

They set off in the morning shortly before seven, leaving Jen and Andy still slightly stunned and busy planning their wedding, and she settled back in the soft leather seat and wondered if she'd completely lost her mind.

'Which way are we going?' she asked as they headed down to Kent.

'The quickest route—northern France, across the Alps in Switzerland, past Lake Como and onto the A1 to Siena. We'll stay somewhere on the way. I don't want to drive through the Alps when I'm tired, the mountain roads can be a little tricky.'

Her heart thudded. They were staying somewhere overnight?

Well, of course they were, he couldn't possibly drive whatever distance it was from Suffolk to Tuscany in one day, but somehow she hadn't factored an overnight stop into her calculations, and the journey, which until now had seemed simple and straightforward, suddenly seemed fraught with the danger of derailing their best intentions.

CHAPTER SEVEN

'LYDIA?'

She stirred, opened her eyes and blinked.

He'd pulled up in what looked like a motorway service area, and it was dark beyond the floodlit car park. She yawned hugely and wrapped her hand around the back of her neck, rolling her head to straighten out the kinks.

'Oh, ow. What time is it? I feel as if I've been asleep for hours!'

He gave her a wry, weary smile. 'You have. It's after nine, and I need to stop for the night before I join you and we have an accident.'

'Where are we?'

'A few miles into Switzerland? We're getting into the mountains and this place has rooms. It's a bit like factory farming, but it's clean and the beds are decent. I'd like to stop here if they have any vacancies.'

'And if they don't?'

He shrugged. 'We go on.'

But he must be exhausted. They'd only stopped twice, the last time at two for a late lunch. What if they only have one room? she thought, and her heart started to pound. How strong was her resolve? How strong was his?

She never found out. They had plenty of space, so he booked two rooms and carried her suitcase for her and put it down at the door. 'We should eat fairly soon, but I thought you might want to freshen up. Ten minutes?'

'Ten minutes is fine,' she said, and let herself into her lonely, barren motel room. It was clean and functional as he'd promised, just another generic hotel room like all the rest, and she wished that for once in her life she had the courage to go after the thing she really wanted.

Assuming the thing—the person—really wanted her, of course, and he'd made it clear he didn't.

She stared at herself in the bathroom mirror. What was she *thinking* about? She didn't want him! She wasn't ready for another relationship. Not really, not if she was being sensible. She wanted to get her career back on track, to refocus her life and remember where she was going and what she was doing. She certainly didn't need to get her heart broken by a sad and lonely workaholic ten years her senior, with three motherless children and a massively demanding business empire devouring all his time.

Even if he was the most fascinating and attractive man she'd ever met in her life, and one of the kindest and most thoughtful. He was hurting, too, still grieving for his wife, and in no way ready to commit to another relationship, no matter how deeply she might fall in love with him. He wouldn't hurt her intentionally, but letting herself get close to him—that was a recipe for disaster if nothing else was.

'Lydia?'

There was a knock at the bedroom door, and she turned off the bathroom light and opened it. Massimo was standing there in the corridor, in a fresh shirt and trousers, his hair still damp from the shower. He looked incredible.

'Are you ready for dinner?'

She conjured up a smile. 'Give me ten seconds.'

She picked up her bag, gave her lips a quick swipe of translucent colour as a concession to vanity and dragged a comb through her hair. And then, just out of defiance, she added a spritz of scent.

She might be travel weary, and she might not be about to get involved with him, but she still had her pride.

The dinner was adequate. Nothing more, nothing less.

He was tired, she was tired—and yet still they lingered, talking for an hour over their coffee. She asked about Isabelle and Luca's baby, and how the children were, and he asked her about Jen's progress and if she'd be off the crutches by the time of the wedding, whenever it would be.

They talked about his time at boarding school, and she told him about her own schooling, in a village just four miles from where she lived.

And then finally they both fell silent, and he looked at his watch in disbelief.

'It's late and tomorrow will be a hard drive,' he said. 'We should go to bed.'

The word *bed* reverberated in the air between them, and then she placed her napkin on the table and stood up a little abruptly. 'You're right. I'm sorry, you should have told me to shut up.'

He should. He should have cut it short and gone to bed, instead of sitting up with her and hanging on her every word. He paid the bill and escorted her back to her room, leaving a clear gap between them as he paused at her door.

Not because he wanted to, but because he didn't, and if he got any closer, he didn't trust himself to end it there.

'*Buonanotte, bella,*' he said softly. 'I'll wake you at five thirty.'

She nodded, and without looking back at him, she opened the door of her room, went in and closed it behind her. He stared at it for a second, gave a quiet, resigned laugh and let himself into his own room.

This was what he'd wanted, wasn't it? For her to keep her distance, to enable him to do the same?

So why did he suddenly feel so lonely?

It was like coming home.

This time, when she saw the fortress-like building standing proudly on the hilltop, she felt excitement and not trepidation, and when the children came tumbling down the steps to greet them, there was no look of horror, but shrieks of delight and hugs all round.

Antonino just wanted his father, but Francesca hugged her, and Lavinia hung on her arm and grinned wildly. 'Lydia!' she said, again and again, and then Carlotta appeared at the top of the steps and welcomed her—literally—with open arms.

'*Signorina*! You come back! Oh!'

She found herself engulfed in a warm and emotional hug, and when Carlotta let her go, her eyes were brimming. She blotted them, laughing at herself, and then taking Lydia by the hand, she led her through the courtyard to her old room.

This time there were flowers on the chest of drawers, and Roberto brought in her luggage and put it down and hugged her, too.

'*Grazie mille, signorina,*' he said, his voice choked. 'Thank you for coming back to help us.'

'Oh, Roberto, it's my pleasure. There's so much Carlotta can teach me, and I'm really looking forward to learning.'

'I teach,' she said, patting her hand. 'I teach you everything!'

She doubted it. Carlotta's knowledge of traditional dishes was a rich broth of inheritance, and it would take more than a few experiments to capture it, but it would still be fascinating.

They left her to settle in, and a moment later there was a tap at the French doors.

'The children and I are going for a swim. Want to join us?'

She was so tempted. It was still warm here, much warmer than in England, although she knew the temperature would drop once it was dark. The water in the pool would be warm and inviting, though, and it would be fun playing with the children, but she felt a shiver of danger, and not just from him.

'I don't think so. I'm a bit tired. I might rest for a little while.'

He nodded, smiled briefly and walked away, and she closed the door and shut the curtains, just to make the point.

The children were delightful, but they weren't why she was here, and neither was he. And the more often she reminded herself of that, the better, because she was in serious danger of forgetting.

She didn't have time to think about it.

The harvest season was in full swing, and from first thing the following morning, she was busy. Carlotta still tried to do too much, but she just smiled and told her she was allowed to give orders and that was all, and after the first two days she seemed happy to do that.

She even started taking a siesta in the middle of the day, which gave Lydia time to make a lot of the preparations for the evening without prodding Carlotta's conscience.

And every evening, she dished up the food to the workers and joined them for their meal.

They seemed pleased to see her, and there was a bit of flirting and whistling and nudging, but she could deal with that. And then Massimo appeared at her side, and she heard a ripple of laughter and someone said something she'd heard a few times before when he was about. She'd also heard him say it to Francesca on occasions.

'What does *bella ragazza* mean?' she asked in a quiet moment as they were finishing their food, and he gave a slightly embarrassed laugh.

'Beautiful girl.'

She studied his face closely, unconvinced. 'Are you sure? Because they only say it when you're near me.'

He pulled a face. 'OK. It's usually used for a girlfriend.'

'They think I'm your *girlfriend*?' she squeaked, and he cleared his throat and pushed the food around his plate.

'Ignore them. They're just teasing us.'

Were they? Or could they see the pull between them? Because ignore it as hard as she liked, it wasn't going away, and it was getting stronger with every day that passed.

A few days later, while she was taking a breather out on the terrace before lunch, Isabelle appeared. She was pushing a pram, and she had a little girl in tow.

'Lydia, hi. I was hoping to find you. Mind if we join you?'

She stood up, pleased to see her again, and hugged her. 'Of course I don't mind. Congratulations! May I see?'

'Sure.'

She peered into the pram, and sighed. 'Oh, he's gorgeous. So, so gorgeous! All that dark hair!'

'Oh, yes, he's his daddy's boy. Sometimes I wonder where my genes went in all of this.' She laughed, and Lydia smiled and reached out to touch the sleeping baby's outstretched hand.

It clenched reflexively, closing on her fingertip, and she gave a soft sigh and swallowed hard.

He looked just like the picture of Antonino with his mother in the photo frame in the kitchen. Strong genes, indeed, she thought, and felt a sudden, shocking pang low down in her abdomen, a need so strong it was almost visceral.

She eased her finger away and straightened up. 'Can I get you a drink? And what about your little girl?'

'Annamaria, do you want a drink, darling?'

'Juice!'

'Please.'

'P'ees.'

'Good girl. I'd love a coffee, if you've got time? And any-thing juice-related with a big slosh of water would be great. We've got a feeder cup.'

They went into the kitchen, and she found some biscuits and took them out into the sun again with the drinks, and sat on the terrace under the pergola, shaded by the jasmine.

'Are you completely better now, after your fall?' Isabelle asked her, and she laughed and brushed it aside.

'I'm fine. My ankle was the worst thing, really, but it's much better now. It still twinges if I'm careless, but it's OK. How about you? Heavens, you've had a baby, that's much worse!'

Isabelle laughed and shook her head. 'No. It was harder than when Annamaria was born, but really very straightfor-ward, and you know Luca's an obstetrician?'

'Yes, I think so. I believe Massimo mentioned it. I know he's a doctor, he met us at the hospital when I had the fall and translated everything for me. So did he deliver him? What's he called, by the way?'

'Maximus—Max for short, after his uncle. Maximus and Massimo both mean the greatest, and my little Max was huge, so he really earned it. And yes, Luca did help deliver him, but at home with a midwife. Not like last time. He nearly missed Annamaria's birth, and I was at home on my own, so this time he kept a very close eye on me!'

'I'll bet. Wow. You're very brave having them at home.'

'No, I just have confidence in the process. I'm a midwife.'

'Is that how you met?'

She laughed. 'No. We met in Florence, in a café. We ended

up together by a fluke, really.' She tipped her head on one side. 'So what's the story with you and Massimo?'

She felt herself colour and pretended to rearrange the biscuits. 'Oh, nothing, really. There is no story. He gave me a lift, I had an accident, he rescued me, and now I'm doing Carlotta's job so she doesn't kill herself.'

Isabelle didn't look convinced, but there was no way Lydia was going into details about her ridiculous crush or their one-night stand! But Luca's wife wasn't so easily put off. She let the subject drop for a moment, but only long enough to lift the now-crying baby from the pram and cradle him in her arms as she fed him.

Spellbound, Lydia watched the baby's tiny rosebud mouth fasten on his mother's nipple, saw the look of utter contentment on Isabelle's face, and felt a well of longing fill her chest.

'He's a good man, you know. A really decent guy. He'd be worth the emotional investment, but only if you're serious. I'd hate to see him hurt.'

'He won't get hurt. We're not getting involved,' she said firmly. 'Yes, there's something there, but neither of us want it.'

Isabelle's eyes were searching, and Lydia felt as if she could see straight through her lies.

Lies? Were they?

Oh, yes. Because she did want it, even though it was crazy, even though she'd get horribly badly hurt. And she'd thought Russell had hurt her? He didn't even come close to what Massimo could do if she let him into her heart.

'He's not interested in an emotional investment,' she said, just in case there was any misunderstanding, but Isabelle just raised a brow slightly and smiled.

'No. He doesn't *think* he is, but actually he's ready to love again. He just hasn't realised it.'

'No, he isn't. We've talked about it—'

'Men don't talk. Not really. It's like pulling teeth. He's telling you what he thinks he ought to feel, not what he feels.'

She glanced up, at the same time as Lydia heard crunching on the gravel.

'Talk of the devil, here they are,' Isabelle said, smiling at her husband and his brother, and not wanting to get involved any deeper in this conversation, Lydia excused herself and went back to the kitchen.

Seconds later Massimo was in there behind her. 'I've come to tell you we've almost finished. The last of the vines are being stripped now and everyone's having the afternoon off.'

'So no lunch?'

He raised an eyebrow. 'I don't think you'll get away with that, but no evening meal, certainly. Not today. And tomorrow we're moving on to the chestnut woods. So tonight I'm taking you out for dinner, to thank you.'

'You don't need to do that. You're paying for my sister's wedding. That's thanks enough.'

He brushed it aside with a flick of his hand, and smiled. 'Humour me. I want to take you out to dinner. There's a place we eat from time to time—fantastic food, Toscana on a fork. The chef is Carlotta's great-nephew. I think you'll find it interesting. Our table's booked for eight.'

'What if I want an early night?'

'Do you?'

She gave in and smiled. 'No, not really. It sounds amazing. What's the dress code?'

'Clean. Nothing more. It's where the locals eat.'

'Your mother's a local,' she said drily, and he chuckled.

'My mother always dresses for the occasion. I'll wear jeans and a jacket, no tie. Does that help?'

She smiled. 'It does. Thank you. Help yourselves to coffee, I need to get on with lunch.'

* * *

Jeans and a jacket, no tie.

So what did that mean for her? Jeans? Best jeans with beaded embroidery on the back pockets and a pretty top?

Black trousers and a slinky top with a cardi over it?

A dress? How about a long skirt?

Clean. That was his first stipulation, so she decided to go with what was comfortable. And by eight, it would be cool, and they'd be coming back at about eleven, so definitely cooler.

Or maybe…

She'd just put the finishing touches to her makeup, not too much, just enough to make her feel she'd made the effort, when there was a tap on her door.

'Lydia? I'm ready to go when you are.'

She opened the door and scanned him. Jeans—good jeans, expensive jeans, with expensive Italian leather loafers and a handmade shirt, the leather jacket flung casually over his shoulder hanging from one finger.

He looked good enough to eat, and way up the scale of clean, so she was glad she'd changed her mind at the last minute and gone for her one decent dress. It wasn't expensive, but it hung like a dream to the asymmetric hem and made her feel amazing, and from the way he was scanning her, he wasn't disappointed.

'Will I do?' she asked, twirling slowly, and he said nothing for a second and then gave a soft huff of laughter.

'Oh, yes. I think so.'

His eyes were still trailing over her, lingering on the soft swell of her breasts, the curve of her hip, the hint of a thigh—

He pulled himself together and jerked his eyes back up to meet hers. 'You look lovely,' he said, trying not to embarrass himself or her. 'Are you ready to go?'

'I just need a wrap for later.' She picked up a pretty pashmina the same colour as her eyes, and her bag, and shut the door behind her. 'Right, then. Let's go get Toscana on a fork!'

It was a simple little building on one side of a square in the nearby town.

From the outside it looked utterly unpretentious, and it was no different inside. Scrubbed tables, plain wooden chairs, simple décor. But the smell was amazing, and the place was packed.

'Massimo, *ciao!*'

He shook hands with a couple on the way in, introduced her as a friend from England, and ushered her past them to the table he'd reserved by the window.

'Is it always this busy?'

His lips twitched in a smile. 'No. Sometimes it's full.'

She looked around and laughed. 'And these are all locals?'

'Mostly. Some will be tourists, people who've bothered to ask where they should eat.'

She looked around again. 'Is there a menu?'

'No. He writes it on a board—it's up there. Tonight it's a casserole of wild boar with plums in a red wine reduction.'

'And that's it?'

'No. He cooks a few things every night—you can choose from the board, but the first thing up is always his dish of the day, and it's always worth having.'

She nodded. 'Sounds great.'

He ordered a half-carafe of house wine to go with it— again, the wine was always chosen to go with the meal and so was the one to go for, he explained—and then they settled back to wait.

'So—are you pleased with the harvest?' she asked to fill the silence, and he nodded.

'*Si.* The grapes have been exceptional this year, it should be an excellent vintage. We need that. Last year was not so good, but the olives were better, so we made up for it.'

'And how are the olives this year?'

'Good so far. It depends on the weather. We need a long, mild autumn to let them swell and ripen before the first frosts. We need to harvest early enough to get the sharp tang from the olives, but not so early that it's bitter, or so late that it's sweet and just like any other olive oil.'

She smiled. 'That's farming for you. Juggling the weather all the time.'

'*Si*. It can be a disaster or a triumph, and you never know. We're big enough to weather it, so we're fortunate.'

'We're not. We had a dreadful year about three years ago, and I thought we'd go under, but then the next year we had bumper crops. It's living on a knife edge that's so hard.'

'Always. Always the knife edge.'

Her eyes met his, and the smile that was hovering there was driven out by an intensity that stole her breath away. 'You look beautiful tonight, *cara*,' he said softly, reaching out to touch her hand where it lay on the table top beside her glass.

She withdrew it, met his eyes again warily. 'I thought we weren't going to do this?'

'We're not doing anything. It was a simple compliment. I would say the same to my sister.'

'No, you wouldn't. Not like that.' She picked up her glass of water and drained the last inch, her mouth suddenly dry. 'At least, I hope not.'

His mouth flicked up briefly at the corners. 'Perhaps not quite like that.'

He leant back as the waiter appeared, setting down bread and olive oil and balsamic vinegar, and she tore off a piece of bread and dunked it, then frowned thoughtfully as the taste exploded on her tongue. 'Is this yours?'

He smiled. 'Yes. And the *balsamico* is from my cousin.'

'And the wild boar?'

'I have no idea. If it's from our estate, I don't know about it. The hunting season doesn't start until November.'

She smiled, and the tension eased a little, but it was still there, simmering under the surface, the compliment hovering at the fringes of her consciousness the whole evening. It didn't spoil the meal. Rather, it heightened the sensations of taste and smell and texture, as if somehow his words had brought her alive again and set her free.

'This casserole is amazing,' she said after the first mouthful. 'I want the recipe.'

He laughed at that. 'He won't give it to you. Women offer to sleep with him, but he never reveals his secrets.'

'Does he sleep with them anyway?'

He chuckled again. 'I doubt it. His wife would skin him alive.'

'Good for her. She needs to keep him. He's a treasure. And I've never been that desperate for a recipe.'

'I'm glad to hear it.' He was. He didn't even want to think about her sleeping with anybody else, even if she wasn't sleeping with him. And she wasn't.

She really, really wasn't. He wasn't going to do that again, it was emotional suicide. It had taken him over a week before he could sleep without waking aroused and frustrated in a tangle of sheets, aching for her.

He returned his attention to the casserole, mopping up the last of the sauce with a piece of bread until finally the plate was clean and he had no choice but to sit back and look up and meet her eyes.

'That was amazing,' she said. 'Thank you so much.'

'Dessert?'

She laughed a little weakly. 'I couldn't fit it in. Coffee, though—I could manage coffee.'

He ordered coffee, and they lingered over it, almost as if

they daren't leave the safety of the little *trattoria* for fear of what they might do. But then they ran out of words, out of stalling tactics, and their eyes met and held.

'Shall we go?'

She nodded, getting to her feet even though she knew what was going to happen, knew how dangerous it was to her to leave with him and go back to her room—because they would end up there, she was sure of it, just as they had before, and all their good intentions would fall at the first hurdle...

CHAPTER EIGHT

THEY didn't speak on the way back to the *palazzo*.

She sat beside him, her heart in her mouth, the air between them so thick with tension she could scarcely breathe. They didn't touch. All the way to her bedroom door, there was a space between them, as if they realised that the slightest contact would be all it took to send them up in flames.

Even when he shut the door behind them, they still hesitated, their eyes locked. And then he closed his eyes and murmured something in Italian. It could have been a prayer, or a curse, or just a 'what the hell am I doing?'

She could understand that. She was doing it herself, but she was beyond altering the course of events. She'd been beyond it, she realised, the moment he'd walked into the tack room at home and smiled at her.

He opened his eyes again, and there was resignation in them, and a longing that made her want to weep. He lifted his hand and touched her cheek, just lightly, but it was enough.

She turned her face into his hand, pressing her lips to his palm, and with a ragged groan he reeled her in, his mouth finding hers in a kiss that should have felt savage but was oddly tender for all its desperation.

His jacket hit the floor, then his shirt, stripped off over his head, and he spun her round, searching for the zip on her dress and following its progress with his lips, scorching a trail of fire down her spine. It fell away, and he unclipped her bra and turned her back to face him, easing it away and sighing softly as he lowered his head to her breasts.

She felt the rasp of his stubble against the sensitised skin, the heat of his mouth closing over one nipple, then the cold as he blew lightly against the dampened flesh.

She clung to his shoulders, her legs buckling, and he scooped her up and dropped her in the middle of the bed, stripping off the rest of his clothes before coming down beside her, skin to skin, heart to heart.

There was no foreplay. She would have died if he'd made her wait another second for him. Incoherent with need, she reached for him, and he was there, his eyes locking with hers as he claimed her with one long, slow thrust.

His head fell against hers, his eyes fluttering closed, a deep groan echoing in her ear. Her hands were on him, sliding down his back, feeling the powerful muscles bunching with restraint, the taut buttocks, the solid thighs bracing him as he thrust into her, his restraint gone now, the desperation overwhelming them, driving them both over the edge into frenzy.

She heard a muffled groan, felt his lips against her throat, his skin like hot, wet silk under her hands as his hard body shuddered against hers. For a long time he didn't move, but then, his chest heaving, he lifted his head to stare down into her eyes.

'Oh, *cara*,' he murmured roughly, and then gathering her against his heart he rolled to his side and collapsed against the pillows, and they lay there, limbs entangled, her head on his chest, and waited for the shockwaves to die away.

'I thought we weren't going to do that.'

He glanced down at her, and his eyes were filled with regret and despair. 'It looks like we were both wrong.'

His eyes closed, as if he couldn't bear to look at her, and easing away from her embrace he rolled away and sat up on the edge of the bed, elbows braced on his knees, dropping his head into his hands for a moment. Then he raked his fingers through his hair and stood up, pulling on his clothes.

'I have to check the children,' he said gruffly.

'We need to talk.'

'Yes, but not now. Please, *cara*. Not now.'

He couldn't talk to her now. He had to get out of there, before he did something stupid like make love to her again.

Make love? Who was he kidding? He'd slaked himself on her, with no finesse, no delicacy, no patience. And he'd promised her—promised himself, but promised *her*—that this wouldn't happen again.

Shaking his head in disgust, he pushed his feet into his shoes, slung his jacket over his shoulder and then steeled himself to look at her.

She was still lying there, curled on her side on top of the tangled bedding, her eyes wide with hurt and confusion.

'Massimo?'

'Later. Tomorrow, perhaps. I have to go. If Antonino wakes—'

She nodded, her eyes closing softly as she bit her lip. Holding back the tears?

He was despicable. All he ever did was make this woman cry.

He let himself out without another word, and went through to his part of the house, up the stairs to the children to check that they were all in bed and sleeping peacefully.

They were. Antonino had kicked off the covers, and he eased them back over his son and dropped a kiss lightly on his forehead. He mumbled in his sleep and rolled over, and he went out, leaving the door open, and checked the girls.

They were both asleep, Francesca's door closed, Lavinia's open and her nightlight on.

He closed the landing door that led to his parents' quarters, as he always did when he was in the house, and then he made his way back down to the kitchen and poured himself a glass of wine.

Why? Why on earth had he been so stupid? After all his lectures to himself, how could he have been so foolish, so weak, so self-centred?

He'd have to talk to her, he realised, but he had no idea what he would say. He'd promised her—promised! And yet again he'd failed.

He propped his elbows on the table and rested his face in his hands. Of all the idiotic things—

'Massimo?'

Her voice stroked him like a lover's touch, and he lifted his head and met her eyes.

'What are you doing here?' he asked, his voice rough.

'I came to get a drink,' she said uncertainly.

He shrugged. 'Go ahead, get it.'

She stayed there, her eyes searching his face. 'Oh, Massimo, don't beat yourself up. We were deluded if we thought this wouldn't happen. It was so obvious it was going to and I can't believe we didn't realise. What we need to work out is what happens now.'

He gave a short, despairing laugh and pushed back his chair. 'Nothing, but I have no idea how to achieve that. All I know that whenever I'm with you, I want you, and I can't just have what I want. I'm not a tiny child, I understand the word no, I just can't seem to use it to myself. Wine?'

She shook her head. 'Tea. I'll make it.'

He watched her as she took out a mug from the cupboard, put a teabag in it, poured on boiling water, her movements automatic. She was wearing a silky, figure-hugging dressing gown belted round her waist, and he'd bet his life she had those tiny little pyjamas on underneath.

'Just tell me this,' she said at last, turning to face him. 'Is there any reason why we can't have an affair? Just—discreetly?'

'Here? In this house? Are you crazy? I have children here and they have enough to contend with without waking in the night from a bad dream and finding I'm not here because I'm doing something stupid and irresponsible for my own gratification.'

She sat down opposite him, cradling the tea in her hands and ignoring his stream of self-hatred. 'So what do you normally do?'

Normally? *Normally?* he thought.

'Normally, I don't have affairs,' he said flatly. 'I suppose, if I did, it would be elsewhere.' He shrugged. 'Arranged meetings—afternoon liaisons when the children are at school, lunchtimes, coffee.'

'And does it work?'

He laughed a little desperately. 'I have no idea. I've never tried.'

She stared at him in astonishment. 'What? In five years, you've never had an affair?'

'Not what you could call an affair, no. I've had the odd liaison, but nothing you could in any way call a relationship.' He sighed shortly, swirled his wine, put it down again.

'You have to see it from my point of view. I have obligations, responsibilities. I would have to be very, very circumspect in any relationship with a woman.'

'Because of the children.'

'Mostly, but because of all sorts of things. Because of my duties and responsibilities, the position I hold within the family, the business—any woman I was to become involved with would have to meet a very stringent set of criteria.'

'Not money-grabbing, not lying, not cheating, not look-ing for a meal ticket or an easy family or status in the com-munity.'

'Exactly. And it's more trouble than it's worth. I don't need it. I can live without the hassle. But it's more than that. If I make a mistake, many people could suffer. And besides, I don't have the time to invest in a relationship, not to do it justice. And nor do you, not if you're going to reinvent your-self and relaunch your career.'

He'd be worth the emotional investment, but only if you're serious.

Oh, Isabelle, you're so right, she thought. But was she se-rious? Serious enough? Could she afford to dedicate the emo-tional energy needed, to a man who was so clearly focused on his family life and business that women weren't considered necessary?

If she felt she stood the slightest chance, then yes, she re-alised, she could be very, very serious indeed about this man. But he wasn't ever going to be serious about her. Not serious enough to let her into all parts of his life, and there was no way she'd pass his stringent criteria test.

No job, for a start. No independent wealth—no wealth of any sort. And besides, he was right, she needed to get her ca-reer back on track. It had been going so well…

'So what happens now? We can't have an affair here, be-cause of the children, and yet we can't seem to stick to that. So what do we do? Because doing nothing doesn't seem to work for us, Massimo. We need a plan.'

He gave a wry laugh and met her eyes again, his deadly serious. 'I have no idea, *cara.* I just know I can't be around you.'

'So we avoid each other?'

'We're both busy. It shouldn't be so hard.'

They were busy, he was right, but she felt a pang of loss even though she knew it made sense.

'OK. I'll keep out of your way if you keep out of mine.'

He inclined his head, then looked up as she got to her feet.

'You haven't finished your tea.'

'I'll take it with me,' she said, and left him sitting there wondering why he felt as if he'd just lost the most precious thing in the world, and yet didn't quite know what it was.

Nice theory, she thought later, when her emotions had returned to a more even keel. It just didn't have a hope of working in practice.

How could they possibly avoid each other in such an intimate setting?

Answer—they couldn't. He was in and out of the kitchen all the time with the children, and she was in and out of his workspace twice a day at least with food for the team of workers.

They were gathering chestnuts this week, in the *castagneti*, the chestnut woods on the higher slopes at the southern end of the estate. Carlotta told her all about it, showed her the book of chestnut recipes she'd gathered, many handed down from her mother or her grandmother, and she wanted to experiment.

So she asked Massimo one lunchtime if she could have some for cooking.

'Sure,' he said briskly. 'Help yourself. Someone will give you a basket.'

She shouldn't have been hurt. It was silly. She knew why he was doing it, why he hadn't met her eyes for more than a fleeting second, because in that fleeting second she'd seen something in his eyes that she recognised.

A curious mixture of pain and longing, held firmly in check.

She knew all about that.

She gathered her own chestnuts, joining the workforce and taking good-natured and teasing advice, most of which she didn't understand, because her Italian lessons with Francesca hadn't got that far yet—and in any case, she was very conscious of not getting too close to his children, for fear of them forming an attachment to her that would only hurt them when she went home again, so she hadn't encouraged it.

But she understood the gist. Sign language was pretty universal, and she learned how to split open the cases without hurting her fingers and remove the chestnuts—huge chestnuts, *marrone*, apparently—and that night after she'd given them all their evening meal, she went into the kitchen to experiment.

And he was there, sitting at the kitchen table with a laptop and a glass of wine.

'Oh,' she said, and stood there stupidly for a moment.

'Problem?'

'I was going to try cooking some of the chestnuts.'

His eyes met hers, and he shut the laptop and stood up. 'It's fine. I'll get out of your way.'

She looked guarded, he thought, her sunny smile and open friendliness wiped away by his lack of control and this overwhelming need that stalked him hour by hour. It saddened him. Greatly.

'You don't have to go.'

'I do,' he said wearily. 'I can't be around you, *cara*. It's too difficult. I thought I could do this, but I can't. The only way is to keep my distance.'

'But you can't. We're falling over each other all the time.'

'There's no choice.'

There was, she thought. They could just go with the flow, make sure they were discreet, keep it under control, but he didn't seem to think they could do that successfully, and he'd left the kitchen anyway.

She sat down at the table, in the same chair, feeling the warmth from his body lingering in the wood, and opened Carlotta's recipe book. Pointless. It was in Italian, and she didn't understand a word.

Frustration getting the better of her, she dropped her head into her hands and growled softly.

'Lydia, don't.'

'Don't what? I thought you'd gone,' she said, lifting her head.

'I had.' He sat down opposite her and took her hand in his, the contact curiously disturbing and yet soothing all at once.

'This is driving me crazy,' he admitted softly.

'Me, too. There must be another way. We can't avoid each other successfully, so why don't we just work alongside each other and take what comes? We know it's not long-term, we know you're not looking for commitment and I'm not ready to risk it again, and I have to go back and try and relaunch my career in some direction.'

He let go of her hand and sat back. 'Any ideas for that?' he said, not running away again as she'd expected, but staying to have a sensible conversation, and she let herself relax and began to talk, outlining her plans, such as they were.

'I've been thinking more and more about outside catering, using produce from my parents' farm. There are plenty of people with money living in the nearby villages, lots of second homes with people coming up for the weekend and bringing friends. I'm sure there would be openings, I just have to be there to find them.'

'It could be a bit seasonal.'

'Probably. Easter, summer and winter—well, Christmas and New Year, mostly. There's always lots of demand around

Christmas, and I need to be back by then. Will the olive harvest be over?'

'Almost certainly. If it's not, we can manage if you need to return.' He stood up and put the kettle on. 'I was thinking we should invite your sister and her fiancé over to meet Anita so she can start the ball rolling.'

'Anita?'

'*Si*. They'll need a wedding planner.'

'They can't afford a wedding planner!'

'It's part of the package. I'm not planning it, I simply don't have the time or the expertise, and Jen can't plan a wedding in a strange place from a distance of two thousand kilometres, so we need Anita.'

'I could do it. I'm here.'

'But do you have the necessary local contacts? No. And besides, you're already busy.'

'Can I do the catering?'

He smiled tolerantly. 'Really? Wouldn't you rather enjoy your sister's wedding?'

'No. I'd rather cut down the cost of it to you. I feel guilty enough—'

'Don't feel guilty.'

'But I do. I know quite well what cooks get paid, and it doesn't stack up to the cost of a wedding in just three months!'

He smiled again. 'We pay our staff well.'

She snorted rudely, and found a mug of tea put down in front of her.

'Don't argue with me, *cara*,' he said quietly. 'Just ask your sister when she could come over, and arrange the flights and check that Anita is free to see them.'

'Only if you'll let me do the catering.'

He rolled his eyes and laughed softly. 'OK, you can do the catering, but Anita will give you menu options.'

'No. I want to do the menus.'

'Why are you so stubborn?'

'Because it's my job!'

'To be stubborn?'

'To plan menus. And don't be obtuse.'

His mouth twitched and he sat down opposite her again, swirling his wine in the glass. 'I thought you were going to cook chestnuts?'

'I can't read the recipe book. My Italian is extremely limited so it's a non-starter.'

He took it from her, opened it and frowned. 'Ah. Well, some of it is in a local dialect anyway.'

'Can you translate?'

'Of course. But you'd need to know more than just classic Italian to understand it. Which recipe did you want to try?'

She raised an eyebrow. 'Well, how do I know? I don't know what they are.'

'I'll read them to you.'

'You know what? I'll do it in the morning, with Carlotta. She'll be able to tell me which are her favourites.'

'I can tell you that. She feeds them to us regularly. She does an amazing mousse for dessert, and stuffing for roast boar which is incredible. You should get her to teach you those if nothing else. Anyway, tomorrow won't work. There's a fair in the town.'

'Carlotta said there was a day off, but nobody told me why.'

'To celebrate the end of *La Vendemmia*. They hold one every year. Then in a few weeks there's the chestnut fair, and then after *La Raccolta*, the olive harvest, there's another one. It's a sort of harvest festival gone mad. You ought to go tomorrow, it's a good day out.'

'Will you be there?'

He nodded. 'All of us will be there.'

'I thought we were avoiding each other?'

He didn't smile, as she'd expected. Instead he frowned,

his eyes troubled. 'We are. I'll be with my children. Roberto and Carlotta will be going. I'm sure they'll give you a lift.'

And then, as if she'd reminded him of their unsatisfactory arrangement, he stood up. 'I'm going to do some work. I'll see you tomorrow.'

She did see him, but only because she kept falling over him.

Why was it, she thought, that if you lost someone in a crowd of that size you'd never be able to find them again, and yet every time she turned round, he was there?

Sometimes he didn't see her. Equally, probably, there were times when she didn't see him. But there were times when their eyes met, and held. And then he'd turn away.

Well, this time she turned away first, and made her way through the crowd in the opposite direction.

And bumped into Anita.

'Lydia! I was hoping I'd see you. Come, let's find a quiet corner for a coffee and a chat. We have a wedding to plan!'

She looked around at the jostling crowd and laughed. 'A quiet corner?'

'There must be one. Come, I know a café bar on a side street. We'll go there.'

They had to sit outside, but the sunshine was lovely and it was relatively quiet away from the hubbub and festival atmosphere of the colourful event.

'So—this wedding. Massimo tells me your sister's coming over soon to talk about it. Do you know what she wants?'

Lydia shrugged, still uncomfortable about him spending money on Anita's services. 'The hotel was offering a fairly basic package,' she began, and Anita gave a soft laugh.

'I know the hotel. It would have been basic, and they would have talked it up to add in all sorts of things you don't really need.'

'Well, they wouldn't, because she hasn't got any money, which is why I'm working here now.'

Anita raised an eyebrow slightly. 'Is that the only reason?' she asked softly. 'Because I know these Valtieri men. They're notoriously addictive.'

Poor Anita. Lydia could see the ache in her eyes, knew that she could understand. Maybe, for that reason, she let down her guard.

'No. It's not the only reason,' she admitted quietly. 'Maybe, subconsciously, it gave me an excuse to spend time with him, but trust me, it's not going to come to anything.'

'Don't be too sure. He's lonely, and he's a good man. He can be a bit of a recluse—he shuts himself away and works rather than deal with his emotions, but he's not alone in that. It's a family habit, I'm afraid.'

She shook her head. 'I *am* sure nothing will come of it. We've talked about it,' she said, echoing her conversation with Isabelle and wondering if both women could be wrong or if it was just that they were fond of him and wanted him to be happy.

'He needs someone like you,' Anita said, 'someone honest and straightforward who isn't afraid of hard work and under-stands the pressures and demands of an agricultural lifestyle. He said your family are lovely, and he felt at home there with them. He said they were refreshingly unpretentious.'

She laughed at that. 'We've got nothing to be pretentious about,' she pointed out, but Anita just smiled.

'You have to understand where he's coming from. He has women after him all the time. He's a very, very good catch, and Gio is worried that some money-seeking little tart will get her claws into him.'

'Not a chance. He's much too wary for that, believe me. He has strict criteria. Anyway, I thought we were talking about the wedding?'

Anita smiled wryly and let it go, but Lydia had a feeling that the subject was by no means closed...

'What are you doing?'

A pair of feet appeared in her line of sight, slender feet clad in beautiful, soft leather pumps. She straightened up on her knees and looked up at his mother, standing above her on the beautiful frescoed staircase.

'I'm helping Carlotta.'

'It's not your job to clean. She has a maid for that.'

'But the maid's sick, so I thought I'd help her.'

Elisa frowned. 'I didn't know that. Why didn't Carlotta tell me?'

'Because she doesn't?' she suggested gently. 'She just gets on with it.'

'And so do you,' his mother said softly, coming down to her level. 'Dear girl, you shouldn't be doing this. It's not part of your job.'

'I don't have a job, Signora Valtieri. I have a bargain with your son. I help out, my sister gets her wedding, which is incredibly generous, so if there's some way I can help, I just do it.'

'You do, don't you, without any fuss? You are a quite remarkable girl. It's a shame you have to leave.'

'I don't think he thinks so.'

'My son doesn't know what's good for him.'

'And you do?'

'Yes, I do, and I believe you could be.'

She stared at Elisa, stunned. 'But—I'm just a chef. A nobody.'

'No, you are not a nobody, Lydia, and we're just farmers like your people.'

'No.' She laughed at that and swept an arm around her to underline her point. 'No, you're not just farmers, *signora*. My family are just farmers. You own half of Tuscany and a *palazzo*, with incredibly valuable frescoes on the walls painted by Old Masters. There is a monumental difference.'

'I think not—and please stop calling me *signora*. My name, as you well know, is Elisa. Come. Let's go and get some coffee and have a chat.'

She shook her head. 'I can't. I have work to do—lunch to prepare for everyone in a minute. I was just giving the stairs a quick sweep.'

'So stop now, and come, just for a minute. Please? I want to ask you something.'

It was a request, but from his mother it was something on the lines of an invitation to Buckingham Palace. You didn't argue. You just went.

So she went, leaving the ornate and exquisitely painted staircase hall and following her into the smaller kitchen which served their wing of the house.

'How do you take your coffee? Would you like a cappuccino?'

'That would be lovely. Thank you.'

Bone china cups, she thought, and a plate with little Amaretti biscuits. Whatever this was about, it was not going to be a quick anything, she realised.

'So,' Elisa said, setting the tray down at a low table between two beautiful sofas in the formal *salon* overlooking the terrace. 'I have a favour to ask you. My son tells me you're contemplating starting a catering business. I would like to commission you.'

Lydia felt her jaw drop. 'Commission?' she echoed faintly. 'For what?'

'I'm having a meeting of my book group. We get together every month over dinner and discuss a book we've read, and this time it's my turn. I would like you to provide the meal for us. There will be twenty people, and we will need five courses.'

She felt her jaw sag again. 'When?'

'Wednesday next week. The chestnuts should be largely harvested by then, and the olive harvest won't have started yet. So—will you do it?'

'Is there a budget?'

Elisa shrugged. 'Whatever it takes to do the job.'

Was it a test? To see if she was good enough? Or a way to make her feel valued and important enough to be a contender for her son? Or was it simply that she needed a meal provided and Carlotta was too unwell?

It didn't matter. Whatever the reason, she couldn't refuse. She looked into Elisa's eyes.

'Yes. Yes, I'll do it,' she said. 'Just so long as you'll give me a reference.'

Elisa put her cup down with a satisfied smile. 'Of course.'

CHAPTER NINE

THE book club dinner seemed to be going well.

She was using her usual kitchen—the room which historically had always been the main kitchen in the house, although
it was now used by Massimo and his children, and for preparing the harvest meals.

She needed the space. Twenty people were quite hard to
cater for if the menu was extravagant, and she'd drafted in
help in the form of Maria, the girl who'd been helping her
with the meals all along.

The *antipasti* to start had been a selection of tiny canapés,
all bite-sized but labour intensive. Massimo had dropped in
and tasted them, and she'd had to send him away before he'd
eaten them all.

Then she'd served penne pasta with crayfish in a sauce
of cream with a touch of fresh chilli, followed by a delicate
lemon sorbet to cleanse the palette.

For the main, she'd sourced some wild boar with Carlotta's
help, and she'd casseroled it with fruit and lots of wine and
garlic, reducing it to a rich, dark consistency. Massimo,
yet again, had insisted on tasting it, dipping his finger in
the sauce and sucking it, and said it was at least as good as
Carlotta's great-nephew's. Carlotta agreed, and asked her for
the recipe, which amazed her.

She'd served it on a chestnut, apple and sweet potato mash,

with fresh green beans and fanned Chantenay carrots. And now it was time for the dessert, individual portions of perfectly set and delicate pannacotta under a spun sugar cage, with fresh autumn raspberries dusted with vanilla sugar and drizzled with dark chocolate. If that didn't impress them, nothing would, she thought with satisfaction.

She carried them through with Maria's help, set them down in front of all the guests and then left them to it. She put the coffee on to brew in Elisa's smaller kitchen, with homemade *petit fours* sitting ready on the side, and then headed back to her kitchen to start the massive clean-up operation.

But Massimo was in there, up to his wrists in suds, scrubbing pans. The dishwasher was sloshing quietly in the background, and there was no sign of Maria.

'I sent her home,' he said in answer to her question. 'It's getting late, and she's got a child.'

'I was going to pay her.'

'I've done it. Roberto's taken her home. Why don't you make us both a coffee while I finish this?'

She wasn't going to argue. Her head was aching, her feet were coming out in sympathy and she hadn't sat down for six hours. More, probably.

'Are they happy?'

She shrugged. 'They didn't say not and they seemed to eat it all, mostly.'

'Well, that's a miracle. There are some fussy women amongst them. I don't know why my mother bothers with them.'

He dried his hands and sat down opposite her, picking up his coffee. 'Well done,' he said, and the approval in his voice warmed her.

'I'll reserve judgement until I get your mother's verdict,' she said, because after all he hadn't been her client.

'Don't bother. It was the best food this house has seen in decades. You did an amazing job.'

'I loved it,' she confessed with a smile. 'It was great to do something a bit more challenging, playing with flavours and presentation and just having a bit of fun. I love it. I've always loved it.'

He nodded slowly. 'Yes, I can see that. And you're very good at it. I don't suppose there's any left?'

She laughed and went to the fridge. 'There's some of the boar casserole, and a spare pannacotta. Haven't you eaten?'

He pulled a face. 'Kid's food,' he admitted. 'My father and I took them out for pizza. There didn't seem to be a lot of room in here.'

She plated him up some of the casserole with the vegetables, put it in the microwave and reheated it, then set it down in front of him and watched him eat. It was the best part of her job, to watch people enjoying the things she'd created, and he was savouring every mouthful.

She felt a wave of sadness and regret that there was no future for them, that she wouldn't spend the rest of her life creating wonderful, warming food and watching him eat it with relish.

She'd had the girls in with her earlier in the day, and she'd let them help her make the *petit fours* from homemade marzipan. That, too, had given her pangs of regret and a curious sense of loss. Silly, really. She'd never had them, so how could she feel that she'd lost them?

And after he'd eaten so much marzipan she was afraid he'd be sick, Antonino had stood up at the sink on an upturned box and washed up the plastic mixing bowls, soaking himself and the entire area in the process and having a great time with the bubbles. Such a sweet child, and the spitting image of his father. He was going to be a good-looking man one day, but she wouldn't be there to see it.

Or watch his father grow old.

She took away his plate, and replaced it with the pannacotta. He pressed the sugar cage with his fingertip, and frowned as it shattered gently onto the plate. 'How did you make it?' he asked, fascinated. 'I've never understood.'

'Boil sugar and water until it's caramelised, then trail it over an oiled mould. It's easy.'

He laughed. 'For you. I can't even boil an egg. Without Carlotta my kids would starve.'

'No. They'd eat pizza,' she said drily, and he gave a wry grin.

'Probably.' He dug the spoon into the pannacotta and scooped up a raspberry with it, then sighed as it melted on his tongue. 'Amazing,' he mumbled, and scraped the plate clean.

Then he put the spoon down and pushed the plate away, leaning back and staring at her. 'You really are an exceptional chef. If there's any justice, you'll do well in your catering business. That was superb.'

'Thank you.' She felt his praise warm her, and somehow that was more important than anyone else's approval. She washed his plate and their coffee cups, then turned back to him, her mind moving on to the real reason she was here.

'Massimo, I need to talk to you about Jen and the wedding. They'll be here in two days, and I need to pick them up from the airport somehow.'

'I'll do it,' he offered instantly. 'My mother's preparing the guest wing for them, but she wanted to know if they needed one room or two.'

'Oh, one. Definitely. She needs help in the night sometimes. Is there a shower?'

'A wet room. That was one of the reasons for the choice. And it's got French doors out to the terrace around the other

side. Come. I'll show you. You can tell me which room would
be the best for them.'

She went, and was blown away by their guest suite. Two
bedrooms, both large, twin beds in one and a huge double in
the other, with a wet room between and French doors out onto
the terrace. And there was a small sitting room, as well, a private retreat, with a basic kitchen for making drinks and snacks.

'This will be just perfect. Give them the double room. She
wakes in the night quite often, having flashbacks. They're
worse if Andy's not beside her.'

'Poor girl.'

She nodded, still racked with guilt. She always would be,
she imagined. It would never go away, just like his guilt over
Angelina slumped over the kitchen table, unable to summon
help.

She felt his finger under her chin, tilting her face up to his
so he could look into her eyes.

'It was not your fault,' he said as if he could read her mind.

Her eyes were steady, but sad. 'Any more than Angelina's
death was your fault. Bad things happen. Guilt is just a natural human reaction. Knowing it and believing it are two different things.'

He felt his mouth tilt into a smile, but what kind of a smile
it was he couldn't imagine. It faded, as he stared into her eyes,
seeing the ache in them, the longing, the emptiness.

He needed her. Wanted her like he had never wanted anyone, but there was too much at stake to risk upsetting the status quo, for any of them.

He dropped his hand. 'What time do they arrive?' he asked,
and the tension holding them eased.

For now.

They collected Jen and Andy from Pisa airport at midday on
Friday, and they were blown away by their first view of the

palazzo. By the time they'd pulled up at the bottom of the steps, Jen's eyes were like saucers, but all Lydia could think about was how her sister would get up the steps.

She hadn't even thought about it, stupidly, and now—

'Come here, gorgeous,' Andy said, unfazed by the sight of them, and scooping Jen up, he grinned and carried her up the steps to where Roberto was waiting with the doors open.

Massimo and Lydia followed, carrying their luggage and the crutches, and as they reached the top their eyes met and held.

The memory was in her eyes, and it transfixed him. The last woman to be carried up those steps had been her in that awful wedding dress—the dress that was still hanging on the back of his office door, waiting for her to ask for it and burn it.

He should let her. Should burn it himself, instead of staring at it for hour after hour and thinking of her.

He dragged his eyes away and forced himself to concentrate on showing them to their rooms.

'I'll leave you with Lydia. If you need anything, I'll be in the office.'

And he walked away, crossing the courtyard with a firm, deliberate stride. She dragged her eyes off him and closed the door, her heart still pounding from that look they'd exchanged at the top of the steps.

Such a short time since he'd carried her up them, and yet so much had happened. Nothing obvious, nothing apparently momentous, and yet nothing would ever be quite the same as it had been before.

Starting with her sister's wedding.

'Wow—this is incredible!' Jen breathed, leaning back on Andy and staring out of the French doors at the glorious view. 'So beautiful! And the house—my God, Lydia, it's fantastic! Andy, did you see those paintings on the wall?'

Lydia gave a soft laugh. 'Those are the rough ones. There are some utterly stunning frescoes in the main part of the house, up the stairwell, for instance, and in the dining room. Absolutely beautiful. The whole place is just steeped in history.'

'And we're going to get married from here. I can't believe it.'

'Believe it.' She glanced at her watch. 'Are you hungry? There's some soup and cheese for lunch, and we'll eat properly tonight. Anita's coming over before dinner to talk to you and show you where the marquee will go and how it all works—they've had Carla's wedding and Luca's here, so they've done it all before.'

'Not Massimo's?'

She had no idea. It hadn't been mentioned. 'I don't know. Maybe not. So—lunch. Do you want a lie down for a while, or shall I bring you something over?'

'Oh, I don't want to make work for you,' Jen said, but Lydia could see she was flagging, and she shook her head.

'I don't mind. I'll bring you both something and you can take it easy for a few hours. Travelling's always exhausting.'

Anita arrived at five, and by six Gio had put in an appearance, rather as she'd expected.

He found Lydia in the kitchen, and helped himself to a glass of Prosecco from the fridge and a handful of canapés.

'Hey,' she said, slapping his wrist lightly when he went back for more. 'I didn't know you were involved in the wedding planning.'

'I'm not,' he said with a cocky grin. 'I'm just here for the food.'

And Anita, she thought, but she didn't say that. She knew he'd turn from the smiling playboy to the razor-tongued lawyer the instant she mentioned the woman's name. Instead she did a little digging on another subject.

'So, how many weddings have there been here recently?' she asked.

'Two—Carla and Luca.'

'Not Massimo?'

'No. He got married in the *duomo* and they went back to her parents' house. Why?'

She shrugged. 'I just didn't want to say anything that hit a nerve.'

'I think you hit a nerve,' he said, 'even without speaking. You unsettle him.'

Was it so obvious? Maybe only to someone who was looking for trouble.

'Relax, Gio,' she said drily. 'You don't need to panic and get out your pre-nup template. This is going nowhere.'

'Shame,' he said, pulling a face, 'you might actually be good for him,' and while she was distracted he grabbed another handful of canapés.

She took the plate away and put it on the side. 'Shame?' she asked, and he shrugged.

'He's lonely. Luca likes you, so does Isabelle. And so does our mother, which can't be bad. She's a hard one to please.'

'Not as hard as her son,' she retorted. 'And talking of Massimo, why don't you go and find him and leave me in peace to cook? You're distracting me.'

'Wouldn't want to do that. You might ruin the food, and I've come all the way from Florence for it.'

And he sauntered off, stealing another mouthful from the plate in passing.

The dinner went well, and Anita came back the following day to go through the plans in detail, after talking to Jen and Andy the night before.

'She's amazing,' Jen said later. 'She just seems to know what I want, and she's got the answers to all of my questions.'

'Good,' she said, glad they'd got on well, because hearing the questions she'd realised there was no way someone without in-depth local knowledge could have answered them.

They were getting married the first weekend in May, in the town hall, and coming back to the *palazzo* for the marquee reception. They talked food, and she asked Anita for the catering budget and drew a blank. 'Whatever you need,' she was told, and she shook her head.

'I need to know.'

'I allow between thirty and eighty euros a head for food. Do whatever you want, he won't mind. Just don't make it cheap. That would insult him.'

'What about wine?'

'Prosecco for reception drinks, estate red and white for the meal, estate vinsanto for the dessert, champagne for toasts—unless you'd rather have prosecco again?'

'Prosecco would be fine. I prefer it,' Jen said, looking slightly stunned. 'Lydia, this seems really lavish.'

'Don't worry, Jen, she's earned it,' Anita said. 'He's been working her to the bone over the harvest season, and it's not finished yet.'

It wasn't, and there was a change in the weather. Saturday night was cold and clear, and there was a hint of frost on the railings. Winter was coming, and first thing on Monday morning Roberto, not Massimo, took Jen and Andy to the airport because *la Raccolta*, the olive harvest, was about to begin.

Jen hugged her goodbye, her eyes welling. 'It's going to be amazing. I don't know how to thank you.'

'You don't need to thank me. Just go home and concentrate on getting better, and don't buy your wedding dress until I'm there. I don't want to miss that.'

'What, with your taste in wedding dresses?' Massimo said, coming up behind them with a teasing smile that threatened to double her blood pressure.

'It was five pounds!'

'You were cheated,' he said, laughing, and kissed Jen good-bye, slapping Andy on the back and wishing them a safe journey. 'I have to go—I'm needed at the plant. We have a problem with the olive press. I'll see you in May.'

She waved them off, feeling a pang of homesickness as they went, but she retreated to the kitchen where Carlotta was carving bread.

'Here we go again, then,' she said with a smile, and Carlotta smiled back and handed her the knife.

'I cut the *prosciutto*,' she said, and turned on the slicer.

He was late back that night—more problems with the *frantoio*, so Roberto told her, and Carlotta was exhausted.

Elisa and Vittorio were out for dinner, and so apart from Roberto and Carlotta, she was alone in the house with the children. And he was clearly worried for his wife.

'Go on, you go and look after her. Make her have an early night. I'll put the children to bed and look after them.'

'Are you sure?'

'Of course. They don't bite.'

He smiled gratefully and went, and she found the children in the sitting room. Antonino and Lavinia were squabbling again, and Francesca was on the point of tears.

'Who wants a story?' she asked, and they stopped fighting and looked up at her.

'Where's *Pàpa*?' Lavinia asked, looking doubtful.

'Working,' she said, because explaining what he was doing when she didn't really understand was beyond her. But they seemed to accept it, and apart from tugging his sister's hair again, even Antonino co-operated.

More or less. There was some argument about whether or not they needed a bath, but she was pretty sure no child had died from missing a single bath night, so she chivvied them into their pyjamas, supervised the teeth cleaning and ushered them into Antonino's bedroom.

It was a squeeze, but they all fitted on the bed somehow, and he handed her his favourite story book.

It was simple enough, just about, that she could fudge her way through it, but her pronunciation made them all laugh, and Francesca coached her. Then she read it again, much better this time, and gradually Antonino's eyelids began to wilt.

She sent the girls out, tucked him up and, on impulse, she kissed him goodnight.

He was already asleep by the time she reached the door, and Lavinia was in bed. Francesca, though, looked unhappy still, so after she'd settled her sister, she went into the older girl's room and gave her a hug.

She wasn't surprised when she burst into tears. She'd been on the brink of it before, and Lydia took her back downstairs and made her a hot drink and they curled up on the sofa in the sitting room next to the kitchen and talked.

'He's always working,' she said, her eyes welling again. 'He's never here, and Nino and Vinia always fight, and then Carlotta gets cross and upset because she's tired, and it's always me to stop them fighting, and—'

She broke off, her thin shoulders racked with sobs, and Lydia pulled her into her arms and rocked her, shushing her gently as she wept.

'—she's the one who bears the brunt of the loss, because when I'm not there the little ones turn to her. She has to be mother to them, and she's been so strong, but she's just a little girl herself—'

Poor, poor little thing. She was so stoic, trying to ease the burden on her beloved *pàpa*, and he was torn in half by his responsibilities. It was a no-win situation, and there was nothing she could do to change it, but maybe, just this one night, she'd made it a little easier.

She cradled Francesca in her arms until the storm of weeping had passed, and then they put on a DVD and snuggled up together to watch it.

Lydia couldn't understand it, but it didn't matter, and after a short while Francesca dropped off to sleep on Lydia's shoulder. She shifted her gently so she was lying with her head on her lap, and she stroked her hair as she settled again.

Dear, sweet child. Lydia was falling for her, she realised. Falling for them all. For the first time in her life she felt truly at home, truly needed, as if what she did really made a difference.

She sifted the soft, dark curls through her fingers and wondered what the future held for her and for her brother and sister.

She'd never know. Her time here was limited, they all knew that, and yet she'd grown to love them all so much that to leave them, never to know what became of them, how their lives panned out—it seemed unthinkable. She felt so much a part of their family, and it would be so easy to imagine living here with them, maybe adding to the family in time.

She squeezed her eyes shut and bit her lips.

No. It was never going to happen. She was going, and she had to remember that.

But not yet, she thought, a fine tendril of hair curled around her finger. Not now. For now, she'd just sit there with Francesca, and they'd wait for Massimo to return.

It was so late.

His mother would have put the children to bed, he thought, but yet again he'd missed their bedtime story, yet again he'd let them down.

The lights were on in the sitting room, and he could hear the television. Odd. He paused at the door, thinking the children must have left everything on, and he saw Lydia asleep on the sofa, Francesca sprawled across her lap.

Why Lydia? And why wasn't Francesca in bed?

He walked quietly over and looked down at them. They were both sound asleep, and Lydia was going to have a dreadful crick in her neck, but he was filthy, and if he was to carry Francesca up to bed, he needed a shower.

He backed out silently, went upstairs and showered, then threw on clean clothes and ran lightly downstairs.

'Lydia?' he murmured softly, touching her on the shoulder, and she stirred slightly and winced.

'Oh—you're home,' she whispered.

'*Si.* I'll take her.'

He eased her up into his arms, and Francesca snuggled close.

'She missed you,' Lydia said. 'The little ones were tired and naughty.'

'I'm sorry.'

'Don't be. It's not your fault.'

'Why are you here? My mother should be putting them to bed. I sent her a text.'

'They're out for dinner.'

He dropped his head back with a sigh. 'Of course. Oh, Lydia, I'm so sorry.'

'It's fine. Put her to bed.'

He did, settling her quickly, earning a sleepy smile as he kissed her goodnight. But by the time he got downstairs again, the television was off and the sitting room was in darkness.

It was over.

La Raccolta was finished, the olive oil safely in the huge lidded terracotta urns where it would mature for a while before being bottled.

The fresh olive oil, straight from the press, was the most amazing thing she'd ever tasted, and she'd used it liberally in the cooking and on *bruschetta* as an appetiser for the family's meals.

Of all the harvests, she'd found the olive harvest the most fascinating. The noise and smell in the pressing room was amazing, the huge stone wheels revolving on edge in the great stainless steel bowl of the *frantoio*, the olive press, crushing the olives to a purple paste. It was spread on circular felt discs and then stacked and pressed so that the oily juice dribbled out and ran into a vat, where it separated naturally, the bright green oil floating to the top.

Such a simple process, really, unchanged for centuries, and yet so very effective.

Everything in there had been covered in oil, the floor especially, and she knew that every time she smelt olive oil now, she'd see that room, hear the sound of the *frantoio* grinding the olives, see Massimo tossing olives in the palm of his hand, or checking the press, or laughing with one of the workers.

It would haunt her for the rest of her life, and the time had come so quickly.

She couldn't believe she was going, but she was. She'd grown to love it, not just because of him, but because of all his family, especially the children.

They were sad she was leaving, and on her last night she cooked them a special meal of their own, with a seafood risotto for their starter, and a pasta dish with chicken and pesto, followed by the dessert of frozen berries with hot white chocolate sauce that was always everyone's favourite.

'I don't want you to go,' Francesca said sadly as they finished clearing up.

Massimo, coming into the room as she said it, frowned. 'She has to go, *cara*. She has a business to run.'

'No, she doesn't. She has a job here, with us.'

Her heart squeezed. 'But I don't, sweetheart,' she said gently. 'I was only here to help Carlotta with the harvest. It's finished now. I can't just hang around and wait for next year. I have to go and cook for other people.'

'You could cook for us,' she reasoned, but Lydia shook her head.

'No. Carlotta would feel hurt. That's her job, to look after you. And your *pàpa* is right, I have to go back to my business.'

'Not go,' Lavinia said, her eyes welling. '*Pàpa, no!*' She ran to him, begging him in Italian, words she couldn't understand.

'What's she saying?' she asked, and Lavinia turned to look at her, tugging at her father and pleading, and he met her eyes reluctantly.

'She wants you to stay. She said—'

He broke off, but Francesca wouldn't let him stop.

'Tell her what Lavinia said, *Pàpa*,' she prompted, and he closed his eyes briefly and then went on.

'*Pàpa* is unhappy when aren't you're here,' he said grudgingly, translating directly as Lavinia spoke. 'Please don't go. We missed you when you went home before.' He hesitated, and she nudged him. 'It's lovely when you're here,' he went on, his bleak eyes locked with hers, 'because you make *Pàpa* laugh. He never laughs when you're not here.'

A tear slipped over and slid down her cheek, but she didn't seem to notice. Their eyes were locked, and he could see the anguish in them. He swallowed hard, his arm around Lavinia's skinny little shoulders holding her tight at his side.

Was it true? Was he unhappy when she wasn't there, unhappy enough that even the children could see it? Did he really not laugh when she wasn't there?

Maybe.

Lydia pressed her fingers to her lips, and shook her head. 'Oh, Lavinia. I'm sorry. I don't want to make your *pàpa* unhappy, or any of you, but I have to go home to my family.'

She felt little arms around her hips, and looked down to find Antonino hugging her, his face buried in her side. She laid a hand gently on his hair and stroked it, aching unbearably inside. She'd done this, spent so much time with them that she was hurting them now by leaving, and she never meant to hurt them. 'I'm sorry,' she said to him, *'mi dispiace.'* And his little arms tightened.

'Will you read us a story?' Francesca asked.

She'd be leaving for the airport before three in the morning, long before the children were up, so this was her last chance to read to them. Her last chance ever? 'Of course I will,' she said, feeling choked. She'd done it a few times since the night of the *frantoio* breakdown, and she loved it. Too much.

They were already in their pyjamas, and she ushered them up to bed, supervised the teeth cleaning as she'd done before, and then they settled down on Antonino's bed, all crowded round while she read haltingly to them in her awful, amateurish Italian.

She could get the expressions right, make it exciting—that was the easy bit. The pronunciation was harder, but it was a book they knew, so it didn't really matter.

What mattered was lying propped up against the wall, with Antonino under one arm and Lavinia under the other, and Francesca curled up by her knees leaning against the wall and watching her with wounded eyes.

She was the only one of them to remember her mother, and for a few short weeks, Lydia realised, she'd slipped into the role without thinking, unconsciously taking over some of the many little things a mother did. Things like making cupcakes, and birthday cards for Roberto. She'd stopped the two little ones fighting, and hugged them when they'd hurt themselves, and all the time she'd been playing happy families and ignoring the fact that she'd be going away soon, going back to her real life at home.

And now she had to go.

She closed the book, and the children snuggled closer, stretching out the moment.

Then Massimo's frame filled the doorway, his eyes shadowed in the dim light.

'Come on. Bedtime now. Lydia needs to pack.'

It was a tearful goodnight, for all of them, and as soon as she could she fled to her room, stifling the tears.

She didn't have to pack. She'd done it ages ago, been round all the places she might have left anything, and there was nothing to do now, nothing to distract her.

Only Lavinia's words echoing in her head.

He never laughs when you're not here.

The knock was so quiet she almost didn't hear it.

'Lydia?'

She opened the door, unable to speak, and met his tortured eyes.

And then his arms closed around her, and he held her hard against his chest while she felt the shudders run through him.

They stayed like that for an age, and then he eased back and looked down at her.

His eyes were raw with need, and she led him into the room and closed the door.

Just one last time...

CHAPTER TEN

'Is IT true?'

He turned his head and met her eyes in the soft glow of the bedside light, and his face was shuttered and remote.

'Is what true?'

'That you don't laugh when I'm not here?'

He looked away again. 'You don't want to listen to what the children say.'

'Why not, if it's true? Is it?'

He didn't answer, so she took it as a yes. It made her heart ache. If only he'd believe in them, if only he'd let her into his heart, his life, but all he would say was no.

'Talk to me,' she pleaded.

He turned his head back, his eyes unreadable.

'What is there to say?'

'You could tell me how you really feel. That would be a good start.'

He laughed, a harsh, abrupt grunt full of pain. 'I can't,' he said, his accent stronger than she'd ever heard it. 'I can't find the words, I don't have the language to do this in English.'

'Then tell me in Italian. I won't understand, but you can say it then out loud. You can tell me whatever you like, and I can't hold you to it.'

He frowned, but then he reached out and stroked her face, his fingers trembling. His mouth flickered in a sad smile, and then he started to speak, as if she'd released something inside him that had been held back for a long, long time.

She didn't understand it, but she understood the tone—the gentleness, the anguish, the pain of separation.

And then, his eyes locked with hers, he said softly, *'Ciao, mia bella ragazza. Te amo...'*

She reached out and cradled his jaw, her heart breaking. *Ciao* meant hello, but it also meant goodbye.

'It doesn't have to be goodbye,' she said softly. 'I love you, too—so much.'

He shook his head. 'No. No, *cara*, please. I can't let you love me. I can't let you stay. You'll be hurt.'

'No!'

'Yes. I won't let you.'

'Would you stop that?' she demanded, angry now. 'The first time I met you, you said I couldn't go in the plane with Nico because it wasn't safe. Now you're telling me I can't love you because I'll get hurt! Maybe I want to take the risk, Massimo? Maybe I *need* to take the risk.'

'No. You have a life waiting for you, and one day there will be some lucky man...'

'I don't want another man, I want you.'

'No! I have nothing to give you. I'm already pulled in so many ways. How can I be fair to you, or the children, or my work, my family? How can I do another relationship justice?'

'Maybe I could help you. Maybe I could make it easier. Maybe we could work together?'

'No. You love your family, you have your career. If I let you give it all up for me, what then? What happens when we've all let you into our hearts and then you leave?'

'I won't leave!'

'You don't know that. You've been here less than three months. What happens in three years, when we have another child and you decide you're unhappy and want to go? I don't have time for you, I can't give you what you need. I don't even have enough time now to sleep! Please, *cara*. Don't make it harder. You'll forget me soon.'

'No. I'll never forget you. I'll never stop loving you.'

'You will. You'll move on. You'll meet someone and marry him and have children of your own in England, close to your family, and you'll look back and wonder what you saw in this sad and lonely old man.'

'Don't be ridiculous, you're not old, and you're only sad and lonely because you won't let anybody in!'

His eyes closed, as if he couldn't bear to look at her any longer. 'I can't. The last time I let anyone into my life, she lost her own, and it was because I was too busy, too tired, too overstretched to be there for her.'

'It wasn't your fault!'

'Yes, it was! I was *here*! I was supposed to be looking after her, but I was lying in my bed asleep while she was dying.'

'She should have woken you! She should have told you she was sick. It was not your fault!'

'No? Then why do I wake every night hearing her calling me?'

He threw off the covers and sat up, his legs over the edge of the bed, his head in his hands, his whole body vibrating with tension. 'I can't do this, Lydia! Please, don't ask me to. I can't do it.'

Why do I wake every night hearing her calling me?

His words echoing in her head, her heart pounding, she knelt up behind him, her arms around him, her body pressed to his in comfort.

'It wasn't your fault,' she said gently. 'You weren't responsible, but you're holding yourself responsible, and you have to forgive yourself. It wasn't my fault Jen had her accident, but I've blamed myself, and it has taken months to accept that it wasn't my fault and to forgive myself for not stopping him.

You have to do the same. You have to accept that you weren't at fault—'

'But I was! I should have checked on her.'

'You were asleep! What time of year was it?'

'Harvest,' he admitted, his voice raw. 'The end of *La Raccolta*.'

Right at the end of the season. Now, in fact. Any time now. Her heart contracted, and she sank back down onto her feet, her hands against his back.

'You were exhausted, weren't you? Just as you're exhausted now. And she didn't want to disturb you, so she went down to the kitchen for painkillers.'

He sucked in a breath, and she knew she was right.

'She probably wasn't thinking clearly. Did she suffer from headaches?'

'Yes. All the time. They said she had a weakness in the vessels.'

'So it could have happened at any time?'

'*Si*. But it happened when I was there, and it happened slowly, and if I'd realised, if I hadn't thought she was with the baby, if I'd known...'

'If you'd been God, in fact? If you'd been able to see inside her head?'

'They could have seen inside her head. She'd talked of going to the doctor about her headaches, but we were too busy, and she'd just had the baby, and it was the harvest, and...'

'And there was just no time. Oh, Massimo. I'm so sorry, but you know it wasn't your fault. You can't blame yourself.'

'Yes, I can. I can, and I have to, because my guilt and my grief is all I have left to give her! I can't even love her any more because you've taken that from me!' he said harshly, his voice cracking.

The pain ran through her like a shockwave.

How could he tell her that he loved her, and yet cling to his guilt and grief so that he could hold onto Angelina?

He couldn't. Not if he really loved her. Unless...

'Why are you doing this to me?' she asked quietly. 'To yourself? To your children? You wear your grief and your guilt like a hair shirt to torture yourself with, but it's not just you you're torturing, you're torturing me, as well, and your children. And they don't deserve to be tortured just because you're too much of a coward to let yourself love again!'

'I am not a coward!'

'Then prove it!' she begged. 'Let yourself love again!'

He didn't answer, his shoulders rigid, unmoving, and after what felt like forever, she gave up. She'd tried, and she could do no more.

Shaking, she eased away from him and glanced at her watch.

'We have to leave in half an hour. I'm going to shower,' she said, as steadily as she could.

And she walked into the bathroom, closed the door and let the tears fall...

He didn't come into the airport building this time.

He gave her a handful of notes to pay for her excess baggage, put her luggage on the pavement at the drop-off point and then hesitated.

'I'll see you in May,' he said, his voice clipped and harsh.

His eyes were raw with pain, and she wanted to weep for him, and for herself, and for the children, but now wasn't the time.

'Yes. I'll be in touch.'

'Anita will email you. She's in charge. I'll be too busy.'

Of course he would.

'Take care of yourself,' she said softly. And going up on tiptoe, she pressed her lips to his cheek.

His arms came round her, and for the briefest moment he rested his head against hers. *'Ciao, bella,'* he said softly, so softly that she scarcely heard him, and then he was straightening up, moving back, getting into the car.

He started the engine and drove away, and she watched his tail lights until they disappeared. Then she gathered up her luggage and headed for the doors.

It was the worst winter of her life.

The weather was glorious, bright winter sunshine that seemed to bounce right off her, leaving her cold inside. She found work in the pub down the road, and she created a website and tried to promote her catering business.

It did well, better than she'd expected, but without him her life was meaningless.

Jen found her one day in mid-January, staring into space.

'Hey,' she said softly, and came and perched beside her on the back of the sofa, staring out across the valley.

'Hey yourself. How are you doing?'

'OK. We've had another email from Anita. She wants to know about food.'

She could hardly bring herself to think about food. For a while she'd thought she was pregnant she'd felt so sick, but she wasn't. The test said no, her body said no and her heart grieved for a child that never was and never would be. And still she felt sick.

'What does she want to know? I've given her menu plans.'

'Something about the carpaccio of beef?'

She sighed. 'OK. I'll contact her.'

It was nothing to do with the beef. It was about Massimo.

'He's looking awful,' Anita said. 'He hasn't smiled since you left.'

Nor have I, she thought, *but there's nothing I can do, either for him or me.*

She didn't reply to the email. Two hours later her phone rang.

'I can't help you, Anita,' she said desperately. 'He won't listen to me.'

'He won't listen to anyone—Luca, Carlotta, his mother—even Gio's on your side, amazingly, but he just says he doesn't want to talk about it. And we're all worried. We're really worried.'

'I'm sorry, I can't do any more,' she said again, choked, and hung up.

Jen found her in her room, face down on the bed sobbing her heart out, and she lay down beside her and held her, and gradually it stopped hurting and she was numb again.

Better, in a strange kind of way.

January turned into February, and then March, and finally Jen was able to walk without the crutches.

'That's amazing,' Lydia said, hugging her, her eyes filling with tears. 'I'm so glad.'

'So am I.' Jen touched her cheek gently. 'I'm all right now, Lydia. I'm going to be OK. Please stop hurting yourself about it.'

'I'm not,' she said, and realised it was true, to an extent. Oh, it would always hurt to know that she'd been part of the sequence of events that had led to Jen's accident, but she'd stopped taking the blame for it, and now she could share in the joy of Jen's recovery. If only Massimo...

'You need to buy your wedding dress, we're leaving it awfully late,' she said, changing the subject before her mind dragged her off down that route.

'I know. There's a shop in town that does them to take away, so they don't need to be ordered. Will you come with me?'

She ignored the stab of pain, and hugged her sister. 'Of course I will.'

* * *

It was bittersweet.

They all went together—Lydia, Jen and their mother and she found a dress that laced up the back, with an inner elasticated corset that was perfect for giving her some extra back support.

'Oh, that's so comfy!' she said, and then looked in the mirror and her eyes filled.

'Oh…'

Lydia grabbed her mother's hand and hung on. It was definitely The Dress, and everybody's eyes were filling now.

'Oh, darling,' her mother said, and hugged her, laughing and crying at the same time, because it might never have come to this. They could have lost her, and yet here she was, standing on her own two feet, unaided, and in her wedding dress. Their tears were well and truly earned.

After she'd done another twirl and taken the dress off, the manageress of the little wedding shop poured them another glass of Prosecco to toast Jen's choice.

As the bubbles burst in her mouth, Lydia closed her eyes and thought of him.

Sitting on the terrace outside her bedroom, sipping Prosecco and talking into the night. They'd done it more than once, before the weather had turned. Pre-dinner drinks when Jen and Andy had come to visit. Sitting in the *trattoria* waiting for their food to come, the second time they'd made love.

'Lydia?'

She opened her eyes and dredged up a smile. 'You looked stunning in it, Jen. Absolutely beautiful. Andy'll be bowled over.'

'What about you?'

'I don't need a wedding dress!' she said abruptly, and then remembered she was supposed to be Jen's bridesmaid, and suddenly it was all too much.

'Can we do this another day?' she asked desperately, and Jen, seeing something in her eyes, nodded.

'Of course we can.'

She went back on her own a few days later, and flicked through the rails while she was waiting. And there, on a mannequin in the corner, was the most beautiful dress she'd ever seen.

The softest, heaviest silk crepe de Chine, cut on the cross and hanging beautifully, it was exquisite. So soft, she thought, fingering it with longing, such a far cry from the awful thing she'd worn for the competition, and she wondered, stupidly, if she'd worn it instead, would she have fallen? And if not, would she have known what it was to love him? Maybe, if he'd seen her wearing a dress like that...

'It's a beautiful dress, isn't it? Why don't you try it on?'

'I don't need a wedding dress,' she said bluntly, dropping her hand to her side. 'I'm here for a bridesmaid's dress.'

'You could still try it on. We're quiet today, and I'd love to see it on you. You've got just the figure for it.'

How on earth had she let herself be talked into it? Because, of course, it fitted like a dream on her hourglass figure, smoothing her hips, showing off her waist, emphasising her bust.

For a moment—just a moment—she let herself imagine his face as he saw her in it. She'd seen that look before, when he'd been making love to her—

'This is silly,' she said, desperate to take it off now. 'I'm not getting married.'

Not ever...

The awful wedding dress was still hanging on the back of his door.

He stared at it numbly. It still had her blood on it, a dark brown stain on the bodice where she'd wiped her fingers after she'd touched the graze on her head.

He missed her. The ache never left him, overlying the other ache, the ache that had been there since Angelina died.

Their wedding photo was still on his desk, and he picked it up and studied it. Was Lydia right? Was her wearing a metaphorical hair shirt, punishing himself for what was really not his fault?

Rationally, he knew that, but he couldn't let it go.

Because he hadn't forgiven himself? Or because he was a coward?

It's not just you you're torturing, you're torturing me, as well, and your children. And they don't deserve to be tortured just because you're too much of a coward to let yourself love again!

Getting up from the desk, he went and found Carlotta and told her he was going out. And then he did what he should have done a long time ago.

He went to the place where she was buried, and he said goodbye, and then he went home and took off his wedding ring. There was an inscription inside. It read *'Amor vincit omnia'.*

Love conquers everything.

Could it? Not unless you gave it a chance, he thought, and pressing the ring to his lips, he nestled it in Angelina's jewellery box, with the lock of her hair, the first letter she'd ever sent him, a rose from her bouquet.

And then he put the box away, and went outside into the garden and stood at the railings, looking out over the valley below. She'll be here soon, he thought, and then I'll know.

Jen and Andy saw her off at the airport.

She put on a bright face, but in truth she was dreading this part of the wedding.

She was going over early to finalise the menu and meet the people who were going to be helping her. Carlotta's nephew, the owner of the *trattoria*, had loaned her one of his chefs and sourced the ingredients, and the waiting staff were all from local families and had worked for Anita before, but the final responsibility for the menu and the food was hers.

None of that bothered her. She was confident about the menu, confident in the ability of the chef and the waiting staff, and the food she was sure would be fine.

It was seeing Massimo that filled her with dread.

Dread, and longing.

She was thinner.

Thinner, and her face was drawn. She looked as if she'd been working too hard, and he wondered how her business was going. Maybe she'd been too successful?

He hoped not—no! That was wrong. If it was going well, if it was what she wanted, then he must let her go.

Pain stabbed through him and he sucked in a breath. For the past few weeks he'd put thoughts of failure out of his mind, but now—now, seeing her there, they all came rushing to the fore.

He walked towards her, and as if she sensed him there she turned her head and met his eyes. All the breath seemed to be sucked out of his body, and he had to tell his feet how to move.

'*Ciao, bella,*' he said softly, and her face seemed to crumple slightly.

'*Ciao,*' she said, her voice uneven, and then he hugged her, because she looked as if she'd fall down if he didn't.

'Is this everything?'

She nodded, and he took the case from her and wheeled it out of the airport to his car.

He was looking well, she thought. A little thinner, perhaps, but not as bad as she'd thought from what Anita had said. Because he was over her?

She felt a sharp stab of pain, and sucked in her breath. Maybe he'd been right. Maybe he couldn't handle it, and he'd just needed to get back onto an even keel again.

And then he came round and opened the car door for her, and she noticed his wedding ring was missing, and her heart began to thump.

Was it significant?

She didn't know, and he said nothing, just smiled at her as he got into the car and talked about what the children had been up to and how the wedding preparations were going, all the way back to the *palazzo*.

It was like coming home, she thought.

The children were thrilled to see her, especially Francesca who wrapped her arms around her and hugged her so hard she thought her ribs might break.

'Goodness, you've all grown so tall!' she said, her eyes filling. Lavinia's arms were round her waist, and Antonino was hanging on her arm and jumping up and down. It made getting up the steps a bit of a challenge, but they managed it, and Massimo just chuckled softly and carried her luggage in.

'I've put you in the same room,' he said, and she felt a shiver of dread. The last time she'd been in here, he'd broken her heart. She wasn't sure she wanted to be there again, but it felt like her room now, and it would be odd to be anywhere else.

'So, what's the plan?' she asked as he put her case down.

He smiled wryly. 'Anita's coming over. I've told her to give you time to unwind, but she said there was too much to do. Do you want a cup of tea?'

'I'd love a cup of tea,' she said fervently. 'But don't worry. I'll make it.'

He nodded. 'In that case, I'll go and get on. You know my mobile number—ring me if you need me.'

She didn't have time to need him, which was perhaps just as well. The next few days were a whirlwind, and by the time the family arrived, she was exhausted.

Anita was brilliant. She organised everything, made sure everyone knew what they were to do and kept them all calm and focused, and the day of the wedding went without a hitch.

Lydia's involvement in the food was over. She'd prepared the starters and the deserts, the cold buffet was in the refrigerated van beside the marquee, and all she had to do was dress her sister and hold her bouquet.

And catch it, apparently, when it was all over.

Jen wasn't subtle. She stood just a few feet from her, with everyone standing round cheering, and threw it straight at Lydia.

It hit her in the chest and she nearly dropped it, but then she looked up and caught Massimo's eye, and her heart began to pound slowly.

He was smiling.

Smiling? Why? Because he was glad it was all over? Or because the significance of her catching it wasn't lost on him?

She didn't know. She was too tired to care, and after Andy scooped his glowing, blushing bride up in his arms and carried her off at the end of the reception in a shower of confetti and good wishes, she took the chance and slipped quietly away.

There was so much to do—a mountain of clearing up in the kitchen in the *palazzo*, never mind all the catering equipment which had been hired in and had to be cleaned and returned.

Plates, cutlery, glasses, table linen.

'I thought I might find you in here.'

She looked up.

'There's a lot to do.'

'I know.'

He wasn't smiling. Not now. He was thoughtful. Maybe a little tense?

He took off his suit jacket and rolled up his sleeves and pitched in alongside her, and for a while they worked in silence. He changed the washing up water three times, she used a handful of tea towels, but finally the table was groaning with clean utensils.

'Better. The guests are leaving. Do you want to say goodbye?'

She smiled slightly and shook her head. 'They're not my guests. Let my parents do it. I've got enough to do.'

'I'll go and clear up outside,' he said, and she nodded. There was still a lot to do in there, and she worked until she was ready to drop.

Her feet hurt, her shoes were long gone and she wanted to lie down. The rest, she decided, would keep, and turning off the light, she headed back to her room.

She passed her parents in the colonnaded walkway around the courtyard, on their way in with Massimo's parents.

They stopped to praise the food yet again, and Elisa hugged her. 'It was wonderful. I knew it would be. You have an amazing talent.'

'I know,' her mother said. 'We're very proud of her.'

She was hugged and kissed again, and then she excused herself and finally got to her room, pausing in surprise in the doorway.

The door was open, the bedside light was on, and the bed was sprinkled with rose petals.

Rose petals?

She picked one up, lifting it to her nose and smelling the delicately heady fragrance.

Who—?

'May I come in?'

She spun round, the rose petal falling from her fingers, and he was standing there with a bottle of sparkling water and two glasses. 'I thought you might be thirsty,' he said.

'I don't know what I am,' she said. 'Too tired to know.'

He laughed softly, and she wondered—just briefly, with the small part of her brain that was still functioning—how often he'd done that since she went away.

'Lie down before you fall.'

She didn't need telling twice. She didn't bother to take the dress off. It was probably ruined anyway, and realistically when would she wear it again? She didn't go to dressy events very often. She flopped onto the bed, and he went round the other side, kicked off his shoes and settled himself beside her, propped up against the headboard.

'Here, drink this,' he said, handing her a glass, and she drained the water and handed the glass back.

'More.'

He laughed—again?—and refilled it, then leant back and sighed.

'Good wedding.'

'It was. Thank you. Without you, it wouldn't have happened.'

'It might have been at the hotel.'

'No. Nobody was giving me a lift—well, only Nico, and we both know how that might have ended.'

'Don't.' He took the empty glass from her again, put them both down and slid down the bed so he was lying flat beside her. His hand reached out, and their fingers linked and held.

'How are you, really?' he asked softly.

He wasn't talking about tonight, she realised, and decided she might as well be honest. It was the only thing she had left.

'All right, I suppose. I've missed you.'

'I've missed you, too. I didn't know I could hurt as much as that, not any more. Apparently I can.'

She rolled to her side to face him, and he did the same, his smile gone now, his eyes serious.

'Massimo,' she said, cutting to the chase, 'where's your wedding ring?'

'Ah, *cara*. So observant. I took it off. I didn't need it any more. You were right, it was time to let the past go and move on with my life.'

'Without guilt?'

His smile was sad. 'Without guilt. With regret, perhaps. The knowledge that things probably wouldn't have been very different whatever I'd done. I'd lost sight of that. And you?' he added. 'Are you moving on with your life?'

She tried to laugh, but she was too tired and too hurt to make it believable. 'No. My business is going well, but I don't care. It's all meaningless without you.'

'Oh, *bella*,' he said softly, and reached for her. 'My life is the same. The only thing that's kept me going the last few weeks has been the knowledge that I'd see you again soon. Without that I would have gone insane. I nearly did go insane.'

'I know. Anita rang me. They were all worried about you.'

He eased her up against his chest, so that her face lay against the fine silk shirt, warm from his skin, the beat of his heart echoing in her ear, slow and steady.

'Stay with me,' he said. 'I have no right to ask you, after I sent you away like that, but I can't live without you. No. That's not true. I can. I just don't want to, because without you, I don't laugh. Lavinia was right. I don't laugh because there's nothing to laugh at when you're not here. Nothing seems funny, everything is cold and colourless and futile. The days are busy but monotonous, and the nights—the nights are so lonely.'

She swallowed a sob, and lifted her hand and cradled his stubbled jaw. 'I know. I've lain awake night after night and missed you. I can fill the days, but the nights...'

'The nights are endless. Cold and lonely and endless. I've tried working, but there comes a time when I have to sleep, and then every time I close my eyes, I see you.'

'Not Angelina?'

'No. Not Angelina. I said goodbye to her. I hadn't done it. I hadn't grieved for her properly, I'd buried myself in work and I thought I was all right, but then I met you and I couldn't love you as you deserved because I wasn't free. And instead of freeing myself, I sent you away.'

'I'm sorry. It must have been hard.'

His eyes softened, and he smiled and shook his head. 'No. It was surprisingly easy. I was ready to do it—more than ready. And I'm ready to move on. I just need to know that you're ready to come with me.'

She smiled and bit her lip. 'Where are we going?'

'Wherever life takes us. It will be here, because this is who I am and where I have to be, but what we do with that life is down to us.'

He took her hand from his cheek and held it, staring intently into her eyes. 'Marry me, Lydia. You've set me free, but that freedom is no use to me without you. I love you, *bella. Te amo.* If you still love me, if you haven't come to your senses in all this time, then marry me. Please.'

'Of course I'll marry you,' she breathed, her heart overflowing. 'Oh, you foolish, silly, wonderful man, of course I'll marry you! Just try and stop me. And I'll never, never stop loving you.'

'I've still got the dress,' he told her some time later, his eyes sparkling with mischief. 'It's hanging on my office door. I thought I'd keep it, just in case you said yes.'

Did the woman in the wedding dress shop have second sight? 'I think I might treat myself to a new one,' she said, and smiled at him.

They were married in June, in the town hall where Jen and Andy had been married.

It had been a rush—she'd had to pack up all her things in England and ship them over, and they'd moved, on his parents' insistence, into the main part of the *palazzo*.

A new start, a clean slate.

It would take some getting used to, but as Massimo said, it was a family home and it should have children in it. It was where he and his brothers and sisters had been brought up, and it was family tradition for the eldest son to take over the formal rooms of the *palazzo*. And hopefully, there would be other children to fill it.

She held onto that thought. She'd liked the simplicity of the other wing, but there was much more elbow room in the central part, essential if they were to have more children, and the views were, if anything, even more stunning. And maybe one day she'd grow into the grandeur.

But until their wedding night, she was still using the room she'd always had, and it was in there that Jen and her mother helped her put on the beautiful silk dress. It seemed woefully extravagant for such a small and simple occasion, but she was wearing it for him, only for him, and when she walked out to meet him, her heart was in her mouth.

He was waiting for her in the frescoed courtyard, and his eyes stroked slowly over her. He said nothing, and for an endless moment she thought he hated it. But then he lifted his eyes to hers, and the heat in them threatened to set her on fire.

She looked stunning.

He'd thought she was beautiful in the other wedding dress, much as he'd hated it. In this, she was spectacular. It hugged her curves like a lover, and just to look at her made him ache.

She wasn't wearing a veil, and the natural curls of her fine blonde hair fell softly to her shoulders. It was the way he liked it. Everything about her was the way he liked it, and at last he found a smile.

'Mia bella ragazza,' he said softly, and held out his hand to her.

It was a beautiful, simple ceremony.

Their vows, said by both of them in both English and Italian, were from the heart, and they were witnessed by their closest family and friends. Both sets of parents, his three sisters, Jen and Andy, Luca and Isabelle, Gio, Anita, Carlotta and Roberto, and of course the children.

Francesca and Lavinia were bridesmaids, and Antonino was the ring bearer. There was a tense moment when he wobbled and the rings started to slide, but it was all right, and with a smile of encouragement for his son, Massimo took her ring from the little cushion and slid it onto her finger, his eyes locked with hers.

He loved her. When he'd lost Angelina, he'd thought he could never love again, but Lydia had shown him the way. There was always room for love, he realised, always room for another person in your heart, and his heart had made room for her. How had he ever thought it could do otherwise?

She slid the other ring onto his finger, her fingers firm and confident, and he cupped her shoulders in his hands and bent his head and kissed her.

'Te amo,' he murmured, and then his words were drowned out by the clapping and cheering of their family.

* * *

Afterwards they went for lunch to the little *trattoria* owned by Carlotta's nephew. He did them proud. They drank Prosecco and ate simple, hearty food exquisitely cooked, and when it was over, they drove back to the *palazzo*. The others were going back to Luca and Isabelle's for the rest of the day, to give them a little privacy, and Massimo intended to take full advantage of it.

He drove up to the front door, scooped her up in his arms and carried her up the steps. The last time he'd done this she'd been bloodstained and battered. This time—this time she was his wife, and he felt like the luckiest man alive.

Pausing at the top he turned, staring out over the valley spread out below them. Home, he thought, his heart filled with joy, and Lydia rested her head on his shoulder and sighed.

'It's so beautiful.'

'Not as beautiful as you. And that dress…' He nuzzled her neck, making her arch against him. 'I've been wanting to take it off you all day.'

'Don't you like it? I wasn't sure myself. I thought maybe I should have stuck to the other one,' she teased, and he laughed, the sound carrying softly on the night air.

It was a sound she'd never tire of, she thought contentedly as he turned, still smiling, and carried his bride over the threshold.

* * * * *

WEARING THE
DE ANGELIS RING

CATHY WILLIAMS

CHAPTER ONE

'You're not going to like what I'm about to say.'

The very second Stefano had called his son and told him that he needed to speak with him as a matter of urgency, Theo had dropped everything and taken the first flight over to Italy, to his father's enormous estate just outside Rome.

Stefano De Angelis was not a man given to drama, and both Theo and his brother, Daniel, had spent the past five years worrying about him. He had never really recovered from the death of his wife, their mother, Rose. The power house who had built a personal fortune from scratch had collapsed into himself, retreating to the sanctuary of his den, immune to the efforts of both his sons to pull him out of his grief. He had continued to eat, sleep, talk and walk, but his soul had departed, leaving only a physical shell behind.

What, Theo thought now, was he about to hear?

Cold fear gripped him.

'Have you asked Daniel as well?' He prowled through the huge sitting room, idly gazing through the window to the sprawling lawns, before finally taking a seat opposite his father.

'This situation does not concern your brother,' Stefano returned, his dark eyes sidestepping his son's piercing green ones.

Theo breathed a sigh of relief. If Daniel hadn't been likewise summoned, then at least a health crisis could be discounted. He had been tempted to phone his brother on the back of his father's summons, but had resisted the impulse because he knew that Daniel was in the throes of a balancing act: trying to close a major deal *and* a minor love affair at the same time.

The deal, his brother had confided several days ago, when he had called from his penthouse apartment in Sydney, was a walk in the park compared to the woman who had been making noises about taking what they had *'one step further'*, and didn't show any promise of retreating without putting up a fight.

'So tell me… What am I not going to like to hear?' Theo encouraged.

'As you are well aware, son…' Stefano's hooded dark eyes gazed off into the distance '…things have not been good with me since your mother died. When my beloved Rose went, she took a big part of me with her.'

'Of us all.'

'But you and your brother are young. I, on the other hand, am an old man—and you know what they say about old dogs and new tricks. Perhaps if her death hadn't been so sudden… Perhaps if I had had time to get used to the idea of her absence…' He sighed. 'But this is not why I called you here, Theo. To moan and complain about something that cannot be changed. I called you here because during the time that I was…shall we say mentally not present, certain unfortunate things took place within the company.'

Theo stilled. His keen eyes noted the nervous play of his father's entwined fingers. His father was the least nervous man he had ever known.

'Unfortunate things…?'

'There has been some substantial mismanagement,'

Stefano declared bluntly. 'And worse, I am afraid. Alfredo, my trusted co-director, has been involved in large-scale embezzlement which has only recently been drawn to my attention. It's a wonder the press hasn't got hold of it. The upshot, Theo, is that vast sums of money—including most of the pension funds—have been hijacked.'

Theo sat back, his lean, handsome face revealing nothing of what was going through his mind.

It was a problem, yes—but a serious one? Not really. At any rate nothing that he couldn't handle.

'If you're worried about the man getting what he deserves, then you can leave that to me,' Theo asserted with cold confidence, his sharp, analytical brain already formulating ways in which payback could be duly extracted. 'And if you're worried about the lost money, then likewise. It will be nothing for me to return what's been misappropriated. No one will ever know.'

'It's not that easy, Theo.'

And Theo knew that now they were approaching the heart of the problem—the reason why he had been summoned.

'I would *never* ask either you or Daniel for financial assistance!' Stefano glowered, his fighting spirit temporarily restored as he contemplated the unthinkable. 'You boys have made your own way in the world and my pride would never allow me to run to either of you with my begging bowl...'

Theo shook his head in frustration at his father's pride—which, he had to concede, both he and Daniel had inherited in bucketloads. 'It would not have been a question of—'

'I'm afraid I went to Carlo Caldini,' Stefano said abruptly. 'There was no choice. The bank was not an option—not when there was a significant chance that they would turn down my request. If that had happened, then the business... Well, what can I say? Everything your mother and I built would have been thrown into the public arena to be picked over by hyenas! At least with Carlo we can keep this between us...'

Theo pressed the pads of his thumbs against his eyes.

Carlo Caldini had once been his father's closest friend and now, for longer than he could remember, was his fiercest adversary. The fact that he had seen fit to go to Carlo for help threatened to bring on a raging headache.

There was absolutely no doubt that whatever his father was going to tell him Theo was not going to want to hear it.

'And what's his price?' he asked, because there was no such thing as a free lunch—and when the lunch was with a sworn enemy then it was going to be the opposite of free.

Exorbitant was the word that sprang to mind.

Stefano fidgeted. 'You're not getting any younger, Theo. You're thirty-two years old! Your mother dearly wished that she would see one of you boys settled... It wasn't to be...'

'I'm not following you...'

'All of this unravelled over eight months ago,' Stefano said heavily. 'During that time it proved impossible to repay the loan. It's been an uphill struggle just picking apart the extent of the losses and dealing with Alfredo...'

'And you kept it all to yourself!'

'There seemed little point in worrying you or your brother.'

'Just tell me what ruinous interest rates Carlo has imposed and I'll deal with it.'

'Here is the part you may not like, son...'

'I'm all ears.'

When it came to money there was nothing Theo couldn't buy, and naturally he would pay the bill without complaint—although he was furious with his father for thinking it necessary to seek help outside the direct family circle.

Pride.

'As you know, Carlo has a daughter. An only child. Sadly there were to be no sons for him.'

Even in the thick of disclosing what he knew his son would not want to hear Stefano couldn't quite conceal the smugness in his voice, and Theo raised his eyebrows wryly. He had never known what had caused the enmity between his father and Carlo, but he suspected that the lifelong grudge stemmed from something ridiculously insignificant.

'What has that got to do with anything?' he asked, frankly bewildered at the tangent his father had taken.

'Alexa… I think you may have met her… Or perhaps not… Well, it seems that the girl is not yet married, and Carlo…' Stefano shrugged. 'He is saddened at that—as I would be had I had a daughter… So part of the repayment schedule—which, in fairness to that sly old fox, is more lenient than at any bank—is that you help him out of his predicament with Alexa. In other words, Theo, I have promised him your hand in marriage to the girl…'

Alexa glared down at the outfit her mother had laid out for her to wear.

Something 'suitable' to meet a man she had no wish to meet, far less marry. A wildly ridiculous frothy dress in startling blue that swept down to the ankles with a plunging neckline and an even more ridiculously plunging back.

She was to be paraded in front of Theo De Angelis like a sacrificial lamb.

She wanted to storm out of the house, head for the nearest port and take a boat to the opposite end of the world—where she would hide out for maybe ten years, until this whole ludicrous situation had been sorted out.

Without her involvement.

At first, when her father had sat her down and told her

that she was to be married to a De Angelis, she had thought that he was joking.

An arranged marriage? In this day and age? To a son of the man with whom he had had a stupid, simmering feud for thirty-five years? What else could it have been but a joke?

That had been a week ago—plenty long enough for her to discover that her father had been deadly serious.

'The poor man is in serious financial trouble.' Carlo Caldini had opened up to her in an attempt to pull at her heartstrings. He had looked at her with a sad expression and mournful eyes. 'True, he and I have not seen eye to eye over the years…'

'All thirty-five of them, Papà…'

'But in the end who else does one turn to but a friend? I would have done the same in his position…'

Alexa had been baffled at this show of seemingly heart-wrenching empathy, but if her father had deemed it fit to rush to the rescue of a man he had spent over three decades deriding, then so be it. What did it have to do with her?

Everything, as it had transpired.

She had been bartered like a…a…piece of meat!

She adored her father, but she would still have dug her heels in and point-blank refused had he not pulled out his trump card—in the shape of her mother.

Cora Caldini, recovering from a stroke, was under doctor's orders to take it easy. No stress, her family had been warned. And, more than that, her father had confided, this last stroke had been the most serious of three… Her heart was weak and all her talk was of her mortality, of her dying before she could see her only child married and settled. What if something happened to her? her father had asked. What if she was taken away from them before her only wish could be granted?

Caught in the eye of a hurricane, Alexa had ranted and

raved, had stood her ground with rousing lectures about modern times, about arranged marriages being a thing of the past. She had pointed out, arms folded, that *they* hadn't had their marriage arranged so why should she? She had waxed lyrical about the importance of love, even though she didn't know the first thing about that. She had darkly suggested that the last thing Cora Caldini would want would be a phoney marriage for all the wrong reasons...

In the end she had gained the only concession that she could. *If* she married the man then it would be on her terms. After a year of unhappy enforced marital misery she would be free to divorce and Stefano De Angelis would be released from his debt. Her father had quickly acquiesced.

Now, with the man due to arrive at their mansion within the hour, she gritted her teeth and returned the elaborate blue dress to the wardrobe from which it had been removed.

She wasn't going to dress up like a doll for a man whose reputation as a commitment-phobe womaniser spanned the country and beyond. There had been no need to look him up on the Internet because she knew all about him—and his brother. Theo and Daniel De Angelis, cut from the same cloth, both ruthless tycoons, both far too good-looking for their own good.

Despite her privileged background, Alexa had made it her life's mission to avoid men like them. She had plenty experience with the superficiality of men who had money and power. She had been surrounded with them for years. She had seen the way they always took it as their God-given right that they could do as they pleased and treat women as they liked simply because *they could*.

She disapproved of everything Theo De Angelis stood for. Certainly the sort of men *she* preferred had always been of the thoughtful and considerate variety.

When she thought about love she thought about her

parents—thought about being swept off her feet by someone kind and humorous, with whom she could enjoy the sort of united happiness her parents enjoyed. When she contemplated marriage she knew that there would be no compromises made. She would marry her soulmate—the man whose hand she would want to hold for the rest of her life. She had met sufficient idle, arrogant, self-absorbed and vain rich guys—guys *exactly* like Theo De Angelis— to know that she would never find her soulmate amongst them.

And look at her now! So much for all her ideals!

She showered, taking her time because she certainly wasn't going to scuttle down to the drawing room to wait for him—like an eager bride-to-be, thrilled to nab a man the tabloid press had once labelled the most eligible bachelor alive.

And she wasn't going to wear the blue dress—or any dress, for that matter. In fact she wasn't going to wear anything that displayed her body at all.

She chose a pair of jeans and a loose-fitting blouse that was buttoned to the neck and then, taut with suppressed anger at her situation, stared at her reflection in the mirror.

Long, wavy dark hair, pulled back into a no-nonsense bun, framed an oval face. Like her father, she was olive-skinned, with dark eyebrows and thick, dark eyelashes, but from her mother she had inherited her bright turquoise eyes. Her best feature, as far as she was concerned— because the rest did little to excite the imagination. She wasn't long and leggy, and she had stopped being able to fit into a size eight the second she had hit adolescence. Hers, to her eternal regret, was an unfashionable five-foot-four hourglass figure—the sort that personal trainers over the years had tried and failed to whip into shape.

She heard voices before she reached the drawing room

because the door was open, and was assailed by a sudden attack of nerves.

It was one thing pouring scorn on the likes of Theo De Angelis from the relative safety of her bedroom.

It was quite another holding on to her self-righteous, justifiable fury when he was perched on a chair, metres away from her, just out of sight.

She had never seen him in the flesh. He lived in London, but even if he had lived in Rome she probably wouldn't have seen him anyway, because she made a point of avoiding society dos whenever possible.

Heart beating fast, she took a deep breath and entered the drawing room.

Drinks were being served and her parents were sitting opposite him, their body language indicating that they were delighted with whatever he happened to be saying.

Conversation came to an abrupt halt.

Alexa had never thrived on being the centre of attention. Along with her background of vast wealth, she had grown up in circles where the girls were catty and where looks counted for everything. Trapped in a figure that had always catapulted her in the direction of baggy clothes, she had learned to leave the attention-seeking to others, and once she had left school had turned her back on it completely.

Right now she found herself riveted by the long, lean man, relaxing in a deep velvet chair which he seemed to dwarf.

Photos could say so much, but they had given her very little indication of just how big and muscular he was. They had also not prepared her for the sheer outrageousness of his looks. He was drop-dead gorgeous. His hair was cropped short and black, his features perfectly chiselled, his eyes lazy and the most peculiar shade of green she had ever seen, fringed with the sort of luxurious lashes any woman would have given her eye-teeth for.

He was as beautiful as any human being had a right to be...and yet the air of ruthless power that surrounded him like an invisible cloak removed him from being just an incredible-looking man to being a man who drew stares and held on to them.

For a few seconds Alexa's heart seemed to stop and she lost the ability to blink.

But that only lasted for a few seconds and then reality resurfaced, rescuing her from standing there like a stranded goldfish.

Her parents had stood up to make introductions. She didn't take a step closer to him, and neither did he make any move to rush forward. In fact he remained sitting just long enough for her to wonder whether a complete lack of manners was also part of his personality.

'Why didn't you wear the lovely dress I laid out for you on the bed?' her mother whispered, in clear dismay at her choice of clothes.

'I decided that the casual approach was better than showing up in a Cinderella frock. Have you noticed that the man is wearing jeans? I wouldn't say *he* dressed for the occasion, would you?'

She directed a cool smile at him as one of the staff got busy with a bottle of champagne and the business of polite conversation began.

With her parents there some of the pressure was removed, but she still found herself sitting like a rigid plank of wood, back erect, body screaming with tension. When, after half an hour, her parents rose and informed them that they were going out for dinner, she glanced up at her mother with undisguised panic.

'You two should have some time to enjoy yourselves!' Cora chirruped brightly. 'Elena has prepared something, and you can dine informally in the blue room...'

Alexa wondered whether her mother had taken complete leave of her senses.

Enjoy themselves?

Didn't she realise that this was an absolute nightmare? No, of course she didn't. She thought that, yes, it was an arranged union—but one that had been happily accepted by both parties. And she wouldn't have questioned that any further because it was so much what she wanted. Her daughter married and settled.

The door clicked quietly shut behind them and Alexa stared down at her half-drunk glass of champagne. She could feel those fabulous green eyes looking at her, and it infuriated her that he felt he had no need to say anything at all.

'So...' She finally broke the lengthening silence. She glanced quickly at him and just as fast looked away.

'So...' Theo drawled, stretching out his long legs and linking his fingers loosely on his stomach. 'Here we are. I never imagined two weeks ago that I would now be sitting in the Caldini living room, gazing at the excited, radiant face of my bride-to-be...'

What had he been expecting? he asked himself. The fact that Carlo Caldini—a man with more millions than he knew what to do with—had been unable to source a husband for the daughter he clearly wanted married off had said it all.

Plain beyond belief, with an insanely boring personality—that had been the prediction his brother had made, when he had been told about the catastrophe, and Theo had privately agreed. He and Daniel might no longer live in Italy, but they were rich and powerful enough to garner invitations from everyone who mattered, and neither could remember ever meeting the girl—which, along with her failure to be married off, had also said it all.

But, finding himself locked in the jaws of a steel trap,

Theo had determined to make the best of things. Because, however odious the woman was, no marriage was set in stone. There was always a window for negotiation when it came to an out clause, and Theo had already located it.

In the meanwhile he had imagined someone unappealing and terminally shy, who would make a suitable background spouse while his father's company was patched up from the inside. All things considered, he had come to the conclusion that his life would hardly have to change at all. She would remain in Italy, dutifully keeping the home fires burning, he would visit occasionally, work permitting, and she would not complain.

When Alexa had walked into the drawing room he had been startled to discover that she was nothing like the woman he had conjured up in his head.

She was…

He still wasn't entirely sure—and that was a first for him. For if it was one thing Theo De Angelis excelled in, it was an ability to read a woman in under five seconds.

She had sat in mute silence for most of the half hour during which laboured chit chat had been made, with both Carlo and Cora Caldini making sure to tread very carefully around the giant elephant in the room: namely the matter of an arranged marriage.

Cora, he had been told by her husband, knew that the marriage was to be an arrangement, but she knew nothing of the financial situation that had propelled it into existence and nor should she find out. She could deal with an arranged marriage… Several of her friends had children who had been diplomatically set up with suitable partners. It would be tactful not to go into more details.

Alexa's mute silence hadn't translated into the meek subservience he had been expecting.

And looks-wise…

He tilted his head and noted the mutinous, challenging stare she returned.

'And *I* didn't think that I would be sitting here gazing at my devoted and adoring husband-to-be!' Alexa retorted, because there was no reason for her to pretend that this was anything but a fiasco.

Besides, the man was so good-looking that he might just be arrogant enough to think that she actually *wanted* to be in this position.

She felt she should rid him of any such assumption from the start.

'So I'm assuming...' he rose fluidly from the chair to refill her glass with more champagne before topping his up with more of the whisky he had been drinking '...that we're both singing from the same song sheet?'

'What did you expect?' Alexa threw at him, mouth down-turned.

'I could either answer that question truthfully or else ignore it altogether. Which would you rather?'

Alexa shrugged and tore her eyes away from his long, muscular frame. 'We might just as well lay our cards on the table,' she said.

'In which case,' Theo drawled, 'I should tell you I had reached the conclusion that you might be a little desperate... considering Carlo is prepared to throw you in as part of his financial negotiations with my father...'

Slow, furious colour crawled into her cheeks.

'You are the most arrogant man I think I have ever met in my entire life!' Alexa said through gritted teeth.

She gauged the level of satisfaction she would get from flinging her glass at him, but decided that the only way to handle this disaster would be not to let him get to her.

She wasn't going to lose her cool. She *never* lost her cool. It was what made her so good at what she did. She worked in the offices of a group of pro bono lawyers and daily dealt with people in need of practical and emotional help. Three evenings a week she volunteered at a women's shelter. She was calm personified!

'Since we're about to be joined in happily married bliss, I suggest you take that on board and don't think of implementing any changes.'

Theo was perversely enjoying himself, and he put that down to the sort of man he was. The sort who could deal with whatever was thrown at him, however unexpected.

'And in return,' he continued, in the same lazy dark drawl that made her toes curl, '*I* won't try and turn *you* into someone charming and well behaved...'

Alexa glared and bit down hard on the riposte stinging her lips. She had no idea how she was going to survive twelve hours with this man, never mind twelve months.

'I've spoken to my father,' she gritted, 'and he has agreed that we only have to carry out this crazy charade for twelve months. After that we can part company and you can return to your life of— You can return to your life and I can get back to mine.'

Theo wondered what she had been about to say but let it go. He, in actual fact, had secured a far better deal— because *his* twelve months also included a substantial acquisition of Caldini company shares and a seat on the board. It would tie in very nicely with his current diversion into telecommunications.

After the initial shock of the catastrophe that had been presented to him, he had very quickly reached the perfectly correct conclusion that marrying his daughter off was only one benefit for Carlo Caldini in helping his father.

The other was glaringly obvious.

Carlo Caldini ran a juggernaut of a family business but there was no male family member to whom he could leave his legacy—and, like many traditional Italians, he wanted his business to remain in the family. By marrying his daughter to Theo he netted one of the most wildly respected and formidable businessmen on the globe.

And for Theo, Alexa Caldini came with a considerable dowry.

'So no doubt we should be discussing the mechanics,' he said.

'What do you mean?'

'I mean that to the outside world we must be a loved-up pair about to embark on the greatest adventure of our lives. I will not have a whiff of scandal surrounding this, because under no circumstances is my father to be subjected to any manner of rumour about a convenient match concocted to save his company.' His green eyes had cooled. 'Are we one hundred per cent clear on this?'

'Or else what?'

'That's a road I would seriously advise you not to go down.'

His voice was icy cold, with deadly intent, and Alexa shivered. Theo De Angelis had not reached the dizzy heights by being kind and avuncular. He'd probably never helped a little old lady cross a road in his entire life. She wondered how he would react to her world when they were man and wife...

'When we're in public,' he purred silkily, 'you will withdraw your claws. You can keep them for when we're alone together.'

'You might find that you don't like being scratched.' Alexa tilted her chin mutinously and he smiled—a slow, curling smile that did all sorts of weird and unexpected things to her body.

'And *you* might discover that I'm very good when it comes to subduing wild cats.'

Suddenly confused, and feeling horribly out of her depth, Alexa blinked and gulped down the remainder of her champagne.

She might talk the talk, but how good would she be at walking the walk?

She had virtually no experience when it came to the opposite sex. She had been sent off to England to an all girls' boarding school and from there to university, where she had buried herself in books, determined to get her law degree.

Of course there had been a couple of boyfriends, but neither had excited her and she had always been determined to hold out for the Right One—never to sell herself short. They had both cleared off as soon as they'd realised that she wasn't going to hop into bed with them.

Now, as her bright blue eyes tangled with his cool, unreadable green ones, she knew that this was a predator, born to lead and accustomed to obedience.

Obedience she would give him—but only within the parameters that suited them both. If he didn't want anyone getting wind of the real reason for their union she, in turn, did not want to embarrass her parents, whom she dearly loved.

He wanted her to put up a public front and she would—but the second they closed the door behind them there would be no more game-playing.

And suddenly a thought rippled through her that made her breathing quicken.

When the front door closed…what happened next?

It was something that she would have to broach, and she licked her lips nervously because the mere thought of this big, domineering man touching her sent her whole nervous system into instant meltdown.

He surely wouldn't expect them to sleep together! Not when this was a farce—a marriage of convenience…a union in which there would be no love lost!

Her breathing steadied.

Panic over.

He might be arrogant and ruthless, but he wasn't an idiot—and besides, she knew the sort of women he dated because she had seen pictures in some of the trashy magazines she had flicked through while she was getting her hair done.

Tall, blonde women who wore the minimum of clothing and whose full-time occupation appeared to be personal grooming.

'You said that we need to discuss the mechanics of this…this arrangement…?'

'Shall we do that over dinner—?'

'Why? We might as well hash it out now.'

He stood up, blatantly ignoring her interruption. 'I wouldn't like to kick off our joyous life together on the wrong note,' he drawled, strolling towards the door, which her parents had tactfully shut behind him on their way out.

'What do you mean?' Alexa followed him, disgruntled.

'I mean your mother has had a doubtless delicious meal prepared for us. What kind of guest would I be if I disregarded her invitation?'

'The kind that's marrying me thanks to parental pressure?' Alexa muttered sourly.

He shot her a brief look of appreciation.

'Besides,' she continued, skin tingling from that momentary look, 'you don't strike me as the sort of man who gives a hoot what other people think of him.'

She swept past him, breathing in his clean, woody scent and determinedly ignoring its impact on her senses.

'I find that I'm willing to make an exception for my in-laws-to-be…'

'Why are you taking this so calmly?'

It was the first thing Alexa said as they sat down at the table in the informal dining room. The blue room was still big enough to fit a ten-seater table, but places had been set for them opposite each another at one end. As always, it was a full arrangement, with dinner plates, side plates and separate silver cutlery for every course to be served—in this case salad, soup, main course and dessert.

Alexa could not have felt less hungry, and she looked with uninterest as salads were brought in and placed in front of them.

He, she noted, had no problem with his appetite.

'How else do you imagine I should react?' Theo looked at her, and across the width of the table she felt his overwhelming presence all the more acutely.

There was something intimate about eating together, and she could barely concentrate on her salad as the flutter of nerves threatened to overpower her common sense.

She put that down to her healthy dislike of the man.

'Do you imagine that this is a situation I *enjoy* being in?' he enquired coolly. 'My father dropped this bombshell and I find I've had next to no option but to take the hit.'

'I never thought I'd end up in a marriage with someone who would walk up the aisle only thanks to having to take a hit from a bombshell he couldn't dodge,' Alexa said bitterly—and that was the stark truth.

She had never followed the pattern of her friends, who had believed in sleeping around. She had never assumed that marriage was something to be taken lightly because it could be unpicked without too much difficulty if the going got rough. Her own parents had had a long and extremely happy marriage. Her mother, Irish by heritage, had been a gap-year student when she had met Carlo, and theirs had been a case of love at first sight. Which made it doubly upsetting that her father had seen fit to put her in this position. He had taken advantage of a situation and *she* was going to have to pay the price.

'I don't think that way of thinking will pay dividends in this particular situation…' Theo pushed his salad plate to one side and sprawled back in the chair to look at her coolly. 'We've both been put in an unfortunate position and now we have to deal with it.'

'And you're not angry...?'

'Like I said, there's no point in wasting energy on emotions that won't get either of us anywhere. We're going to present the perfect picture of a couple in love. Naturally there will have to be an engagement and a public announcement. Doubtless there will be cameras. You will smile and gaze adoringly up at me.'

'And what will *you* be doing while I'm smiling and gazing adoringly?'

'Controlling the situation.'

'And this so-called engagement is supposed to last... how long?'

'It'll be brief,' Theo asserted with the sweeping assurance of someone who had given the details a great deal of thought. 'We can't wait to tie the knot.'

'And how is this supposed to make any kind of sense?' Alexa demanded. She lapsed into silence as their salad plates were removed, to be replaced with soup. 'Have you suddenly had a transformation and gone from being a womaniser to a one-woman man who's desperate to get married?'

'And *that*,' Theo said in a hard voice, 'is just the sort of approach I am warning you to avoid.' Then he smiled—a slow, lazy smile that made the breath hitch in her throat. 'I never imagined that you were a spitting cat...' he mused. 'Do you think that's the reason your parents think you'll end up on the shelf...?'

CHAPTER TWO

'I CAN'T BELIEVE you just said that.'

Never had a meal seemed so interminably long. Interrupted by the arrival of their main course—a fish casserole—Alexa could only glare at him with simmering resentment. No one had ever riled her to this extent. His air of superior cool got on her nerves and made her rantings seem childish and petty.

'You have no right to say stuff like that! You don't *know* me!'

Theo dug into his food. She might not be his type, but there was a certain arresting quality to her face. Anger suited her, and he was startled at this reaction—because temper tantrums were things he had always actively discouraged.

Her dig about his womanising had annoyed him, and as far as he was concerned what was good for the goose was likewise good for the gander. If she wanted to throw accusations at him, then her shoulders should be broad enough to take it when he threw a few home truths back at her in return.

Not his style, admittedly, but then again since when had he ever been placed in a situation like this? On every single level she was just the sort of woman he would never naturally be drawn to. Physically, she was nothing like the tall, leggy supermodels he dated and, appearances aside, he liked his women to be obliging and accommodating. His work life was intense enough without having to do battle with a woman.

'Aren't you going to eat?' he asked. 'It's excellent. Maybe I'll get the name of your mother's chef... Do you think she would object if I poached him?'

'Elena isn't a chef,' Alexa muttered. 'She's the house-keeper we've had for centuries. And, yes, I think my mother *would* object if you decided to poach her. For your information, I have never considered myself as *on the shelf*. I'm not one of those women who thinks that the be-all and end-all of life is to get married as fast as you can and start having children.'

'I'm guessing that both your parents *do*.'

Alexa pushed her plate to one side. 'There's no point discussing this. What my parents think or don't think... How long before we get married?'

She was forcibly struck by the surreal situation she was now wading through—and by the fact that her con-tented life had been turned upside down in the space of a few days.

So she hadn't been leading the most thrilling of lives... But it had taken her ages to get used to being back in Italy after first boarding school and then university abroad, fol-lowed by a stint in London, where she had worked for a small law company before her mother's illness had called her back home.

She had spent the past year and a half easing herself into a life that felt foreign. Was it any wonder that excitement and thrills weren't high on her agenda? Once she found her feet, she was sure that the slightly zoned out feeling she lived with much of the time would disappear.

She hadn't banked on excitement landing on her door-step in the form of a forced marriage.

'Max—two months. And, to return to your question

about the plausibility of my settling down at the speed of light... We both need to agree that it's a case of love getting the better of me.' He shrugged elegantly and stood up, tossing his serviette onto the table and prowling through the room as he thought.

Alexa followed him with her eyes. His movements were economical and graceful. He was wearing black jeans, a white linen shirt which was cuffed to the elbows and loafers, and he exuded elegance. He certainly hadn't dressed for the occasion, but he still managed to look every inch the powerful tycoon that he was. He was obviously one of those people who could pull off elegance wearing anything... If he swapped clothes with a tramp he would still manage to look cool and sexy.

'I broke up with my last girlfriend over three months ago—during which time I've been out of the public eye...'

'You're telling me that the press usually follow everything you do?'

Theo paused, leaned against the window ledge, then looked at her and kept looking at her as the dishes were cleared away. He signalled in a barely discernible gesture that they should be left alone for a while, and the door was duly shut as the last dish was removed. The oak table was left with just the wine decanter and a bottle of champagne.

'I'm high-profile,' he agreed. 'I don't ask for it, but it seems that some reporters have little else to do but take pictures of the rich and famous. It's just a fact of life, and I've become accustomed to dealing with it.'

'I would absolutely *hate* that.'

'It's something to which you might find you have to become accustomed—'

'On top of everything else,' Alexa muttered.

Her eyes flickered towards him and she found that she had to tear them away, because he was just so unfairly compelling to look at.

Theo chose to ignore her interruption. He had anticipated someone plain, docile and quite possibly grateful
to be rescued from the prospect of spinsterhood. A traditional Italian woman who would welcome the abundance
of riches suddenly deposited in her lap—because he knew
without a trace of vanity that he was a good catch.

It would have been hard to locate someone *less* grateful
than the girl now glowering at him, and he banked down
a sudden flare of irritation.

'At any rate,' he pressed on, 'no one will raise eyebrows about the timeline, and the fact that at least on paper
this would appear to be the perfect match will certainly
help things along. We both come from prominent Italian
families... I have found the woman of my dreams, someone close to home, and have decided to steer my life in a
different direction... Both families are overjoyed by the
match...'

'Even though our fathers haven't been on speaking
terms for years?'

'All the more touching. Everyone likes a fairy-tale ending.'

'You're so cynical, aren't you?'

'Realistic and practical.'

'And how are we supposed to have met? We don't even
live in the same country.'

'I don't think it will require great feats of the imagination to come up with something.'

Was she going out of her way to get on his nerves? he
wondered. Did she honestly think that *his* life hadn't also
undergone a seismic change? Less than two weeks ago
he had been a free man—free to go where he pleased, to
have whatever woman he wanted. No one was waiting in
the wings, expecting him to put in an appearance. That
freedom had disappeared in a puff of smoke, but was *he*
whining and complaining? No. He was solution-orientated

and, like it or not, plans had to be made so that this pretence could be seamlessly accepted as nothing short of the absolute truth.

'Let's have your thoughts on this,' he said.

An edge of irritation had crept into his voice and, hearing it, Alexa scowled, once again reduced to feeling petty.

'I suppose we could have met here,' she said, a little ungraciously.

'I occasionally *do* come to Italy to see my father. . It's a realistic enough scenario. You happened to be somewhere… Suddenly my life shifted on its axis… If a reporter asks you for details you can always tell him *no comment* and then gaze adoringly at me. Probably safer than getting tangled up in a lie.'

He looked at her glum face, then down to her baggy, unappealing outfit. No doubt she had pointedly dressed down for a confrontation she didn't want, but it was something that would have to be discussed whether she liked it or not. He suspected not, but treading delicately round the issue wasn't going to do.

'Is that how you normally dress?'

'I beg your pardon?'

'Jeans…baggy tops… And what are you wearing on your feet…?'

Alexa looked at him indignantly and stuck her foot out. 'Trainers.'

'Running shoes? To my mind, they're for running. Are you running anywhere? Have you just come from the gym?'

'What are you getting at?' Her voice had risen a notch. His levels of arrogance were in the process of escalating.

'Credibility,' Theo said succinctly. 'We may make the ideal match, and when our engagement hits the news much will be made of our backgrounds, but even the least observant reporter might question the fact that I've fallen head over heels in love with someone who doesn't appear to give a damn how she looks...'

Alexa's mouth dropped open. She contemplated throwing something at him.

'That is the most insulting thing that has ever been said to me in my entire life!'

'It's not meant to be insulting,' Theo informed her drily. 'I'm looking at this situation from all angles and simply bringing one of those angles to your attention. The women I've dated in the past—'

'There's no need to go into that.' Alexa was mortified, and outraged that he should be tactless enough to criticise her choice of clothing. 'I know *exactly* what sort of women you've dated in the past.'

'How so?'

'I've seen the occasional picture in a trashy mag.' She liked the way the words *trashy mag* rolled off her tongue.

'You read "trashy mags"? You surprise me. I thought I might be getting a highbrow intellectual for a wife. I'm disappointed.'

There was a thread of amusement in his voice which she decided to ignore, because it seemed to point to a side of his personality that wasn't part of the package she had conjured up.

'They're the only things to read at the hairdresser,' Alexa told him airily. 'Great big stacks of silly magazines, full of useless gossip. I saw a picture of you in one of them a couple of months ago. A tall, blonde woman was clinging to you as though she might fall flat on her face unless you kept her propped up. Maybe she'd had too much to drink...' Alexa mused, enjoying herself for the first time that evening. 'I hadn't thought of that. But I suppose those society dos usually involve a lot of alcohol. I've been asked to several over the years,' she inserted, truthfully enough, because as the daughter of a prominent Italian family she had occasionally been asked to some event or other in aid of a good cause, 'but I try and avoid them.'

'How virtuous.'

'So, yes, I know that you date tall model-types. A bit like your brother. *He* also pops up in those kinds of magazines, with some drunken supermodel hanging on to him for dear life...'

Theo thought of Daniel and for a second tried to imagine what the mouthy little brunette facing him would have thought of his brother. His brother was the essence of a playboy—which was why he had laughed uproariously when Theo had told him about the situation he was stuck in.

It would have been Daniel's ultimate nightmare, and he had been overjoyed at the prospect of being able to remain free, single and unattached, without having to worry that their father might start making noises about him settling down. One son who had settled down would be plenty good enough.

'I like the way you think the supermodel was drunk...' Theo murmured, temporarily distracted by her digression and thinking that, yes, there was a very high chance that whoever she had seen clinging to him *had* had too much to drink. 'Maybe she was clinging to me because she liked the sensation of being pressed up against me... A lot of women do...'

Alexa blinked and blushed. 'Well...' the conversation had meandered, and she had only herself to blame '...in case you hadn't noticed I'm not six-foot-two and blonde, so you can't turn me into one of your supermodels...'

'You know exactly what I was talking about, Alexa...'

'Do I?' The way he said her name sent little shivers through her, and her eyes glazed over as she tried to fight off the unusual sensation.

'Show up next to me in a pair of jeans, some trainers and

a baggy sweatshirt and people are going to scratch their heads in bewilderment. And show up next to me you're going to have to—because we're going to spend the next couple of months convincing whoever needs convincing that we're a loved-up couple.'

'I have a *job*...' Alexa stared at him in horror.

'I'm not asking you to shadow me twenty-four hours of the day,' Theo clarified. 'In fact I won't even be in Italy for significant periods of time. My work is primarily in London. I will, however, try and arrange my business dealings so that I can be here more often than I normally would. I don't see that I have much choice in the matter. At any rate, when I'm in London you're going to have to drop whatever you're doing and put in an appearance. Two people who are supposed to be madly in love should be madly in love enough that they actually want to spend time in the same country together.'

'Are you telling me that I will have to give up my job?'

Theo looked at her pensively. 'You work in a law office. Am I right?'

'How did you know?'

'Your parents told me before you came down,' Theo said wryly. 'They thought a little background information about you would be a good idea.'

'What else did they say?'

'That you don't seem particularly enthralled by it...'

Alexa was dismayed. She liked what she did well enough, but her liking it only 'well enough' would not have gone unnoticed by her parents. She was their only child, and they could tune in to her moods in ways that were scary.

Was that why they had jumped to the conclusion that she was somehow unhappy with her life?

Like a detective in possession of clue number one, Alexa could begin to see why they might have also come to the conclusion that if she wasn't happy in her job, she wasn't happy in her life—and her mother, traditional as she was, would have instantly decided that it was because there was no guy in the picture. She was now twenty-six years old—at an age when so many Italian girls she had grown up with were married, some with kids. Her mother wouldn't have understood that she was just missing the independence she had had in another country.

'I haven't been there very long.'

'A year and a half is long enough to decide whether you like a job or not. My point being that it won't be any great sacrifice for you to be flexible with it while we indulge in our passionate love affair. And when we do tie the knot it won't be any great sacrifice either for you to jack it in altogether and return to London with me. There's no way I can live out here.'

Alexa's head was spinning. It didn't get worse than this. Not only had her life been overturned, but she felt as if she were on a rollercoaster ride and someone else had complete control of the on/off switch.

'I don't just work at a law firm,' she said tightly, 'I also volunteer three evenings a week at a local women's shelter, and that's something that I *do* happen to like—very much!'

That came as a surprise to Theo. Her parents hadn't mentioned it, and he wondered whether they'd thought it was something he might find a little embarrassing.

He didn't.

In fact he was intrigued. There was no need for her to do anything but enjoy living in the lap of luxury. There was certainly no need for her to have a job, but he could understand her wanting that well enough. However, helping out at a women's shelter was way beyond the call of duty, and he felt a twinge of curiosity about this woman who was going to become his wife.

Since curiosity and women didn't tend to go hand in

hand for him, he allowed himself a few seconds to enjoy
the novel sensation.

'Doing what?' he asked with genuine interest.

Alexa hesitated. Determined that total detachment was
the only way to deal with a situation she didn't like, convinced anyhow that someone like Theo De Angelis was
just the sort of man she could only ever view as an adversary, she was wary of this brief lull in warfare.

He was leaning forward, frowning slightly, his head
inclined to one side, waiting for her to reply.

And just for a split second she glimpsed the ferocity of
his charm—the charm that drew women like magnets and
ensured that his face was always plastered somewhere inside one of those trashy magazines she had told him about.

For a split second it was as if she were the only woman
in the universe who interested him. That was how it felt.
And even though she knew that it was an illusion, and it
didn't change her fundamental opinion of him, she was
still...

Sucked in...

'I... You probably don't get this...' she tried for defen-
sive and belligerent but achieved breathless '...but I *am*
actually interested in putting back into the community...'

'I'd like to argue that one with you, but go on...'

'I did Law at university, and my experience has been
working with pro bono legal teams. I like the thought of
being able to help people who need legal aid but haven't
got the money to hire some fancy, expensive lawyer. I like
thinking that the little guy can get as much from the system
as someone with money.' Her voice picked up with enthusiasm. 'One thing led to another, and I found out about a
women's shelter that needed volunteers. I thought it would
be just the sort of thing I might like—and I do. I help out
there on every level...from mucking in with the general
work to giving some of the women there legal advice...'

She stopped abruptly, a little embarrassed at the way she had opened up, even though she was hardly divulging state secrets.

'Anyway,' she said, her guard back up and firmly in place, 'there's no need to dress up for my job *or* for my volunteer work—not that I feel comfortable dressing up anyway. You asked me if jeans and baggy jumpers and trainers are the clothes I like wearing and the answer is *yes*.'

Theo didn't say anything for a few seconds. He was still chewing over the picture she had painted of herself and marvelling that he could have been so far off target in his assumptions about this person who had been dumped on him.

Then he shook aside the moment of introspection.

Back to the matter in hand.

'That's as may be,' he said, in a voice that allowed no wriggle room, 'but you'll need a new wardrobe.'

Alexa was happy to fume once again, even though she could see the sense of what he was saying. Who was going to be convinced that he'd fallen in love with a girl who avoided parties and society affairs and whose wardrobe consisted of varying shades of denim? It just demonstrated how far apart they were in everything aside from their backgrounds, and as far as she was concerned similar backgrounds would never be good enough to bridge the gaps.

Thank goodness there was a time limit on this charade!

'And what sort of clothes would you suggest?' she asked politely. 'Do I have a say in what I wear as the radiant bride-to-be, or are you going to take over that aspect of things as well?'

'Would you like me to? I've never been shopping with a woman in my life before, but I'm more than happy to test-drive the experience with you...'

'I'll choose my own clothes,' Alexa said hurriedly as

her head was filled with images of him sitting on a chair in a boutique and looking at her as she paraded different outfits in front of him. Short, over-endowed on the breast front, and lacking in the legs-up-to-her-armpits arena, she could just imagine the comparisons he would make and inwardly cringed.

'And leaving Italy...?'

He let that very important question drop and wondered what ripples it might cause. She was extremely close to her parents. He knew that. Just as he knew that she had returned from working in London post-haste the moment she'd felt she needed to be by her mother's side.

Alexa shrugged. It wasn't a depressing thought. In fact it might be just about the brightest thing on an otherwise nightmarish horizon.

Of course it would entail living with the man now scrutinising her...

Which brought that awkward subject she had shoved aside back to the surface.

What, exactly, would their married life entail? It would be a silly academic question, of course. She wasn't his type any more than he was hers. But she would have to clarify things—draw a line in the sand, so to speak.

'I would want to carry on working wherever I happened to be,' she told him, and he nodded.

'Do you imagine that I'm the sort of dinosaur who would stop you? At any rate...' He shrugged and glanced at his watch, to find that they had been talking for a lot longer than he had imagined. It wouldn't be long before her parents would return. 'At any rate...' he picked up the thread of what he had been saying '...within the constraints of our so-called marriage you would be free to do whatever you wanted to do.'

Alexa nodded, and wondered what sort of woman he would have liked to marry, and what his expectations might have been. Would he have wanted a little stay-at-home wife? She couldn't picture him as a guy who could ever be domesticated. There was something essentially untamed about him. She'd been pushed into this, but so had he. He must have had thoughts about marriage and now he was stuck with her—at least temporarily. His life had been equally disrupted and yet you wouldn't have guessed.

She had noted the way he had looked at his watch. So they might be talking business, but it still felt like an insult to be in a man's company and to find him clock-watching because he wanted to get away.

'Fine,' she said crisply. 'In that case I would look for work as soon as I moved to London. Which…er…brings me to… I feel I ought to get a few things straight…'

'Spit it out.'

'This isn't going to be a *normal* marriage.'

'That's somewhat stating the obvious.'

'We probably won't see much of one another, which suits me just fine, and it'll just be for a few months anyway, but during that time I would appreciate it if you didn't bring women to the house.'

Theo looked at her incredulously. '*"Bring women to the house…"*?'

'I know…' Alexa felt addled by the way those cool green eyes were resting on her face, making her feel as though she had made one big, enormous gaffe. Which she hadn't. She was just getting things straight. 'I know that behind closed doors…you know…we will be able to drop the act… But I would rather I didn't have to bump into any of your supermodels on the staircase…'

'You think I'm going to bring women back to the house I will be sharing with you? Put them in the room next door for easy access?'

'You're going to be with me for a year. I expect you will have…needs…so to speak…' Her cheeks were flaming red and she licked her lips nervously. 'And of course,' she ploughed on into thick silence, 'our marriage will be for show only. I mean…there will be no question of us… sharing a bedroom…or anything. I just want to make that clear.' She gave a high laugh. 'Just stating the obvious! So, when it comes to…er…' Her voice petered out and she looked at him in helpless frustration.

'To…er…?' he encouraged.

'You know what I'm saying!'

'You're giving me permission to have sex with any woman I want, just so long as I don't bring them into the house I will be sharing with you?'

'Yes!'

'That's very considerate and generous of you, but I'm not the sort of man who believes in fooling around outside marriage.'

'But it won't be a *real* marriage…'

'Are you magnanimously giving me permission because you want me to respond in kind?'

'I—I don't know what you mean,' Alexa stammered.

His eyes were chips of ice. 'Then shall I spell it out for you? Are you telling me that I can have sex with any woman I want because you want me to tell you that you can do likewise with any man?'

Alexa's mouth dropped open.

'You can drop the innocent act,' Theo said drily. 'I may be older than you, but I don't hark back to the Dark Ages. You're in your mid-twenties, and I'm guessing that you have a boyfriend stashed away somewhere. Your parents didn't mention anyone on the scene, in which case he probably isn't socially acceptable…'

'Not *socially acceptable*?' was all Alexa could parrot in bewilderment.

Of course—he was judging her by *his* standards. A bolt of white-hot fury lanced through her. She clamped her lips tightly shut and waited to hear where he would go next with his crazy assumptions.

'If he was the sort of guy you wanted to show off to your parents you would have trotted him back home for a sit-down meal and a meet-and-greet evening by now...'

'Because that's what you've done with your girlfriends in the past?'

'I've always discouraged that.' Theo waved aside her interruption. 'But we're not talking about me. We're talking about you.'

'So he's "socially unacceptable..."?' She stifled a bubble of hysterical laughter.

If only he knew! But to a man like Theo De Angelis the thought of being a twenty-six-year-old virgin would have been unthinkable. It wouldn't even have crossed his radar! It would never have occurred to him that there were some people on the planet who actually weren't interested in jumping into bed *for the fun of it*—people who were willing to hold out for the real thing...people who believed in love and were willing to wait till they found it before they had sex. People who wanted to share the precious gift of their body with the person they truly loved.

'He's not married...?' he mused, for the first time wondering what her social life was like.

His eyes skimmed over her flushed face and, yes...there was definitely something curiously appealing about her—something that would definitely be considered attractive by any number of men.

What would she look like with her clothes off?

Just like that his imagination fired up. Her clothes revealed nothing, but the jut of her breasts suggested that she had more than a generous handful. Big breasts, with big nipples.

He frowned and shifted as his libido, dormant since he had dispatched his last girlfriend, sprang into enthusiastic life. His thick, hard erection pushed against his zipper and he shifted again, annoyed at the way his body was reacting without his permission.

Hell… He had no intention of complicating an already complicated situation by getting curious about a woman who wasn't his type.

But his body was refusing to play ball and he focused on her face, driving inappropriate thoughts from his head.

'What a relief!' Alexa said with thick sarcasm. 'It's nice to know that you think I have *some* morals.'

Theo's eyes narrowed, because the suggestion was there that what she had he obviously lacked in abundance.

What woman had ever insinuated anything like that to him in his life before? It was outrageous. She knew just how to antagonise him, whether deliberately or not, and it took willpower not to waste his energies rising to the bait.

He wondered whether he had touched upon a sensitive issue. Had he hit a home run without even trying? *Was* there some man waiting in the wings? No matter. He would have to be dispatched—and that was certainly something he wasn't going to waste time apologising about.

'I suppose he's one of your do-gooder pals?' Theo asserted flatly. 'Maybe someone working with you at whatever shelter you work at. Am I right? I don't suppose you would want to introduce someone like *that* to your parents. You might enjoy putting the world to rights, but cut to the chase and you're the only child of one of the most important families in the country. You might be allowed freedom of movement to pursue whatever career you want, but when it comes to settling down don't tell me that your parents wouldn't be alarmed if you chose someone who couldn't make ends meet…'

Alexa didn't know whether to be insulted or amused by his freewheeling assumptions. She certainly wasn't going to set him straight—because why should she? She stoutly reminded herself that whilst it was in her nature to be utterly honest this was a novel situation—there was no need for her to account for herself.

'My parents aren't that small-minded,' she told him with saccharine politeness. 'They wouldn't *care* if I brought home someone who couldn't make ends meet.'

'I beg to differ,' Theo said, in just the kind of tone of voice that set her teeth on edge. 'Why do you think your father is so keen for me to marry you?'

'Apparently because he wants to get me down from the shelf before I take up permanent residence there.' Her cheeks were burning and she was clutching the sides of her chair, leaning forward, every muscle in her body rigid with angry tension.

'He sees me as his natural successor,' Theo informed her smoothly. 'He sees me as the perfect match for you— someone who can run his empire. It's what he wants for you…and of course for himself…'

Alexa whitened. It all made sense now, and she suddenly felt like a pawn caught up in a game that was much bigger than her. Their feuding fathers had sealed a bond and all the players had won except her. Theo's father would have his family name kept intact and his company rescued from the threat of public disgrace. Her mother would have her daughter married and, after her stroke, would have what she had wanted for the past few years. She wouldn't see it as an act of selfishness. Arranged marriages were perfectly acceptable in certain social circles. Her father would likewise see his daughter married off, and in return… Yes, he would have the perfect son-in-law.

And Theo would have…

He didn't have to spell it out for her, because it was obvious now that she was putting two and two together. Theo would wangle part-ownership of her father's company. Maybe not all of it, but his portfolio would increase substantially—not that he needed it.

And she, Alexa, would get one year of gnashing her teeth and trying not to commit homicide.

Right now she could dig her heels in and refuse to go along with what everyone else wanted. But she knew that she wasn't going to do that. She wouldn't stress her mother and risk another health problem which might prove far more serious than the last.

Theo could see the play of emotions on her face as comprehension dawned and he squashed the sickening suspicion that he was responsible for that. She was an adult and she had made her choice. True, she hadn't asked to be put in this unenviable position, but neither had he. Tough situations always made a person stronger, more resilient.

Matter sorted, he said bluntly, 'I know this situation isn't ideal, but if you have a boyfriend he's going to have to go into hiding while we're together. I have no intention of sleeping around behind your back. The press follow me like hyenas and I don't plan on giving them any carcasses to chew on—and you're going to do the same.'

He heard a rustle of activity and the distant sound of voices marking the return of her parents.

'There's an event tomorrow evening.' He stood up and raked his fingers through his hair. 'Formal. I've been invited and you'll be my…guest. It will be our first public appearance together and the perfect opportunity to get the gossip mill at work…'

Feeling as though she had been through several wars and only managed to survive by the skin of her teeth, Alexa stood up as well.

'And of course I'm to dress the part…' she muttered, feeling even more powerless standing in front of him, because he was just so…*big*…

'I intend to stay in the country for at least the next fort-night. There will be several high-profile functions.'

'I'll make sure my wardrobe is overflowing with stuff I wouldn't normally wear in a million years!' she snapped.

Theo smiled slowly. 'I look forward to seeing them… I'll pick you up tomorrow evening at seven. Get ready to be the centre of attention…'

CHAPTER THREE

'DARLING, YOU LOOK BEAUTIFUL...'

Alexa tried hard not to grimace. She had spent a restless night. Her entire mind had seemed to be filled with images of Theo, leaving no room for anything else.

First thing in the morning she had telephoned her boss at work to advise him that she would have to take a temporary leave of absence. She hated leaving him in the lurch, but he would find out soon enough the reasons for her abrupt departure. When pressed, she had only muttered that it was of a personal nature.

Then she had spent the day, at her mother's excited instigation, at various beauty parlours and clothes shops.

She had had her nails done, her face done... She had gone to the hairdressers, where they had trimmed her hair, suffused it with highlights and then insisted she look and admire what they had created... She had traipsed from one shop to another and allowed herself to be guided by personal shoppers...

Alexa knew that it was just the sort of day most girls of her background would have taken for granted. But by the end of the afternoon, laden with bags which had quickly been taken to her room, each elaborate dress carefully hung in her wardrobe while her precious casual clothes had got second billing, she had felt utterly spent.

Now, looking at her mother's thin, beaming face, she

reminded herself why she had embarked on this crazy scheme. Her mother was positively radiant.

She hadn't accompanied her shopping, but had greeted the sight of each purchase with gratifying squeals of delight. Alexa was forced to concede that at long last Cora Caldini had managed to get the doll she had wanted rather than the tomboy she had been stuck with.

'I look…' Alexa stole a glance at her reflection and for a few startling seconds, now that she was seeing the complete and finished product, was lost for words '…different…' she eventually managed to croak.

Neither the mirrors she had cursorily glanced in at the various shops nor the face she had politely and very briefly scanned at the hairdressers seemed to have done justice to the person now reflected back at her.

Different was an understatement, and she was honest enough to acknowledge that.

Her curves were still all there, but for some reason the dress took them, held them, shaped them in some way so that she was…*sexy*…

'I know,' her mother said with immense satisfaction. 'Fabulous! And the colour suits you perfectly.'

That colour was a shimmering pale duck-egg-blue that brought out the brightness of her eyes. Perfectly fitted to slightly below the waist, clinging to her torso like a second skin, the dress flared softly to the ground. The neckline was scooped, but not outrageously so, just affording a tantalising glimpse of the soft swell of her breasts, and the back was equally scooped. When she moved, it flowed in gossamer-fine layers of silk around her, so that every movement she made was as graceful as a dancer's.

The highlights she had ignored at the hairdressers picked up rich copper threads in her hair that she had never noticed. Only a fraction of her hair had been trimmed so that, loose, it tumbled down her back and cascaded over her shoulders.

Her mother had brought in some of her jewellery, and the next half an hour was spent trying on several pieces.

Alexa discovered that she actually enjoyed that half an hour...

She was hardly aware of time passing until there was a knock on the door and she was told that Theo had arrived and was waiting for her by the stairs.

Alexa snapped out of her reverie and smiled at her mother. 'This is the most excited I've seen you in ages. Do you think I should have been going around dressed like this for the past few years?'

'You've never been one for dressing up...' Her mother sighed, still smiling. 'And I wouldn't have changed that for the world. But now and again... Well, my darling, you can see for yourself how wonderful it is to just try something new once in a while. Theo is going to be stunned.'

Theo won't notice what I wear unless I turn up in dungarees and trainers, Alexa wanted to retort as she slipped her feet into stilettoes that were precariously high but absolutely suited to the outfit.

'You're going to be *engaged*—and *married*. Such an exciting time... I know you've been nudged a little in that direction—but, darling, a mother knows best, and I just *know* that the two of you are going to be soulmates. When your father told me that Stefano had mentioned his son had seen you, wanted to meet you... Well, I was over the moon. And, having met him for myself... Well, he's just perfect—and I can tell you feel the same...'

So that's how this little charade is being played out, Alexa thought. Theo had supposedly wanted to set up a meeting with her. Her mother probably had visions of love at first sight, if not at first meeting.

Of course she didn't know of his deal made with the

devil. One year of self-sacrifice and in return shares in their sprawling family company. And, added to that, *his* father's company would be saved from public ruin.

Love and respect for her mother stopped her from prolonging the conversation and hammering the truth home like a battering ram. But it was just so frustrating.

She grabbed a little sequinned bag from the dressing table and then followed her mother along the corridor towards the staircase. Pausing at the top, she looked down to see Theo and her father chatting. Theo's back was to her, but the powerful force of his presence still struck her like a physical blow.

He was dressed as formally as she was. One hand was shoved into the pocket of black hand-tailored trousers, and she could see the pristine white of his shirt-cuff peeping out from beneath his immaculately fitted black jacket.

His body's posture was loose…relaxed. He was a man looking forward to an evening out with the woman he would show off to the world as his wife-to-be.

No wonder her mother thought that the man was the next best thing to sliced bread. Theo had his act down pat. He was so socially adept at handling any situation that anyone looking in would have just seen a prospective son-in-law dedicated to charming his in-laws. Anyone looking in would have probably thought that he had asked her father for her hand in marriage and proposed on bended knee. Which just went to show…

She took a deep breath and began walking down the winding staircase.

Theo turned slowly. Carlo Caldini was proving to be both amusing and intelligent. In fact he reminded Theo of his own father. He could understand why they had been inseparable friends for such a long time. Without much time to spare there had seemed little point in having a drink, so they had remained at the bottom of the staircase, chatting.

It had come as no great surprise that Alexa had not been waiting for him when he arrived. As long as she wasn't hiding out in the broom cupboard in the hope that he would leave without her, then that was all right. He was prepared to wait for as long as it took—whether they arrived on time or not was of little importance to him. In fact the later the better, to some extent, because not only would that limit the hours spent in tedious chatter but it would also ensure that the maximum number of people would witness their arrival, arm in arm.

In Rome, even more than in London, news of the happy couple and their impending nuptials would spread faster than the speed of light.

With his mind toying with the question of how best he could assimilate a wife into his lifestyle without having to alter his day-to-day routine very much, it took Theo a few seconds to focus on the woman gliding with effortless grace down the stairs.

So she'd taken him at his word. He hadn't known what to expect—whether she would actually do what was necessary or else jump aboard her independence bandwagon and don some paint-spattered overalls and hiking boots for the social event to which he had been invited.

Where had that figure come from? She'd hidden it well… With the dress clinging lovingly to her, he could see that she had the perfect hourglass shape. Full breasts narrowed to a slender waist, and even in the floor-length gown he could see that her legs would be shapely. She was the absolute opposite of the stick insects he was accustomed to dating.

Their eyes met and she pursed her lips—just sufficiently to remind him that she was doing this under duress.

If either of her parents had noticed that little show of rebellion they were hiding it well under their broad smiles and proud gazes, but as soon as he had followed her into the chauffeur-driven limousine, Theo turned to her.

'You're going to have to do a bit better than that…' he drawled, making sure that the privacy partition between the driver and the rear seat was firmly up.

She had pressed herself as far away from him as she could physically get without falling out of the car.

'And the evening isn't going to kick off on the right footing if you behave as though I'm carrying the plague,' he went on, keeping his voice even and detached.

'I'll be fine once we get there,' Alexa told him defiantly.

She had noticed that he hadn't complimented her on her outfit. Whilst her father had been holding her at arm's length and showering her with over-the-top compliments Theo had stood back, face impassive. Anyone in that situation would have felt hurt, so it wasn't strange that she had.

Clearly when there was no pressing need to make an impression he wasn't that bothered, so why did he expect her to cosy up against him now? Just in case the driver got suspicious?

'I'm not even sure where we're going,' she said, because yet again his show of good manners had made her feel like a silly kid.

'Art exhibition,' Theo said succinctly. 'Under normal circumstances I would have been in London, but as I happen to be here…'

'An art exhibition…?' She had gone to a couple of those ages ago, with her parents. The art had been incomprehensible and the crowd had been shallow and overdressed.

'There will be no need to stay long,' Theo said mildly. 'Just long enough to create an impression. Although…'

'Although what?' Alexa tensed and looked at him.

In the blue-grey twilight his face was all angles and shadows. She felt a dangerous ripple of response snake through her body and she caught her breath and held it for a few panicked, confused seconds before slowly releasing it.

'Although perhaps we might stay a bit longer than absolutely necessary. After all, it would a shame to waste a dress like that on a forty-minute appearance...'

Alexa was lost for words. He had paid her a compliment, in a backhanded sort of way, and his lazy velvety voice swirled around her like a mind-altering drug. He was leaning against the door, utterly relaxed, and his eyes were broodingly sexy as he watched her, obviously not caring that it was rude to stare.

Of course, she told herself feverishly, what he had *meant* was that it was a dress designed to grab the headlines, so why waste it? Why not stay as long as they could so that it had maximum effect? It hadn't been a compliment directed at her *personally*.

At any rate, it didn't matter one way or the other. This was a business arrangement. They were co-workers, so to speak.

'I've never liked those sorts of things.' Alexa rushed into nervous chatter. 'I think that was the best thing about being away from Italy...not having to go to openings and art shows and film premieres... Not that I was ever forced to, you understand, but I think my parents enjoyed showing me off. The hardship of being the only child of a rich family!'

She was blabbering, but she couldn't seem to stop herself because she knew that if she did she might have to analyse the rush of giddiness that had assailed her on the back of his stupid compliment. And then she would have to link it up with the weird way her body seemed to behave in his presence.

Did it all stem from her lack of experience with the opposite sex?

Blabbering on seemed an easier option than wrestling with those kinds of questions.

'Most people would kill to endure that sort of hardship.'

Cheeks flaming, Alexa turned to look through the window before glancing back at him. The space between them was as big as it could possibly get on the back seat of a very big car, but it still felt tiny. If she reached out she would be able to touch him.

'I get that,' she said stiffly. 'I wasn't complaining. I was talking too much because…'

'Because you're nervous?'

'Aren't you?'

Theo shrugged. He liked the way her hair fell in waves around her. It was much longer than he had originally thought, and it wasn't poker-straight, which seemed to be the only style women below the age of thirty-five wore their hair in the circles he mixed in. A year out from them might be a pleasant break in the monotony. She looked as though she had just climbed out of bed and run her fingers through its length and then left it to its own devices. She was dressed to kill and wearing war paint, but there was still something lacking in artifice about her. She would do those cameras proud.

'Why would I be nervous?'

'Because we're pretending to be something we aren't,' Alexa said bluntly.

'You never did tell me,' he murmured, 'whether you have a boyfriend or not.'

'Because it's none of your business.'

'Of course it's my business,' Theo returned smoothly. Was it? *Really?* Probably not. But he was suddenly curious to find out. 'Reporters will do anything to get background material so that they can flesh out a non-existent story, and you'd be surprised at the efforts they go to to rake up mud. If they uncover a lovelorn pro bono lawyer weeping in a corner somewhere they'll have a field-day. I'm going to have to be prepped with a suitable story.'

'Are you telling me that you're as pure as driven snow when it comes to…to…women? That there are no skeletons in your cupboard that can be uncovered?'

'My love-life is an open book!'

Theo grinned, and she was fascinated at how that open grin could be so engaging. She was as nervous as a kitten and he couldn't have been cooler.

Did *anything* rattle the man?

'We're here.'

Alexa realised that the limo was slowing in front of an impressive white building, fronted with imposing stone columns and a bank of shallow stairs leading up to double doors, which were open. In front of them two uniformed men were checking invitations.

'Boyfriend or no boyfriend?' Theo pressed, circling her wrist with his hand, staying her before she could get out of the car.

'No boyfriend! Okay?'

Theo shot her a smile of such satisfaction that she wanted to smack him. Instead she gritted her teeth and returned his look of satisfaction with one of simmering resentment, which just made him smile a little more.

'No boyfriend. Good. The fewer complications, the better. And stop scowling. Our relationship is too fresh for us to be having arguments in the back seat of a limo. We're still in the honeymoon phase… The way I leave the toothpaste uncovered and forget to put the toilet seat down hasn't started getting on your nerves just yet… So let's smile a lot and face the music…'

He laughed softly at her indignant, helpless expression and gently urged her out of the car as her door was opened for her.

It was a big deal. Cameras flashed at the throng of people clustered outside or making their way in. Even as the car had stopped Alexa had been able to recognise faces. A couple of high-profile politicians, celebrities clinging to other celebrities, as if terrified of moving out of their comfort zones, businessmen in suits, accompanied by wives dripping in diamonds…

Just the sort of crowd she preferred to avoid.

They stepped out of the car and every reporter with every camera seemed to turn, as one, in their direction.

This was the difference between being rich and being rich and newsworthy. The blinding flash of bulbs going off dazzled her, and the steadying arm of Theo, curving around her waist, felt like a solid rock of support in turbulent waters. She knew that she was actually leaning against him. Loathing the man, yet still finding his support strangely comforting.

There was an excited babble of voices and heads turned in their direction.

'You look amazing.'

Theo leant to whisper huskily into her ear and she looked up at him, sensed the popping of cameras taking a picture of their whispered conversation.

'So don't be nervous. I'm right here.'

He felt her automatic protest and his hold on her tightened. He laughed softly under his breath.

'Remember,' he murmured, still pressing close to her, so that no one could overhear what was being said, 'what I told you about retracting those claws in public… Don't forget that we're in love…at the honeymoon stage…you can't get enough of me…'

Alexa had no idea how she managed to deal with the next hour and a half. She drank two glasses of champagne and ate some of the canapés that were passed around. Questions peppered her from various quarters, including from several people—friends of her parents—who wanted to know what was going on.

The gossip mill was in full swing, and they couldn't have announced their togetherness in a more public manner.

Theo didn't leave her side. His arm was around her at all times. She was conscious of that with every step she took.

'Had enough?'

Theo tilted her chin up and their eyes met. Alexa found that she could do little else but stare. His eyes were truly amazing and she felt giddy, sucked in by their green depths. She saw those fabulous, mesmerising eyes flicker and then he was leaning towards her and his mouth was covering hers, grazing it, and then he was delicately teasing his tongue between her lips.

Never in her life had she felt anything like this before. It was as if a series of fireworks had exploded in her head. Every single thought vanished. Indeed, there was no one else in the room—no crowds of people chattering around her, no waiting staff weaving through with trays balanced on hands, no curious eyes boring a hole into her back.

There was just the two of them, and the feel of his tongue meshing with hers, eliciting a soft shudder of response.

Simultaneously the flash of a camera captured the moment, and she knew instantly that Theo had foreseen that.

Everything had been timed to perfection. He had held her with just the right amount of possessiveness, had been attentive to just the right extent, had led the charade, expecting her to follow in his lead—and she had.

They left the still-packed art exhibition and the babble of noise eventually subsided as they moved out into the open foyer outside the room where the main event was taking place, which was far less crowded.

'Well done.'

Theo released her, and without his arm around her reality was re-established.

'What choice did I have?' Alexa asked stiffly as they made their way outside.

The chauffeur had already been summoned and was waiting for them, with the passenger door open and thankfully, no prying cameras to chart their sudden lack of affection.

She was taut with anger. Anger at herself, for having become swept up in that kiss—and not just the kiss. The whispered encouraging compliments…the way he had spent the evening touching her in some way or another… the way he had been the perfect newly loved-up boyfriend.

'About as much as I had.'

The ferocity of his body's response to that well-timed kiss, which would doubtless be in print somewhere by the following morning, had shocked him. He prided himself on being in control of the situation that had been foisted upon him, and he was annoyed with himself for the unrestrained surge in his libido. *Again.*

He propelled her into the waiting car and then slid the partition up so that once again their conversation could not be overheard by their driver.

'Our engagement will be publicly announced in the next few days,' he informed her matter-of-factly. 'So our next bonding session will be at a jeweller's.'

Every trace of affection had disappeared. His cool washed over her like freezing water. He had detached. There was the man who could show one face to the public, and then there was the man who could remove that mask and be someone completely different in private.

This was a lesson she should learn, Alexa thought feverishly. While *her* feelings were all over the place, his had never shifted. He was completely lacking in all emotion—

which was why he had no problem going along with the farce.

Considering she had always thought of herself as a restrained person—someone who could stand back and laugh at the weaknesses of other members of her sex, who got their emotions all tangled up, who ended up being ruled by them—it came as a shock to realise that she wasn't quite the person she had thought herself to be.

She would have to learn fast.

'When shall I pencil that in?' she asked.

'Whenever I tell you to. It will take full precedence over everything else.'

'And I assume there will be some sort of stupid engagement party?'

'I prefer the word *lavish* to *stupid*.'

Alexa glumly pictured the extravagant affair it would no doubt turn out to be. Lots of important people, and among them the friends she had made in her job—who would stick out like elephants in a tea shop.

'I can't see your father having a great time being entertained by my parents,' she said snidely.

'You'd be surprised. They may have their simmering feud, but they have still carried on mixing in the same social circles. You know well enough what it's like over here.'

'Not really. I've spent most of my time abroad. And anyway I never attended those events.' Curiosity got the better of her. 'You've seen our fathers interacting?'

'On a couple of occasions. They bristle in each other's company and yet end up having conversations—like a married couple who can't help fighting but find it hard to stay away from one another. In a room of five hundred people, somehow they'll end up right next to one another. And in between the fraught relations there's usually a fair amount of gossip, which they can't seem to help divulging. Which, in turn, is probably why my father turned to Carlo before heading to the nearest bank. It's a strange case. So I shouldn't worry over-much about your father at our engagement party…it won't be a case of fisticuffs at dusk.'

'Do you know why they fell out?'

'Your guess is as good as mine.'

This lull in hostilities was a temporary soothing balm, but she shook herself free and recalled that this was just a business arrangement with a man she didn't even like.

The limousine was pulling up outside her house, but she remained sitting in the car for a few moments after the car had come to a stop in the courtyard.

'Perhaps you could text me with details of when this visit to the jeweller's is likely to be?' she offered politely.

Theo dragged his thoughts away from the way she was sitting, her body towards him, leaning in so that the soft mounds of her breasts were temptingly on show.

'Let's say I pass by for you at noon tomorrow. The sooner the better, as far as I'm concerned. We can choose a ring and then go somewhere to have lunch.'

Alexa couldn't hide her dismay. 'Lunch? Is that really necessary?'

'Your constant shows of reluctance are really beginning to get on my nerves, Alexa! Yes, *lunch*! What exactly is your dilemma with that? We're newly engaged. Has it occurred to you that as a newly engaged couple we might just want to celebrate together before scuttling off in opposite directions? Scuttling off in opposite directions would be more suited to a couple on the verge of divorce!'

Alexa glared, but this was her life for the time being and she knew that he was right. It was a game that had to be played to the full or not played at all.

She had embarked upon it, and it was too late now to start trying to renegotiate the terms of the contract.

'I can meet you at the jeweller's,' she offered.

'Not good enough. We're browsing together. No need for hiking boots, though…'

'Don't worry,' she sniped in return. 'I know my trainers wouldn't be suitable wear for being seen in public with you.'

'You have to be the most argumentative woman I have ever met in my entire life,' Theo mused in a driven undertone. 'Are you this argumentative with all the men you've been out with?'

Alexa was momentarily caught on the back foot, because the number of men she had dated could be counted on the fingers of one hand and none of them had provoked her the way this man did.

'I've never been out with anyone like you,' she finally gathered enough wit to respond, and Theo grinned.

'Are you telling me that I'm one of a kind?'

'If I'm argumentative, then *you're* downright impossible,' she muttered. 'I should be going in. The lights are on. My parents are probably waiting to hear how our first outing in public went—although judging from the amount of reporters there, they can probably find out in the papers tomorrow.'

'If I've failed to mention it, you handled the evening incredibly well.'

Of their own volition, his eyes dipped to her full and still mutinous mouth.

'Thank you. So did you,' she responded in a stilted voice.

When she glanced down she could see her breasts, too big and too exposed for her liking—especially now that she was in the intimate confines of a car with him—and she surreptitiously adjusted her dress, hoping that he wouldn't notice.

'My mother will ask about this stupid…sorry, this *lavish* engagement party. I expect she'll need time to sort it out. Could you give me an approximate…er…date? And I agree with you—the sooner the better.'

Theo marvelled that here was a woman who, only just engaged to be married to him, was clearly already thinking about the divorce papers being signed. Incredible. The fact that these were not normal circumstances did little to assuage his male pride.

'At the outside…a fortnight.'

'Will your brother attend as well as your father?' she found herself asking, because she knew that his brother lived on the other side of the world and that during these transactions he hadn't been a player on the scene.

Theo frowned. 'All bets are off when it comes to that,' he commented wryly. 'Daniel is in the process of buying himself a toy, and it may remove him from the scene of the action while this drama is being played out.'

'Buying a toy?'

'He has his eye on a small cruise ship.'

Much as he loved his brother, Theo was quietly relieved that Daniel wouldn't be around for the engagement party, such as it would be. Daniel could be counted on to respond with nothing but laughter at the fact that his big brother had found himself tying the knot prematurely. Actually, tying the knot at all.

'I had no idea that cruise ships could be called *toys*…' Alexa was distracted enough to say.

'In which case you don't know my brother.'

Alexa thought that that was just as well, because coping with one was bad enough. Two alpha males didn't bear thinking about.

She pulled open the car door and stepped out into a balmy night. Of course he walked her to the door. No protective arm around her shoulder this time, though! Instead both hands were firmly thrust in his trouser pockets.

'Isn't your chauffeur going to think that we're not behaving the way two nearly married people should be behaving?' she couldn't help but ask sarcastically, reaching into her bag for the house key, even though she knew that her mother was probably hovering very close to the front door so that she could pounce the second it was opened.

Theo lounged indolently against the door frame, looking down at her as she pulled out the key to insert it into the lock.

'Is that an invitation?' he asked softly.

Alexa raised startled eyes to his.

'What—what on earth are you talking about now?' she stammered, as her wide-eyed gaze was caught and held.

She had the oddest sensation that the oxygen was being sucked out of the air she was breathing as she continued to stare up at him. Her heart was fluttering madly, like a caged bird in a desperate bid for escape.

'What do you think?' Theo asked, in that same soft, lazy drawl that gave her goosebumps.

'Are you suggesting that I actually want you to…to…?'

'Kiss you? That's exactly what I'm suggesting…'

'Then you couldn't be further from the mark!' she snapped, blushing furiously and hating him for reminding her of their kiss, which *she* would rather have forgotten. 'I'm fine with you being…being attentive when we're out together, but the last thing I want is to be *kissed* by you! Do you know something, Theo De Angelis? You're the most egotistical, arrogant man I have ever met!'

'I know. I think you've told me already. But you make a valid point… Just in case…'

She sensed what he was about to do and yet it still took her by surprise—and this time there was an urgency to his kiss that hadn't been there before. His mouth assailed hers, his tongue seeking out hers. He curved a big hand behind her back and pulled her towards him.

He could feel the softness of her breasts squashing

against his chest and knew that he was losing his cool. *Again.* But her mouth was nectar-sweet—and after all, he told himself, it was all for the benefit of a driver who might or might not be taking note. Why take chances…?

'I'll see you tomorrow.' He straightened. 'Engagement ring shopping. Who would have thought…?'

With which he headed back to the car and Alexa, thoroughly unnerved, let herself into the house.

CHAPTER FOUR

As PREDICTED, THE next day the centre pages of all the newspapers had been printed with at least half a dozen pictures of the loving couple. Whoever had taken the photos couldn't have done better when it came to capturing angles that actually seemed to *prove* the lie that they were in love.

Theo's arm was always around her. In several pictures Alexa was looking up at him, mouth parted, the very picture of an enraptured girlfriend—as opposed to wearing the teeth-clenched, resentful expression, which was a lot closer to the truth.

Cora Caldini, who was waiting for her when she emerged at a little after eight, had all the papers spread out on the massive dining room table and Alexa stifled a sigh.

'I know this has all been unexpected for you,' her mother said gently, 'but there's so much to be said for a whirlwind romance—and looking at these pictures…my darling, you *sparkle*.'

Alexa helped herself to coffee and a croissant from the basket of fresh bread on the sideboard. Sparkle? Did minnows sparkle in the presence of hungry, prowling sharks?

'He's certainly a force to contend with,' Alexa forced herself to say. 'And you're right. It wasn't…er…exactly what I had in mind when I thought about meeting the man of my dreams. In fact I'm a little dazed—because he's just the sort of guy I never thought I'd...um...fall for. But... well...life is full of surprises, I guess...'

Unable to be more effusive than that, she scanned the photos once more and wondered whether the reporters had bothered with any other guests at all, or whether they had just decided to trail along behind Theo, snapping pictures.

'Isn't it...?' Her mother beamed. 'And sometimes surprises turn out all the better for being unexpected. It reminds me of when I met your father, as a matter of fact. Of course I'd seen him out and about, but at a distance, and when my parents arranged for us to meet face to face... Well, it really was love at first sight. He was nothing like what I'd expected, and I just fell for that rogue on the spot.'

Always mindful of the consultant's warning words several months ago, in the wake of her mother's third stroke, Alexa reluctantly decided to backtrack.

'Theo's...er...certainly not what I expected,' she conceded. 'I suppose he's quite intelligent, and he has a certain amount of...er...charisma...'

'Funny...your father likes him very much.'

Then perhaps *he* should marry Theo, Alexa thought nastily, surprising herself because she wasn't an uncharitable person by nature.

'That's good.'

'And I know you, my darling. You're as headstrong as I was at your age. If you really didn't like Theo I think we'd all know about it by now! You just don't want to jinx anything—which is why you're being reticent—and I completely understand. It took your father and I ages to have you, and I didn't tell a soul I was pregnant until I couldn't hide it any longer! So I won't press you. Now, tell me what your plans are for today.'

Alexa told her mother and could immediately feel her tummy clench at the prospect of a few hours browsing for a ring and then having lunch in a trendy restaurant with him.

The memory of that blistering kiss the night before had preyed on her mind all night, and she had awoken determined to make sure that they kept a cool distance from one another when there was no one around.

Her thoughts drifted while her mother chatted about rings and reflected on how fast she and Carlo had progressed from that first meeting—marrying within three months and never regretting a day of their long and happy marriage.

Naturally Alexa had known that the man was good-looking. But why did he have to be *so* good-looking? Averagely good-looking would have been all right. She felt that she might have been able to cope with that. But something about Theo De Angelis sparked a reaction in her that burned as fierce as a conflagration.

She didn't understand it. It didn't make sense, And it unsettled her. Scared her, even—although what was there to be scared about?

She surfaced to catch the tail-end of her mother informing her that Theo was going to be dashing off to New York—apparently called away on business. Carlo had wanted to show him around the electronics plant later in the week, talk men stuff, but unfortunately it was a visit that would have to wait.

'He never mentioned that,' Alexa murmured, brightening. 'When? Exactly?'

'Tomorrow, I believe. Your father called him first thing this morning about a visit to the plant and it seems that an emergency blew up overnight. So he wouldn't have mentioned anything to you when you were out.'

'I don't suppose you know how long he'll be away, do you, Mother?'

'A week at the very least… I'm sure he'll be most apologetic when he sees you later and will explain it all himself.

If there's one thing I can say for Stefano's son it's that he's an extremely polite young man…'

Good humour restored on the back of the heartening news that she was going to have a break from Theo, Alexa spent the remainder of the morning looking through her law books, making sure her brain was still ticking over. She dealt with a variety of problems at the shelter on a daily basis, and some of them were practical—questions pertaining to government allowances, retrieving cash from runaway partners, applying for social housing. It paid to keep abreast of the law, and it was no great hardship because she enjoyed it anyway.

At precisely eleven-thirty she got dressed, but she didn't rush.

This time, her spirits light because with Theo out of the country for maybe as long as a fortnight she would at least have some respite from his dangerously incendiary personality, choosing what to wear was far less of a chore than it had been the evening before.

Jeans, but smart black ones, a cream silk camisole top, because it was beautifully warm outside, and flat black pumps. Everything was brand-new, and she was in a good mood when, at twelve sharp, the doorbell rang and she forestalled her mother to answer it.

This time there was no driver, which was even better—because with Theo driving she would be spared those intense, speculative green eyes on her.

'You're in a good mood,' he said flatly, starting the engine of a Ferrari and easing it out of the courtyard towards the buzzing town centre. 'Why does that make me instantly suspicious?'

Alexa relaxed against the passenger's door, her head resting on the window, rolled up thanks to the air-conditioning which kept the temperature wonderfully cool. She absently noted his strong jawline and the sharp beauty of his lean face, in profile now as he focused on the road. He was wearing black sunglasses and a navy blue polo shirt and cream trousers. He looked impossibly elegant.

She tugged her eyes away from him, simultaneously deciding that this was just the sort of thing that had to stop—this mindless staring at him—and again applauding the fact that he was going to be away for the next few days. Plenty of time during which she could recover her equilibrium.

'I have no idea,' Alexa said chirpily. 'Doesn't *every* girl like going out shopping for her engagement ring?'

Theo glanced narrowly at her, then relaxed and smiled. 'Indeed. That *would* explain your good mood. You're right. I have yet to meet a woman whose heart doesn't beat faster at the prospect of all things bridal…'

Alexa scowled, because her saccharine-sweet sarcastic rejoinder had clearly backfired. 'I honestly don't think we should waste much time traipsing through shops in search of a diamond ring,' she told him loftily.

'Agreed.' He put the fast car into cruise mode and relaxed in his seat. 'There's no need for us to be seen going from one shop to another in search of the perfect ring. We've already got all the press coverage we need. Speculation is rife that marriage is in the air… If we went to the corner shop and bought a plastic washer it would probably be enough.'

Alexa grimaced as she recalled the spread of newspapers her mother had neatly laid out on the table for her perusal. 'Maybe they'll leave us alone now?' She breathed a sigh of relief at the thought.

'I expect they'll only leave us alone when there's a chunky wedding ring on your finger. Before then there are infinite possibilities for our relationship to crash and burn—and disasters always make better headlines.'

'Why would they assume that it will crash and burn?' How on earth did *real* celebrities survive? she wondered. Without going completely mad? 'And who *cares* if our relationship crashes and burns anyway? Who's interested?'

Alexa was genuinely bewildered, because she might come from a wealthy background but—of her choosing— she was as noticeable as wallpaper. Theo might be similarly rich, with the added bonus of his looks, but he wasn't a *star*…was he…?

Theo shrugged. 'Don't know. Don't care. I just know how the world of media operates and I deal with it. So if you don't want some trigger-happy reporter to shoot you leaving the house without your make-up, be warned.'

'I honestly don't care.'

Theo found an empty space in a crowded square around which designer shops extended outwards in ripples—layers of them, sandwiched between cafés and restaurants. In the centre of the square a trio of mythological creatures figured in bronze cavorted in the centre of an enormous fountain.

He turned to her and said, with utter seriousness, 'You don't, do you?'

'No. Do you?'

'I'm a man. I don't tend to go out wearing make-up. Well, not unless I have to. Sometimes after a long night at work I find a bit of foundation under the eyes…'

Alexa felt her mouth twitch and she grinned shyly and reluctantly at him.

He killed the engine, but she got the impression that there were more questions he wanted to ask her. It felt as if he had been testing her boundary lines…placing one foot over the perimeter of her electric fence, threatening to make inroads. That made her shiver a little.

'Right,' he said briskly. 'Engagement ring.'

In case she started falling behind him he curled his fingers into her hair and pressed his hand to the nape of her neck, gently making sure she kept up with him and slowing his naturally long stride to accommodate her much shorter one.

People turned and looked.

They clearly didn't know exactly who Theo was, but Alexa could almost see their brains churning, trying to figure out why he was famous—because he just *had* to be, looking the way he did.

Something weird rippled through her. A surge of pride. That he was with *her*.

They bypassed the first three jeweller's they came to and went directly to the fourth, which was little more than a nondescript door leading into a shop that was barely visible from the street outside.

'How on earth do you know about this place?'

'You're a woman. How on earth do you *not*?' From behind his dark shades Theo looked down at her upturned face, amused. 'Have you made it your life's mission to avoid leading the sort of life you were expected to lead?'

'I'm not into expensive jewellery. Do you come here with your girlfriends?'

She was acutely conscious of his fingers, still in her hair, absently stroking her neck. It sent shivers racing up and down her spine, and she had to forcibly remind herself just how over the moon she was that he would be disappearing to salvage his business deal and she wouldn't have to put up with these public shows of phoney affection.

Theo paused. 'Quite some time ago a woman I was dating dragged me here and made a point of telling me how exquisite and expensive the jewellery was.'

'So you bought her a diamond ring?' Alexa squeaked.

'Quite some time ago' implied that the woman he had been dating might have been *her* age, and she was struck again at just how sheltered a life she had led—more inter-

ested in her studies than in getting a guy to buy her baubles and trinkets…waiting for love to knock on her door and refusing to spread herself thin in the meanwhile…

'I broke off the relationship,' Theo returned wryly. 'I didn't like the direction it was taking.'

Alexa stopped dead in her tracks. 'You must *hate* this,' she said with sudden force. 'Being trapped into marrying me.'

'The rewards outweigh the inconvenience,' Theo said, fighting an urge to brush the hair blowing softly around her face from her eyes. 'And your dowry is certainly a healthy incentive.'

Feeling like cattle that had been successfully bartered to a new master, Alexa spun round on her heels and pushed open the door to the jewellery shop—which was as unprepossessing on the inside as it was on the outside.

'Take your time,' Theo urged as they were ushered into comfortable chairs and the process of displaying rings began.

The owner of the shop was small, thin and extremely knowledgeable. He seemed to know everything there was to know about diamonds, and tray after tray was brought, with rings nestling in beds of velvet, unpriced and therefore probably priceless.

Since it wasn't a real engagement Alexa didn't care which ring she wore, but it would be ridiculous to choose something that was big and ostentatious.

'What is *your* preference?' She turned to look at Theo, who was lounging in the chair, his long legs stretched out to one side, lightly crossed at the ankles. 'Why don't *you* choose?'

Theo linked his fingers on his washboard-flat stomach and looked at the proprietor with a knowing, man-to-man grin.

'Women!' He shook his head with an expression of rueful indulgence. 'As if *my* opinion would count for anything!'

He stroked her back with one possessive hand and his fingers lingered for fractionally too long on her bra strap. Alexa kept a smile pinned to her face and wriggled a little to dislodge his over-inquisitive hand.

'The women do usually take the lead when it comes to choosing jewellery, sir.'

The proprietor returned Theo's smile and Alexa gritted her teeth as Theo patted her a couple of times on her back and then linked his fingers lightly on his lap once again.

'And this feisty little lady knows that she can have whatever she wants! So what *do* you want?' He looked at her with lazy, sexy bedroom eyes. 'Your wish is my command…'

'If only *that* were true,' Alexa returned pointedly.

She bared her teeth in a smile and hoped that he was sharp enough to read the hidden message, which was along the lines of *If my wish was your command, you would be on the other side of the world…*

Without warning, Theo leaned forward and quickly, but far too effectively, planted a kiss on her mouth.

Their eyes tangled and she realised, heart beating frantically, that he knew exactly what she had been implying and had duly punished her with that kiss.

To add insult to injury, as she returned her attention to the tray in front of her, she felt his big hand rest on her leg and then, shockingly, move upwards, curving over the sensitive skin of her inner thigh and sending a frisson of electric response through her.

Perspiration beaded her upper lip. She snapped her legs shut and pointed to any ring on the tray—she didn't even notice which one she had chosen.

'That'll do!'

Theo's hand on her thigh tightened.

'Perfect choice, if I may say so myself...'

The proprietor reverently removed it from its velvet bed and they listened to his rhapsodies about the purity of the diamond and the rarity of its setting. They were asked to pay attention to the tiny details in the band, which marked it out as a one-off. Alexa was made to try it on. Measurements were painstakingly taken.

The ring cost a small fortune, so it wasn't hard to understand why the whole process was taking for ever.

'That'll do...?' It was the first thing Theo said as they made their way out of the shop.

'Your hand was on my leg,' Alexa said stiffly. And his arm was around her shoulders now. The public face of unity was back in place, although her body was as rigid as a plank of wood.

'Perfectly natural,' Theo purred, giving her shoulder a little squeeze as he guided her to one of the hippest cafés in the area—a place where people went to be seen. 'You're my fiancée. Of course I'm going to want to touch you. Frankly, I can't keep my hands off you...'

It was a load of nonsense, but Alexa still shivered with an illicit little thrill.

Her treacherous mind wondered what it must be like to have this sinfully sexy guy say those words and mean them...

What would it feel like to actually *know* that he couldn't keep his hands off her...?

Her eyes skittered across to him—a quick glance at his face, once again shielded behind his sunglasses. Then, rebelling against all common sense, she noted the width of his shoulders, the lean muscularity of his body, the strength of his forearms and the way his dark hair curled around the dull metal of his watch strap.

She found herself drinking him in and felt her nervous system ratcheting up a notch.

In a couple of days she would be wearing a large diamond rock on her finger. Speculation, such as there was, would be over and she would be officially engaged to the guy now attracting stares from every single woman under the age of eighty and over the age of eighteen.

She was short and unspectacular. He was physical perfection. Even if he did get under her skin in ways that made her want to scream, there was no way that she could deny the sheer beauty of the man.

Was it any wonder that he was taking all this in his stride? He was accustomed to women. A phoney engagement wouldn't faze him and he would be particularly incentivised by the carrot at the end of the stick. He didn't need yet more money, but since when did the wealthy ever turn down the opportunity to add to their bank vaults? *Never.*

As expected, every head swivelled in their direction, and Alexa saw one very leggy blonde disengage herself from her group of friends and make a beeline in their direction.

She stifled a groan.

The blonde stalked towards them, her sharp bob expertly cut and dropping squarely to her shoulders. Even in flats she was close to six foot, and wearing next to nothing. She was rake-thin, flat as a pancake, and had the longest legs Alexa had ever seen—and most of those long legs were exposed because her skirt barely covered her underwear.

Her body language said it all as she chose to ignore Alexa completely, focusing one hundred per cent of her blue-eyed attention on Theo. *Surely it couldn't be true?* The blonde ran her china blue eyes dismissively over Alexa. *The press had it all wrong, hadn't they?*

'I mean, I just can't believe it!' she squeaked, sliding him a naughty smile that was designed to eliminate Alexa from the conversation.

She placed a flattened palm on his chest and shimmied

a little closer. Her hair was so silky and so unbelievably blonde that Alexa could only stare in wonder.

'Andrea…' Theo caught the blonde's hand, halted it firmly in its tracks and held it slightly at a distance before dropping it. It was a gesture that was cool and indifferent. Alexa would have been mortified. The blonde remained perky and upbeat. 'I'd like you to meet Alexa…'

'You're really *short*, aren't you?'

'Alexa is my fiancée.' Theo's voice was soft, silky, glacial. 'And now, before I start getting annoyed at your interruption, I suggest you take yourself back to your group of friends.'

For a few seconds the blonde was nonplussed. Alexa almost, but not quite, felt sorry for her. In her world she would rule supreme, but with a few words from Theo she was reduced to a woman of no standing.

'You don't mean that…'

She tried for provocative and Alexa, with a stab of pure womanly satisfaction, could have told her that she had made a mistake. One look at Theo's shuttered face should have sent the blonde running for cover.

'I mean it, Andrea. I'm giving you two seconds. You don't leave…you see that big guy, standing on the corner…?'

Andrea left, head held high, long, slim body taut with anger and wounded pride.

'I don't mind leaving if you feel that you might be uncomfortable here…' Alexa hovered, uncertain as to what to say in the wake of that dramatic scene.

Theo looked down at her, bemused. 'Why would I feel uncomfortable?'

He signalled with a nod to a hassled-looking waitress, who immediately patted her hair and plastered a smile on her face when she spotted him. Every other customer apparently forgotten, she dashed over to them and cleared a path to a table at the back of the restaurant.

'It's reserved,' the waitress confided with a giggle, 'but I'll sort something else out for the women who reserved it…'

Alexa automatically opened her mouth to protest, but Theo was already sitting and ordering a bottle of wine for them to share without looking at the menu.

'Why do you think I would feel uncomfortable?' he asked again, as soon as she was seated. 'And stop looking guilty because someone else had reserved this table. That charming little waitress said she'd sort it out—let's let her do her job.'

'Her job isn't to pander to customers who haven't booked a table.'

'Not my problem.' He shrugged. 'Now, moving on…'

Alexa sighed. The man was utterly impossible. The more time she spent in his company, the more cemented that impression became.

'I guess that woman must be one of your girlfriends and I just thought it might be awkward for you to be in the same place as she is when you know she'll probably be gossiping about you to her friends…'

Theo was looking utterly relaxed. 'You guess correctly,' he said, pushing back his chair to accommodate his long body. '*Ex*-girlfriend. Barely lasted a month, if you want the truth. The woman turned out to be a bunny-boiler. What started as a little bit of fun with a reasonably attractive woman turned into a dozen phone calls a day and attempts to get into my diary to make sure I wasn't seeing anyone else…'

Andrea had wanted a hell of a lot more than he had been prepared to give. Big mistake. On the love front… he had *nothing* to give. He'd seen what unrestrained emotions did to a guy—had seen the way his mother's death had destroyed his father…the way it had left a great gaping hole in his and Daniel's lives. No. Frothy, dewy-eyed looks from women were the ultimate turn-off to him, and trying to get anything more out of him than passion was their fastest way to the exit.

Alexa's mind had become stuck on his description of the blonde bombshell as a *'reasonably attractive woman'*.

What on earth did he consider *stunning*? Were his values so much different from everyone else's because of the way he looked? What on earth must he think of *her*?

'Some women are possessive, I guess…' she said.

Wine had been brought to the table and poured into oversized goblets and she took a sip of the chilled liquid and then stared at the glass—which seemed less fraught with potential danger than staring at *him* and getting into a mental muddle.

Theo nodded. He found it amazing that a life of luxury and wealth appeared to have had so little effect on the woman sitting opposite him. The privileges which should have turned her into the sort of vain, self-obsessed young woman he met every day of the week in his social circles seemed to have had the opposite effect. Frankly, and against all odds, she roused his curiosity.

'I've always found it a healthy option to stay away from those,' Theo drawled. 'Life's too short to waste any of it with a woman who wants to micro-manage my life. No, I don't give a damn if Andrea is sitting five inches away from us, gossiping with her friends.The only thing Andrea will tell anyone is that I am now engaged.'

'Engaged to someone short.'

He laughed, and his cool green eyes skirted over her flushed face. 'There's no law about falling in love with someone who doesn't fit the insane prototype other people have come up with,' he murmured.

No, Alexa thought, and as he had pointed out they made

the perfect society match. Two prominent families united in marriage. Who would think to scratch beneath the surface to see two individuals who couldn't have been less suited?

'How is it that you have never settled down?' she asked with blunt curiosity.

It was an extremely personal question—but why not? There would be occasions they spent together away from the spotlight, and they couldn't lapse into silence whenever they were together, could they? It would make living together extremely difficult—even if their living together would be taking place in opposite wings of whatever house they ended up living in…

She wondered whether they might not end up being friends, and then nearly laughed hysterically at that notion—because the man was just too *much*, too *larger than life*, to be considered a potential buddy. Potential buddies didn't make you feel as though you were standing on the edge of a precipice, looking down. Buddies were comfortable to be around, unthreatening, safe…

Theo looked at her consideringly. Out of the corner of his eye he could see his ex-girlfriend shooting venomous looks in their direction. He wanted to grin, because he knew that the single thing that would enrage Andrea and all those women like her—all those beautiful, arrogantly self-assured women he had dated in the past—was the fact that he was engaged to someone they would consider downright plain.

The fact that Alexa had been born to privilege would make little difference. Beautiful women were notoriously superficial when it came to judging other women, by standards that were almost always according to looks.

He felt a sudden surge of protectiveness towards his fake wife-to-be.

He reached forward and stroked the side of her face, linking his fingers through hers at the same time.

Another public display of affection, Alexa thought as her heart picked up a frantic pace. And particularly appropriate given that their actions were being minutely watched by an ex-girlfriend who would be busy spreading the news that the most eligible man on the planet had been caught.

An ex-girlfriend who was probably appalled and stunned that he had been stupid enough to fall for someone *like her*...

Alexa had always known that when it came to looks she could only ever aspire to be average. She didn't have razor-sharp cheekbones or long, thirty-four-inch legs or shiny poker-straight hair. She had never felt comfortable in revealing clothes and largely avoided wearing anything that was too bright or too eye-catching.

And yet here she was. Engaged to a man who could have any woman he wanted with the crook of one imperious finger.

Okay, so it might all be pretend, but just for a moment she felt something wicked steal into her. A purely feminine response kicked into gear. His fingers were still entwined with hers and she slowly lifted them to her lips and grazed his knuckles with her mouth.

Heat flared in Theo's eyes. She could almost hear his sharply indrawn breath.

Alexa felt a rush of unfamiliar daring. She raised her eyes to his and held his stare, watched the way his slow smile transformed his face and tried hard not to panic when he leaned in close to her, creating a little bubble of intense intimacy between them.

Nerves threatened to overtake her, but she could feel the blonde's glassy blue eyes boring into her back and that gave her the impetus she needed to lean right into him. To offer her lips to him.

And when he kissed her she responded with an enthusiastic lack of inhibition. She slid her tongue against his and stifled a little moan as, eyes closed, she indulged in naked, forbidden desire.

This was what was expected of her. She was his fiancée. He had confirmed that to an ex-girlfriend, who would have been surprised if they had continued sitting opposite one another making polite conversation. Theo De Angelis was an intensely physical man. You just had to look at him to know that. So kissing him like this, curling her hand into his hair, was only to be expected.

She was just playing the part she had been commissioned to play!

It was liberating to think that she wasn't doing anything out of the ordinary.

It was permission granted to sink into a kiss that was... *explosive.*

When she pulled back she knew that she was shaking a little, and she licked her lips and forced a smile.

'Just for show,' she mumbled, and Theo raised his eyebrows.

'I like it,' he murmured softly. 'I sense a change from all those other displays of affection you didn't seem to enjoy—or was I wrong about that...? Were you actually burning up and looking for a few encores?'

'Of course not!' Her mouth was still tingling from that searing kiss. 'But...'

'But you thought you'd take the opportunity to get one up on the delectable ex-girlfriend who's been shooting you daggers behind your back...?'

'Of course not!' But she blushed furiously.

Theo grinned. 'Trust me, I don't have a problem with your reasoning.'

'I...I hope you don't think that was anything but acting,' Alexa breathed forcefully. 'It's just that you've announced that we're engaged… I thought it would look odd if we didn't act like a newly engaged couple. I mean… you're the one who's kept telling me that we have to make this stupid charade look real…'

'Of course…' He paused, wondering just how real he would like the charade to be. Complications aside… 'And I'm heartened that you're now in such a positive mindset,' he told her, 'because I should tell you that I've been called away on business. I will be out of the country for a week. Maybe a bit less…maybe a bit longer. It's hard to tell because this is a complex deal…'

'I know.'

'You do?'

'My mother broke the news while she was poring over all the pictures of us together at that art opening we attended last night. Don't worry…' Now, more than ever, Alexa was looking forward to a few days on her own— away from his powerful, charismatic personality and the weirdness of their situation. 'I'll make sure to keep the home fires of the newly engaged couple burning…'

'You won't have to do that,' Theo informed her kindly.

'I won't?'

'Don't be silly. How could you think for a moment that I would want you out of my sight for an hour, never mind a week…? No, there will be no need to keep those home fires burning, because you will be right there with me… by my side…'

CHAPTER FIVE

ALEXA WAS APPALLED. She stared at him in open-mouthed consternation, forgetting that her every move was being watched by an interested party.

'Coming with you?' she stuttered.

'Step one in assimilating into my lifestyle,' Theo said smoothly. He leaned back and slouched elegantly in the chair. 'You may hate premieres and art gallery openings, but there will be a certain amount of socialising that you will have to do—like it or not.'

He signalled for the bill without taking his eyes from her face. 'I'm not a fan of meeting and greeting people I have no intention of forming any sort of relationship with,' Theo said drily, 'but it's all part and parcel of the game.'

'Why do I get the feeling that everything about this arrangement is on *your* terms?'

'Explain.'

'Your father is the one who needed a bail-out,' Alexa muttered, feeling terrible at having to remind him of that little detail, because she liked what little she had seen of Stefano De Angelis and was sorry that he, a proud man, had found himself in the position of having to ask for financial assistance from a man he was not on speaking terms with. Although she was beginning to suspect that their so-called feud had petered out into two old men warring through habit over something both had long forgotten about.

Theo's mouth tightened. His father might have taken his eye off the ball, but he didn't need to rehash that misfortune. And he certainly wasn't interested in anyone rehashing it on his behalf.

'He is—but that's old news now. I don't see the point in moaning about what can't be changed.'

'I'm not moaning.' Alexa fiddled with the stem of her wine glass and wondered where all the contents had gone. She'd barely been aware of drinking. Or eating, for that matter. She raised her eyes to his and struggled to look away. 'I just think that *my* life has been completely disrupted while you continue to carry on as if nothing much has happened…'

'Stop feeling sorry for yourself. It makes sense for you to move to London after we are married. I can't conduct my business from here. And remind me… As far as I am aware you don't currently have many ties to this place. You've quit your job and your only other interest appears to be helping at a shelter somewhere. Nothing that can't be left behind at a moment's notice.'

Alexa felt rage rush through her with tidal wave force. If they'd been anywhere but here she would have been tempted to chuck something at him.

How dared he take her life, sum it up and write it off in a handful of words?

But perhaps that was how he treated all women? she thought with scathing distaste.

'Are you like this with all women?' she asked tightly.

'How do you mean?'

Theo frowned, puzzled. How had they gone from a perfectly rational conversation about the dynamics of their married life to some opaque query about his treatment of women? He realised that never before had he had to hold himself to account with anyone—far less a woman.

Her bright eyes glittered as she waited in silence for a response.

Theo raked his fingers through his hair and muttered an oath under his breath. 'I have no idea where you're going with this...'

'It's a simple question,' Alexa said stubbornly.

'I'm extremely fair in my treatment of women,' he said impatiently. 'Exemplary, some might say.'

'Really?'

'Time to go, I think.'

'Only if you answer my question.' She didn't know why it was important to her. She just had a vague feeling that she had to have some say in what was going on or else he would take control of the reins and she would find life as she knew it disappearing even faster than it already was.

'I already have.'

'I feel like you're bullying me.'

Theo shot her a look of pure incredulity. 'I don't believe I'm hearing this!'

'You expect me to change my whole *life*! You don't even bother pretending that I have any say in the matter!'

'I'm cutting through the red tape,' Theo pointed out, with irrefutable logic as far as he was concerned. 'There's nothing you have here that ties you down.'

'What about my parents?'

'Your parents can come to London any time they want,' Theo pointed out. 'In fact I assume they already do, given that your father has business interests there...'

'That's not the point.'

'It's exactly the point—and if you would stop looking at the big picture with irrational feminine logic you would agree with me.'

'Sometimes,' Alexa gritted, 'I really want to hit you.'

'Who knows...?' he replied without hesitation. 'Maybe you will. Although if you do, it won't be in anger...'

'What are you talking about?'

Colour crawled into her cheeks as he raised his eyebrows and shot her a slow, deliberate smile. Her treacherous body tingled. Try as she might, she couldn't bank down the sudden tightening of her nipples, achingly sensitive as they grazed against her lacy bra. And she was aghast to feel spreading dampness between her legs.

'Never tried a bit of bondage?' Theo asked, enjoying the hectic flush in her cheeks. 'I admit I do prefer my women to fully participate in the action—although who knows...? I'm a man who has always been open to new experiences...'

'I've already told you...' Alexa could barely get the words out because her mouth was so dry. 'We won't be... That won't be part of the deal...'

Did she have *any* idea how much he disliked being told that there was something he couldn't do? Theo thought that if she did she might refrain from that approach.

'Anyway, we're straying off the topic.' She cleared her throat. 'I don't like feeling that I have no input.'

'And you're implying that that's the way I treat women generally? You're telling me that you think I'm a bully who takes advantage of women...?'

Alexa cringed because, put like that, it seemed a crazy accusation. If he was a mean bully who took advantage of women why would they care if they were dumped? That blonde who had sidled up to him still had the hots for him. That had been *very* obvious. And she was the sort of woman who could have any man she wanted. If money had been the only thing keeping her in a relationship with Theo, there was no way she would have looked at him the way a starving man eyed up his next meal.

'I'm just saying—'

'I have never bullied a woman in my life before,' Theo interrupted coldly. 'I have extremely healthy relationships with the opposite sex. I am honest to a fault. I have never pretended that commitment and marriage is a possible destination. I have always told them upfront that I'm in it for fun and that fun doesn't last—that beyond that I have nothing to give. But while they're with me they couldn't be treated better. Andrea, as a case in point, was showered with presents and taken to the sort of glittering social dos that have gone a long way to kick-starting her career in film.'

Alexa didn't say anything, because he seemed to expect congratulations for being the sort of guy most women who wanted something other than a ten-second fling would run a mile from. And she was sure that a lot of those women who had been given his rousing speech on not getting thoughts of permanence wouldn't have been quite as cheerful when they were dispatched as he liked to think.

'What do you mean that you have nothing to give beyond *fun*? Why?'

Theo flushed darkly and immediately decided that he had imparted enough information on the subject of his private life. Inside, where the soul stored love, his soul was empty. No reserves left. That place, instead, stored the pain of his father's reaction to loss and the hurt of his own loss…all the result of that big thing called love.

'I'm not laying down laws,' he said snappily, bringing the conversation back to the matter in hand. 'Feel free to tell me if you think it's feasible for me to set up camp here for the duration of our short marriage… Even when you have no strenuous objections to moving to London aside from the fact that it was a decision you feel you didn't reach of your own free will.'

'I've never had anyone make decisions on my behalf.'

She stuck stubbornly to her guns, but she knew that her moral high ground was being eroded from all directions.

'Then maybe you should sit back and enjoy the novelty.'

Theo knew that that remark was tantamount to waving a red rag at a bull with an axe to grind, but he couldn't help himself. Something about the way she reddened and pursed her lips and glared made for addictive watching.

Alexa refused to rise to the bait. They exchanged a brief look, during which a lot seemed to be said without any words passing between them. She communicated with a slight tilt of her chin that she knew exactly what game he was playing—knew that he was trying to rile her because it amused him—and he, in turn, acknowledged the truth in that.

The moment unnerved her.

'I don't like being told what I can wear and what I can't,' she confessed shortly.

'So I'm taking it that part one of your complaint has been dealt with? You're in agreement with me that London would be the best base for us?' He sighed. 'Decisions have to be made,' he said heavily, 'whether you like it or not. Your parents are more than welcome to come and stay with us whenever they want and let's cut to the chase: we'll only be together for just as long as it takes for the ink to dry on our marriage certificate...'

'It's awful. I never thought that I'd end up getting married for all the wrong reasons...'

It was a sobering thought. An arranged marriage—a marriage of convenience—was a marriage without love, and she had always imagined love and marriage as two words inextricably bound together. Yet to some extent her parents' marriage had started on lines very similar to those she was now having to endure.

This tangent threatened to lead them down all sorts of unfamiliar paths, and meandering chat about emotional issues just wasn't his forte, but when Theo looked at the heartfelt expression on her face he found it hard to feel exasperation.

'Love disappears,' he said gruffly. 'And even when it doesn't it burns so strong that it consumes everything around it and ends up self-imploding.'

They were leaning into one another, unconsciously promoting a space around themselves that excluded everyone else in the restaurant, and for that he was glad—because a bride-to-be with a downcast, near to tears expression could in no way be interpreted as a bride-to-be contemplating the happiest day of her life.

As it looked from the outside, they were two people huddled and whispering sweet nothings to one another.

He entwined his fingers with hers and absently stroked her thumb with his to promote the illusion.

'I prefer not to think that way. I prefer to think that you can really find your soulmate and, yes, live happily ever after without everything "self-imploding", as you say. Or else disappearing like water down a drain. That's not how love works. I might be stupid, but I'd like to think that the man for me, the man who can make me happy, is out there…and I'll find him. *We'll find one another.*'

'And who's to say that won't happen…?'

'What do you mean?' For a few seconds Alexa was genuinely disconcerted. Was he talking about *them*? Insinuating that their marriage of convenience could end up becoming the real thing?

'I mean you will move on from me and find this man of your dreams—maybe a little later than you originally planned, and not quite in the order you might have anticipated, but who knows…?'

'What's made you so cynical?' she asked, flabbergasted at the casual way he was happy to dismiss their marriage and divorce as just something a little inconvenient—

something that could be swept aside in the future as though it had never happened.

Whether they were married for twelve months or twelve minutes, and whether she liked him or not, he would leave an impression. She would not be the same person she had been before.

'Let's leave that thorny subject for another day,' Theo told her wryly. 'I'll let you know when we'll be leaving for the States…'

'I didn't say that I was coming with you.'

'Are you going to argue with each and every small thing until we finally part company and go our separate ways? Because if that's your intention it's going to be a very long twelve months.'

'I'm not being argumentative.' She glared at him mutinously and in return he raised his eyebrows in cynical disagreement. 'But if I'm obliged to fall in line and never complain then I think it's only fair that *you* fall in line a bit as well.'

'Are we about to have another bracing conversation about the "separate bedrooms post-marriage" clause?'

'I'd like you to sample how *I* live,' Alexa continued doggedly. 'You want me to go to all sorts of stupid fancy social dos—'

'Don't write them all off. You might find that you actually *enjoy* some…'

Alexa chose to ignore that interruption. 'The least you could do is try and understand what I'll be sacrificing.'

Theo raised his eyebrows and began standing up. He was at a loss to understand what she was talking about. Of course the 'pause' button would have to be pressed on her fairy-tale love and perfect soulmate, but she was young. Plenty of time for her to find that once their committed spell together was at an end.

Frankly, he could tell her that airy-fairy dreams were a

certain recipe for disappointment—but what would be the point of that? She would find out soon enough. She was an enduring romantic, while he…he had about as much faith or interest in romance as a turkey had in signing up for centrepiece duties next to the carving knife on Christmas Day.

She had asked him why he was cynical. He could have told her that he'd had a close-up view of just the sort of pain love could bring—the sort of pain that no one in their right mind would want inflicted on them.

It tended to turn a guy off marriage. Although, in fairness, he knew the day would come when marriage would make sense, and when that day came he anticipated something very much like what he now had—but without the complication of a partner in search of the impossible. Emotions would not take over, leaving him vulnerable to going through what his father had gone through.

Of course he was a very different man from his father. Stefano had met his wife when they had both been young. They had fallen in love when they had both been green around the ears. Theo was anything *but* green around the ears. The opposite. And he prided himself on having the sort of formidable control that would never see him prey to anything he didn't want to feel.

An arranged marriage with the right woman—a woman who wasn't looking for anything that wasn't on the table—would be the kind of marriage he would eventually subscribe to. It made sense.

'Do tell me what that would be. What great "sacrifices" will you be making? Tell me. I'm all ears…'

They were outside now, walking in the balmy sun. He had a case load of documents to read before his trip to New York, but he didn't think that a few minutes prolonging their conversation would hurt.

'I can show you.'

She hailed a cab and leant forward to give the taxi driver

an address. It was on the tip of his tongue to tell her that time was money, but he desisted. Why provide her with another excuse to stage an argument? He had never met a woman as stubborn and as mulish as she was, and those were traits he had no time for. His life was stressful enough, without having a woman digging her heels in and finding objections to every single thing he said or suggested.

'We're here.'

'Here? Where?' The designer shops and smart cafés had been left behind, to be replaced with dingy shop fronts and fast food outlets. It was the sort of place Theo had only ever passed with the windows of his chauffeur-driven car rolled up.

'The shelter where I volunteer,' Alexa told him.

She pointed to a building next to a pawn shop. A grim concrete block fronted by a no-nonsense black door that would have deterred anyone but the most foolhardy.

'I want you to come in and see it—meet some of the other volunteers I work with.' She sprang out of the car, only realising that he hadn't followed when she had slammed the door behind her, at which point she reopened her door and peered inside at him.

'You're not *scared*, are you?' She smirked, because for the first time since she had boarded the rollercoaster ride that had become her life she felt as if she had the upper hand. 'I promise I won't let anything happen to you…'

Theo looked at her, partly outraged because no one had ever dared accuse him of being scared of anything in his life before, partly amused because she had wrong-footed him and not many had done that either.

'What do you think I might be scared of?' he murmured as they headed into the shelter.

'A new experience?' She blushed, hearing the teasing tone in her voice.

'You've broken the ice on that one,' Theo pointed out

drily. 'When it comes to new experiences, you rank right up there as a first.'

'I'll take that as a compliment,' Alexa threw back at him, because she knew that a compliment it certainly hadn't been meant to be.

He smiled slowly, his amazing eyes skirting over her flushed face and doing a lazy inventory of everything else.

'You should,' he murmured. 'I have a jaded palate, and new experiences are always welcome...'

'Even unpleasant ones?'

'What are we talking about, here? The shelter...or you...?'

He was leaning against the door, towering over her, and she felt her heart begin to race. His voice was as smooth as the finest dark chocolate and his eyes were doing all sorts of weird things to her nervous system, muddling her thoughts and stripping her of that momentary feeling of triumph she'd had moments earlier.

She rang the bell and turned away, although she could still feel him staring at her, and suddenly the memory of all those convenient kisses slammed into her, depriving her of breath.

She didn't like him, she reminded herself fiercely. Not only did she not like him—she didn't like the situation she was in.

But he was so sinfully good-looking. He had the sort of face that made her want to stare with helpless fixation and keep on staring. He had that effect on every woman. She had witnessed it for herself. And, whilst she had thought herself immune to that sort of thing, she had to accept the galling truth that she wasn't as immune as she wanted to be.

That was why she found it so unsettling whenever he got too close to her, and why the thought of those kisses kept her awake at night. She was human, and she lacked the necessary experience to deal with a man like Theo De Angelis.

All her old-fashioned ideas about only ever being attracted to her soulmate had been turned on their head...

Which didn't mean that they had disappeared! No, it just meant that she responded to him on a purely physical level, and it was only now that she was accepting that unpalatable truth. She'd always assumed that, for her, physical attraction would only be possible when it was to the guy who had stolen her heart, but she'd been wrong. She could see that now.

Which was a good thing.

Once you knew your enemy, you knew how to arm yourself—and *her* enemy was her treacherous body. She would just have to make sure that she maintained as much distance as she could and never, ever repeated the mistake she had made at the restaurant, when she had initiated that kiss and totally lost herself in it.

It was great that she was going to introduce him to what she did, because it was the one area in which he would be at sea—and that was something she would really enjoy watching.

'You're smiling...' he leant in to whisper as footsteps were heard on the opposite side of the door. 'Private joke or something you'd care to share?'

'Private joke,' she told him promptly.

She looked away as the door was opened and felt a lump in her throat, because she knew that she was going to miss the shelter beyond words when she disappeared off to London.

The prospect of the lifestyle awaiting her there made her want to burst into tears.

Not that *he* would ever understand.

She sneaked a sideways glance at him and, introductions made, took a background seat to watch the spectacle of the great Theo De Angelis fumbling awkwardly in a situation of which he would have had no experience.

He didn't fumble. He charmed all the women there, Franca and Louisa and Marie and Ndali. He introduced himself to some of the women who came to them for practical and emotional help. He pried and prodded into all the rooms and asked so many questions that anyone would have thought that he was an expert on women's shelters.

He talked finance with the guy who ran the place, and made a show of looking at the books. He even went so far as to make suggestions on how small improvements could be made!

She had hoped to watch him squirm, and instead he had dumbfounded her with lots of phoney interest.

'So what exactly is your role there?' was the first thing he asked when they were back outside an hour and a half later.

The work awaiting his attention would have to wait and he had resigned himself to that. Allowing work to take second place to anything was an alien concept to him, but he had watched her as they walked through the premises, watched her interaction with her colleagues, and the casual, friendly, concerned manner with which she had spoken to the some of the women waiting in queues to be seen or chatting to the other volunteers.

Everything about her had breathed open sincerity. Her laughter with her colleagues had been rich and infectious. Frankly, it was the sort of laughter that had been conspicuously absent between *them*, and he had been irked by that.

He had been tolerant of her hostility, even though he privately thought that she should have taken her cue from him and dealt with the whole unfortunate situation with a bit more aplomb—because why rail against the inevitable? And besides, it wasn't destined to be a lifetime situation. He had gritted his teeth at the patently grudging reluctance in her responses to him and the ease with which she accepted as fact the thought that he was deplorable.

But here he had glimpsed a side to her that he hadn't seen before.

It was rare for any woman not to respond to him. Even when he was uninterested in them they still tried hard around him. He had made exceptions for her because of the circumstances of their forced relationship, but only now was he accepting that her indifference was an offence to his pride.

On a more basic level, he wanted what he had seen of her at that shelter. It was human nature to desire the things that are denied. Fact of life.

Alexa was making sure to keep as much distance between them as was acceptable, considering they were supposed to be madly in love. People who were madly in love didn't necessarily have to hold hands everywhere they went—and besides, no one in these streets knew who they were.

Niggling away at the top of her mind was the uncomfortable thought that she fancied the man, and that her plan of seeing him out of his depth and floundering in unfamiliar surroundings—which she had hoped might put the brakes on her stupid attraction to him—had spectacularly backfired.

She should have guessed. He could pull that charm out when it was needed like a magician pulling a rabbit out of a hat.

'Are you *really* interested?' she asked, then belatedly remembered what he had said about her arguing with everything he said. 'Sorry,' she apologised. 'Even if you're not really interested, it's thoughtful of you to pretend to be.'

She was determined to stop letting him get under her skin and rattle her. If she could reach a higher plane of being cool and controlled when she was around him, then her wayward responses could be harnessed and quickly killed off. Fancying someone because of the way they looked was so superficial that it surely couldn't last longer than two minutes.

'And,' she continued, 'you put on a really good show of being interested in what went on there.'

Theo's mouth tightened. Whatever he said or did, she was determined not to give him the benefit of the doubt and it was really beginning to get on his nerves.

'So what exactly is your role there?' he repeated, keeping his voice even and neutral.

They were heading back in the direction of the bars and shops and cafés, looking out for any passing taxis and walking until they could hail one. They had quickly left behind the insalubrious neighbourhood where they had just been, and the houses to either side of them now were well maintained but small and all exactly alike.

Theo realised that this was a part of town he had never actually visited. He wasn't in the country a lot, and when he was his visits were fleeting, because he far preferred to import his father to London.

Having always considered himself a man of the world— widely travelled, the recipient of far more global experiences than most people could ever dream of achieving in a lifetime—he now wondered when and how he had managed to isolate himself so entirely in a very specific social circle that was accessible only to the very, very wealthy. He was delivered to and from places in chauffeur-driven cars, never flew anything but first class, always had the most expensive seats at the opera or the theatre…

Alexa, having come from a very similar background to his own, should have followed the same route—maybe without the high-powered career—but she hadn't and that roused his curiosity.

'It wasn't quite the sort of thing I was expecting,' he expanded truthfully.

'And what *were* you expecting?'

She turned to him and was dazzled by the glare from the sun, which threw his lean, handsome face into a mosaic of shadows. She shielded her eyes and squinted against the sun. Overcome by a sudden feeling of vertigo, she took a couple of small steps backwards.

'A soup kitchen and people waving begging bowls at you?'

She took a deep breath and told herself that sniping and bristling was just a symptom of the stupid attraction she felt for the man, against all odds. If she carried on like that he would begin to wonder why he got under her skin the way he did, and the last thing she wanted was for him to suspect that he got to her, that she was so horribly alert to him.

'I guess *shelter* might be the wrong word...' She fought to inject polite indifference into her words. 'Most people do think of the homeless when they hear the word *shelter*. It's more of an advice bureau. Women come to us with all sorts of problems. Financial, personal... Often we redirect them to other services, but there are people on hand who are really experienced at listening and getting the desperate off the path they've gone down. We also have contacts with companies who offer jobs wherever possible, to help some of them get back on their feet...'

What she had really wanted to show him, Theo mused, were the sort of people she liked. He hadn't been able to help noticing that the men there had been a 'type'.

Caring, soft-spoken, touchy-feely...

Had she subconsciously wanted to show him the sort of guys she liked—was attracted to? Had her intention been to draw comparisons, so that she could underline how far short he fell of her ideal? Just another way of reinforcing her dislike for the position she was in and the man she would be forced to marry—like a Victorian bride being dragged to the altar, kicking and screaming.

And yet…

When she had pulled him towards her in the restaurant and kissed him… Hell, he knew enough about women to know that loathing and dislike hadn't been behind that kiss. She might not want to admit it, but he had felt an urgency there and it intrigued him.

Why wouldn't it?

'Those are the people I enjoy being around,' she carried on, pausing as his driver cruised up alongside them and stopped.

When had he summoned a driver? But of course that would suit him far better than a normal taxi, because there was the option of sliding up that partition so that their conversation could not be overheard. He was always one step ahead.

'Is that your not so subtle way of telling me that those are the sort of *men* you enjoy being around?' He slid into the seat alongside her and predictably slid up the partition, locking them into complete privacy.

Work hard, play hard. Alexa was beginning to understand that, for Theo, the priority was business and after that came sex. He didn't do love and emotion but he did do *sex*. It was why he could be so cool about the situation they were in. He could detach.

'Yes.'

She took a deep breath and thought she had been gifted a golden opportunity to make it perfectly clear to him that those were just the sort of guys she was attracted to. And by attraction she knew that she meant a lot more than just a passing physical tug.

'Their priorities are all in the right places…'

'Heart-warming,' Theo drawled. 'Not the most aggressive of men, though, are they…? One had his hair in a ponytail. I'm thinking that he might be the type to strum a guitar and sing a haunting ballad by way of entertaining a woman...'

'Jorge is absolutely wonderful! Hugely caring! Besides, I don't like aggressive men!'

'And yet your father didn't get where he is by being the sort of man who gets walked over...'

'He's not ruthless...'

'He bartered you in marriage so that he could get *me* as a bonus prize...' Theo pointed out flatly, because he didn't do well when it came to accepting unfavourable comparisons.

'He did it for Mum,' she contradicted. 'I admit he saw an opportunity and seized it, but are you telling me that you wouldn't do the same thing? He's been desperately worried about my mother and he was convinced that her health and her spirits would improve if...if she had *this* to focus on. And that's why I agreed to...to go along with the pretence.'

'And when the pretence comes to its inevitable crashing halt?'

'A year is a long time,' she mumbled, because that thought had occurred to her as well. 'My mother's health will be in a better place and she'll be able to accept that the marriage didn't work out. She'll no longer spend her days thinking that she's on her way out and will die before she sees me settled down.'

'That's *very* optimistic projecting,' Theo declared, in just the sort of arrogantly self-assured voice that got on her nerves. 'She might have a nervous breakdown when we tell her that, sadly, we're joining the statistics of the happily divorced...'

'That's a risk my father was prepared to take and so am I,' Alexa told him sharply. 'Wouldn't *you* have done the same if it had been *your* mother?'

Theo's face closed down. 'I don't deal in pointless hypotheses.'

But it was *just* the sort of solution his father would have hit upon. Deal with today and let tomorrow be a bridge yet to be crossed. And, yes, Theo would have gone along for the ride. He would have done anything for his mother. He and Daniel both.

'All that's beside the point,' he said, and shrugged elegantly. 'Now, our little detour has eaten a chunk of my time. I'm going to get my driver to deliver you to your house and you can pack your bags for our trip to the States. And no protest-packing please...' he added, for good measure. 'During the day you can amuse yourself, but the evenings will be formal occasions. I expect we will be entertained on a fairly lavish scale.'

'Fine—but I insist that we check in to separate rooms,' Alexa told him.

'Already done,' Theo returned smoothly. 'My person in New York has booked us a penthouse suite. Adjoining rooms...'

'But...'

'But what...? Do you think I might try and break down the door between us so that I can ravish you?'

Alexa felt hot colour rush into her cheeks. She had been so intent on laying down her ground rules that she hadn't even considered the obvious—which was that he didn't even fancy her.

'You're getting a little ahead of yourself,' he said kindly. 'Aren't you?'

'I was just...just...making sure... Of course I don't think that!' She thought of the stunning blonde and the nuisance she had eventually turned into and mortification made her skin tingle.

'Then I'll text you our timings and get my driver to collect you...'

They were pulling up outside her house and Alexa felt physically and emotionally drained. She was gripping the door handle before the car had even pulled to a stop.

'Till tomorrow...' he directed at her as she flipped open the door to step out.

Alexa turned and watched helplessly as the car pulled away. A week in New York, where thankfully their time together would be limited, but then would come their engagement party, and then, in short order, a wedding.

By then she would have to make sure that she...

That she was in control...

CHAPTER SIX

ALEXA KNEW WHAT to expect in New York. She had been there several times before and had always loved the buzz of the city that literally never slept.

She met Theo at the check-in desk at the airport, where he was waiting for her, chatting to the woman who had checked him in, who was trying to ignore the fact that there were two other people impatiently waiting in the queue behind him.

'Is that all you've brought with you?' were his opening words as he strolled towards Alexa, who had joined the back of the queue.

Unlike every other woman he had ever travelled with, Alexa had made absolutely no concession to the fact that they would be travelling first class and he liked that. She was in a pair of loose culottes and a T-shirt, with a cardigan lightly draped over her shoulders and flat ballet shoes. There wasn't a scrap of colour in her outfit, and she had braided her long, untamed hair into a neat French plait which hung over one shoulder.

'I have enough for a week—although you haven't mentioned just how long I will be expected to stay.'

In response to that incendiary way of phrasing her question, Theo slung his arm over her shoulder and felt her tense.

'What are you doing?' Alexa squeaked as the line shuffled forward.

'I'm getting you in the mood.'

'In the mood for what?'

'For being my adoring fiancée… And in answer to your question about how long we will be staying…my plans are fluid.'

'What do you mean…?' she asked, hopeful that his 'fluid' plans might entail a reduction in the time they would end up spending in the city. 'Might we be there for less than a week…?'

Alexa looked up at him, eyes wide, and he shot her a half-smile before lowering his head and kissing her—a delicate kiss that feathered over her lips with just the lightest touch from his tongue. He pulled back and turned to the woman who had checked him in.

'Newly engaged,' he explained, giving Alexa a little squeeze so that she was pulled against him.

'How romantic.' The woman eyed Alexa with a look that shrieked, *Lucky you, how did you manage that…?* 'When is the big day?'

She fiddled on her computer, checking her in and ticketing her bag at the same time.

'Not soon enough,' Theo answered on Alexa's behalf. 'The engagement ring is in the process of being altered. Who knows…? We might tie the knot even before the diamond is on your finger—mightn't we, my darling?'

His low, throaty husk made her blood heat and she stared at the woman with a glassy smile.

'Maybe not,' she said gently. 'I don't think my mother would stand for that. She's a stickler for tradition,' Alexa expanded chirpily, 'and by *tradition* I mean taking her time over the wedding arrangements! None of this crazy sprinting up the aisle!'

But then the sooner they tied the knot, the sooner they

would *un*tie it. It wasn't a case of delaying something in the hope that it might disappear altogether if the delay was long enough. No such luck.

'Speaking of diamonds...' Theo told her as they headed towards the first class lounge and away from the chaos of the tax-free shopping area, which was packed.

'*Were* we speaking of diamonds?' Alexa used the pretence of stopping to peer into one of the shop windows to disengage herself from his embrace.

'I've brought something for you...'

He left that teaser hanging in the air as they reached the lounge and were waved through towards a couple of cosy chairs, with a table in front of them on which a few business magazines were fanned out.

'Have you? Alexa looked at him suspiciously. 'What?'

Theo laughed and crossed his legs. 'When are you going to stop fighting me? I've never met anyone with more of an appetite for arguing.'

'As I've told you before—you're the only one I argue with.'

'Sign of a vibrant, lively relationship...'

'It's a sign of two people who don't get along,' Alexa corrected him. 'Which is probably why you've never argued with any of the women you've been out with. And I'm sure they've *all* been vibrant, lively relationships!'

Theo cocked his head to one side and appeared to give her statement a great deal of serious thought.

'Yes,' he agreed eventually, 'I suppose there's been a certain amount of liveliness in the women I've dated...'

'And no arguments,' Alexa persisted, drawn to prolong the conversation and prove a point. 'I can't imagine *any* of your supermodels arguing with you.'

'It's true.' Theo threw his hand up in a gesture that implied rueful but graceful defeat. 'I don't like argumentative women.'

'So it's a good thing that we don't have to like one another, isn't it?'

She had felt just the merest flash of hurt—because who enjoyed being told that they weren't liked? Especially when his job of pretending that he did indeed like and fancy her was so polished and so convincing. And especially when she had grudgingly been forced to concede that she had become just another member of the long list of women who found him physically compelling.

Who wanted to fancy a guy who didn't even *like* them?

Theo didn't bother to get involved further in a conversation he knew wouldn't end up going anywhere, because he was pretty sure that when it came to arguments there was a mighty one brewing like a storm just over the horizon.

It would certainly pay to broach that thorny subject as soon as possible and get it out of the way. Give her the duration of the flight to assimilate and accept.

He grunted something that might have been anything when it came to a response and Alexa banked down a sigh of frustration.

'What is it that you've brought me?' she reminded him briskly.

'I'll show you when we're on the plane,' Theo said, because there could be no available exit door when they were twenty thousand miles up in the air. 'Your bag looks heavy. What have you got in it? Heavy club for beating me over the head?'

'I'm glad you think this is funny,' Alexa told him coldly.

Theo's lips thinned. 'Lighten up, Alexa. Do you take *everything* in life so seriously?'

'This isn't just any little thing.'

'As I've said to you on a number of occasions, it's inevitable—so why don't you just kick back? Or is that something you don't quite know how to do?'

He watched the slow colour crawl into her face. Hard-working, diligent, involved in the caring profession, pointedly making sure to avoid things she considered frivolous... In her own way, it was a statement of rebellion against her privileged background. She had bucked the tide of every other woman in her social circle, who would have settled into a life of pampered predictability and been married by the age of twenty-one to someone not very different from themselves.

The people he had met where she volunteered her services were all very nice indeed, but none of them had struck him as a bundle of fun.

So *did* she ever kick back?

'I kick back.' Alexa heard defiance in her voice.

'Who with? I haven't met the people you used to work with...what were *they* like?'

'Lots of fun,' she told him edgily. 'But you'd probably think they were dull as dishwater.'

'Why?'

'Because they're not the sort of people who think that "fun" is all about nightclubs and being in the public eye.'

'And have *you*? Ever?'

'Have I ever what?'

They were having a perfectly normal conversation, but Alexa still felt as though she was trying to find a foothold on thin ice. Maybe because when she was in his company, try as she might, she never seemed to *feel* normal.

'Thought nightclubs and being in the public eye are fun? Scrap the being in the public eye. No one in their right mind considers *that* fun.'

Although, if he were to be honest, most of the women he had dated in the past had basked in the glare of paparazzi flashbulbs.

'I'm not a nightclub type of person,' Alexa muttered, wondering how the conversation had managed to get here.

'When I meet up with friends we all prefer to go to places where we can actually hear ourselves think.'

Theo had a vision of a group of earnest individuals, solving the problems of the world over cups of espresso. She was positively the *last* sort of person he would ever have been drawn to normally. Frankly, he had little use for people who solved the world's problems over cups of coffee. If the problem was too big to solve, then why waste time talking about it? And if it was solvable then why not just get out there and solve it? Cut out the middle man, which came in the form of pointless discussion.

On the other hand he had watched her in that shelter place of hers—had seen her interaction with the people there and for a fleeting instant had actually caught himself thinking of the supermodels who had graced his arm in the past with a certain amount of distaste.

'And those friends would be your colleagues at work?'

'I've kept in touch with a couple of school friends,' she admitted. Both were married, and one was the proud mother of a baby boy. 'Why are we talking about this anyway?'

She heard the announcement of their flight over the Tannoy. Travelling first class, she knew they would be the last to board the plane, and sure enough, after a brisk ten-minute walk, they were taking their very comfortable seats in the first class section.

'Books,' she said, and Theo shot her a quizzical look as he made himself comfortable.

Flutes of champagne were brought to them and he sipped the drink while he continued to look at her, waiting for an explanation.

'You asked me what I had in my bag. Books. So that I have something to do on the flight over.'

Theo smiled slowly at her and wondered whether her

definition of *kicking back* might involve having some fun on a long-haul flight...

He'd done that once—a long time ago—and had since come to the conclusion that planes were inappropriate when it came to certain activities for a man as big as he was.

Although *private* planes certainly redefined the options...

His thoughts veered off and he held her gaze steadily. 'Books...?' he murmured. 'Let me guess... Non-fiction for the serious reader?'

'Wrong,' Alexa told him triumphantly. 'Romance and crime! Holiday reading...'

'So you're thinking of this as a *holiday*?' He was quick to pick up her stray remark, although he didn't add to that as their champagne was gathered up by a flight attendant and then, mere seconds later, the plane began its ascent. 'Excellent,' he continued heartily, once they were airborne. 'Big improvement on your lack of enthusiasm! A holiday spirit is just the thing.'

It wouldn't last, but he enjoyed watching the way she blushed at the slightest provocation.

He was almost tempted to swing the conversation back to her mission to read books so that he could ask her whether she had ever done anything more adventurous on a plane...with a man...

She might explode with embarrassment.

'I won't be working.' Alexa rushed into hasty explanation. 'So while I wouldn't call it a holiday in the strict sense of the word...'

'Too much detail, Alexa. Let's stick to the holiday spirit theme. But before you dive into one of your books...' Theo sighed and allowed a telling silence to gather momentum until she chewed her lip with sudden anxiety.

'What?'

'There's been a slight change of plan…'

Sudden scenarios flashed through Alexa's head in Technicolor glory. Change of plan? But they were still en route to New York…

But what if New York for a few days was going to expand into other cities across the globe for an indefinite period of time?

What if her one small suitcase with a few essentials ended up being five large trunks to cater for *a change of plan*…?

What if he was going to surprise her with an impromptu wedding so that the baying nosy press could be satisfied?

What if…? What if…? What if…?

The single certainty she had was that she knew she wasn't going to like his change of plan.

He was looking at her with the expression of someone who truly regretted having to say what they were about to say—except Theo De Angelis was immune to any feelings of true regret about anything. Of that she was *very* sure.

'The hotel we were booked into…'

Alexa exhaled a sigh of silent relief, because hotels could always be changed at the last minute—especially when money was no object. And maybe there wouldn't be a penthouse suite available. In which case they would end up sleeping in separate rooms on separate floors. Fingers crossed…

'Don't worry about it,' she told him kindly. 'It's a great hotel, but there are loads of other hotels in Manhattan if for some reason they've double-booked the suite…'

'Double-booked the suite?' Theo laughed shortly. 'Colin Clark wouldn't *dare* do anything of the sort. I'm a frequent enough guest for him to know which side his bread is buttered. Not only have I used that suite on a number of occasions, I have frequently rented it for members of my staff and have held several conferences at the hotel. No… I'm a valued and cherished customer—as I've been told in the past. And *as* a valued and cherished customer, I know that suite will always be available for my use.'

'Then what's the change of plan?'

'Brace yourself...'

They were briefly interrupted by yet more drinks, and a menu which Alexa didn't even look at.

'My brother going to be in that part of the world...'

'Your brother? Daniel?'

'Special detour before he buys his toy,' Theo informed her drily. 'So that he can meet the radiant bride-to-be...'

'But he knows that— Well, there won't be any need for us to pretend around *him*, will there?'

Alexa had banked on exploring the art galleries on her own during the day and getting through the evenings as best she could. The pressure to be loved-up would not be nearly so intense as it had been at home, because who in New York really cared?

With Theo's brother on the scene she would have to re-sign herself to a little more than mere polite conversation with people she had no intention of ever seeing again. But no matter. In truth, she was curious about his brother—curious to see whether it really *was* possible for two alpha males to be brothers...

She shrugged and rested back, half closing her eyes. Strangely, she could still see Theo's lean, dynamic face, even though her eyes were closed.

His image was imprinted on her retina with the force of a branding iron. No good fighting it. Sooner or later, once she became accustomed to the inconvenience of fan-cying the man, indifference would begin to trickle in, and before she knew it she would be able to look at him with-out a flicker of emotion. He would be just someone she'd happened to share space with for a short period of time—much to her mother's joy and delight.

'Will he be working with you?'

'Oh, no…' Theo drawled. 'My brother is as successful as I am, but his area of expertise is not mine.'

Alexa turned and looked at him. 'You mean *you* wouldn't think about buying a cruise ship as a toy?'

Theo grinned. 'I'm more of a financial guy,' he said. 'I enjoy numbers. Daniel likes the leisure side of things. If he weren't such a successful businessman in the leisure industry there's a strong possibility he would be a beach bum somewhere hot.'

Alexa heard the warmth in Theo's voice and realised that he was in exactly the same position as she was. A devoted child from a close-knit family, willing to make a ridiculously huge sacrifice for the sake of a parent or, in her case, *parents*.

It had been so much easier to pigeonhole him as a one-dimensional cardboard cut-out, and she was shaken at the tangent her thoughts had taken.

'So he'll be there? No big deal.' She closed her eyes once more and tried to block out the silent fizz of electricity radiating from his body.

'Indeed. He will be staying for a matter of just one night, but not, it would only be fair to tell you, at the hotel…'

'That's a shame.' Alexa couldn't stop herself from being just a tiny bit sarcastic. 'You'd think that as you're a *valued and cherished* customer, they would be able to rustle up a room for your brother.'

'Oh, I'm sure they would—if I asked…'

Eyes still closed, Alexa allowed herself a smug little smile. 'But you'd rather he stayed somewhere else? I guess, however close you might be to a sibling, there's still always a part of you that doesn't want them in your pocket…'

'*Not* really where I was going with this conversation,' Theo murmured. 'And, before we get lost in a series of misunderstandings, you should know that Daniel will be staying exactly where *we* will be staying. It just isn't going to be at the hotel, as originally planned...'

Alexa's eyes flew open and she sat up and looked at him. 'Okay... So...?'

'So we'll be going to The Hamptons instead,' Theo told her bluntly. 'Bob, a mutual friend of ours, has something of a mansion there, and I've been persuaded to take him up on his offer to accommodate us...'

'What? *Why?* When did this happen?'

Theo waved his hand in a soothing manner and she only just resisted slapping it away.

Her thoughts were swirling all over the place. None of them were comfortable or pleasant. What was going to happen to her time out, browsing the art galleries, if she was closeted in a house out in The Hamptons? What was going to happen to the peace and quiet she knew she would need just to deal with the wretched man every evening?

She felt physically sick at the unfolding and newly altered scenario.

'Got the call last night. Arrangements were sprung on me. What can a guy do?'

'A guy could have picked up the telephone and called to let me know of the change of plan!' Alexa snapped.

'And risk you bailing on me? No chance. It would have looked very suspect indeed if my beloved fiancée couldn't be bothered to meet her potential brother-in-law, her fiancé's best friend and three top clients who will all be adjusting their schedules for flying visits to the Hamptons to sort out the deal I'm going across to nail...'

'You've told *all of them* that we're engaged...?'

'It would have been peculiar to keep such momentous news to myself—and besides, who knows how far the news has already travelled? You would be surprised how small a world it is, with the internet and Facebook. It would have been downright discourteous for news of my engagement to reach their ears via a third party.'

'I don't have Facebook,' Alexa muttered, feeling well and truly trapped.

'Nor do I. But you can bet that we're in a minority... Bob's wife, Felicity, almost certainly *is* on Facebook—to keep in touch with their daughter in Australia.'

'What am I going to do with myself all day for days on end in a house with people I've never met in my life before?' Alexa was on the verge of undignified sobbing. 'It's just not *fair* that you couldn't even be bothered to tell me until we were in the air...'

'It will be fine,' Theo said. 'Although you might have to adjust your wardrobe a little bit...'

'Meaning...?'

'Those smart outfits might not be appropriate for a house visit.'

'I just can't believe you've done this to me.'

'Let's move on from that. It will be hot in The Hamptons. Outdoor eating is probably going to be the order of the day. Formal long dresses won't work. There's also a swimming pool, and I'm guessing that you didn't pack any swimwear...'

In actual fact Alexa *had* packed a bikini. There was a rooftop pool at the hotel, and she had intended to make use of it during the day when she wasn't out and about busying herself. She hadn't banked on parading in it in front of Theo, and she certainly, even in her wildest nightmares, hadn't envisaged staying at a private house, where she would be expected to hang around a pool with the rest of the guests in nothing but a sheer sarong and the bikini.

'Before we head to Bob's place we can fit in a whirlwind shop in Manhattan...'

'*We...?*'

'I can't say that shopping with a woman is something I ever do, but I'm willing to make an exception...'

'That's very considerate of you, Theo, but I'll manage just fine with what I've brought with me.'

Thank heavens for the two big books. She anticipated doing a *lot* of reading. Although she wouldn't be able to hide away—not when there would be other people around whose mission it was to entertain the newly engaged couple.

'I think I'm going to get some sleep now.' She pointedly turned away and nestled herself into a suitably dormant position, although her mind was still all over the place.

She didn't want to think about it. What was the point?

'Don't wake me for food,' she muttered, turning her head, and Theo, who had already extracted his laptop from his case, grinned at her.

'Are you *sulking*?'

'I don't like plane food.'

'It will be far more relaxing at a house...away from the noise and chaos of the city...'

Alexa didn't bother to answer, because she just *knew* that he was having a laugh at her expense. Instead she snatched the airline blanket and covered herself as much as she could without ducking under it completely.

Relaxing? How much 'relaxing' did a mouse do in a lion's den?

But she was far more tired than she had thought. She had had a sleepless night... The low thrum of the plane's engine, the dimming of the cabin lights...

She fell asleep for the duration of the seven-hour flight and was pleasantly surprised to be shaken awake when the sign flashed on for seat belts to be fastened.

Her mouth was dry, her hair had rebelled against its restraining braid and was a tousled mess, and she knew that her skin would look as rumpled as the rest of her did.

Too bad.

'Somehow,' Theo greeted her as she struggled into an upright position and stifled a yawn, 'we got lost in conversation about our change of plan and I forgot to give you my little present...'

The man looked unfairly bright-eyed and bushy-tailed. Had he worked solidly for the entire flight? Alexa hoped that she hadn't flopped against him accidentally, or snored or dribbled, and she hastily undid her plait and sifted her fingers through her hair in an attempt to get it looking a little less like a bird's nest.

'I'm not sure I can deal with any more surprises,' she told him truthfully.

Her nostrils flared as she breathed in his woody aftershave, and when she glanced down she was momentarily mesmerised by the dark sprinkling of hair on his forearm. She could see the strength of muscle and sinew when he flexed his fingers, and she wondered...

Appalled, she tore her eyes away to find him holding a box out to her. He flipped open the lid and there, nestled in a bed of dark blue velvet, was an engagement ring. Not *the* engagement ring, which was currently being altered, but a smaller version.

Alexa had privately thought the original one was a bit on the gaudy side, but she loved the tiny diamond twinkling up at her from this one.

He didn't give her time to protest. Instead he simply stuck the ring on her finger and then looked at it with satisfaction. 'That will do,' he said, holding her finger between his and examining it.

'What on earth is *this* for?'

'Something to wear until the one you chose at the jeweller's is returned.'

'Why do I have to wear something in the meanwhile?' She furtively looked at her finger. It was weird, but this much smaller, less conspicuous ring actually made her feel more *engaged*.

'Humour me. I'm a traditionalist. I like the world knowing that you're my woman...'

Their eyes tangled and he smiled slowly.

Laughing at her again! Yet Alexa couldn't halt the liquid heat pooling between her legs or the tight pinch of her nipples scraping against her lacy bra. She couldn't ignore the effect that low, husky, amused voice had on her weak, weak body.

Her breath caught in her throat and she turned away quickly, hoping that those shrewd, knowing eyes wouldn't gauge her spontaneous reaction.

Thankfully, the plane was descending. She would focus on that, and on checking her bag—which she hadn't opened at all, so there was absolutely no point in making sure that everything was correct and present. But it was a distraction.

They weren't going to be driven to the Hamptons. Instead they would be whooshed there by helicopter, because Bob had extensive gardens—big enough for several helicopters to land and take off, it would seem.

Theo told her all this as they were whisked through Immigration and on to where they could collect their bags.

'I really was looking forward to going to all the art galleries,' Alexa returned wistfully as they were transported like royalty to where the helicopter was waiting for them.

It was hot and sunny and a perfect day for sightseeing.

'Something can be arranged, I'm sure, if you're really desperate. Felicity would probably love to accompany you. If my memory serves me right, she's into that sort of thing... I shall be preoccupied during the day, at any rate...'

Alexa shuddered at the prospect of trekking down to Manhattan in the company of someone else. Strolling through art galleries had always been a pleasurable thing to do on her own—a time for quiet reflection and a bit of peace and quiet.

'How many people are going to be there?' she asked, gazing idly around her as the stretch limo removed them from the main airport,

'A handful.' His phone buzzed and he picked up the call and remained talking, only cutting short his conversation when their helicopter was within sight.

'Work,' he said crisply.

'Is that all you ever think about?' Alexa asked, eyeing the helicopter with trepidation. She had been on a helicopter twice in her life and had hated both experiences.

'Not *all*...'

There was a small, knowing smile on his lips and she shook her head with exasperation.

'Work and flings, then...'

Theo burst out laughing and made a big show of stepping back and helping her into the helicopter. He exchanged a few pleasantries with their pilot and then turned to her, the smile still lingering on his lips.

'Don't knock a good fling. Flings can be very satisfying—as I'm sure you've discovered for yourself, considering you've never married...'

'I can't see anything satisfying in meaningless sex!' Alexa had to half shout as the scream of the rotor blades threatened to drown out conversation.

'I prefer to call it *no strings sex*. And what about *fun*?' Theo prompted. 'Or is that something you disapprove of? Along with kicking back?'

'I just think it must get very boring after a while,' she bristled.

'In which case your "meaningless sex" can't have been very exciting.'

Alexa ignored that. Did he think that she spent her time

hopping in and out of bed with random men? Hadn't he seen for himself that she wasn't like that? She didn't know whether to be relieved or insulted at his one-track mind, but she did know that it was hardly surprising, because he was simply judging her according to his own standards.

He had no problem disengaging his emotions from the act of sexual intercourse. For him it was no more meaningful than a physical workout at the gym. And his relationships, if they could be called that, probably didn't last much longer.

Thankfully, *she* had never been like that—which was some consolation considering she fancied the man.

At least she knew where her priorities were, and would never allow the physical to take over.

She didn't reply to his provocative statement. Instead she stared down at the wispy clouds and thought that in a week's time all of this would be over—and thank goodness for that.

CHAPTER SEVEN

ALEXA HAD NO time to let panic get a grip because the helicopter ride was over practically before it had begun, and then it was buzzing and lowering itself down to a section of lawn which had been converted into a neat helipad.

She had no idea what to expect, but she did know that if Theo had referred to his friend's house as 'a mansion', then it was going to be pretty spectacular—and it was.

She had seen there was a pool from above—a rectangle of pristine bright blue—but the view of the top of the house didn't do justice to its splendour, which only became apparent as they were transported in something resembling a motorised golf buggy to the curving courtyard.

On either side of the drive immaculate lawns stretched towards hedgerows that had been clipped with razor-sharp precision, high enough to ensure perfect privacy. The house was fronted by a series of striking columns that threw the sprawling veranda at the front into cool shade. On the first floor a similar veranda mimicked the one below, but circled the entire house, providing a massive outdoor deck space on which she could spot clusters of shaded furniture. The top floor was more modest, sheltered by an overhanging terracotta roof, and at the four corners of the house massive chimneys advertised indoor fireplaces.

'Huge…' Alexa was duly impressed, even though she

was accustomed to grand houses. 'How many people live here?'

'Four, once upon a time. Now just two, because both kids have left home. As you might gather, they're not my contemporaries. I met them a long time ago, when my father was involved in lending Bob cash to fund his dream of building a golf and country club. The golf and country club is now one of the most frequented by top professional golfers, and he's dabbled in a series of other successful ventures since those heady days.'

'You must have been very young at the time.'

Theo looked down at her and grinned. 'I challenged Bob to a game of golf and whipped him. Since then we've been firm friends...'

'*That's* something else you do,' she couldn't resist murmuring.

'Come again?'

'By way of relaxing... You play golf.'

'Would you like to know which form of relaxation I prefer?'

'No, I wouldn't!'

'You're so predictable in your responses...'

Suddenly he pulled her towards him and tucked her against his body—and, sure enough, waiting in the open doorway was a small blonde woman in her fifties, her face wreathed with smiles.

'Bob never thought you'd do it, you great big lug! But I *knew* that a woman would come along and sweep you off your feet! I'm Felicity, by the way, and you have to excuse my shrieking like a crazy person but we were just so darned *surprised* when we heard that our favourite boy in the *whole wide world* was finally going to settle down!'

In between speaking at rapid-fire speed and introducing herself Felicity managed to plant a friendly kiss on both their cheeks while hustling them into the house and calling out for 'Stanley' to take their bags up.

Alexa had no time to say any of the usual polite things about the house or about their trip or about anything at all.

'Like it or not, you're gonna tell all! *Bob!* Bob's in the middle of one those darned conference calls!'

This to Alexa, with a woman-to-woman wink.

'You make sure when you've got a ring on this guy's finger that you ban all conference calls! And make sure he doesn't take up golf! I've had to start taking lessons or else lose that lug of a husband of mine to fairways and putting greens!'

No concessions were made to the fact that they had been travelling for several hours. Felicity dragged them through the house at breakneck speed, towards a massive kitchen which was the last word in high-tech. Glossy white built-in cupboards concealed everything, and the gleaming marble countertops were bare of all but the essentials. She led them on towards some comfortable seating in a conservatory that overlooked the manicured lawns, and once they were seated offered tall glasses of homemade lemonade whilst promising them that they could 'go freshen up' just as soon as they'd spilled the beans.

'I've got to grab you two kids before the house becomes a hotbed for dull businessmen!' She settled comfortably into one of the chairs and peered at them with lively curiosity.

Alexa could see fine laughter lines around her eyes and mouth. This was a warm, giving woman who loved to laugh and have fun. That was apparent in the way she spoke and the way she punctuated everything she said with a little breathless laugh.

'So, what does it feel like to be in love?' She directed the question to Theo, but her twinkling eyes darted between both of them. She was obviously delighted at their engagement.

Next to her, Theo still had his arm around her shoulders and it took a lot of effort not to shuffle a few inches away. Now that she had faced up to her inconvenient attraction Alexa was finding it impossible to keep her body's responses under control.

'A refreshing change,' he said.

Alexa kept her smile pinned to her face and tried to wax lyrical when Felicity looked at her for more of a gushy explanation. 'Wonderful!' she chirped. 'We never thought in a million years that...er...when we met we would end up...well...'

'In the throes of heady love? Is that what you were going to say, my darling?'

Felicity needed no more encouragement to launch into an impassioned speech about the wonders of love, after which she quizzed Alexa about her family, about what she did, expressing earnest approval of her volunteer work. Everything was interspersed with smug, smiling nods that said Theo had indeed found the perfect woman.

At that point Bob appeared, and there were more introductions and an excited synopsis of everything that had been said in his absence.

These were Theo's good friends and, looking at their interaction, Alexa could see a side of him that had not been in evidence before. He was warm, thoughtful, interested...and utterly, utterly charming. He had ensured that their daughter in Australia was introduced to a social network, thanks to his brother. He had personally chaperoned their youngest daughter when she had travelled to Europe as a sixteen-year-old, making sure that the family to whom she had been sent on an exchange visit was vetted and ticked all the boxes.

She had a new picture of him, and it wasn't the sarcastic, ruthless guy who provoked her and rubbed her up the wrong way.

'I feel like I've been tossed into a cyclone,' she said, when they finally left their hosts to prepare a barbecue for later.

Theo grinned. 'They like you. And you'll get used to their high-octane energy.'

Ahead of them Stanley, one of the staff, had disappeared along the corridor. The house seemed bigger on the inside than it did on the outside, and it was furnished in a beautifully airy, plantation style. The paintings on the walls were bright and eclectic, and the marble flooring on the ground floor gave way to rich, deep wood on the first floor.

She was so preoccupied with admiring the rooms they passed that she only realised that they had arrived at a bedroom when she noticed Stanley disappearing back towards the stairs, and then, as she entered, she looked around her with mounting panic.

'It's a bedroom,' she said in a high voice.

Theo had strolled towards the window, and now he turned to look at her for a few seconds, before moving to quietly close the door behind them. 'Well observed.'

'I'm not *sharing* a bedroom with you.'

Had it crossed her mind that they would be put in the same room? If it had, then the thought hadn't registered long enough to take root. She had glibly assumed that they would be housed in separate rooms... The place must have dozens of rooms, for heaven's sake!

'That is exactly what you'll be doing,' Theo told her, his voice hard.

He stood in front of her, an implacable rock, until she had no choice but to look up at him.

'Furthermore, you're going to compliment Felicity on the room and tell her how fantastic it is being here instead of in a boring, impersonal hotel in Manhattan. Bob and Felicity have bent over backwards to have us here and you're going to be suitably grateful.'

'I'm not sharing a bed with you,' Alexa said, stubbornly holding her ground.

Just thinking about that made the hairs on her hand stand on end. She could imagine his big, muscular body rolling accidentally against hers in the middle of the night and she cringed. She didn't care whether he fancied her or not. She didn't care that she wasn't his type. She cared about the fact that she would combust if they were in the same bed together.

And furthermore... *Did he even sleep with anything on?* He didn't strike her as the flannel pyjamas type...

Theo eyed the chaise longue by the window. 'Fine. In that case the chaise longue is all yours... I'm way too big for that thing.'

'A gentleman would offer to sleep on the floor,' Alexa gritted through pearly white teeth.

'Considering you've already written me off as not being one of those, it's fair to say that I won't be sleeping on the floor. However, you're more than welcome to make *your* bed down there if you like. Now, I'm going to have a shower.'

For a few seconds Alexa remained staring at him in sheer, angry frustration—until it dawned on her that he was beginning to take his clothes off, at which point every nerve in her body was galvanised into horrified action and she spun round to speak with her back to him.

'Do you mind getting undressed in the bathroom?' she hissed, and she heard his throaty chuckle in response.

'Why? Don't tell me that you've never seen a man's naked body before?'

Alexa seethed. 'I won't even bother to answer that!'

Not only did he continue chuckling, he actually *whistled* as he disappeared into the bathroom, thankfully closing

the door behind him and giving her time to unpack her
clothes at the speed of light.

He emerged ten minutes later, a towel casually wrapped
round his waist.

Alexa, about to reach for her bundle of clothing, was
frozen to the spot. Background noises faded and all she
could hear was the frantic thud of her heartbeat.

The man was…*spectacular.*

Bronzed, muscled, broad-shouldered. Not an ounce of
body fat. He was utterly, utterly perfect and she could feel
her skin prickle with heat. It was as if something alien and
unfamiliar had invaded every nook and cranny of her body.

'I'm going to have a bath now!' Her voice was high-
pitched and she cleared her throat. 'I'll meet you downstairs.'

'Oh, I think it would far more fitting if we were to head
down together. Hand in hand.'

Right now *his* hand was reaching to hook the edge of
the towel and she fled, slamming and locking the bathroom door behind her.

She barely noticed the over-the-top luxury of the marble
bathroom suite, or the little touches that had been given
to make it welcoming. The fragrant pot-pourri, the fluffy
white towels, the dinky soaps and shampoos…

She couldn't concentrate on anything but the fact that
Theo was in the next room…*probably strolling around in
his birthday suit while he decided what to wear…*

She took as long a bath as was humanly possible, and
then dressed and applied her make-up in the bathroom,
peering into the steamed-up mirror and finally abandon-
ing the effort because she could barely make out her reflection. Her hair she left just as it was, long and tangled,
and she finally emerged with only her shoes to put on.

He was sprawled on the bed, half naked, just his trousers on, with a book casually propped on his bare stom-

ach. He peered at her over the top of it as she walked into the room.

'How *dare* you go into my bag?'

Theo inspected the book cover and grinned. 'Shall I tell you how it ends or will that spoil the surprise?'

'I thought you might have got dressed!'

'I was about to put my shirt on but this gaudy book jacket grabbed my attention. Of course I figured out who did it by page four, but I thought I'd check to confirm—and, sure enough, I was right.'

He chucked the book and it landed neatly back in her bag, which was on the ground, half open.

'Nice outfit.' Taking his time, he slid his legs over the side of the bed and sauntered towards the wardrobe to extract a shirt. 'The bed's very comfortable. Shame you won't be experiencing it. You'll be trying to find a comfy position on the chaise longue or on the floor...'

'You're... You're...'

'Shall we head down?'

He waited by the door for her, watching as she stepped into some sandals with little wedge heels. He didn't think she realised just how damned sexy she looked in that strappy little sundress, with her long hair tumbling all over the place. Even her scowl couldn't detract from the picture.

Difficult, feisty, mulish and prickly as hell. Who would have thought that *sexy* could come in that package?

He offered his arm and Alexa stormily hooked her hand in the crook as they descended the stairs. He was as cool as the proverbial cucumber, telling her about the history of the house and the antics of the infamous gardener who had landscaped the grounds. Admittedly it was very interesting, and she was big enough to tell him so before Bob and Felicity took over the rest of the evening.

It was relaxed, and they made charming, inquisitive and interesting hosts. Bob had hundreds of amusing anecdotes about the famous golf players he had met over the years…a golf game was arranged…the barbecue was exquisite and informal and champagne flowed. Alexa was even aware that she was laughing at one point as glasses were raised to toast the couple.

But could she relax? Not a bit of it.

Every nerve in her body was stretched to breaking point because all she could think about was that room…that bed…and Theo lying with the duvet half on, half off, possibly clothed but more likely not…

She was spent by the time the evening was at an end. She liked both their hosts, and she could see that they were thrilled at what they considered a wonderful love match. If only they knew!

'So…' Theo flung open the bedroom door and stood aside to let her pass, then shut it behind him and lounged against it, arms folded, a slight smile curving his mouth. 'Did you enjoy the evening?'

The confines of the bedroom and the daunting prospect of the night ahead, not to mention all the other nights ahead, slammed into her with the force of a sledgehammer.

'I…I really did, as a matter of fact,' Alexa replied nervously. She remained standing by the window on the opposite side of the bedroom, with the yawning space of rug-covered floor between them. 'I had no idea what to expect of your friends, but they're incredibly nice and hospitable…'

And that, by association, said something about the man towering in front of her. She relaxed. She had nothing to fear in sharing a bedroom with him. He'd been nothing but decent in accepting her terms and, frankly, putting up with her moods. She'd sniped and argued and fought him every inch of the way when *he* hadn't been the one who had dumped her in this situation. She had used him as a scapegoat for her own frustrations and, arrogant though the man was, he had not retaliated in kind.

'I…er…just want to apologise…'

Theo looked at her in surprise and pushed himself away from the door to kick off his shoes. He began unbuttoning his shirt and Alexa fought to stay calm and hold on to her relaxed frame of mind.

'Apologise for what?'

'I haven't been the easiest person to be around…'

'Really?' Theo said drily. 'I'm glad you brought that to my attention. I wouldn't have noticed otherwise.'

'Not that *you've* been plain sailing!'

Theo burst out laughing and Alexa reluctantly smiled.

'Some men might find your fighting spirit a little challenging, but I admit that I'm growing to rather like it. And now that we've established a fragile truce I wouldn't want to ruin it by forcing you to build your nest on the chaise longue, so I'll take the floor.'

Alexa nodded.

Good.

But it was a super king-sized bed, and the floor was going to be an uncomfortable resting place even for a guy who probably survived on only a couple of hours sleep a night.

She escaped to the bathroom, washed her face and brushed her teeth and changed into her pyjamas. Feverishly she decided that whilst she *could* continue ranting and railing and behaving like a child, she could also just… trust that new side of him she had seen. He wasn't going to make a pass at her just because they happened to be lying on the same mattress, was he? She had been superimposing her own anxieties on to him and it was foolish.

He took the bathroom after her and she pretended not to notice the fact that he was already half naked…that the button to his trousers was undone…that she could see a sliver of his underwear where the trousers dipped down over his lean hips.

In the fifteen minutes during which she heard the whoosh of water and the sounds of him getting ready she tried to get her racing heartbeat under control, and she was burrowed down under the duvet by the time the bathroom door was flung open.

She sneaked a glance and heaved a sigh of relief that he was still in his boxers.

'Well, well, well…' Theo strolled into the room and registered that she was in the bed but that there was no pile of linen on the floor, waiting to be turned into a sleeping area. Instead she had banked some cushions down the middle of the mattress in a neat dividing line.

Alexa flipped over and feigned a yawn of exhaustion. 'It's silly for either of us to sleep on the floor. The bed is huge and there's no reason why we can't share it like two adults.'

'I like your definition of sharing *like two adults*…' He nodded at the military march of cushions along the middle of the bed.

Reluctantly she grinned. 'I thought it might be a good idea to have separated sides.'

'Of course.'

Theo was amused at just how innocent that gesture was. He climbed into bed, his antennae noting the way she shifted ever so slightly away from him. She was clearly awake, but she wasn't reading her book and she certainly wasn't about to engage in conversation. He reached for his laptop, propped it on his lap and casually asked if it would bother her if he worked for a couple of hours. He was even more amused when she didn't answer.

Bother her? It bothered her that he was even *breathing* next to her, far less working.

Her body was rigid. She would never manage to get a

wink of sleep. She knew that. Nor would she be able to toss and turn. If she tossed and turned he would guess that she was awake, plus she would keep *him* up, and then they'd both be awake…in a bed…just the two of them…

Sleep overcame her. It had been a long and tiring day and her exhausted body at last won the battle over her hyperactive mind.

She dreamt that she was skimming over the clouds, looking down. And then, as she looked behind her, over her shoulder, Theo was advancing, getting closer and closer. Part of her wanted desperately to run away, but another, stronger part was holding her fast and *liked* the fact that she couldn't move, that he would get closer and closer, and their bodies would fuse… She would be able to skim her hands over his broad chest and feel the rough surface of muscle and tendon…

The dream was so real that she could almost feel his hands on her, brushing against her thigh and then curving between her legs. She moaned softly.

Her eyes fluttered open and…she wasn't dreaming.

For a few seconds Alexa was completely disorientated. The strategically positioned cushions had hit the floor at some point during the night, and not only had she rolled towards Theo but right now the palm of her hand was flat against his hard chest and he was as awake as she was.

And holding her against him as if it was the most natural thing in the world.

Her limbs felt heavy and lazy and, just like in her dream, whilst a part of her desperately knew that she should pull away, another part of her felt heavy and warm and lazy, utterly incapable of doing anything but revelling in the feel of his equally warm body.

'Shh…' Theo murmured, as if she had spoken.

After lying in complete silence while he had tried to focus on work Alexa had eventually fallen asleep. He had known by the change in the rhythm of her breathing and, oddly enough, having her asleep next to him had made *him* a little jumpy.

He had managed to subdue his disobedient libido when it had reared its head and he had done that by rationalising it out of existence. He was in an unnatural and forced situation—heading down the aisle and not by choice. He was with a woman whose emotionalism was not the kind of thing he sought or appreciated in *any* woman—certainly not in a woman to whom he was to be married. And, physically, since when had he *ever* gone for small, curvy girls? That had always been his brother's domain.

But just knowing that she was next to him in the bed had kept him awake. At one point he had seriously considered slipping out of bed and heading for a cold shower—especially when those cushions had been kicked away and, like a little mouse gravitating towards the source of warmth, she had wriggled closer and closer until she had been touching him.

'You were moaning,' he whispered. 'Having a bad dream? Or a really good one?'

Alexa squeezed her eyes shut and remembered exactly how erotic that dream of hers had been. Heat was still making her want to snap her legs together.

'I'm sorry if I woke you,' she whispered back. 'The cushions…'

'Turns out that soft furnishings don't make very successful fortifications…' He sifted his fingers through her hair. His body was raging, his libido in full surge—a primitive response over which he had no control.

Right now, right here, Theo wanted her in a way he had never wanted any woman in his life before. This wife-to-be he had never asked for and from whom he knew he should keep a safe distance. Because if he slept with her…slept with someone who was looking for a guy who was most certainly *not him*…that single act of passion would make the next year even more impossibly awkward than it was already showing signs of being.

And yet…

'Why did you feel the need to stick a row of cushions between us?'

His hand dipped to the curve of her waist. She wasn't pulling back with a screech of maidenly outrage and more than anything else *that* was a massive turn-on—because it was proof that despite all her protests she wanted him. She didn't *want* to want him…just as *he* didn't want to want *her*…but their bodies were not on the same page as their intellects.

In a life that was formidably controlled this lack of self-control felt good…satisfying…addictive.

How the hell was he going to endure twelve months of wanting her and banking down his desire?

They were both adults, he reasoned. They fancied one another, and he knew from experience that it was a very short journey between fancying a woman and boredom setting in. He had no doubt that if she fancied him it was something she was fighting to ignore, which meant that the same would apply to her. If they slept together they would rid themselves of an inconvenient lust—a bit like taking the right medicine to kill a fever.

'Did you think…?'

His voice was low and soft, and Alexa knew that it was no shock that she was finding it impossible to pull away from him when he was hypnotising her with his deep, dark, sexy drawl.

'Did you think that if it weren't for some scatter cushions you might have found yourself wanting to touch me?'

'No!'

'Liar.' He laughed softly under his breath. 'I've felt the way your body tenses up every time I've touched you and seen the way you slide hot little glances over at me when you don't think I'm watching you... Except I've been watching you a hell of a lot more than you probably thought. In fact a lot more than I ever anticipated...because I'm feeling what you're feeling...'

'I never said...' Her voice was so feeble and unconvincing that she wasn't surprised when he laughed again.

'Sure about that? Because there's a foolproof way of proving whether you're telling little porky-pies...'

He was going to kiss her—and she wasn't going to fight it. Her body was on fire and she wanted him to touch it... she wanted to touch *his*...and she had never wanted to touch any guy like that—hadn't even come close...

She'd never suspected—not for a second—that lust could trample all over her principles and turn them to mush.

She closed her eyes on a sigh, leaned into him, and Theo, trailing the most delicate of caresses along her jawbone, simultaneously slipped his finger under the baggy nightie and beneath her underwear and into her wetness to finger her.

It was shocking and unexpected, and Alexa wriggled away from the touch, reaching down to push his hand away, squirming free, but knowing that she didn't want to create space between them—she wanted to abolish it.

She shouldn't want this but she did. She *wanted* his fingers exploring her and she burned with mortification. When he slid his hand along her stomach desire held her fast, stopped her from breaking their connection. It felt like an extension of her dream, weird and surreal and somehow *not really happening*—at least not in a way that felt dangerous or threatening.

Her breathing quickened. She heard herself pant a desperate *'No!'* but it felt so good. She slid her treacherous, trembling hands over his chest, yanked them away, repeated the caress, this time tracing the broad, muscled width of his shoulders.

The sexless nightie felt itchy and uncomfortable, and she wanted to squirm out of her underwear—and was immediately horrified and panicked by the impulse.

So she fancied him. And he, to her amazement, fancied *her*. Maybe it was the strangeness of the situation into which they had both been thrown. In fact that was probably it—because if she had bumped into him under normal circumstances, at one of those social events which *she* hated and which *he* saw as part and parcel of being who he was, then she was sure that she would never, ever, have been attracted to him. And he would have had one of those leggy, supermodel airhead types clinging to him like ivy. He wouldn't have given *her* a second glance.

But here they were...

She tentatively let her hand stray to his waist, and then a bit lower, and she shivered as she felt the massive bulge of his erection pushing against the boxers. It was terrifying, and she withdrew her hand as though she'd suddenly plunged it into an open fire.

But she wanted to touch him *so badly*...

'Theo...this is crazy...'

'Is it? I don't think so. In the whole crazy charade, this feels like the least crazy bit...'

'I don't do this sort of thing.'

'You mean make love to your fiancé?'

'You know what I mean.'

'I know what you mean, my dearest wife-to-be. But do you *want* to...?'

'Yes! No... Oh, I don't know... Theo! I can't think straight...not when you're touching me...'

'Not thinking straight suits me—and what does "Yes! No... I don't know..." mean?'

'It means I find you attractive. Okay?'

'Okay.'

He'd never had to ask a woman if she wanted him, had never received such a grudging response, but hearing her say that put him on top of the world.

He gradually pushed up the nightie. He was as out of control as a horny teenager about to lose his virginity. *Crazy.* He cupped the fullness of her breast and then rubbed his thumb over her stiff nipple, over and over, until she was moaning and moving restlessly against him.

'We shouldn't…' In the grip of the sensations that were bombarding her on all fronts she could barely get the pathetically weak protest out.

'Life is too short for *shouldn't…*'

'That's easy for you to say.'

You're experienced. You haven't spent your life welding sex to love and waiting for them to come along at the same time. You're relaxed and carefree about this sort of thing. Not like me.

And yet for all that she couldn't have shifted out of his reach if she'd tried.

'You've done nothing but fight me,' he moaned softly. 'Now I want you to tell me that you need this as much as I do…'

'I…'

'*Say it*, Alexa…'

'I want this so much,' she confessed shakily, thrilled at the hot urgency in his voice.

'Good.' His voice was thick with satisfaction.

He lowered his head, angling her body so that he could lick and kiss her neck, her shoulders. He nearly lost it completely when he felt the hitch in her breathing as he trailed kisses over her breasts, until finally he clamped his mouth over the big, pink circular disc of her nipple.

Her whole body tensed, and then relaxed into the caress. He was dimly aware of the fluttering of her fingers in his hair as he continued to draw the stiffened bud of her throbbing nipple deep into his mouth, nipping and suckling on it. He was a big man, with big hands, and the abundance of her breasts was a good fit as he cupped her other breast and massaged it.

'Touch me,' he commanded roughly, pulling her hand down and clasping it hard over his erection. 'Just hold me. *Tight*, for God's sake. I don't want to spoil the party prematurely...'

He reared up as she obeyed and took a few deep breaths, fighting to recover some of his lost self-control. When his breathing finally levelled out he resumed where he had left off, this time devoting his attention to her other breast, but not until he had looked at her nakedness, feasting his eyes on the paleness of her skin and the contrasting rosy flush of her nipples.

Alexa gazed up at him through half-closed eyes. He had rid himself of his boxers and his erection was a thick, hard, pulsing rod of steel. There wasn't a shred of self-consciousness in him as he watched her gazing at him. She was scared, thrilled, massively turned on...all at the same time.

'Would you like to sample the fare...?' He asked, and when she frowned in bewilderment he grinned. 'Taste with your mouth what you're busy tasting with your eyes...?'

He couldn't understand her... She was enthusiastic, turned on, and yet curiously shy and hesitant. But, then again, the women he slept with were all so experienced that perhaps he had forgotten what it was like to be with one who didn't see sex as an exercise in impressing him with gymnastics. He liked it. He knew that.

'I... I'm not... I don't... This is all so far out of my comfort zone...'

'Then I'll let you set the pace...'

He was moved by the nervousness in her voice. She

wanted him, but she wasn't going to jump on him, and he got that. She needed to be treated like a delicate piece of porcelain china. He needed to let her have control. And that turned him on.

She covered him with tentative little kisses. She clearly liked him to touch her breasts and he did. But he wanted her to hold his erection, and after a while, after she had trailed delicate little kisses over his stomach—kisses that were driving him mad, had she but known it—she garnered the courage to take those delicate little kisses lower down.

She whimpered softly, and those little whimpers were a turn-on beyond belief. To a man with a fairly jaded palette when it came to the opposite sex and their bedroom antics, this was uniquely refreshing. She was shy. He wanted her to feel comfortable with his body, comfortable to touch him wherever she wanted, but the way she took her time... *agony.* He could barely breathe.

To Alexa, witnessing this big, utterly confident and controlled man lose it a little was as heady as a dose of adrenaline shot straight into her system.

Her faltering self-confidence strengthened into a growing sense of liberation. A guy who was restless and impatient, who took what he wanted whatever the cost—a guy for whom *tomorrow* was not a word in his vocabulary if it could be replaced by *today*—was letting her take charge, and that felt so good to her.

She straightened and looked down at him. She'd never been naked in front of a man in her life before, and her skin tingled and burned as he gazed at her with open, unashamed desire.

When he reached forward to graze his thumbs across her stiff nipples she moaned softly and closed her eyes. Her whole body was trembling.

*She wanted more than this. She wanted him inside her,
moving inside her, filling her up...*

She guided his hand between her legs and even as she did
so was shocked at her forwardness. When he began mas-
saging her there she covered his hand with hers, groaned
as he slid two fingers inside, unerringly finding her clitoris and sending her into spiralling, ever-increasing zones
of sexual pleasure.

She felt like a rag doll. As her pleasure grew...and grew...
and grew...she opened dazed eyes and levelled them at him.

'I want more, Theo.' She barely recognised her own
voice, which was husky with desire.

'And so do I... You have no idea... But...' He reached
for his wallet on the dressing table to extract a condom.
'Life right now,' he murmured, catching her heated gaze
and holding it, 'is complicated enough without adding to
it...'

CHAPTER EIGHT

HE DROPPED THE condom on the side table and settled over her, grazing between her legs with his erection, nudging, but not too much. And then he slid his hands under her back, arching her up towards him. Nerves mingled with wicked anticipation, and anticipation won.

She had disposed of her nightie—flung it over the side of the bed. She knew that she should be feeling timid, quailing at his frank inspection of her body, but there was open heat in his lazy gaze. No mistaking the fact that he was hot for her. She didn't think that his heat could match her own.

'I'm fat…' she confessed, burning up like straw flung to a struck match.

'Whoever told you that? Surely not your parents…?'

He didn't normally do pillow talk, but the openness of her admission touched him. He lay down next to her and pulled her against him. He could feel the steady beating of her heart and the squash of her breasts against his chest.

A slight delay to proceedings. There was nothing un-cool about that. In fact it made sense, gave his body time to adjust to its normal tempo.

'Gosh, no.'

This intimacy felt good. Not so much sex for the sake of sex as two people in bed about to make love. She had a gut feeling that he wasn't the kind of guy who slowed down to accommodate anyone, and that included the women he took to his bed. But he was slowing down for *her*. And whilst the logical part of her knew that it meant nothing, it still felt good.

Plus... Rushing into sex...

Yes, her body was on fire for him, but her mind was tentative, filled with her own shortcomings and what he might say about them. If he'd made some great big show of trying to get her into bed she might have stood a chance at resistance, but like this...in the dead of night...here in this bed...she was powerless to fight her body's urgings.

Talking like this might relax her...

'The opposite.' She traced the outline of his shoulders, liking its tough ridges and contours. 'My parents always told me that I was beautiful and that I could do anything I wanted.' She laughed a little breathlessly, because confiding wasn't something she was accustomed to doing. She marvelled that she was doing it now, with this man. 'Of course most parents say that, and I wasn't a complete idiot. I knew I wasn't beautiful.'

'And you knew that because...? You had a magic mirror on your wall...?'

Alexa laughed, but there was a telling catch in her laughter and Theo experienced a moment of disorientation during which he felt weirdly tender and possessive towards this prickly, argumentative woman who had given him nothing but a hard time ever since their paths had crossed.

'I overheard a conversation when I was eleven,' she confessed. 'I was in a toilet cubicle at school and I overheard some of my friends giggling about me. I'd never thought I was fat but it seems that I was...and I had also developed way ahead of everyone else. That's a big deal when you're a kid. Whilst all the girls in my year were busy shooting up like beanpoles I was getting...well...*a figure*... It seems I was something of a figure of fun...especially to boys...'

'Boys that age can be idiots,' Theo told her fiercely. He dropped a kiss on her forehead and held her against him, her face pressed against his neck. 'In fact…' he angled her so that he could look down at her seriously '…quite a few idiot boys grow up into idiot men.'

Was that her opinion of him? A guy who judged by appearances only?

He sensed that that was just the sort of introspective question that might not benefit from too much in-depth analysis. Her whole persona now made sense to him. Her defensiveness…her passionate interest in the intellectual as opposed to the physical…her mulish aversion to the sort of high society affairs where she might feel herself judged, yet again, on appearance instead of personality.

The fact that she was here now, playing at a relationship with the sort of man she had probably spent her entire adult life erecting walls to keep out, spoke volumes about her close relationship with her parents.

'I suppose…' She laughed a little self-consciously. 'Thanks for listening…'

Theo was highly offended. 'Of course I listened to you! Why wouldn't I?'

'Because you don't listen a lot when women moan and whine?' she suggested teasingly.

Theo had the grace to flush. 'Maybe that whining and moaning always had a certain predictable flavour…'

'What do you mean?'

'We're having a conversation,' Theo heard himself say.

Alexa nestled against him, nerves temporarily banished. 'Isn't that what you told me we *had* to do, considering we're about to tie the knot?'

'I don't do a lot of that either,' he admitted with a wry smile.

'Talking in bed with a woman?'

Theo thought that it might have been more accurate to

say *talking*, and leave it at that, but of course he *did* talk to women... Regrettably, the conversations were not usually of an inspiring nature and, having never—not once—thought about that, he now wondered whether he had set his standards a little on the low side in the past. At least insofar as intellectual stimulation was concerned.

'There always seem to be far more exciting things to do than chit-chat...' He shoved aside the niggling moment of introspection and returned to the business of making love—his comfort zone.

He curved his hand along her side, smoothing it over her rounded hip and confidently inserting it between her legs, parting them and laughing under his breath at her little pant of anticipation.

This was *definitely* more like it.

'Now it's time for you to lie back and think of England...'

'Is that an order?'

'Of course it is. Haven't we already established that I'm the arrogant sort, who gives orders and expects them to be obeyed...?'

Alexa giggled breathlessly and closed her eyes—although she knew the last thing she would be doing was thinking of England...

He explored her body and took his time doing it, suckling on her swollen nipples, arching her body up so that he could enjoy them all the more. The longer he spent there, the more she frantically wanted him to go further, and her whole body was tingling as he made his way down, inch by inch, until his mouth found the dampness between his legs.

Alexa gave a little yelp and tried to wriggle away, but Theo pinned her down by her hips and glanced up at her.

'What's the problem?'

'There's something you should know...'

She had debated whether to say anything or not. Could

a man tell the difference between a virgin and a woman who was not? Alexa didn't know, but she knew that she would reveal the full extent of her inexperience the very second he started getting too intimate.

As he had just been doing.

'Hasn't anyone been intimate with you like that?' Theo was tickled pink by that. 'Shh… Time for me to show you what you've been missing…'

He didn't want her to think about this. He just wanted her to *enjoy*. He gently parted her legs and felt her tense. He licked the inside of her thigh and she relaxed with a soft moan, and then, so slowly, he began to explore her.

She tasted of musk and honey, fragrant and seductive. He licked her, and then darted his questing tongue, touching the protruding nub of her clitoris. After gently smoothing her thighs he parted the lips concealing her womanhood with his fingers, so that her sensitive clitoris was even more exposed to the erotic dance of his tongue.

Alexa groaned. She could barely breathe, the pleasure was so intense.

She shielded her face with her arm and twisted away. She was so wet down there…melting like candle wax.

The pleasure became more and more intense, spiralling until she was hurtling towards the edge, and only then did Theo slowly ease his rhythm, leaving her begging for more, pleading with him to bring her to orgasm.

By which time he was so shockingly turned on that he could barely steady his hands to apply the condom. More than anything else, he wanted to come inside her, to feel her wet tightness wrap around his erection…

Alexa stayed him with one trembling hand and gulped. 'There's something I should tell you…'

'Alexa… Not now… I want you so much I'm not sure I'm going to be able to withstand another conversation—

not unless we pause for an intermission and I have a cold shower…'

'It's…it's something you really need to know, Theo,' she said with wrenching urgency.

Theo stilled and gazed down at her flushed cheeks. He couldn't imagine what she might have to say that couldn't keep. She was as turned on as he was and he could barely think straight. Add to that the fact that he was highly experienced and you didn't need to join too many dots to work out how explosive her effect on him was.

Was she about to tell him that she was involved with someone else? It was a question he had asked of her before and she had given a negative response—but that might have been a diplomatic denial, intended to halt a sticky conversation.

With a jolt of surprise he realised that he had already formed assumptions about her, and one of them was that he believed she was genuine—and that annoyed him, because he was cynical when it came to members of the opposite sex.

'If you're going to break my heart by telling me you've got the hots for another man, then it's a conversation I have no interest in having.'

He lay back and felt her nestle against him, propping herself up against his chest. Her long hair hung on either side of her heart-shaped face, a jumble of curls.

'What are you talking about?' Alexa was genuinely puzzled. 'If I had the hots for someone else why would I be…? Well…'

Theo dealt her a slashing grin, relieved at the earnestness in her voice. He curled his fingers into her hair and tugged her down to kiss him.

'Then what…?' he murmured huskily. 'Spill the beans…'

'I've… I'm probably not as experienced as you think I am…'

'What are you telling me?'

'I've never…never done this before…' Alexa said bluntly, holding her breath for his appalled reaction.

'You're a *virgin*?'

'And you're shocked.' She miserably filled in the blanks.

Shocked? No. Surprised? Yes. In his experience virgins in their twenties were about as common as sightings of the dodo. But he was also massively turned on at her admission.

He flipped her over so that he was looking down at her. *His woman*. He should have been turned off, but he wasn't. The opposite.

'I'll take my time,' he murmured. 'And by the time I'm ready to enter you, Alexa, you'll be so wet and ready for me…'

Words failed him.

Who needed words? He was going to give her an experience that would live with her for ever.

He explored her body all over again. He nuzzled and licked her nipples until they were warm and throbbing in his mouth. He trailed languorous kisses along her stomach and as he did so slowly rubbed her clitoris with his fingers, readying her for his mouth.

Alexa raised her legs, squirming as he nuzzled between her legs. Just watching his dark head there was the most erotic thing she could ever have imagined. True to his word, he took his time, and she knew, inexperienced as she was, that it would require a lot of willpower for him to do so.

'I don't want to…to come like this…' she gasped, as her body began sweeping her towards the edge.

Theo looked up from where he had been busy and shot her a lazy smile. 'You won't…'

He'd also promised to be gentle, and he was. He nudged his way into her and she felt herself open up for him, and when he began to thrust into her she was crying out for him, her hands curling into his hair, her body arching up so that he could take her completely. Any fleeting discomfort was quickly overwhelmed by a surge of *want* and she came with soaring intensity. It was an out-of-body experience that left her shaking.

She didn't want to let him go. She wanted to cling, to feel his perspiring body pressed up against her. She felt him as he came, shuddering inside her on a broken groan of satisfaction. There were no barriers between them in that moment of total surrender and she wished that she could hang on to the moment for ever.

When he reared up to discard the condom, she *missed* him.

'Did the earth move for you?' Theo teased, settling down next to her and pulling her into position so that they were both on their sides, bodies pressed close together. He could have done it all again, but he would have to exercise restraint even though her nakedness was continuing to drive him crazy.

Alexa lowered her eyes, because the feeling of sudden tenderness confused her. He'd stopped being a cardboard cut-out, and that was worrying, but she felt helpless to do anything about it. She couldn't seem to recover her anger at the situation she was in.

'So, no men before me?' Theo mused. 'Tell me why...'

Alexa shrugged.

'You're not going to get away with that. Didn't you have boyfriends at university?'

'Honestly...?' she mused pensively. 'Like I said, I wasn't all that confident about the way I looked. I have an old-fashioned figure...'

'Hourglass. It's a shape that never goes out of style.'

Alexa laughed, liking the compliment even if it wasn't true. 'I guess I watched what my peer group was getting up to from the age of fifteen and knew that I couldn't compete, so I decided I was just going to find my own path and that was academic. I really threw myself into my degree. Yes, of course I went out—but in a group. I'd already decided that I would only give myself to someone if I was in a loving relationship that was going somewhere…'

With dismay, she heard just how that sounded and was quick to rescue him from any false misconceptions. Marriage or not, he wasn't in this out of any genuine feelings for her and she knew that. It was the same for her!

'I didn't think that I could be physically attracted to a man unless I had deeper feelings for him,' she admitted.

'Are you telling me you don't have deeper feelings for me?' Theo drawled, amused. 'Tut-tut… Any self-respecting husband-to-be might be offended by that! Don't underestimate the power of attraction, Alexa. You'd be surprised how many good intentions get trampled on when two free and consenting adults find that they can't keep their hands off one another…and *I* find that I can't keep my hands off *you*. In fact I'd quite like to take you again. Right now. But I won't. I'm a big man, and you'll be sore down there…'

'Theo!'

She traced the outline of his shoulder blade with her finger. *What happens now?* she wanted to ask, but when she thought about that she knew what would happen… They'd have a lavish engagement party, they'd get married and then they'd get divorced. Why did it seem so muddled when it was actually so straightforward?

'I think we need a little time alone to get this out of our systems…' Theo broke through her soul-searching silence.

'What do you mean?'

'Neither of us signed up for this,' he told her matter-of-factly. 'And I'm not just talking about the arranged marriage scenario. *That* particular bombshell was definitely not on the radar for either of us.' He lay back and stared up at the ceiling. 'Neither of us expected that this attraction would jump out at us, did we? But it has, and it's something we have to deal with.'

'Yes…' Alexa parroted faintly, brow furrowed.

Saying that they would *deal* with it somehow removed the element of emotion—turned an unfortunate situation that had taken them by surprise into one that had a solution. He was right. She knew that. But she couldn't stifle the sudden hollowness that settled in the pit of her stomach.

Theo had paused. *A virgin.* She had just discovered that unbridled lust had an unstoppable momentum of its own but he wasn't a fool. She was an incurable romantic and she had lost her virginity to *him*. And he was destined to marry her. The last thing he needed was for her to get in too deep with him.

He fancied her, but he was all wrong for her—in the same way that *she* was all wrong for him. He could never give her what she wanted. He could never give *any* woman the sort of love that took away the ability to think clearly and behave logically. He just didn't have it in him.

He didn't *do* emotions. He played hard, but he always played with his head. She deserved someone who was willing to give her what she wanted. That man wasn't him, and unless they established some ground rules a year might prove a very long time indeed. For both of them.

Being married to someone who might end up expecting more than he was prepared to give would be a recipe for disaster.

'We get this out of our system,' he said flatly, 'and I see no reason why we won't have a harmonious year together.'

'Get it "out of our system"?'

'We can't fight this. We will be in one another's company all the time…'

'What if we weren't?'

'Then it would run its natural course. Lust fades as fast as it comes. That's always been my experience.'

'And you just walk away when that happens?'

'I'm not looking for deep emotional connections, Alexa,' he told her gently. 'For me, a permanent partner will be someone who is prepared to accept that my work will always come first.' He sighed.

'A marriage of convenience with someone who is emotionally switched off…?'

'I wouldn't necessarily describe it like that…'

'Would you fancy her, or would that not matter?'

'We're veering off topic, here.'

'I hear your warning.'

Her drowsy contentment was fading fast. She knew what he was telling her, but just in case she missed the message he was making sure he spelt it out in words of one syllable. *Don't confuse lust with love.* He could give her lust, but love wasn't on the table, and he was probably horrified at the possibility that he might be stuck with someone who'd fall for him.

He was telling her that his boredom threshold would be reached quickly, and that once that happened they would settle into playing the game they were destined to play, with no nasty surprises along the way.

Like unnecessary emotion.

She knew exactly what she should tell *him*. That this had been a one-off. One of those curiosity things… Something that she had succumbed to but which she did not want to repeat.

She opened her mouth and he smoothed his hand over her, between her thighs, and her body suddenly had other things in mind.

'But…' he said.

'But what?' She tried to inject some defiance into her

voice but she heard the way she sounded—helpless and breathy.

'We have options.'

'What are you talking about?'

He had found the damp patch between her legs and was stroking her, finding her sensitive nub and playing with it so that she couldn't think straight.

'You can either retreat back into fighting with me and put this down as a one-night stand...'

Alexa flushed, because that had been her first thought. She had foolishly betrayed all her principles but maybe she could persuade herself that she had put the lapse behind her—because you didn't have to keep repeating a mistake just because you'd made it once.

But how easy was *that* going to be when he could do this to her?

'I can't...can't think...when you're...'

'Let me do the thinking for you.'

'You're so incredibly bossy. Do you *always* have to take charge?'

'Taking charge suits me. I happen to do it very well.'

But this wasn't a decision he wanted her to make on the back of her arousal—even though watching the dazed heat in her eyes and the hectic flush in her cheeks was immensely satisfying. He reluctantly withdrew his hand and rested it in the curve of her waist.

'You'd like to write this off and pretend in the morning that nothing really happened.'

'You can't say that—'

'I can, because I know the way you think, Alexa. You had a fairy-tale dream wedding and a dream guy all mapped out in your head, but instead here we are...'

It irritated him just to voice that, because playing second fiddle to any man—even a fictitious one—just wasn't his thing, but there was no avoiding the truth.

'You know what those marriage vows say...' he drawled, carefully averting his eyes from the tempting glimpse of one pouting pink nipple peeping at him. 'For better or for worse. Loosely interpreting them, I say we should focus on the better side of things for the moment... We fancy each other, incredible though that might be...'

'Thanks very much, Theo.'

'You'd be the first to agree,' he returned wryly. 'You were *horrified* to find out that you would be walking up the aisle with me.'

Alexa didn't want to turn that flat statement back to him—didn't want to hear that he had likewise been horrified to find himself saddled with an emotional and inexperienced girl who—horror of horrors—didn't even have the decency to look like all his supermodel clones.

Truth hurt, and she had faced too many awkward truths recently—not least being this...her attraction to him.

'I would have been horrified to find myself walking up the aisle with *anyone* who wasn't of my own choosing.'

Theo shrugged, because one way or the other it didn't matter.

'I think that instead of denying what's between us we exhaust it—after which the duration of our time together should be as plain sailing as it can be, given the circumstances.'

'We *exhaust* it...?'

'Correct.'

'And do you have a timeline on that?'

If he got bored with all his beautiful conquests after a couple of months, then she gave herself a couple of *weeks*. Oddly, something inside her twisted.

'I prefer to play things by ear—and that cuts both ways. *You* could be the one who gets tired of me...'

Alexa wasn't dim enough to think that he seriously believed that for a minute, but she nodded in agreement.

This wasn't her at all, but he had cut through all the red tape and produced the bald truth of the matter, shorn of all emotion. They carried on having sex until that side of things dwindled away, at which point they would be able to function in one another's company without that sizzle of electricity—which was something he seemed able to handle but which she had found she just couldn't.

She couldn't imagine ever being around him without the hairs on the back of her neck standing on end and her imagination shaking its reins and running wild. It would be like spending a year doing a high wire act without a safety net. Just thinking about it exhausted her.

He was presenting her with a choice. And why not? She couldn't see herself wanting a man indefinitely when he basically wasn't her type anyway. It *would* fizzle out. Of course it would. In the crazy, surreal world into which she had been catapulted it was the one thing that made sense.

And also...

She would be able to give herself permission to enjoy him.

She felt a guilty rush of pleasure at the thought of that.

'I suppose it makes a weird kind of sense...'

She drew that sentence out and filled it with lots of doubt and uncertainty. She didn't want him to feel that she was a push-over simply because she was inexperienced, or that she had become a member of his worshipful fan club. She wanted—*needed* him to think that it was an arrangement that suited her as much as it suited him...that he was as much a virus in her system which she wanted to dispel as she was in his.

'I suppose we can't help the people we're attracted to—even though I always thought I could. I've been edgy around you...and not just because of the circumstances that threw us together. I haven't *liked* being attracted to you, but I'm honest enough to admit that I am. Stupid, and—as you say—passing.'

Theo wasn't sure he liked the word *stupid*, but he wasn't going to get hung up on detail.

Frankly, the faster it passed, the better for him. She was unreasonably distracting and he didn't like distraction—at least not a distraction that seemed to attack without warning and at any given time.

'I have my guys coming tomorrow,' he said. 'My original plan involved a prolonged stay here, with work taking a bit of a back seat to relaxation. This…change in circumstances…requires a change of plan…'

He accompanied that with a slow, curling smile that reminded her just how dangerous a temptation he could be, so thank heavens it wasn't going to be long-lasting.

'How do you mean?'

'We'll just stay for the day. I'll get my business done and then we'll head to Manhattan—finish our stay there. And no adjoining rooms in a penthouse suite…' He stroked the pink, peeping nipple and the little bud hardened under the abrasive rub of his thumb.

'We can't!' Alexa gasped, responding on cue, pulses racing, her whole body slowly heating up once again and then going into meltdown as he continued to rub her nipple.

'Why not?'

'Because it's *rude*! Your friends…they'll be disappointed…'

'They'll be the first to understand. They think this is a love match and they've been trying to brainwash me into the joys of married life for far too long… They'll be over the moon when I tell them that we have to escape for some private time because we can't get enough of one another… I can already hear the violins in the background…'

Little will they expect that this is just a pretend game, and that this so-called need for private time will just be about sex, Alexa thought, with the sort of cynicism she'd never thought she had.

'And your brother's making a big effort to come over… I was quite looking forward to meeting him, maybe going to one of the local art galleries while you were busy during the day…'

Theo burst out laughing. 'Daniel and art *don't* go hand in hand. I think it stems from the fact that an art teacher once told him when he was a kid that he would be doing the world of art a service by staying as far away from pencils and paintbrushes as he could…'

'Whereas you…?'

'*I* was smart enough to work out that if I couldn't paint anything remotely realistic then I'd paint whatever the hell I wanted and call it abstract… It worked… I'll message my brother—tell him to skip the meet-and-greet detour and head directly to the cruise ship he wants to buy…'

'So we go to New York,' Alexa said slowly, 'spend a week there…after which we should both be over this… this…situation between us. Then we return to Italy as a happy, platonic couple and serve our one year's penance before walking away from one another…' She forced a bright smile to her face. 'You're right, of course. Enjoy one another for a few days…get this inconvenient attraction out of our system…and once that little hiccup's dealt with we'll be able to…to look at one another without any stupid awkwardness…'

Since that was pretty much what Theo had had in mind, he was a little unnerved to hear it stated so bluntly.

'Enough talking…' He tilted her head and when she arched back kissed her neck, worked his way to her breasts and then levered himself up and stared down at her flushed face. 'Now I'm going to give you a little lesson on taking charge…'

He did.

She touched him as he had touched her. She straddled him and worked her way meticulously down his body, loving every inch of muscle and sinew under her exploring hands. She marvelled that her shyness had evaporated. Something about the way he looked at her, with a sort of lazy, lingering, heated intensity, stripped her of her inhibitions and invested her with self-confidence she'd never known she possessed.

When she took him in her mouth and heard his throaty groan a heady sense of power invaded her.

There had been moments in her adult life when she had thought about her virginity. She had never been bothered by it, but there had been a nagging worry that when the time came she would be so nervous that she wouldn't be able to enjoy the experience. Sex would have become a big thing she had built up and would fail to deliver on the night.

The only consolation in that scenario had been the certain knowledge that the guy she fell in love with would be someone kind, thoughtful and patient enough to guide her slowly.

As she felt this big, arrogant, sinfully good-looking man shudder as she continued to caress his erect sheath with her mouth and her tongue a thought flew through her head, as lightning-fast as quicksilver...

He might not be a shining advertisement for kind, thoughtful or patient, but he has been kind and thoughtful and patient with me...

The roughened feel of his thighs under her fingers as she continued to arouse him with her mouth took her own physical response to a level she could barely control, and she drew back from her lingering exploration so that she could rub herself against his erection.

Theo was having to take long, even breaths to keep his control in place. He opened his eyes and inhaled sharply as he looked at her astride him.

With one hand firmly on his erection, she flung her head back as she moved her body sensuously against him. Every shudder of pleasure was reflected in her soft moans as his hardness played against her clitoris.

Her long hair was in utter, sexy disarray and her generous breasts bounced as she moved like ripe fruit, gently shaking, too succulent to pass up.

He tugged her towards him so that those breasts were closer to his mouth, and as she knelt over him, still enjoying his erection against her, eyes still shut, breathing still coming and going in little gasps and groans, he flicked his tongue over one engorged nipple and then stilled her slightly so that he could suckle more thoroughly on it.

Hands on her slender ribcage, he carried on pleasuring himself at her breasts until neither of them could handle the build-up any longer.

They were so hot for one another—but she was still cool enough to fumble through his wallet and extract his last condom, which she took her time stretching over him.

Theo was riveted in a way he had never been with any woman by the sight of her voluptuous nakedness…the satiny smoothness of her shoulders and the soft paleness of her skin in such contrast to the perfect circular deep rose of her nipples.

His feeling of absolute possession was second to none, but he easily explained that away by the fact that she had come to him a virgin.

He was going to enjoy being her teacher, and she was showing all the signs of being an A class student…

Who knows? he thought, before his mind emptied of all thought and the primitive responses of his body took over. *Maybe a week might not be quite long enough after all…*

CHAPTER NINE

Lying on the bed, Alexa drowsily watched Theo, sitting at the desk in the hotel bedroom, wearing only his boxers, frowning at whatever he was looking at on his computer.

Their last night in Manhattan.

She couldn't quite believe how fast the time had flown since they had left The Hamptons. As predicted, Bob and Felicity had not been at all fazed at their early departure.

'Completely understand!' Felicity had carolled. 'It's been a while—hasn't it, Bobby?—but I can still remember what it was like to be young and in love…!'

Alexa had had to inwardly admit that she and Theo were certainly giving the impression of two people who couldn't keep their hands off one another, and she could understand how that might have led to the misconception that they were in love.

How ironic that now, when there were no reporters around, furiously snapping pictures, the physical contact between herself and Theo was one hundred per cent genuine.

Every time she glanced at him her imagination took over, and she remembered what it felt like to have those hands all over her body and his mouth kissing every enthusiastic inch of her.

They had checked into the penthouse suite which had originally been booked for them—the adjoining room was now redundant—but, frankly, they could have been any-where in the world. Any hotel in the world. Just so long as there was a bed, because they spent an inordinate amount of time making love.

For a couple of hours every day Alexa had insisted on going out on her own, so that Theo could work.

'I can work perfectly well with you around,' he had drawled, in the sort of dark, persuasive voice that had made her almost but not quite revise her determination not to submerge herself entirely in him. 'In fact I find I work better, because I can touch you whenever I need a break...'

This was just the sort of heady flattery that she knew could so easily go to her head. It was the stuff she loved hearing—just as she loved hearing him tell her how desirable she was, how irresistible, how he couldn't see the bed without wanting her in it, naked and pressed up close to him.

But flattery was all it was, and Alexa knew that she had to steer clear of reading anything else behind it. Because she was getting seriously hooked on touching him, on hearing all those softly murmured words that did wonders for her self-confidence, making her feel utterly desirable...the most desirable woman on the planet.

He'd swept into her life, bringing with him all his worldly experience, and he had used that worldly experience and his unimaginable charm to captivate her.

He had found fertile ground in her, because nothing in her past had prepared her for the impact of their involvement. Had she had *some* experience with the opposite sex she might have had sufficient ammunition to see his charm for what it was...practised, well-used...the same charm that had turned all those other women's heads...

But she'd lacked the necessary experience. And now...

He was completely oblivious to the fact that she was staring at him. It was still only six fifteen in the morning, but she would have bet that he'd been up for at least an hour—maybe more. He seemed to need very little sleep to function.

She gazed at the way his dark hair curled at the nape of his neck, at the muscled width of his shoulders and the tiny mole on his right shoulder, which she could just about make out in the pool of light from the desk lamp he had switched on. He hadn't yet shaved and there was a definite shadow along his jawline. He was frowning, and she knew that in a second he would gently tap his fountain pen on the desk—a habit he had when he was utterly focused on something.

She had asked him why he had a fountain pen when all his work was done on the computer, and he had twirled it in his fingers and told her that it had been a present from his mother when he was eleven. It was his talisman.

There were so many things she felt she now knew about him, and there were so many physical details she had absorbed too, lodging them in her brain the way information was stored on a computer, lying there, ready to be accessed at the flick of a button.

She could recognise the sound of his soft breathing when he was in deep sleep...could tell from the clipped tone of his voice on the phone when he was talking to someone he wanted to get rid of as fast as possible. She had watched him shave in front of the mirror and had come to realise that, although he must surely know just how good-looking he was, he did very little to enhance his looks. No manly moisturisers. He barely looked in a mirror at all.

Her heart began a steady, anxious thud in her chest.

When exactly had she stopped seeing him as the enemy she was shackled to and started seeing him as someone who was witty, beyond intelligent, wickedly charming...?

She knew when she had owned up to her guilty fascination—when she had acknowledged the chemistry between them. But when, exactly, had that undeniable chemistry turned into something deeper for her?

They had strolled through Manhattan, gone to the famous Museum of Modern Art, walked along the High Line and visited the gallery district. She had forgotten that this wasn't a real-life courtship. She had forgotten that those piercing, lazy eyes that roved over her body with rampant appreciation had no intention of lingering there indefinitely.

What had started out for both of them as a perfectly reasonable way of dealing with the inconvenient attraction between them had morphed into something else—*for her*.

She had...

The steady, nervous thud of her heart picked up pace as the enormity and horror of her realisation hit her with the force of a runaway train.

When had she fallen in love with him?

'You're up. Why are you up?'

His dark drawl made her jump, because she had been so busy being dismayed and horrified at her thoughts that she had blanked him out of her line of vision. Now she sat up and feigned a yawn.

'The light must have woken me...' She burrowed back down into the duvet, so that she could take up where she had left off and carry on chewing over her plight—which couldn't have been worse as far as she was concerned.

'In that case I'll switch it off...'

Theo stood up and stretched, and then headed back to the bed—which was just where, for once, Alexa *didn't* want him. Because she still had so much thinking to do, still had to work out how she had managed to give her heart to a guy who had no intention of looking after it—not in the long term and not, if she were to be honest with herself, in the short term either.

'No—don't!' She tempered the sharpness of her reply

with a little laugh. 'I know you've had a pretty distracted time when it comes to work, and that you get a lot done early in the morning. I'm still very sleepy anyway.' She yawned on cue. 'So I shall try and grab a couple more hours...'

'Sex is very good for guaranteeing restful sleep...' He slid into the bed alongside her and eased her to face him, so that they were both on their sides, looking at one another, perfectly level.

'In which case you should get back to work,' Alexa told him crisply, although her firmness was somewhat undermined by the hand that was now lying between her legs, cupping her down there and moving ever so gently. 'You don't want to fall asleep on the job, do you?'

Theo sighed and reluctantly removed his hand. 'Unfortunately that's the last thing I can afford to do,' he conceded. 'Several million pounds rests on my making sure I stay awake on the job—at least for the next couple of hours...'

He swung his legs over the side of the bed and strolled back towards the desk and the blinking of his computer. When he glanced over his shoulder it was to see that she was on her side, turned away from him, her long hair hiding her face, doubtless on her way back to sleep.

It seemed peculiar that he was going to be marrying a woman who, in the normal scheme of things, would not have excited his interest—and even more peculiar that she had not only excited his interest, but that his interest was showing no signs of petering out just yet.

He wondered what the chances were of a continuing sexual relationship for the duration of their imposed marriage, but dismissed the idea before it had taken root.

He just didn't have it in him to ride the crest of physical attraction for longer than a couple of months, and he knew without the shadow of a doubt, that to sleep with her for any continued period of time would be a big mistake.

He had always been able to deal with broken hearts, but this was a special case. When he and Alexa parted company they would still see one another, because he would have shares in her family company and would, on occasion, be working alongside her father. Her father was a sociable man. There would be instances when he would be invited over for a meal—special occasions, some family do—and there would be instances when she would be there too.

The last thing he wanted was to find himself in the firing line for recriminations should she get more involved with him than necessary. The last thing he wanted was her broken heart. Because she wasn't a tough, sexually experienced woman of the world and her broken heart might not mend quite so easily.

He heard her soft, even breathing and frowned, because thinking of her suffering did something to him.

Which, he concluded, was all the more reason to make sure what they had ended before it could become a problem. No big deal for him, but he might have to gently guide her in the same direction, just to make sure...

Alexa, her thoughts all over the place, actually fell asleep, and woke to the sound of her mobile buzzing next to her on the bedside table.

She could hear the sound of the shower in the bathroom. Predictably, the bathroom door was wide open, because Theo was anything but a shrinking violet when it came to flaunting his nudity.

It was her father, and their conversation was brief and puzzling. She waited until Theo was back in the bedroom, his hair damp and tousled and a towel hooked precariously around his waist.

'That was my dad...' She looked at him anxiously.

'What did he want?'

'He said that he has something to tell me but I'm not to

worry.' She sat up, heels tucked beneath her rear, and she chewed at her lip.

Being told not to worry was the fastest way to make sure that someone got worried—especially when it came to her father, who was the master of understatement.

Had her mother's health scare not been quite as severe as it had been, Alexa was sure that her father would have not deemed it necessary to contact her and ask her to return to Italy sixteen months ago. She'd been protected and sheltered as a child and that was the way it remained.

'What if something's wrong with Mum?' she asked in a quiet, wobbly voice.

Theo crossed over to the bed and looked at her uncertainly for a few seconds. The Alexa he had first met had changed over the brief but intense time they had spent together. Having expected a frumpy little doormat, he had been presented with a firebrand...

A feisty, outspoken, mutinous firebrand, who was also a ridiculous romantic...

Who had been a virgin...

He could sense her making a big effort not to cry, and he fought against his instinct to bracingly tell her to pull herself together.

'He'd tell you,' Theo informed her calmly. 'When it comes to health, people tend to avoid beating around the bush.'

'You don't know my father,' Alexa said ruefully. She suddenly realised that she wasn't wearing anything, and she hurriedly dragged the duvet over her and slumped back against the pillows.

'Fill me in.'

Alexa paused. This was what it meant to be in love, she thought. She could no more fight the urge to confide in him than a starving man could have fought the urge to feast at the banquet. Her head was telling her one thing—telling her to protect herself and back away—but she was drawn to him like a moth to the flame that threatened to kill it.

Being in love meant waving goodbye to common sense—to everything that had been her compass through her life.

'He's always hated the thought of worrying me,' she confessed. 'They wanted more kids, you know, but Mum had a terrible time when she was pregnant with me and was told that to risk having another would be endangering her life.' Alexa sighed. 'You could say that I've lived a pretty sheltered life. Not that I wasn't allowed out of their sight, but I was always protected from what they considered *too much information*. I only found out just how bad Mum's stroke was by cornering the consultant and demanding the details. Left to Dad, he would just have tutted and told me that everything was going to be fine. Which is why for him to call me here and say that he's got something to tell me… Well…'

Theo sat down on the bed, and she toppled a little towards him before steadying herself. For once he was with a woman, in a bed, and sex was not uppermost in his mind.

'I can only think that he's readying me for something big—that it's serious. And the only serious thing I can think of is that Mum… Well…'

Unaccustomed to soothing crying women, Theo pulled her towards him and smoothed her hair clumsily with his hand. She was crying against his chest but trying hard to stifle it, and that more than anything else touched him.

He hadn't had to dig too deep to find the soft-as-mush girl beneath the tough, outspoken exterior. And that was something he felt he should have sensed from the very beginning.

'So chewing over it and coming up with lots of worst-case scenarios…is that going to alter the reality?'

'Well, no…'

'If your mother was seriously ill your father would tell you—however much he didn't want to worry you—and if *he* wouldn't, then my father would call me and say something. You forget—they're back in touch now. And my father, I assure you, has *never* been backward when it comes to being brutally honest...'

'What do you mean?'

She was feeling better already. She liked the way he was holding her—as if she were a piece of fragile porcelain china. It felt good to be held like this, without sex being their final destination. It scared her how much she liked it...

'That art teacher might have been a bit forthright with Daniel,' Theo joked lightly, 'and I may have passed the litmus test with her by painting nonsense and talking my way into an explanation, but I remember my father taking one look at one of my productions and bursting out laughing. He said that it was the biggest load of rubbish he had ever seen, and then he patted me on the shoulder and told me that if *he* couldn't give me a few home truths then who could? So rest assured that he wouldn't shy away from phoning me if there was a crisis over there...'

'And has he?'

Theo looked at her with a frown. 'Has he what? Phoned me? To tell me about a crisis with your family? No.'

Alexa breathed a sigh of relief—because she believed him. It was as simple as that. She would wait and see what the problem was when she returned. Hopefully it would be something to do with the wedding or the engagement party.

Which brought her back to the thoughts that had momentarily taken a back seat.

She edged away from him and shuffled out of bed. Just now, knowing what she knew about her feelings for him, she felt that a bit of distance between them would be a good idea.

'So...' she said, gathering herself. 'It's our last day...'

She was well and truly up and awake now, and the thought of trying to pretend to go back to sleep wasn't going to work.

What happened next? she wondered.

The longer she carried on having sex with him, the more hurt she would be building up for herself. But how on earth was she going to last a year of wanting him and having to hide that want? How was she going to survive when he looked at her with polite indifference because what had started as lust for him had dwindled and disappeared?

The stakes were never going to be even between them, and just thinking about that made her head ache.

More than anything else she wished she could run away and take cover until this crazy love had blown over—except she knew that it never would.

She might no longer be able to keep her heart intact, but she felt she could try and keep her dignity intact—and to do so she would have to guard her expression and never allow him to see just how much he had finally ended up getting to her.

She wondered if this was the fate that had befallen all those women he had dated in the past. Having heard him give them his warning speech about not getting involved, had they, like her, found themselves being sucked into something that was bigger than them?

Had that been the fate of the striking blonde who had confronted him in that restaurant?

Alexa could only hope that, however hard she had fallen for him, she wouldn't be one of those women who kept trying to grab his attention whenever they happened to bump into him—who let him think that what he had once taken from them was still on offer should he decide to pay them another visit.

She had seen the way he had looked at that blonde, with

veiled contempt in his eyes—the same contempt that had been in his voice when he had talked about her.

There was no way Alexa would allow herself to become someone like that.

'I think we should do some sightseeing,' she said lightly. 'I'll just grab a shower and then we can think about heading out…maybe have breakfast at one of those bagel places by the hotel… Or we could go to Central Park… There's still so much to see… The earlier we leave, the better, don't you think?'

Theo inclined his head to one side, his antennae picking up invisible signals and trying to decipher them. 'Don't rush,' he told her with a little shrug, 'I'll have to wrap up these documents. It'll take at least half an hour…'

Alexa took longer than that, and emerged fully dressed an hour later. Theo, likewise, was in a pair of black jeans and a cream polo shirt that did amazing things for his athletic, muscular body.

She licked her lips and tried not to stare. Staring had been permissible when it had been about lust. Now that it was about love, staring was a weakness she could not afford.

Her heart was still beating fast and she frantically wondered how she could carry on sounding normal when everything inside her felt so *abnormal*.

She need not have worried. Theo's charm and the breadth of his knowledge proved irresistible.

She had, of course, travelled—but not nearly as extensively as he had, and he didn't allow her to be introspective as they had breakfast in a noisy bagel café before jumping on the subway—something she had to persuade him into doing—so that they could explore Williamsburg.

At one point he grabbed her hand and continued holding it. She knew that it was just one of those throwaway gestures of his, but also knew that would be one more thing she would store in her memory bank, to be extracted for examination at a later date.

She couldn't resist.

And she couldn't resist when he pulled her towards him and casually dropped a kiss on her parted lips.

She couldn't resist the way he took it for granted that her body belonged to him. Every passing touch was like the heavy brand of possession, but if he'd known the effect he had on her he would have been quailing at the thought of their year-long pretend union.

She hoped she'd kept everything on a light level, and by the time they'd headed back to the hotel and begun packing for their trip back to Italy she even managed to ask the question that had been uppermost in her mind for the past few hours.

'Should we discuss how we…er…move forward now…?'

About to fling the last of his clothing into his suitcase, Theo paused and stared at her. Something was off, but he couldn't quite put his finger on it.

'Come again?'

'Well, the week is up,' Alexa pointed out nervously. 'And I know that was the time limit we both agreed for us to…er…get this thing between us out of our system…'

'I don't recall agreeing to any such thing,' Theo pointed out.

She had come to him a virgin and yet now it seemed that she was keen to draw her experiences with him to a close. He clenched his jaw as it was brought home to him how little they had in common, aside from the obvious bond of their similar backgrounds, and how much, fundamentally, she still disapproved of him. He had the feeling that he'd been used, and it wasn't a feeling that he liked.

His cell phone buzzed and a text message popped up, saying that their limo had arrived to take them to the airport.

She had certainly started a tricky conversation at the

right point in time, he thought drily. Did she think that he would be too embarrassed to continue in the back of a taxi?

'Taxi's here,' he said curtly.

He phoned through to Reception to ask for their bags to be taken down to the limo and then waited until they were inside the spacious car before he picked up their conversation.

'Well…I know we didn't *exactly* set a time and a date,' Alexa said, when he lazily asked her to finish what she had started saying. 'I mean, I do understand that it's hard… impossible…'

'To set a time and a date when it comes to lust?' he interrupted smoothly. 'You're right. It is.'

'But,' she persisted valiantly, 'I do think we need some kind of clarification here…'

'Why?'

They did. He knew that. However, for some reason he had a perverse desire to dig his heels in. He wasn't ready to give up what they had, and there was nothing worse than unfinished business, as far as he was concerned.

True, when it came to women that was pure conjecture, but he couldn't see the point of self-denial and that was precisely the road she was trying to head down right now.

'Because this marriage of ours isn't going to be real,' Alexa mumbled. 'And if it's a business arrangement—'

'You can try.'

'I beg your pardon?'

'You can try to fight this thing between us, but you won't be getting any help from me.'

'What—what do you mean?' Alexa stammered.

'I mean that I'm not ready for this to end yet. And don't forget—we may have had a little respite from the cameras but we're heading back into the lions' den, and with our engagement those pesky reporters are going to be snapping away to capture the happy couple. I just want you to know that when I kiss you it won't be for the cameras…'

'I'd forgotten about them,' Alexa said in dismay.

He grinned wolfishly at her. 'Don't worry. It'll soon come flooding back…'

'So in other words,' Alexa said tightly, 'you want this to carry on until *you* get tired of it?'

'In other words, I have no intention of fighting what's between us.'

The taxi ride was completed in silence. Typically, Alexa thought, he had said what he had to say and then, rather than continue driving his point home, had dismissed the topic by spending the ride to the airport with his laptop open, sifting through dozens of emails and ignoring her completely.

He was just so damned *sure* of himself—just so *convinced* of his own monumental appeal that he didn't envisage her standing a chance of saying *no* to him.

She despaired.

Would she be able to withstand an onslaught? Even though she knew that he was not in it for more than just sex? Even though she knew that she would end up being desperately hurt? That she would turn into one of those clingy, needy women he had no time for? The sort who never forgot him and staged scenes whenever their paths chanced to cross?

All her resentment and anger, her conviction that she could never in a thousand years fall for a guy like him, now seemed like naïve stupidity. She had been able to hate the one-dimensional cardboard cut-out, but the minute the three-dimensional man had emerged she had not been able to resist.

She'd turned into just another one of his conquests, and she shivered at the prospect of those lips touching hers and her knowing that she wanted more. She was terrified of being betrayed—not just by her own weak body, but by her emotions.

Her head buzzed with so many scenarios that she was barely aware of the flight. He left her to stew. In fact she was certain that he wasn't even aware of her presence next to him. He was utterly absorbed in his work, and sex, however compelling, played second fiddle.

Only as they were taxiing on landing, and after having fitfully dozed for part of the trip, did she find other concerns settling—and the main one was whatever it might be that her father had to say to her.

All over again she felt anxiety begin to claw at her insides. Theo had calmed her fears by telling her that if her mother's health was involved *he* would have known about it. Now, Alexa could see all the flaws in that argument. Why would her father advertise something like that to his dad? It was a personal problem and he would surely want to keep it to himself. The fact that his instincts had always been to protect her from anything unpleasant meant that whatever he wanted to say must be of grave concern. It must be something he couldn't keep from her.

'What if something's really wrong with Mum?' she couldn't help asking as they disembarked.

She hated herself for appealing to Theo for reassurance, but she had had time to contemplate the worst and she *needed* to hear the strong conviction in his voice. It was irritating—especially considering she should be trying to erect whatever fragile defences she still had at her disposal to protect her pathetic, foolish heart—but she needed his logical explanation. Even though she had already convinced herself that it made no sense.

'It won't be.'

Theo had had plenty of time on the trip to try and work out why he was in the process of breaking his own self-imposed rule never to chase any woman. She was backing away, and instead of shrugging his shoulders and moving on he was intent on pursuit. Ego and pride, he presumed. Not exactly the most endearing traits in the world, but he wasn't going to pretend that there was anything more to it than that.

'But you don't *know*...'

Theo stared down at her flushed, earnest face and his libido kicked into gear with surprising ferocity. What *was* it about this woman that made him want to drag her off to the nearest empty room and take her?

He actually caught himself doing a brief mental tour of what he could recall of their route towards Immigration, trying to figure out if there were any cubbyholes he could pull her into, so that he could yank down those oh, so prim and proper trousers, taking her underwear with them, and have sex with her in the most basic way possible.

Reluctantly he gave up the idea, but this, he thought, was precisely why he would carry on his pursuit... Because to back off now, when neither of them wanted to, whatever she said to the contrary, would be like having to endure an indefinite erection without the benefit of a cold shower to get rid of it.

'Nor do you,' he said with a hint of impatience. 'Now, don't forget that we're back in the public eye. Try not to trail behind me—and it would help if you wiped that anxious expression off your face.'

With his free hand he massaged the nape of her neck, underneath her silky hair—which Alexa knew was unnecessary because there was no one with a camera around. But he had warned her that he wasn't going to play by her rules... He was just proving to her that he had meant what he said.

And right now, in these crowds, she was powerless to do anything about it.

Even when they were in the back of his chauffer-driven

car—he had called from the airport for it to come for them—she still had an insane urge to close the gap she had studiously put between them.

Like a predator, with all the time in the world to hunt its prey, he made no move to get closer to her, contenting himself with watching her through brooding, speculative eyes that gave her goosebumps.

Finally she hissed, with one eye on the driver, although the screen, as always, was up, 'I wish you'd stop staring at me!'

'Why?' Theo drawled.

'Because I don't like it!'

'Liar. You like it—and so do I.'

His words floated around her like a physical caress. There was lazy intent in his eyes and she looked away hurriedly, her body turned on to screaming point. Because he was one hundred per cent right... *She did like him staring at her—liked the way it made her whole body tingle, as though it had been plugged into an electric socket...*

She heard herself launch into nervous chatter, babbling even while her body recalled how and where it had been touched, and fought against the seductive temptation to think about how and where it would be touched again...

She was surprised that they made it to her house with her nervous system still intact. Of course he hadn't opened his computer once, or checked his phone at all. He'd just leaned against the door, limbs loose, his fabulous green eyes pinned to her face, fully aware that he was unsettling her and amused by it.

'I'll come in with you,' Theo murmured, pressing a button and talking to the driver once the partition was lowered.

'There's no need,' Alexa said hastily.

He didn't bother to answer, instead stepping out of the car and moving round to wait for her as she followed suit.

'There's no need to pretend now that we're here,' she muttered as he neatly tucked her arm into the crook of his.

'Oh, I know *that*,' Theo murmured silkily, 'but remember what I said to you?'

Alexa's breath caught in her throat, because she knew that she just didn't have the weapons for a sustained assault.

'And remember what *I* said to *you*!' But her voice was weak.

He actually laughed under his breath. Laughed and patted her on her arm. 'You want me. Don't fight it, Alexa. Enjoy it while it lasts. Now...' his tone changed from lazy to brisk as he rang the doorbell '...why don't we see what all the fuss is about with your father?'

CHAPTER TEN

NOT ONLY WAS her father waiting for her, so was her mother. And, even more ominous, so was Theo's father. All three were hovering by the door, and she got the uneasy feeling that they had been waiting for their arrival.

Alexa automatically stepped a shade closer to Theo, who had sized up the situation and taken charge, smoothly querying their joint presence by the front door with the quirk of an eyebrow but not commenting on it, instead leading the way into the kitchen while conducting a running commentary on their trip, omitting the salacious details and focusing on filling his father in on Bob and Felicity.

They followed him like sheep.

The man was a born leader, and she could understand why her father had dangled the carrot of shares in the family firm, ensuring that he would oversee holding its reins in the years to come. A true marriage of convenience.

'So…'

Somehow, without her noticing, Theo had managed to pour their collected parents glasses of wine and put the kettle on for coffee for both of them. He sauntered towards the kitchen table, which was a long oak affair that could comfortably seat twelve. He looked perfectly relaxed and utterly in charge.

'Which lucky family member gets to tell us what's

going on…?' he drawled, patting the chair next to him, into which Alexa sank with a sigh of relief, because nervous tension at this new, unsettling situation had piled up on top of the nervous tension already wreaking havoc inside her. He looked narrowly from face to face and his father cleared his throat.

'We have been talking, son—' Stefano said, sitting at the head of the table while the other two followed suit, flanking him on either side. Alexa's mother nervously twirled the stem of her wine glass and looked at her daughter,

'Let *me*, Stefano,' Cora interrupted. 'Now, Alexa, your father's come clean and told me everything. I know you two have been worried sick about me, and I understand that you reached this…this…*arrangement* with poor Theo for the best possible reasons, but I don't need protecting as much as you think.'

She looked lovingly at her husband, who looked away sheepishly.

Alexa's brain had stopped at the description of Theo as 'poor', as in *helpless*, and she wanted to burst into hysterical laughter.

'I've had health problems, all three of you know that, but they've been physical—not emotional. Yes, I'll admit that I may have told your father, Alexa, that I longed for a grandchild—longed to see you settled down with a nice man—but what mother doesn't wish that for her child? There was no need for you to concoct this silly scheme…'

'So what are you saying?' Alexa looked between the three parents in bewilderment. She was trying to follow what her mother was saying, but it was like walking in treacle. When she looked at Theo he was frowning, his brooding eyes speculative. It hit her just how much she had come to admire the silent strength of his personality, and was floored by how much it hurt to love him when her love wasn't returned.

Stefano picked up the thread of the conversation. 'We're saying that there's no need for this charade any longer. Certain things will remain in place...'

'I promised you shares in my company,' Carlo said, addressing Theo, 'and that stays in place. I won't pretend that I didn't...' he cleared his throat '...see certain advantages to helping your father out financially...'

'Because you're a manipulative old man.' Cora smiled indulgently at her husband. 'But, Alexa, darling, I don't understand why you didn't put your foot down and refuse to go through with this silly pretence. No...' She sighed. 'I *do* understand, and for that I have only love for you...'

Alexa's head was swimming. She was now grasping exactly what was being said. She had been looking at the prospect of a year with Theo—a year trying to fight the impulses that were so much bigger than her...a year knowing that every time he crooked his finger it would take all the strength at her disposal not to go running...a year of knowing that she would walk away from their relationship battered and hurt beyond comprehension.

That year wasn't going to happen now. She was being given her *Get Out Of Jail Free* card—and so was Theo.

And the future yawned in front of her like a black, empty void.

'So...' she said slowly.

'Yes, my darling.' Cora reached across the width of the kitchen table to pat her daughter's hand. 'And of course the press have hounded you both. You will simply tell them that the engagement's off and so is the marriage...'

Alexa headed for the most secluded seat in the first class lounge at the airport. She didn't want to be near anyone because she didn't want to be dragged into making small talk. She'd been operating on automatic for the past three weeks and she planned on carrying on doing just that—at least until she reached London, when she was banking on new surroundings and the thrill of her new job to rescue her from the zombie-like torpor into which she had sunk.

Where had Theo gone? She didn't know, and of course she had been too proud to ask her parents. She had moaned and railed against the situation in which she had found herself, and yet when that situation had been whipped out from under her feet she had been lost because she had become so dependent on him.

In the blink of an eye he had gone from being just the sort of guy she would run a mile from to being just the sort of guy she couldn't imagine living without.

But live without him she would, and it hurt more than she could ever have contemplated in those carefree first few days when she had actually disliked him.

The press, predictably, had passed a few days speculating on the break-up of the perfectly matched couple and then, just as predictably, new scandals and gossip had drawn them away.

Now, staring down at the book on her lap, and with two hours of waiting ahead of her because she had been itching to leave, she thought back to the brief conversation she had had with Theo after his father and her parents had fled the scene, leaving them stranded in the kitchen like a couple of castaways, washed up on a beach after being stuck on a raft together but with nothing to say now that the storm had passed.

The passionate lover had gone. He had carefully asked her what her plans were now. One minute he hadn't been able to keep his hands off her—the next minute, freed from the shackles of a union he'd never asked for, he'd been coolly indifferent.

Of course *she* had gone on about the relief of not hav-

ing to face a marriage neither of them had wanted. The
more indifferent he'd seemed, the more she had sparkled,
voicing the joys of her newfound freedom.

And then he'd gone, and she'd been left in an empty
kitchen contemplating the horror of her newfound freedom.

London. Her parents had an apartment there. It was
where she had lived before she had left for Italy and she
would go back there. She had phoned her old company,
who had remembered her, and after a million calls they
had found her a job.

The change of scene would do her good—she knew that.
Just being in her parents' house had reminded her of Theo.
And in the dead of night, her whole body ached for him.

Right, she thought severely, *think about the good stuff.*

No falling deeper and deeper in love with a man who
didn't love her. No agonising year together, during which
time he would have grown tired of her body and settled
back into enduring the time he was forced to spend in her
company. He had simply been her lover, and she knew that
she would eventually meet someone else—someone she
could entrust with her heart.

She forced herself to read a few pages of her book and
was totally unaware of anyone approaching her until a
shadow fell over her. When she looked down she saw a
pair of very expensive loafers and didn't bother to look any
higher, because if she didn't then whoever it was wouldn't
ask her if she'd mind if he sat next to her.

'Alexa.'

For a few seconds Alexa was convinced that she'd mis-
heard her name being said—and had definitely miscon-
strued that rich, mellow voice she had come to love.

She hunkered down and ignored whoever it was—
because he *hadn't* spoken, and it was just her feverish
imagination playing tricks on her.

'Are you going to acknowledge me or are you going to carry on reading…? What are you reading?'

The book was whipped out of her hands and there he was, standing right in front of her, as cool as a cucumber and as devastatingly sexy as every single memory she had of him.

In a pair of cream trousers and a black T-shirt, with a cream linen jacket hooked over one shoulder, he was drop-dead gorgeous.

'Still on the crime novels, I see. Would you like me to predict the end?'

'What are you doing here?'

Her voice was a hoarse whisper and she cleared her throat, then fidgeted as he took the empty chair next to her and pulled it in, so that there was no way she could avoid looking at him.

Theo wished there was an easy answer to that question—something glib that he could pull out from up his sleeve—but there wasn't. He had spent the past three weeks unable to focus, unable to concentrate—unable to do anything but think about her, even though he had told himself that it was great that he had been released from the obligation of a marriage he hadn't wanted…great that he could resume his life as he had always wanted it…great that his routine would be returned to him.

His address book was bulging with names and phone numbers of women, and all of them without exception would have welcomed a call from him. He had known that.

He hadn't called any of them because he'd had too much catching up to do on the work front. That was what he had told himself. Until he'd been forced to face the fact that he missed *her*. Not just her warm, welcoming body, which he had known for such a brief period of time, but he missed the whole package. He missed the way she bristled and glared at him…the way she never obeyed any of his 'No

Trespassing' signs but got stuck in and told him just what she thought of him anyway. He missed her shy, hesitant smiles and the ready way her eyes filled up with tears. He missed the softness underneath the feisty scrapper. Most of all he just missed the woman who had been born to have it all and had chosen to do her own thing and ignore the life she had been conditioned to lead.

Except he had no idea how to put any of that into words, and he could feel her blazing eyes on him—could feel her willing him to just *go away*.

'How have you been?' he asked, in a lame attempt to kick-start the conversation.

'Fine,' Alexa said coldly. 'Are you travelling to London? I had no idea.'

'And if you had you would have checked on to a different flight…?'

Alexa shrugged. 'Probably,' she told him truthfully. 'You can't deny that this situation is a little uncomfortable at the moment. I do realise we'll probably bump into one another in the years to come, but right now…'

'I get it. From being lovers and engaged to…nothing…'

Resting his forearms on his thighs as he leaned forward, Theo raked his fingers through his hair and took some small comfort from the delicate blush that bloomed in her cheeks at the mention of their having been lovers.

'I don't want to talk about that,' Alexa said stiffly. 'In fact I'd rather you left me alone,' she continued, barely able to look at him. 'I have lots of planning to do for my new job in London and I really would like to do that in peace and quiet.'

'No.'

Alexa's mouth dropped open and she stared at him. 'What do you mean, *no*?' she demanded furiously.

'I haven't come here so that I can disappear without telling you what I've come to say.'

'Which is what?'

'I liked being engaged to you.' He looked around him at the crowded lounge. 'I have my driver outside.'

'I *beg* your pardon?'

Alexa was frantically trying to analyse what he had just said about liking being engaged to her. What did *that* mean? She didn't want to dwell on it, because it meant nothing coming from a man who had spent the past three weeks avoiding her and who didn't have a committed bone in his body—a man who had a block of ice for a heart.

'I want to talk to you and I can't do it here.'

'Well, *I* don't want to talk to *you*.' Alexa's body was ramrod-straight and as stiff as a board. She dreaded that one of those hands loosely dangling between his thighs might accidentally brush against her, because if it did then she knew the already uphill task of projecting indifference would be even harder.

'Please.'

That single word was wrenched out of him and for a second she hesitated, because *please* was not a word that passed his lips very often.

'What do you want to talk about?' she asked, relenting a little.

Theo glanced at her and kept his gaze on her face.

'I've missed you,' he said roughly, and Alexa tried to hold on to some of her gritty determination not to melt.

You've missed having sex with me.

'Are you travelling to London as well?'

'I will if I have to. I'm booked on the same flight as you, although I'd rather we didn't have this conversation on a plane or in an airport lounge...'

'Look, I can't think that there's anything to talk about, Theo. I mean, you've got your freedom, and I know that was all you wanted when you thought you'd lost it for a year. So maybe you miss having sex with me? You said that you wanted to carry on sleeping with me until… Well, until you got bored and dispatched me to wherever it is you dispatch women you no longer want hanging around. Some locked cupboard in your head, I expect. Of course, physically I'd have still been around, until the year ran out, but as far as sleeping with me went I guess it would have been separate rooms and you discreetly returning to your diet of leggy blonde supermodels…'

Her voice was brittle and she looked away and stared straight ahead.

'So I'm not going to jump into bed with you again just because you're not bored with me yet, Theo.'

Theo heard what she was saying and knew that she was describing the man he had thought himself to be. Even when they had walked away from one another he had still thought himself to be a guy who worked hard, played hard and avoided commitment.

'And I wouldn't ask you to,' he said quietly. 'Are you sure you won't dump your flight so that we can have this conversation somewhere a little less…frantic?'

'No one's paying us a scrap of attention.' She sighed with heartfelt longing. 'I just want to get to London and begin a new chapter in my life.'

Theo's jaw hardened. He had heard a lot about this wonderful new chapter in her life on the night they had returned from the best time he had ever had with a woman, to discover that the charade was over and they were free to go. She couldn't have waxed more lyrical when it had come to letting him know how relieved she was that the pretence was over.

Pride had turned his responses then to ice, and pride had kept him away for three weeks, but now he had discovered that there was something more powerful than pride and that had been a bitter pill to swallow.

'Your mother tells me that you have a new job lined up.'

'You spoke to her?'

'That's how I knew that you would be leaving for London today. She told me a few days ago...'

'*A few days ago?* Since when have you and my mother been having cosy chats behind my back? She never mentioned a word about talking to you!'

'Because I asked her not to.' Theo flushed darkly.

'You *asked her not to*? Why would you do that?' Alexa was genuinely bewildered.

'I...' He hunkered down.

Never in his life had he felt less cool, more in danger of making a complete fool of himself and more exposed to rejection. Indeed, when it came to women he had *never* felt exposed to rejection, and he loathed the feeling of vulnerability. He had never been vulnerable. He had always had the direction of his life firmly within his controlling hand.

Alexa was even more bewildered at his discomfort. It just wasn't *him*.

'I never thought I wanted involvement with a woman,' Theo surprised her by saying. His eyes met hers and held them. 'Don't interrupt me,' he continued, returning to some of his usual form. 'I...I didn't have any crash-and-burn relationships that turned me off commitment. I never lost my heart to a gold-digger only to find out in the nick of time. I suppose I was simply a product of my background—just as my brother is. I was ambitious, and in my upward climb I enjoyed women but never invited any of them further than the front door, emotionally speaking.'

Alexa gave him an encouraging look. She was all ears.

'I was in no hurry to settle down—in fact it never crossed my mind what sort of woman I would end up with, or even if I would end up with one at all.' He paused and thought about the relationship his parents had had. 'When my mother died Daniel and I watched my father fall apart at the seams. Actually,' he confessed heavily, 'we *all* fell apart. And that was when I realised just how destructive all-consuming love can be.'

'Empowering,' Alexa corrected in a staccato voice. 'I'm sure your father would agree that it was better to have had all those wonderful years with your mother than to have lived the sort of life *you* want to carve out for yourself.'

Theo smiled crookedly at her. 'And that's why I thought that, whether I married you or not, you and I were poles apart. I admit that the only kind of marriage that ever crossed my mind after my mother died was one that would have been very similar to the one we found ourselves pushed into—a marriage of convenience. But not with a woman who was all about romance and love and happy-ever-after endings... What I anticipated was a relationship where I couldn't be hurt—a relationship that was a mutually convenient business arrangement...'

'So you've come here to tell me what I already knew?'

'No. I've come here to tell you that I was wrong.'

Hope flared inside her, suffocating everything else and shooting up blooms that she couldn't squash.

'What do you mean?' Alexa asked in a stifled voice.

'You *know* what I mean,' Theo said drily. 'I was wrong. I might have *wanted* a relationship I could control, but in the end I *needed* the relationship that I couldn't. I needed *you*. I still do...'

Alexa masked her disappointment, because need was very far from love. 'And that's why you're not the man for me,' she said softly. 'You've learned to be cynical and I've learned the opposite. I don't want something that stops at *need* or *desire* or *lust*. I want the full package and I always did.'

'And why can't that be *me*?' Theo demanded with muted belligerence.

He had never had to justify how he felt to anyone in his

life before, and even if he left now, without her, he was driven to lay himself open to that possibility.

'Because—'

'I love you, Alexa. I never expected to, but somehow it just…happened. Without even realising it I let you into my life, and I came here to tell you that I don't want you to leave it. I came here to ask you if you'd be mine for ever. Hell, Alexa, I came here to propose to you now that we're no longer engaged…'

'You *love* me…?'

The words hitched in her throat and she tentatively stroked his knuckles with her finger, wishing now that she had abandoned her flight and gone somewhere else with him for this conversation—but how was she supposed to have known what he had come to say?

'You have no idea how much I've longed to hear you say that,' she whispered tremulously. 'I didn't think I would ever fall in love with you. You didn't make sense. I'd always assumed that the guy I fell for would be…well, just the *opposite* of you, to be honest. And I hated it that I was being forced into marrying you…'

'Tell me about it. I've never known a woman fight me as much as you did…'

Alexa laughed. She believed him. She'd dug her heels in. But even when she'd thought that she was refusing to budge an inch more than necessary she had already been shifting in places she hadn't begun to understand.

'I was so desperate for you to be the horrible, arrogant person I wanted you to be, but it felt like with every day that passed you escaped the box I'd shoved you in just a little bit more—until I realised that I'd fallen in love with the three-dimensional guy I never thought you could ever be.' She frowned as a sudden thought occurred to her. 'Did you tell my mother why you were coming here?'

'It was the only way I could find out what sort of reception I might expect,' he confessed, with such humility that she wanted to kiss him and keep right on kissing him. 'I swore her to secrecy,' he further admitted. 'She was to say nothing if it turned out that you wanted me out of your life for good.'

'I love you so much, Theo,' Alexa whispered, half giggling, because this was such an inappropriate place for such a wildly wonderful marriage proposal.

'So you'll marry me...?'

'Try and stop me...'

* * * * *

We Love Romance

with MILLS & BOON

Available at
weloveromance.com

LET'S TALK
Romance

For exclusive extracts, competitions and special offers, find us online:

- facebook.com/millsandboon
- @MillsandBoon
- @MillsandBoonUK

Get in touch on 01413 063232

For all the latest titles coming soon, visit
millsandboon.co.uk/nextmonth

MILLS & BOON
A ROMANCE FOR EVERY READER

- **FREE** delivery direct to your door

- **EXCLUSIVE** offers every month

- **SAVE** up to 25% on pre-paid subscriptions

SUBSCRIBE AND SAVE

millsandboon.co.uk/Subscribe

WANT EVEN MORE

ROMANCE?

SUBSCRIBE AND SAVE TODAY!

'Mills & Boon
books, the perfect
way to escape for an
hour or so.'

MISS W. DYER

'Excellent service,
promptly delivered and
very good subscription
choices.'

MISS A. PEARSON

'You get fantastic special
offers and the chance
to get books before they
hit the shops.'

MRS V. HALL

Visit millsandboon.co.uk/Subscribe
and save on brand new books.

JOIN THE
MILLS & BOON
BOOKCLUB

* **FREE** delivery direct to your door

* **EXCLUSIVE** offers every month

* **EXCITING** rewards programme

50% OFF
YOUR FIRST
PARCEL

Join today at
Millsandboon.co.uk/Bookclub

MILLS & BOON

MODERN

Power and Passion

Prepare to be swept off your feet by sophisticated, sexy and seductive heroes, in some of the world's most glamourous and romantic locations, where power and passion collide.

Eight Modern stories published every month, find them all at

millsandboon.co.uk/Modern